THE SANDBOX

BOOK THREE IN THE VICTOR WELLS SERIES

JORDAN ALLEN

For those who never give up.

1

My footfalls were unsteady in the rough undergrowth. I still wasn't accustomed to the tangled mess of roots, leaves, and ferns that made up the ground. The mandatory backpack and bracelet weren't helping any, either. I stumbled but caught myself before losing any momentum. I glanced ahead to plot my course and then returned my eyes to the branches above.

She was around here somewhere...

I ducked a tree limb and came to a halt. I was nearing the perimeter. Things were quiet, relatively so. Tree branches creaked, leaves rustled in the tops of the trees, but on the forest floor, all was calm. A pair of flies chased one another through a shaft of light that managed to pierce the canopy. I watched their chaotic aerial dance until they passed through the protective hologram and immediately disappeared beyond the perimeter.

I walked slowly, not caring to make my footfalls silent. I was tired of running, but I was ready to fight.

I slapped a vine out of my path with my saber. It made virtually no noise thanks to Zeno's new sound-dampening coating that covered the triangular blade.

I paused to listen.

Still, nothing. Did I dare call out? Would it really alert the searcher drones?

Behind me, a twig snapped, and the hair on the back of my neck stood tall. I turned and brought my saber up and across my body, and not a moment too soon.

Pria's saber clashed against mine with surprising force, nearly knocking me off balance.

"What took you so long?" she said, a wicked smile on her face.

"I don't know why you're in such a hurry to get beaten," I said, grunting as I held her back. Without warning, I dove to the side and came up in a crouch. Pria staggered forward without my weight to brace her. She recovered almost immediately and gave her saber a twirl.

"If I recall correctly," she said, "there's never been a winner in one of our little matches."

"Well," I said, matching her saber twirl, "we should probably do this more often then."

I rushed her. I feigned left and parried right. Noiselessly, our sabers collided as she blocked my move. She hopped back and began to circle my position.

"We would if you weren't otherwise occupied eight hours a day." She raised her eyebrows at me. "I assume things are going well with Daphne?"

"Well, it's only been a few weeks, but..." I rushed her again.

Our blades crossed in a blur of movements. A quick instep from me left her saber hand exposed. With blinding speed, I grabbed her wrist with my free hand and brought my saber down in a heavy arc. I would have said her saber clattered to the ground, but instead, it fell silently to the earth. For some reason, it wasn't quite as gratifying when it didn't make any noise. "I think so," I said.

I let go of her wrist, and she shoved me away.

"You *think* so?"

"What, you think you know better?"

"Yes, because Daphne and I talk."

I waited expectantly.

She let out a sigh. "Of course, it's going well. You think she'd spend all that time with you if it wasn't?"

I allowed myself a smile.

"That counts as a win, right?" I took a few steps back, ready for another round.

Pria bent over to pick up her saber.

"Are you tired of wearing all of that yet?" She motioned with her saber to my wrist.

"I barely notice it," I said, glancing down at the thin, black band around my left wrist. "Alex says it clashes with Mort's arm—"

"He's still calling it that?"

"That, or the Bounty Hunter's protégé's most impressive weapon, but BHPMIW doesn't roll off the tongue like 'Mort's arm,' or so I'm told. Speaking of the Bounty Hunter," I said, "have you heard anything from Kratos?"

Pria lowered her saber, the fire of combat leaving her expression. The last several weeks in this place had changed her.

We had made the decision early on to keep the fact that she was Tyrann Kane's daughter under wraps. No one knew except for the five of us and my grandfather and Augustine. As a result, a different version of Pria had started to show up, who I assumed was the real Pria Kane. The guarded persona she used to wear was nearly gone. She smiled more frequently, and her perpetual scowl and sarcasm had started to disappear. Well, the scowl, maybe, but not the sarcasm.

With her vast medical knowledge, she had become not only useful, but helpful, and willingly so.

After a few dislocated fingers, some poison oak incidents, and a myriad of other ailments had occurred, Pria quickly gained notoriety among the group. Unofficially, she was the doctor of the camp. She had also received regular updates from Ville on Kratos's health status. At least, she had, until a week and a half ago.

"According to Jahko," Pria said, bringing me back to the present, "Kratos was completely healed as of ten days ago. Zeno gave him the coordinates. I honestly thought we would have heard from him by now." Pria paused. "Jahko did mention that something was off with him, though. Physically, he's perfectly healthy, but psychologically"—Pria brought her saber back up and shrugged—"if I had learned that my mother was evil, and I had been shot by a poisoned bullet by one of her henchmen, and then weeks passed while I was in a needlessly prolonged coma... I would have skipped coming here and just sought my revenge. Maybe that's why he's not here yet."

Pria nodded at my saber, ready for another go. I brought my own blade up but then let it dip.

"If only... but he's not doing that. He's too rational, right?" Part of me wished he wasn't. Part of me hoped that he was in the process of dealing out justice to Rosewood right now, but I knew it wasn't the case.

Pria shrugged. "I don't know if I'd be rational after all that has happened."

"Yeah, but he's—"

"The Bounty Hunter?" Pria said, giving me a knowing look.

"Well, yeah. He's one of the toughest people we know. He'll be all right, right?"

"I guess we'll see." In that moment, Pria sprang, bringing her arms back in a powerful overhead stroke. I moved to block it, but my bracelet buzzed.

My heart started to race, and our sparring match was forgotten.

I held my body still, not bothering to block Pria's onslaught. She landed almost level with me to my left, her saber at her side, and froze. We locked eyes.

She nodded behind her. I scanned the forest behind her. Nothing.

I gave a slight shake of my head and then returned the gesture.

Her eyes focused past me, darting left and right. She shook her head, too.

My heart continued to race. It had to be here somewhere.

With my free hand, I slowly pointed to my ear. It was as if the whole forest had gone still. Gone were the periodic sounds of birds chirping. A definite stillness had arrived. I closed my eyes and focused on my hearing, letting out a long, slow breath as I did so.

There.

An almost imperceptible hum penetrated the quiet. My eyes popped open, searching for the source of the sound. We had to be careful. They followed sound and movement, and I assumed a whole array of other indicators. I swiveled my head, eyes searching for the owner of that electric hum.

To my left, mere feet away from where I assumed the perimeter was, a lone searcher drone hovered in midair, no doubt looking for me.

"Pria," I whispered, motioning with my eyes. "Behind you."

With her free hand, she reached delicately into the small pack on my back, my body shielding her movements. I felt her grab hold of the lead-lined sack in my pack. We had to time this right. The drones sought out facial scans or physical DNA, and they wouldn't stop until one or the other was obtained.

Pria gave me an almost imperceptible nod and began to count down, her voice still a whisper.

"Three, two, one—Now!"

We both turned to sprint back the way we had come.

I briefly heard the electric motor of the drone intensify before the crunching under my feet and the wind in my ears drowned it out.

Pria was close on my heels, the lead-lined sack on hand.

"Where is it?" she said.

I glanced over my shoulder.

"It's close!" I ducked under a branch and continued to sprint. The drone zipped through the air ten feet behind Pria's flowing hair. If the drone caught even a single strand, we were done.

"Switch places with me!"

Pria put on a burst of speed, and I jumped in behind her, my feet nearly touching her heels with each bound. We couldn't sprint forever, and I was already somewhat drained from our sparring matches. Adrenaline could only take us so far.

"I'm going to try and draw it after me," I said. "You know what to do."

I was close enough to hear her labored breathing.

"Just say when. And don't trip!"

I glanced behind me—the drone had gained ground. Five feet was all that separated us. I gave up half a step to create some space between me and Pria.

I could hear the buzz of the drone's rotors now. I couldn't let it get any closer than it was.

"Go!" I yelled.

Pria made an abrupt left turn while I stayed straight.

Stay with me, stay with me!

A quick glance told me that the drone hadn't deviated from its course. If I could have breathed a sigh of relief, I would have, but instead, I gulped down another breath of air and willed myself to go faster. The drone was relentless. I just had to keep at this long enough for Pria to circle back around.

I zigged and zagged before turning right, taking myself into a denser part of the forest.

The trees cast a thick, dark shade on the forest ground. I swatted a vine out of my way and chanced another glance behind me.

And that was when I tripped.

2

The mossy, plant-filled forest floor broke my fall. I rolled and immediately got back to my feet and found myself face-to-face with the drone.

My breathing was ragged. My hands, knees, and elbows were covered in mud and damp from the fall.

Less than a foot from my face hovered the searcher drone, its dark-brown frame nearly blending in with the shaded surroundings. Other than the dull hum of the rotors, the forest was calm around me.

Where was Pria?

I strained my ears for the faintest sound of her approach.

Silence.

So this was it. Rosewood would find us out. I blinked away the shame I felt.

There was no way Pria could make it to me before the drone finished its scan and left. There was no way I could capture the drone myself. My saber lay somewhere among the undergrowth nearby, and Pria had my lead-lined sack.

A beam of light emitted from the drone, scanning up and down my face. I turned away, but the drone swiftly matched my position. In a matter of moments, the drone would zip off to join its comrades, and the information would be transmitted back to Rosewood.

I would have to alert the rest of the camp, or more likely Pria would. They would have to leave, start over, regroup. As for me...

The drone continued to hover in front of me, finally finishing its scan in a confirmatory beep. The scanning light disappeared, but the drone stayed put.

Why hadn't it left yet? Maybe this wasn't over?

I struck out, hoping to catch it off guard, but it dodged my fist with ease. The drone inched closer. I struck out again and took a step back. It dodged and followed. A small needle seemed to grow out of the brown metallic frame.

I took another step backward, realization dawning on me.

DNA, it needed my DNA. The facial scan wasn't enough. Anyone could have printed a Victor Wells mask, right?

Could I stall this? Was Pria close? My heart pounded. I could hear nothing but the blood pumping in my ears.

I searched the ground for my saber. If I could just get to it, maybe I could disable the drone. If I had been wearing my gloves, I could have used some of the spray to trap it. I could have stopped it before it pierced me with its needle, but I didn't have my gloves.

I spotted my saber, nearly ten feet away, partially hidden beneath a fern.

Could I get to it? I knew my odds were slim. I knew I needed help. The drone had found me, scanned me, and was about to try and stick me. Any pretense of stealth was useless at this point. I gave one last-ditch yell.

"PRIA!"

The drone shot forward.

I dove for my saber.

A sharp, stinging sensation burned in my arm. I stretched my other arm toward my saber, but I was still short. From my view of the forest floor, the drone rose slowly, as if in triumph, into the air. It almost seemed to gloat in victory. Another confirmatory beep sounded, sealing my fate, maybe sealing everyone's fate.

I reached over, grabbed the pommel of my saber, and pushed myself to my feet. The whir of the drone's rotors grew louder. It began to move.

I cocked back my arm and hurled my saber at the fleeing drone with all my might. Time slowed as I realized that this throw was my only hope in preventing Rosewood from finding out our hiding place. My heart stopped, and I held my breath. The blade somersaulted through the air pommel over the tip, seeking the drone like a targeted missile.

And then the drone turned.

I yelled as my saber disappeared into the forest floor. The drone course corrected and continued onward.

My heart fell. I watched it fly away, becoming smaller and smaller, but that was when I heard something—the frantic pounding of feet through the underbrush.

Pria appeared, almost by magic, her lead-lined sack in hand, her course set to intersect the searcher drone.

Her silver hair streaked out behind her. Branches, vines, and leaves did little to slow her down. And then she was airborne, the sack above her head until it began moving down, faster and faster, until it swallowed up the drone.

3
———

"You understand that counts as me winning, right?"

She was smiling as she swung her prized bag over her shoulder, the captive drone inside. Her face was red from the effort, and sweat had dampened and darkened the hair around her temples.

"I owe you," I said with a shake of my head, "more than you know. I thought that was it—it scanned me! And then it stung me!" I showed her the raised bump on my arm with the pinprick spot of dried blood.

Pria looked down her nose at it.

"So you're saying that not only did you let it run facial recognition, you *also* let it get a DNA sample?" She raised her eyebrows. "I think you're losing your edge." She started walking back toward camp.

"For the record, you catching the drone doesn't equate to you beating me in a saber fight."

"So you're saying I only beat you in things that matter?" Pria glanced over.

"All right, fine, I'll give you this one. But seriously," I said, "thanks. That could have ended everything if you hadn't shown up."

"Agreed," Pria said. "And as a show of your gratitude, why don't you carry this for me? The stupid thing keeps trying to fly around inside the bag."

I looked over as a drone-sized bulge bounced around the sack. She forced it into my hands. I held it out in front of me, doing my best to keep it away from my head.

"Annoying, isn't it?" Pria said. "Hold it right there."

I did so, and in a flash, Pria's saber made contact with the drone inside.

It stopped trying to fly immediately. She continued walking.

"Zeno's going to love that," I said, slinging the bag over my shoulder. "What's he going to do with another broken drone?"

"Next time you catch a drone, you get to decide what to—"

Pria's reply was cut off, and we both stopped in our tracks. The bracelet on my wrist buzzed again. I dropped my voice to a whisper.

"Another one?" I said, scouring the area.

"Can't be, can it?" Pria said. "Zeno said their search patterns keep them separated by nearly half a mile."

Pria and I exchanged looks. We hadn't traveled far from the perimeter. I thought I could still make it out through the trees, but I didn't see anything. My bracelet buzzed again.

"Do you think our drone had a chance to transmit before I caught him?" Pria said, eyeing my bag.

My mind filled with the vision of an army of drones breaching the perimeter.

"No," I said, "the drones have to be within a few feet of each other to link up. At least, that's what Zeno said. This has to be something else, right?"

My eyes raced up and down the perimeter, searching for anything remotely out of place.

"Victor," Pria said, raising her arm to point. "Is that...?"

I followed her finger to a lone figure, clad entirely in black, making his way through the trees. The pale, blurred facial features—I would have recognized them anywhere.

Kratos.

All pretense of stealth forgotten I started to run, questions filling my mind as I did so. Where had he been? Why had it taken so long for him to get here?

Alex was going to be beside himself—I wouldn't be surprised if he fainted.

As we closed in on him, something felt off. I slowed to a jog but kept moving toward him.

Kratos had stopped in his tracks, which was odd, but it was almost like he didn't see us. He didn't really appear to be looking in our direction.

I called out to him.

"Kratos!" I said, slowing even further. He looked up at us, almost as if he was startled by our sudden appearance. "We've been worri—"

"Stop!" Kratos yelled, holding up his hands.

Pria and I came to a tentative halt and exchanged looks.

"It's me, Victor," I said slowly, holding up my hands. "And Pria." I nodded to my left.

Pria's brow was furrowed, a look of concerned intrigue on her face.

"Prove it."

Kratos's stance changed. I felt it more than I saw it. His eyes danced back and forth between us. He was ready to fight.

"Kratos," I started, "I, um, we—"

Pria shushed me. I looked over at her. She maintained her gaze on the Bounty Hunter.

"Prove what?" Pria said.

"That you're real," he said, his words fading almost to a whisper. Finally, his eyes slowed their rapid movement and locked with mine.

A chill ran down my spine. The piercing blue I had come to associate with strength and intelligence, and ultimately trust, had been replaced by something else. What exactly it was, I wasn't sure. I shifted uncomfortably and looked at Pria.

She ignored me and kept her eyes on Kratos.

"Your mother is Victoria Rosewood." Kratos's eyes snapped over to her. Pria continued. "She carries TIID. You were shot with poisoned bullets by one of her henchmen. We took you to Ville, where you were placed in a coma. We left you with friends to make sure you were completely healed. Jahko gave you the coordinates to this location."

Her words seemed to break down his walls. His posture relaxed.

"Now, how do we know *you* are who we think you are?"

Her words hung in the air.

Kratos continued to stare at her. His eyes jumped back and forth between the two of us again. I stood like a statue, feeling like any extra movement might spook him. After a moment, his eyes became still again. I watched as he took a deep breath and exhaled slowly. Then, with trembling hands, he reached up and removed his mask.

His golden hair brought a stark contrast to the rest of his appearance. What I saw was a man that was lost and confused. Several days' worth of stubble adorned his chin. His shoulders slumped.

"Help me."

4

————

We watched on as Kratos sat in Pria's medical tent. It was a small space made entirely of green canvas. Inside were a couple of rickety-looking but stable chairs, a table where patients would sit, and a single shelf with an assortment of vials and instruments. Due to a lack of space, we all stood while Pria worked.

Kratos's eyes were unblinking as she moved around him, taking his pulse and checking his eyes. It was like he was catatonic. I'd never seen anything like it.

"So he just"—Daphne glanced over— "showed up in the woods?"

"He's been through some stuff," Alex said, "but he's got an awesome internal compass. I mean, the fact that he knew you and Pria would be fighting in that exact spot at that very time..." He let out a low whistle. "That's good."

Pria let out an exasperated sigh.

"Alex, this is serious," she said, glancing over at him. "He could be seriously—"

"In good shape?" Alex said. "Come on, it's Kratos. He'll be fine."

I gave Alex a sidelong glance, which he missed. He grabbed a fistful of shirt and polished his prosthetic forearm. It was, if possible, even shinier than the day Ivy had given it to him. It was often a topic of conversation, and Alex certainly didn't shy away from the spotlight, but as I turned my gaze back toward Kratos, I couldn't help but wonder if Alex knew just how bad off Kratos was.

He had been mostly incoherent while Pria and I dragged him back to camp, and that wasn't even the worst of it. At points, he simply refused to walk, while at others, he attempted to break off in his own direction. I was glad he was here, but I was definitely worried. I'd rarely seen Pria so troubled about anything medical, and since arriving back at camp, her demeanor hadn't improved.

"Should we see where Zeno's at with that drone?" Daphne said, grabbing my hand as she did so. A tingle ran up my arm. I still wasn't completely used to us, but she gave me a smile as I caught her gaze. I looked back over to Kratos as Pria continued her assessment.

"You guys go," she said, lifting up Kratos's left hand and letting it fall limply back to his side. "I think we'll be here for a little bit."

"I'll stay," Alex said. "You know, for moral support. I never liked doctor's offices. He probably doesn't either."

Pria gave him a withering look.

"It'd be better if you left too," she said. "I don't want there to be any distractions for him."

Alex shrugged.

"Fine, guess I'm going with you guys."

I turned back to Daphne.

"All right, let's go."

***

Zeno's tent was one of the only structures in the camp that was built from something other than canvas. It was dome-shaped and made up of a complex series of heavy gauge steel cords. Apparently, the design made it impossible for any sort of electromagnetic signal to get in or out, which made it an ideal location for Zeno to tinker with our captured drone. A heavy fabric had been draped over the structure to protect it from the elements, but it didn't quite cover the whole thing.

"Zeno! It's us!" I stepped back as the rustling noises of fabric emanated within. Moments later, the door swung out to greet us.

"Well, those are new," Daphne said as Zeno appeared in the opening, a small, bright light shining from in between his eyes.

"What's up, team?"

In place of his regular glasses, he had what looked like a miniature set of binoculars inset into a pair of lenses with a small light situated directly over his nose.

"I knew he'd try and go all cyborg on us," Alex whispered to me. "It was just a matter of time." He patted his arm and strode past me to give Zeno a fist bump.

"My metal-armed bro, come on in, and, per our agreement, please keep your palm pointed at the ground."

"It was one accidental discharge, Zeno! One! There's nothing in here to shoot anyways." Alex's shoulders slumped as he shuffled inside, his arm noticeably stiff at his side.

"That's what you said last time," Zeno muttered. "I nearly lost part of my afro again."

I couldn't help but stifle a laugh. Zeno looked over at Daphne and me, the light on his contraption coming to rest on our interlocked fingers.

"Look at you two taking it to the next level." A smile spread across his face. "This is some serious stuff."

I felt Daphne's grip loosen. This was something I had been worried about over the last few weeks. Zeno used to have feelings for Daphne, and even though that was all in the past, I still felt a little weird about it.

"Come on, Zeno, my dad is supposed to be the one who makes this awkward," Daphne said. "And don't even get me started on you and Ivy."

"No idea what you're talking about," Zeno said lightly. "But since ol' Augustine is busy with all the new colony talk, someone's gotta make sure there's a healthy dose of awkward here. I'm told it's good for a new relationship." Zeno winked at me, blinding me with his light in the process.

I held up my hand and looked away.

"Sorry, bro, these are so light I almost forget they're there." He reached up, switched off his light, and motioned for us to come inside.

"So what exactly are they?" I said, making my way across the threshold. The dome enclosed a single large room with a very cluttered table in the center. On the table, partly disassembled, lay the most recent searcher drone. Even disabled, it made me wary.

"Pria's idea," Zeno explained. "Apparently, back before cameras and robot-assisted medicine, surgeons used to wear them so everything they looked at would be enlarged." He motioned to the drone components. "The circuits on this thing are pretty intricate, not to mention tiny. Nothing I haven't dealt with before," he added, closing the door behind us, "but these do help, especially when I'm doing it all by hand. Or when I'm repairing significant damage." He gave me a look, which I ignored.

"Any news on this thing?" I said, walking over to the table.

"Just finished erasing its memory," Zeno said. "It'll be a little bit before it's flying again, but I'll get it there. What I really need is a drone that hasn't been damaged, one that hasn't had any of its safety protocols activated. I could make some real headway if I—hey!"

Alex dropped an intricate metal piece back onto the table and quickly shoved his hands behind his back.

"Anyways," Zeno said, turning back to us, "I'm going to try and bug this one and then send it back out to join the rest of Rosewood's floating army. Maybe then we can figure out exactly what she's up to.

The one from last week was burnt to a crisp. I couldn't do anything with it except use it for scrap metal." Zeno looked over at Alex, whose hand was hovering over something else over the table. He froze.

"All I know is that if I didn't blast it, it would have reported back to Rosewood, and we all would have been in trouble." Alex shrugged. "And when I see trouble, I blast it."

"Pretty good plan, my man, except when we're in here!" Zeno held his hands wide, his voice escalating as the phrase ended.

"Fair point," Alex said simply and then returned his focus to the many pieces of the drone on the table.

Zeno shook his head.

"I should be able to finish up with the drone in the next hour or two. If Ivy were here, we would have cracked it already—"

"Or you wouldn't have even started," Alex chimed in, smiling as he did so. It wasn't often he got a jab in, but when he did, he knew it.

Daphne and I laughed.

"All right, my man, twenty-four-hour ban!"

"That's it?" Alex said.

"Out!" Zeno pointed to the door. "And leave that piece here."

Reluctantly, Alex dropped the piece in his hand back onto the table and made his way toward the door.

"Oh, and don't forget about the meeting," Zeno added. "I know they're boring, but Augustine wants us all there."

"Oh, right," he said. "I almost forgot. Thanks, Zeno." He paused for a fist bump, which Zeno reluctantly gave. Alex took a step outside. "I'll save you guys a seat!" He smiled and waved before closing the door behind him.

"I swear his new arm is going to his head," Zeno said.

"It does keep things entertaining," Daphne said.

"It's been good for him," I said. "He's definitely more confident, and he might even care less about other's opinions than before."

Zeno smiled to himself.

"A feat in and of itself. How's Kratos?"

Daphne and I looked at each other before I spoke up.

"We'll see. Pria's doing her exam now, but between you and me, I'm worried she's out of her depth here."

"Yeah," Daphne said, "he seems to be in pretty rough shape. It actually reminded me a lot of Jahko before he turned normal."

"Except that I don't think this is a part of Kratos's grand plan," I said. "And he didn't yell insults at us as we walked."

Zeno returned his magnified gaze to the partially dismantled drone.

"I can't imagine what he's been through. I hope Pria can do something for our black-clad brother. But it looks like we'll have to wait to find out," Zeno said, nodding to mine and Daphne's bracelets, which had just pulsed with white light three times in a row. Not only did they alert us of a perimeter breach, but they were also the primary means of calling everyone together. "Looks like the meeting is starting a few minutes early."

5

———

Alex waved us over as we approached. It looked as if the entirety of the camp was in attendance. Around a hundred people stood or sat in a small clearing between the trees. Everyone was oriented in a sort of semicircle, all listening to one man—Reginald Boone.

He wasn't a friendly person, and he definitely wasn't someone I enjoyed hearing speak. He was a shorter man, probably a good three inches shorter than I was, who kept his full head of gray hair closely cropped. He had strong opinions and ideas, and he was well-respected within the camp. He was a retired businessman who had done well for himself years ago. Grandfather knew him fairly well and seemed to like him, but there was something off-putting about him that I just couldn't place.

"...fool's errand," he was saying. Some agreeable muttering broke out in the crowd. "I see one way forward, and it is not back to that city."

Alex scooted over to make room for us as we sat down beside him. He and Zeno fist bumped. Daphne sat down next to me, her hand on mine.

"Yeah, you guys didn't miss much," he said a bit too loudly. "Just old Reggie talking about the city being a lost cause again."

If I knew anything about Boone, it was that he wouldn't appreciate being called "Reggie." Or at least the stern look he always wore led me to believe that was the case.

A few people nearby turned toward us to see who was talking. I hadn't spent much time getting to know people at the camp, but I did recognize one of the faces. She broke out in a smile as soon as our eyes met.

"Mrs. Supart," I whispered, leaning forward, "how are you?"

"Not nearly as good as you are," she said, pumping her eyebrows as she motioned with her eyes to mine and Daphne's hands. "Not that it matters, but I approve." She winked before turning back around.

I looked over at Daphne, who shrugged.

"People just like me," she said.

I looked back at Mrs. Supart. The stunner she had let me borrow after kidnapping her son, Jeffrey, was tucked into the waistband of her pants. It still bore the scuffs I'd given it. She was a very interesting lady, and although our interactions had been minimal, having her approval did feel good.

I searched the crowd for Augustine. He had to be around here somewhere. I had noticed over the past few weeks that he had an incredible knack for networking. Nearly everyone in the camp knew who he was and liked him. I imagined years ago, he must have been an effective senator, at least before he was slandered into exile by Rosewood.

I spotted him on the far side of the group with several people I didn't know. He seemed happy here. He caught my eye and smiled. I returned it. But my smile didn't last long as Reginald Boone continued his speech.

"Unfortunately, the destruction of a portion of the Innerbelt only served to bolster President Rosewood's allies. He," Boone continued, his eyes darting to me for a long, uncomfortable moment, "of course, he had no way of knowing the consequences of his actions, but facts are facts."

Several heads turned my way, and a scattering of mutters and nods floated around the group. The muttering grew louder, and Boone stood taller, puffing out his chest as he continued to talk. "Thanks to his reckless actions, the city's view of people like us has only deteriorated and done so quickly." He fixed me with a stare. "It is too big a mountain to climb. We must not deny the reality of the situation."

Color rushed to my face. Boone was blaming *me* for our current predicament as if I were the person solely responsible. He was ready to abandon friends and family alike if it meant he could start somewhere new.

He motioned to his right, and Trevor, the same Trevor who had met us at stunner-point when we first arrived several weeks back, held out a small box that projected a holographic video into the air. The muttering died off as the footage played.

Dozens of Nobles and Sinisters stood on opposite sides of a dividing fence between the Heights and the Flats. Men and women on both sides screamed and yelled at each other. Some held signs. All were angry. The video was uncomfortable to watch. If the "Nobles" were supposed to operate on a higher ethical plane than the "Sinisters," it wasn't showing.

"That was footage from yesterday." He turned slowly in a circle. "I believe that solidifies my point. Thank you, Trevor."

Trevor closed his hand around the holographic projector and returned to his previous spot. He was an odd man—very obedient to Boone, almost subservient. Otherwise, he was quiet and kept to himself.

"Trevor," Alex said, with a shake of his head. "Complete buzzkill. He's always around when Boone gets on me about firing my energy blasts at birds."

Zeno shook his head but didn't bother holding back a smile.

"Since the destructive events of several weeks ago," Boone continued, shooting another quick glance toward me, "Rosewood's support has grown significantly. The Noble population has become more and more vocal about their disdain for the Sinisters, and those who had been on the fence about the Sinisters have seemed to tip their support for Rosewood as well." He paused here, for effect I guessed. "The Sinisters have likewise increased their vocality. A confrontation is coming, and unfortunately, Victoria Rosewood has the upper hand."

He surveyed our group. "If we had months to plan and gain allies, perhaps there would be some small chance we could win back our city and eliminate the lies it was founded on, but I doubt it. On top of that, we don't have months. We don't have allies. We have each other. Our resources are best utilized in the creation of something new, not the destruction of something old." He said that last sentence slowly, deeply, and with a measure of emotion that was clearly fake. He ended with a slight bow of his head. "Thank you."

A general muttering broke out as he ended his speech. I heard my name mumbled more than a few times. Was I really to blame for Rosewood gaining more support?

Zeno leaned in close.

"You okay, bro? That was a little rough, him calling you out like that."

Daphne lightly squeezed my hand.

"It's fine," I said, letting out a breath.

I took a deep breath and evaluated the evidence. It was frustrating, but Boone made some logical points. Rosewood had more resources than we did. We had no allies, and any future allies would be exceptionally difficult to come by—especially because the bulk of our group was previously known as Nobles, and the bulk of our potential allies were currently Sinisters. Clearly, trust issues would arise. And lastly, Rosewood *had* capitalized on our haphazard escape from Ville.

Grandfather had explained to us a few days later the impact we had had on the Flats—the Innerbelt was shut down for over two weeks, something that had never happened before. Rosewood had placed a mandatory stay-at-home order for all of the Flats as a safety precaution. And, Rosewood's support, as well as everyone's disdain for Sinisters, had increased.

But it still felt like Boone was running away from the problem. Not to mention, 'the creation of something new' meant living essentially how we had been living indefinitely. There wasn't another city we could go to for hundreds of miles, and they more than likely wouldn't want us joining them. There was, however, a bunch of wilderness we could claim. Life in a tent without running water or permanent shelters didn't seem too appealing. And knowing Rosewood, would she ever stop searching for us?

Fleeing due to fear and then remaining in fear for the rest of your life wasn't a life. It was a prison.

Running away was the wrong move.

Grandfather stepped into the center as Boone stepped out.

"Thank you for your words, Reginald. Certainly, we have much to think on." He motioned to Trevor. "Trevor, can you give everyone a security update for the camp?"

"Absolutely, I can. "

Grandfather stepped aside as Trevor strutted forward importantly. He reached into one of his many pants pockets and pulled out a small screen.

"Current safety rating out of one hundred"—he thumbed his screen several times—"thirty-seven."

Another round of muttering broke out among the gathering.

This was not good. For the last few weeks, I had been seeing a general trend in the camp toward Boone's ideas. Numbers like this scared people, and as I had learned from my saber fights, people made bad decisions when they were scared.

Trevor continued. "This is a decrease of over twenty points from two weeks ago. I cite the following items as reasons." He looked down to his screen. "One. An extremely high number of drones—twelve, to be precise—have managed to breach our perimeter, or roughly one per—"

"Sorry, my man, that's not right, it's more like forty," Zeno said, speaking up.

"Excuse me?" Trevor said, looking up from his screen and peering around.

I elbowed Zeno in the ribs. He gave me a startled look. I glared.

"Right, I mean, yes, twelve *is* the number that we've captured and sent back out to Rosewood without her knowing."

Trevor narrowed his eyes but returned to his screen.

More muttering broke out, including me.

"What was that?" I said through the side of my mouth.

"Sorry, bro, dude's off by a factor of three! I've been using some tech that gently distorts their search patterns to go around us. There's been like forty that touched our perimeter, spent thirty seconds inside, and then left, but a few have gotten through."

"You mean twelve?" I whispered.

Zeno opened his mouth but didn't get a chance to respond.

"Two," Trevor said. The muttering ceased. "Increased activity in the camp due to boredom has a greater chance of alerting the searcher drones. Three. The algorithms used by the drones are learning algorithms. The more time we spend here, the more likely it is we will be found out."

Trevor shoved his screen back into his pocket.

"Each additional day we spend here will equal a decrease of at least one point on the security scale."

I felt the atmosphere change. Everyone was doing the math. We had even less time than we originally thought.

"Which is why a path must be chosen and chosen quickly!" Boone said. "The time for a decision is upon us. Safety does not lie behind us. It lies ahead and away from our former homes."

I let go of Daphne's hand and pushed myself to my feet.

"Do you really think that Rosewood is going to stop looking for us if we move to a new spot?" I said, taking a few steps into the clearing.

Boone's eyes bulged as I stood, incredulity and anger marking his face.

"Says the one who has given Rosewood additional leverage." Boone stood firm. His face relaxed, his signature crease forming between his eyes. "Your actions have brought Rosewood closer to her goal."

"My actions are also the reason we even have a chance at survival," I said. "Rosewood isn't going to stop looking for us. And if we allow her to gain complete control of the city, then what? The searcher drones will be the least of our worries." I paused briefly to look around. "Our knowledge is a threat to her. She's not going to leave us alone."

"She won't leave *you* alone," Boone said. "She very well may leave the rest of us be."

Silence fell over the group.

"Clearly," Grandfather said, taking a step forward and clearing his throat, "we have much to think about. I suggest we take what we've heard and—"

Grandfather paused and looked down at his wrist. We all did. The combined buzzing of all of our bracelets brought a certain hum to the air and, with it, fear. The meaning was clear—a searcher drone was close—but normally, only those in close proximity to the drone would feel the vibrations.

It could only mean one thing. My heart began to race. In response, a few of our numbers started to run.

"Stop!" I yelled. "They track movement better than sound. Everyone stay still."

The fleeing ceased, and the silence grew heavy.

"If you spot it," I said, loud enough for all to hear, "point it out."

My bracelet continued to hum. The vibration had never lasted so long.

"Correction, bro," Zeno said. "A vibration this long means there's more than one. We're talking drones plural."

As if confirming Zeno's words, the gentle sound of rotor blades speeding through the air met my ears. I followed the sound to the edge of our camp. What I saw made me wish I still had my lead-lined bag. Or a saber.

The drones weren't searching a grid pattern. They were in formation.

6

Four drones sped toward us in a box formation. They were a couple of hundred feet out but closing fast. One thought consumed my mind.

None could escape.

"There they are!" I yelled, abandoning my former plan. Stealth no longer mattered. Speed did. We had to catch them, and fast. If so much as one drone completed one scan and got away, that was it— Rosewood would know exactly where we were.

At my words, the whole camp began to scatter. Screams and yelling erupted around me.

"Alex!" I looked around, finding him right next to me. "Alex, we're going to need your arm."

"On it."

With a flourish, Alex pointed his arm to the sky, palm out, mechanical fingers splayed, his back to the drones.

"Six o'clock!" I said, pointing in the opposite direction.

"It's only four-thirty. Dinner's not for another hour and a—"

"No, behind you!"

"Right!" Alex swiveled, closing one eye as he did so, a little bit of his tongue sticking out of the corner of his mouth. "I see them, and I am locked on."

Around us, people continued to flee, most heading for their tents. The drones flew in a straight line toward us, completely ignoring anyone in their path. It's as if their course was set. And it probably was. On me.

I had had this suspicion before. When we had encountered other drones, they had always seemed to come after me, no one else. I assumed Rosewood had built something into their programming that scanned for my height and build or something, but whatever it was, it was accurate.

The drones continued to make a beeline straight toward me.

"What are you waiting for! Shoot!" I yelled.

"Someone is blocking my shot," Alex said, "but I'm just going to let her do her thing for a minute." He let his arm relax.

Pria appeared, sprinting straight at the drones, a long stick in her hand. She vaulted at them, wielding the stick like a saber, her makeshift blade coming down in a wide arc. The drones were quick, but not quick enough. In a shower of sparks and smoke, Pria brought one of the drones to the ground.

"She's clear!" Alex said. Without another word, a burst of energy erupted from his palm. The front most drone absorbed the blast and crashed into the drone behind it, bringing them both down.

"Boom! Two for one protégé special! Now for the last one, you tricky little—"

"No!" Zeno yelled, pulling Alex's arm down. We all stared at him. "We need one of them alive."

"What are you waiting for?" Pria yelled, sprinting toward us. "There's one more!"

"On it," Daphne said. She made a beeline away from the drone.

"Me too," I said, taking off after her, "but if it gets near the perimeter of the camp," I yelled, looking back, "you shoot it down!"

Alex nodded his understanding, and I adjusted my focus to the task at hand. As I started to run, the drone switched its course. Apparently, it *was* tracking me.

I ran faster.

Daphne continued her sprint toward... somewhere. I scoured the path ahead, but I wasn't sure where she was headed. I followed anyway. And then I saw it, or him. Trevor stood in his same spot, lead-lined bag in hand, his head turning this way and that in search of the final drone.

"Trevor!" Daphne yelled. In a single motion, she swiped his bag and changed her direction a hundred and eighty degrees.

I knew exactly what she was thinking.

I glanced over my shoulder and slowed my pace, letting the final drone gain on me. Daphne continued her sprint, our paths set to collide.

I could hear the rotors whirring behind me, a sound I was becoming far too familiar with. It was close, but so was Daphne.

"Now!" she yelled.

I threw my weight back and went into a skid, one leg out, one leg tucked underneath. Daphne jumped, soared over top of me, and bagged the drone mid-flight. She landed triumphantly and cinched the bag shut against her struggling captive.

"Zeno!" she yelled. "We got it!"

"And exactly how long do you plan on letting it fly around in here, identifying each and every one of us?"

Zeno didn't bother to look up when Boone finished his question, his eyes fixated on the task at hand. We'd been in here for half an hour, and I had started to wonder the same thing, but I assumed Zeno had things under control. This drone was pivotal—we finally had a fully functioning drone to work with—and that equated to information, good information. I wished for nothing more than for Boone to take his impatience elsewhere.

About fifteen of us, mostly the pseudo-leadership of the camp, stood in Zeno's dome-shaped hut. Grandfather, Augustine, Daphne, Pria, Alex, and I stood on one side, while Boone, Trevor, and their crew stood on the other.

The drone came back and turned away from us, almost like it was continuing its search pattern. It looked a little bit like a self-directed kite with a thin cord connecting it to Zeno's table. It was the latest gadget Zeno had conjured to attempt to truly hack the drones.

Any time we managed to capture one, usually by destroying it, Zeno had taken what was left and done his best to reverse engineer it. Bit by bit, we had learned how to catch them, how they searched for us, and how they communicated with one another (hence the lead-lined bags). But we didn't know much else. That was about to change. Or at least I hoped that was the case.

Boone, a look of annoyance on his stern, weathered face, stepped back as the drone buzzed past his head again. Zeno stood at his table, a small legion of screens casting a pale glow over his face as he typed rapidly on a keyboard while glancing periodically at the drone. I could see the reflection of the screens in his glasses. Pure gibberish. Was he even using English anymore?

"Right, two things, boss," Zeno said, finally looking up at Boone and setting his phone down as the drone continued to soar around the space. "Thing number one: its database is useless until it syncs up with the rest of the searcher drones like I've been telling you. They can't transmit data through all the trees or out of my faraday dome, so it can search and identify all it wants. And two: you see that cord that's connected to this table?"

Zeno rapped his knuckles on the surface and pointed at the taut cord that held the drone like a leash. "It's a reinforced mix of a nickel-titanium alloy embedded with chromium, bro. I call it 'Super Rope.' That drone isn't going anywhere." Zeno returned his focus to his phone, his fingers flying over the screens.

Boone cleared his throat and shook his head with an unintelligible mutter.

"And for three," Zeno raised his voice suddenly and locked eyes with Boone. "I'm experimenting here, and your negativity is bumming out my faraday bungalow dome." He held his arms wide. "Let's give me some space."

Boone's group took a collective step back. I couldn't help but smile, something Boone rarely ever did.

"All right, all right, that's good," Zeno said, working his shoulders almost like a dance. "I can feel it now."

"Feel what?" I gave him an odd look, and he smiled.

"The Chi, bro! I've never had to work with Chi before. Normally, it's concrete walls and wires and screens—not much Chi there. But here? Tons of Chi."

Boone shook his head again. Zeno's face became stern.

"Maybe another step back," he said. "You know, for the Chi?"

Begrudgingly, Boone and his team took another step back, nearly pressing themselves up against the wall.

"Thanks, my man." Zeno closed his eyes and took a deep breath in through his nose, which he then exhaled loudly. "Yep, it's really flowing now."

Zeno swayed a few times in place before his fingers returned to the keyboard.

I couldn't help but feel as though his act was just that—an act. He'd been working on the drones for weeks. He'd been optimistic, but really, though, how much closer *were* we to taking down Rosewood? Were we closer at all, or did each day we spent here put her that much further out of reach?

Boone eyed Zeno's progress. For some reason, he didn't seem too impressed with Zeno, unlike almost everyone else in the camp.

With his normal, easy demeanor and affable nature, Zeno had gotten to know just about everyone here. He had a reputation for his brilliance and his ability to get excited about and improve almost anything, but he had steered clear of Boone and his crew.

Secretly, I thought they feared him a little bit, a fact I could tell Zeno enjoyed.

Next to me, Augustine leaned over and lowered his voice.

"Never a dull moment, is there?"

I nodded in agreement.

"I've always been amazed by Zeno's many abilities," he continued. "I've often thought his talents were more useful than mine, but, well, to each his own."

I watched Zeno's fingers as they flew across one of the keyboards, the plastic keys chattering as their inputs appeared on the screens in front of him. It was true that Zeno had been immensely helpful since the very beginning, but it hadn't been his gadgets or knowledge that had gotten us this far. No doubt they had helped, and without them, we probably wouldn't be here, but that wasn't what that kept us going. It was a set of ideals. It was the belief that people were worth saving, that good existed in all people, that hope was never lost—that's what hadn't let us give up. That's what really moved people to action.

If only we could convince Boone of those same ideals, maybe we could get out of this forest and go after Rosewood.

"I don't know, Augustine, I—" I started to respond but was cut off by the sound of Zeno slapping his palms on the table.

"All right, ladies and bros," he said, nodding to Daphne and Pria. The drone continued to circle overhead. "On previous attempts, I disabled the drones before I started working on them, or at least what was left of them. The technological wizard that I am, I learned a lot, but not enough. I knew, somewhere, embedded in the drones, a protocol existed that directed their actions. And if I could find that, then maybe we could get a glimpse into what Rosewood is planning. If she's invested this type of time into these drones, she's probably using them for other things too, you follow?"

This was nothing new. Zeno had told Daphne, Alex, Pria, and me the very same thing at least a hundred times already.

"You're saying, Mr. Zeno, that the drones may hold some strategic value if we can extract the appropriate information?" Grandfather said.

"Grandpa Wells!" Zeno nodded appreciatively. "Exactly. And while this drone has been flying around identifying all of us, I've been accessing its inner workings through the cable because that's what the increased Chi allows me to do."

I stood up a little straighter. Would this actually amount to something?

"To answer your unspoken question, bro," he said to me with a smirk, "yes, this is about to blow your mind."

With a single finger, Zeno turned one of the larger screens on the desk around so we could all see.

"All semi-intelligent machines have a basic set of commands or objectives that guide them. Without further ado, I present to you Rosewood's main objectives for these drones in three, two, one."

He emphatically pressed one of the keys, and the screen in front of us began to fill with text.

My heart began to race. I couldn't read the words fast enough.

Almost as one, we all rushed forward to get a better look.

Execute objective display

<u>Low Priority</u>

1. Locate and detain Victor Wells and his allies

<u>Mid-level Priority</u>
2. Identify weak spots in Sinister infrastructure

<u>High Priority</u>
3. Exterminate all Sinisters

Timeline to extermination movement. 25 hours, 8 minutes, 56 seconds.

I read the text again. Timeline to extermination movement. 25 hours, 8 minutes, 32 seconds.

It continued to count down.

31 seconds. 30 seconds. 29...

I stared at the last line for several seconds.

She couldn't... How many people lived in the Heights? How many innocent people? I knew Rosewood was bad, but this amounted to genocide.

I felt a mix of anger and fear rushing up inside of me like I hadn't felt before. This was her plan all along. Get rid of the people who hated her, the only people who would challenge her, and then what? Permanent life extension? President to benevolent dictator?

"Bros, what's it say?" Zeno said, his smile faltering. "I gave you guys the only display screen for dramatic effect."

When none of us answered, he stepped around the table, the silence in the dome interrupted only by his footsteps and the soft whir of the circling drone. A moment later, Zeno broke the silence.

"Oh, dang."

"Yeah," I said.

"Call a meeting," Boone said gruffly. "We have some decisions to make."

7

———

"The protocol is extermination, not assimilation. Thousands will die. And we'll be included in that number if we return."

Boone stood resolute in the center of the clearing, yet again, as a series of muttered agreements made their way around the circle. The entire camp had come out to hear arguments.

A decision needed to be made, and made quickly. The time to act had arrived.

As Boone paused, side conversations broke out around me.

"He's hitting this whole 'we're going to die if we go back' thing pretty hard, isn't he?" Alex said, rolling his eyes. "But I have to tell you —my Bounty Hunter instincts are telling me that a lot of people agree with him."

As much as I disagreed with Boone's plans, people listened when he spoke. His demeanor commanded respect, and his ideas, unfortunately, appealed to many. More than half, if I were being honest with myself. A lot more than half.

"Speaking of the Bounty Hunter," I said.

"I told him about the extermination plan," Alex said.

"How'd he take it?"

"Tough to say," Alex said. "I think I caught him mid-meditation, but message received. Or at least delivered." He shrugged. "It's in his subconscious. It'll resurface soon."

Boone continued.

"There is but one alternative here, and it is to move on. We can take our meager resources and build anew."

"Where?"

Boone paused and looked around, finally locating the source of the question—Mrs. Supart. Beside her, Jeffrey shrunk as all eyes turned to her.

"Where shall we go?" Boone asked. "Away from here, far aw—"

"Yes, yes, I know you want to go 'far away,'" Mrs. Supart said, cutting him off, "but I want to know exactly what your plan is. Our resources won't last forever, and I'd rather die fighting for a noble cause than starve to death in a wasteland."

A few scattered "yeahs" were heard in the group.

"And what about the dead zones and radiation?" someone else said. "We don't have all the protective equipment!"

Boone's face fell to one of irritation as more and more people began shouting out their opinions.

"We can make a new place exactly how we want i—"

"We're not making it how *you* want it."

"And what about an energy source? There's no infrastructure out there! We'll be living in huts without running water."

I checked Boone, who glanced over at me, making brief eye contact. His irritation was turning to frustration.

"Listen!" The chattering stopped. "These details are just that—details. We can and will build something better than where we came from. We have brilliant people here. In the beginning, will things be as comfortable as they once were?" Boone looked around. "Of course not. But things will not be any less comfortable than this." He gestured to a small collection of tents nearby. "I can see it now—we will only make progress from here."

"And what about the people we're leaving behind?" I said, taking a step forward.

Boone continued on as if I hadn't spoken.

"There is incredible ingenuity and resolve in this group!" he said. "I would go so far as to say that our group consists of the finest our former city had to offer."

"Half of the city."

Heads turned as Pria's voice cut into Boone's speech. She stood, arms folded, about ten feet from me, a look of poorly veiled resentment on her face. Boone inclined his head in agreement.

"Yes," he said slowly, "half of the city. But this is what we have. This is the hand we have been dealt. I am confident in our ability to brave the elements and build something that will last."

Boone paused as some muttering broke out. He held up a hand, and things quieted down once more. He continued. "I am not confident in our ability to withstand whatever lethal means President Rosewood has planned for her city. To go back, even for a worthy cause, spells death."

A hush fell over the crowd. The momentum had shifted. I saw the corner of Boone's mouth twitch. He knew he was moments away from delivering the final blow. I couldn't let him make it. Our eyes locked for a brief moment before he began to speak.

"For our own survival—"

"For our own survival?" I said, stepping forward to face Boone. "Survival? Is that what we're doing here, hiding out in the woods, fearing for our lives every moment of every day?" I broke my gaze with Boone and looked around. "Do you think that someone like Rosewood, someone with nearly unlimited resources with a vendetta against us, will leave us all alone if we just set up camp somewhere out of the way?"

"It would be a waste of resources for her to come after—"

"You don't know what Rosewood is or isn't willing to do, Boone," I said, cutting him off and facing him once more. "You haven't looked her in the eyes while she told you that she would murder every single one of your family members, all of your closest friends, to maintain her secret. You haven't seen her stand by as her biological son was shot by one of her henchmen."

I turned to address the camp. "I have, so I know that she won't leave us alone. If you choose to leave and live the rest of your life in fear, knowing that one day Rosewood will come for you, so be it, but I'm going to go back to our home, and I am going to fight."

All eyes rested on me, but I had nothing more to say. The silence continued for a few more seconds, almost to the point of awkwardness. I took a step backward, hoping to signal I was done.

Mrs. Supart gave me a subtle nod and a tight smile. Daphne's jaw was set. She knew this was the only way. Alex stood nonchalantly admiring his gleaming prothesis as if he'd known we'd get to this point eventually. I moved to go stand by my friends, my family.

"You will be outmanned and outgunned," Boone said in the silence that followed.

Before I could answer, a raspy, ragged voice entered the conversation.

"And you think that will be different when she comes for anyone who leaves?"

I whipped my head around. A few gasps accompanied the appearance of Kratos. Like an invisible wedge, members of the camp parted to let him through as he trudged forward, dressed in his customary Bounty Hunter attire. Most wouldn't be able to tell, but to me, Kratos looked haggard. His walk was off, the way he held himself was different, but at least he was coherent. Or at least appeared to be.

"Victor is right," he continued, laboring through his words. "She will stop at nothing to destroy you, all of you. Anyone who is a threat.

So whether we face her now when she only has control of half of the city or later when she has complete control is up to you." He shifted his weight to his other foot. "I choose the former."

At his words, Boone deflated. Even here, the Bounty Hunter's words carried additional weight.

Grandfather stepped forward.

"It is the logical choice," he said. "Of course, none of you will be forced to aid in the fight, but any able hands will be helpful." He surveyed the camp. "It appears as though we must move quickly. And to do so, we will need a plan."

8

After riding in the sweepers of Ville, our new transportation was kind of a letdown. The sweeper we had arrived in was loaded up with as many supplies and heavier items as we could shove into it. Zeno had rigged it to drive on its own, so we were here, instead of with the sweeper.

Outside, and sometimes inside our vehicle, branches slapped by at what felt like a glacial pace. Trees lined either side of the dirt path. If only we had vehicles with enclosed cabins. I held my arm out the window and sprayed a blast of invisible beads to block an incoming leafy appendage.

Alex, Daphne, and I sat in the back of a, well, wheels with seats. Augustine drove, following a line of similar vehicles, some towing a few of our supplies, some merely hauling people. Our vehicle had no doors, no protection, and apparently couldn't move very quickly. The dirt ruts we drove in didn't do our lack of suspension any favors either. It was a wonder our "car" hadn't fallen apart already.

"It doesn't feel like this is enough," Daphne said quietly.

I looked out over the procession of vehicles, all in varying stages of disrepair. I knew that our return to the city was the right call, but our chances against Rosewood weighed on me. Would we even make a difference? Could we?

I imagined the people in the Heights. How would they respond to a group of mostly former Nobles showing up in just a few hours' time?

I shook my head, trying to force out the negativity. Daphne squeezed my hand. I squeezed back.

"We'll find a way," I said.

We had to.

"Hey!"

Behind me, Alex had his hands over his face.

"You're getting beads all over me!"

"Oh, sorry," I said, relaxing my finger position on my gloves. My absent-minded spraying stopped.

"Do you think Rosewood knows where we are yet?" Daphne said.

"I don't know," I said. "Zeno told me her DNA locator device doesn't work outside of the city, and I haven't seen any drones, but that doesn't mean much."

I nodded to our convoy.

Augustine chimed in from the front seat.

"I imagine she knows. We haven't been particularly stealthy these last few hours."

"You're probably right," I said, grunting as we bounced over a particularly large branch in the path. I looked behind us at our meager convoy, then back to the dash next to Augustine. Zeno had rigged up a timer to match the extermination countdown. Twenty-one hours, eighteen minutes, and seven seconds before Rosewood initiated genocide in the Heights.

"You don't like our odds," Daphne said, quiet enough that her dad couldn't hear us.

"We just need to figure out the rest of the plan," I said.

"You mean the remaining ninety percent?" Daphne raised her

eyebrows. "We'd almost be better off winging it—that's basically what we're doing."

I couldn't argue with that. We had left a good chunk of our food and supplies at camp, we had enough sabers for half of us, and as of our departure, the plan was to travel to the southern end of the city and attempt to get into the Heights undetected, provided that we had someone on the inside willing to help out, which reminded me:

"Augustine, any updates on our contact in the Flats?"

"Nothing yet," Augustine replied. "Your grandfather is hopeful that we'll have help once we reach the city's perimeter."

"Thanks," I said. I lowered my voice. "We need to have a strategy once we're in the Heights."

"I never thought I'd say this," Daphne said, "but I really wish Tyrann was still alive. He'd be the perfect person to rally everyone together."

"Or force them," I said. "But yeah, you're right."

Behind us, the sound of a small engine puttered along, getting louder with each second.

"Hey, Pri, what's up?" Alex said as Pria motored up beside us on a two-wheeler.

"My name is four letters long, please trouble yourself to enunciate them all." She gave Alex her customary glare.

Alex leaned over toward me.

"Secretly, she loves it."

"You think so?"

Alex nodded confidently.

I knew he couldn't be more wrong, but I was grateful she hadn't heard us talking about her dad. It was still a sore spot for her, and I assumed it would be for a while. We hadn't talked about it, but I was starting to think that Rosewood was responsible, not someone else in the Heights.

I looked at Daphne and Alex. Rosewood wasn't afraid to kill to protect herself. She would use any weapon at her disposal. It was a recurring thought, but I couldn't help but wonder if my attachments to other people were more dangerous than they were helpful.

"Anyways," Pria said, bringing me back to the present, "have you seen Kratos anywhere?"

"Wasn't he with you?" I asked.

"Nah," Alex said. "You guys all saw him at the meeting. He was better, right? He didn't need to stay with Pria." Alex looked down at her. "No offense."

"He was *not* better," she said. "He's acting like he's had a psychotic break, there's some psychosomatic thing going on—you all saw how he was moving— and he's repressing part of his speech. He needs to be under observation!"

"Wait, so Kratos is missing?" I said. "You lost Kratos?"

"Kratos is never *lost*," Alex said. "Purposeful wandering is a useful tool in the belt of a—"

"No," Pria said, cutting him off. "Kratos is lost."

I turned to Augustine.

"Hey, can you send a message to Zeno? Kratos is—"

"I've already tried that," Pria said, impatience showing in her voice. "Zeno's been running a search for the last thirty minutes but hasn't found anything yet. I've been circling in and out of the woods trying to find him."

A sinking feeling had started to develop inside of me. Something wasn't right.

Alex didn't seem too concerned. Granted, in his eyes, Kratos could do no wrong, but I had seen him. I had interacted with him. Everything was not all right. The fact that he was missing was worrisome.

At that moment, we all careened forward. A few of our belongings went flying into the back of Augustine's seat as our vehicle came to a standstill. Up ahead, the rest of the convoy seemed to have stopped as well. I noticed a break in the trees. And was that the distant glimmer of buildings I noticed in the waning sun?

"Sorry!" Augustine said. "I've just gotten word—we're stopping here to regroup. Boone wants to talk. We're about thirty minutes from the outskirts of the Flats. It's time to put our plan into action."

A small clearing overlooked the gentle downslope that led to our former home. The sun had begun to set through a mostly cloudless sky. Distant hues of purple and pink added color to the darkening nightscape. As the colors began to outline the taller buildings in the Heights, I looked to the Flats, to the Capital. I could just make out the one lone skyscraper there. A chill ran down my spine.

It was the only move, but we had had so little time to prepare.

Boone was talking, outlining what he thought was the best way to proceed.

"We need to gain contact with our friends in the Flats and find a way to stay in the Flats undetected."

I let loose a scoff. Daphne shook her head while Pria pity-laughed. Alex polished his arm while Augustine gave reproachful looks all around. Boone continued, unabated.

"From there, we can draw a division within the Nobles and—"

"It'll never work," I said.

Boone, exasperated, sighed and took a step closer, fixing me with his best withering gaze.

"Mr. Wells, I grow tired of your constant disagreement."

"Then come up with better plans," Daphne said.

Boone swiveled his gaze to her.

"We have less than a day to make a stand against Rosewood," I said, drawing his attention back to me. "We don't have time to divide a group that's loyal to her. Our only chance is uniting everyone who's already opposed."

"That, or disrupting Rosewood's operation to the point that she has to reschedule," Pria added. "But because Zeno couldn't get more information out of the drones, I doubt that is possible."

I could hear the annoyance in her voice, but our lack of info wasn't Zeno's fault, and she knew that.

A few horns honked behind us, an annoying reminder of our lack of time.

"I suppose you're right," Boone said slowly. "On both counts."

Pria gave me a quick look—almost an "I told you so."

Boone continued. "How, then, do you propose we go about creating unity between all of—" He crinkled his nose but quickly realized his error and tried to scratch at his nose to hide it. "All of them?"

"*They* happen to have a common enemy," Daphne said.

"But they don't have a history of being united," Boone responded.

I could see the wheels turning behind Daphne's eyes. Augustine stood off to the side, content to watch, at least for now.

"What are you thinking?" I said.

Daphne glanced at Boone and then back to me.

"The playmakers in the Heights will need a show of good faith, something to let them know we're on their side, but it has to be something quick and easy for us and meaningful to them." She looked up for a few moments before continuing. "Many of them have been wanting to make a move against the Flats for years but haven't had the resources or encouragement to do it."

I looked out over the city. From this distance, at dusk, everything seemed so peaceful, so normal. Even the weather—the temperature, the stillness of the oncoming evening—everything pointed toward safety and comfort.

"I take it you have something in mind?" Boone said, clearly annoyed with her vagueness.

"I do."

"Care to share?"

Daphne stared at Boone for a few seconds, her eyes narrowing. "No," she said, then continued along. "After we've proved we're useful to them, we'll have leverage, and then..." She trailed off. "Do you guys hear that?"

I didn't hear anything.

Without warning, the leaves of the surrounding trees began rustling as if we were in the midst of a windstorm, but around us, the air was calm.

Horns started honking, lights flashed. People screamed and pointed to the sky, to the trees, everywhere. Daphne was the first of us to notice them.

"Drones!" she yelled.

Like a coordinated swarm of ill-intentioned birds, dozens and dozens of them appeared, seeming to line the pathway of our convoy as far as I could see.

They flew and dipped and dove, moving in a way we hadn't seen before. These drones were different.

Alex looked to me for direction, and so did the others.

A feeling overtook me, an intuition.

"Get out of your cars!" I yelled, taking off in a sprint down the row. "Get out! Out!"

I ducked and let loose a steady stream of invisible beads overhead. Terrified faces stared at me as I ran past them. "Get out! Get out!"

We were like sitting ducks on the path. All of the vehicles were blocked in by each other. The surrounding forest was the safer bet.

I looked to the sky. More drones were coming.

The jig was up—Rosewood had found us, all of us. There was no use trying to hide. We had to fight back, and for that, we needed our only sweeper, the sweeper that carried all of our sabers, all of our offensive measures.

A few drones whirred overhead, but most had disappeared into the trees, following people as they fled. I kept a steady stream of invisible beads pointed above my head, just in case, and slowed my jog to a walk. Where was the sweeper?

Daphne arrived at my side.

"We've got to fight back," I said.

Up the path, a few bursts of light shot through the air, one of them sending a drone crashing to the ground.

"Boom!"

Alex let loose another yell as a near continuous stream of energy bursts left his outstretched arm.

"Where's the sweeper?" I said.

"It's bringing up the rear," Daphne said, pointing to my right. "Let's go!"

About twenty cars down, I saw it, its metal panels almost appearing to shimmer in the waning light. It had been our savior before, and perhaps it could be again.

We started running, but it was at that moment that I noticed a drone hovering above it, not moving like the rest of them. Alarm bells sounded in my mind.

I yelled for Alex, but it was in vain. There wasn't enough time.

A small blinking light detached itself from the drone, falling in what seemed like slow motion in perfect alignment with the roof of our one and only chance to fight back.

On impact, the sweeper burst into flame, metal panels and all. Even the arms caught fire, the metal tentacles seeming to melt before my eyes. I could feel the heat, even from this distance.

And then, the fading sky was alight with a long row of blinking lights. Lights that lined up perfectly with our convoy. They fell through the sky, and in moments, nearly every car in our company was aflame.

The fire consumed everything it touched. Our transport, our

weapons, our food—everything was on fire. I just stood there and watched.

Screams echoed and mingled with coughing from all the smoke. Daphne grabbed my arm, shaking me from my shock.

"We need to get—" She broke into a coughing fit and ducked down, but there was no hiding from it. "To the others," she rasped, pulling her shirt up over her mouth and nose.

I followed suit, but it didn't do much.

The smoke stung my eyes, but I blinked it away.

"Let's go."

We jogged through the haze. Most of the screaming had died out as everyone came to accept what had happened. The drones were nowhere to be seen, but whether that was due to the smoke or because their mission had been completed, I wasn't sure.

"Dad!" Daphne yelled.

"Alex!" I yelled.

"Over here!"

A burst of light shot upward through the haze twenty feet in front of me.

Alex.

I ran toward him.

"Alex!" I yelled once more.

"Victor!"

The smoke was so thick I collided with him, but I didn't care. I didn't apologize. I was too relieved to see him.

"Are you hurt?" I said, grabbing him by the shoulders. His face was covered in soot and ash, but I didn't see any pain in it.

"No, we're all fi—" He doubled over, coughing and wheezing vehemently. "Fine," he continued, his voice hoarse. "My arm still works, so I'm good. You?"

"Fine," I said. "Where's everyone else?"

"We took cover when you started to run. It looked like a lot of people made it out safe, but, well, come on, we're over—"

Alex paused and looked up.

"Do you feel that?" he said.

It was light at first, a few wet drops here and there, and then it intensified.

Like a gift from the heavens, water began pouring over us.

Rain, heavy, clothes-drenching rain, fell from the sky.

Alex punched me in the arm and smiled.

I looked at Daphne, the water droplets leaving streaks down her smoke-stained face. She attempted a smile, but her heart wasn't in it. The rain meant nothing. It saved nothing. It had come too late.

As the rain continued, the fires began to die. The smoke started to clear, and the smell of wet soil mixed with the charred aroma of ash.

Hesitantly, members of our group started appearing at the edges of the trees, holding their hands out as the water poured down. The drones appeared to be gone. They had disappeared as quickly as they had come.

I heard a few noises of delight or thanks, but as steam and smoke rose from what remained of our meager fleet, the toll the fires had taken sank in. There wasn't a single vehicle that hadn't been ravaged by the flames.

It had taken mere minutes, and there was nothing we could have done. The sheer firepower Rosewood had created to deal with us... We were lucky to have our lives.

Was this what she had in mind for the Heights?

"Daphne!"

Augustine called out from somewhere nearby.

"Dad!" Daphne yelled, turning to see him. He jogged over, a smile of relief working its way onto his face.

"Thank goodness you're all okay," he said, wrapping all three of us into a hug. He let go and then embraced Daphne separately. His eyes were red from the smoke, and his clothes were wet from the rain, but he looked unharmed.

"From what I can tell, no one was seriously injured," he said. "Although, Pria is already making the rounds, to be sure. Thank goodness for this rain," he said, holding out his hands. "I can't imagine what would have happened to the forest without it."

As if to contradict his words, the pitter-patter of the rain suddenly ceased.

I looked up, expecting to see clouds. Instead, all I could do was yell.

"EVERYBODY RUN!"

A canopy of darkness composed entirely of drones hovered above us.

I pushed Alex and Daphne toward the trees. The drones began to swarm, many of them making a line straight for us. Hysteria broke out anew. Screams filled the air as realization hit all of us.

The rain had come from the drones.

Sprinting toward the tree line, I could hear a mass of fluttering rotors behind me.

The trees were close but not close enough. I felt something slam into my ankles, sending me tumbling into the now slick mud. Daphne and Alex continued to run, unaware I had fallen.

A contingent of drones flew past me and formed a wall, cutting off my escape.

More drones surrounded me, their black bodies completely obscuring the trees, forcing me to turn around.

But in front of me, there was no way out either. They had formed a huge enclosure around me, blocking everyone else out, and me in. But I wasn't alone—another contingent of drones of all sizes swirled around in front of me inside the enclosure. Slowly, they flew into their places, packing themselves tightly together to form a horrifying, larger-than-life shape.

At least ten feet tall, a metal incarnation of Dr. Rosewood's head floated in front of me, and it began to speak.

"Victor Wells."

Rosewood's voice boomed from the formation, sure to reach the ears of every member of our camp.

"What a nice little parade you organized. I'm sure there's something to be said, what with all of the rain, hmm?"

She laughed—a cold, hideous sound that echoed through the now silent forest. I balled my fists.

"I knew you were planning something." She smiled. "But honestly, I expected more."

"We're not done yet!" I yelled, having no idea whether or not she could hear me. But I didn't care. "You'll never get away with it! We won't let you!"

The drones rearranged her face into one of innocent confusion.

"We, Mr. Wells? Do you mean you and the Pendleton girl?"

I felt like my mind had plunged into a bucket of ice water. Cold, constricting, fear-inducing ice water.

"How quaint—you think the two of you can stop my, what was it I put in those drones? Oh yes! The extermination order! Yes, about that."

Immediately, I felt like I was sinking.

"Clearly, you can see the whole purpose of letting you find that bit of code was to flush you out along with all of your precious resources, can't you?" She paused, letting her words sink in. "Tsk, tsk, Mr. Wells, there *is* no extermination order. Well, at least not this week."

I felt ill. How had we been so stupid? How had we not questioned what we had found? How did she know about Daphne and me?

"Things will proceed as I direct," the floating metal apparition continued. "Your company is free to go, derelict vagabonds that they now are. You are free to wander the wastelands until your dying days.

However, if that is the path you choose, you will not be welcome when you want to return.

"However, I am not without mercy. Those of you who fear the outside world, those of you who would have our city be your home once more, are welcome to return. Conditionally, of course—you will be stripped of any former Noble status, but you will live. Let today serve as a warning to those who displease me."

She nodded to her right.

"Those of you who choose to return will be escorted to the Heights by my mobile army. They will disperse once you've reached the other side of the fence. You will become Sinisters. Beyond that, I do not care. Any small uprising you create will be nothing more than a small annoyance, like an unwanted spider scurrying across my floor, a spider I will stomp on quickly, violently, and without any remorse. You have four minutes to decide. At that time, my offer to return expires. There will be no second chances."

Behind me, the drones broke formation as Rosewood's face dissolved into individual drones. The forest was still. Slowly, I turned around. The entire camp had gathered sparsely behind me. I took in their faces, their horrified, defeated faces. They were scared. They were beaten.

Boone stepped forward.

"Three minutes and thirty seconds left. It's time to make a decision."

9

I needed more than three minutes.

In light of what had just happened, Boone was too persuasive, and everyone was too scared.

Three groups had formed—mine was the smallest, and Boone's was the largest. Those who were undecided remained in the middle, but as the seconds counted down, that group grew smaller and smaller. My group did not get bigger.

"Rosewood will never allow us to live full lives," Boone was saying. "We will be captives to an oppressive government, and if today's display was any indicator, we would sooner become martyrs than die of old age. The more we stick together, the greater success we'll have."

Two minutes.

Daphne, Alex, Zeno, and I stood resolute as several more people made their way over to Boone's side.

Less than an hour ago, there were over a hundred people willing to take the fight to Rosewood. Now, that number was less than ten, and I couldn't help but feel as though with each person who joined with Boone, our chances against Rosewood became that much slimmer.

"Our home isn't lost yet," I said, raising my voice. "There are thousands of people still there, people you know, people worth fighting for. We can save them. We don't have to abandon them to save ourselves."

My plea fell on deaf ears. A few more people made their way to Boone's group. He and I exchanged glances. I had expected to see triumph, but instead, I saw sadness. At that moment, it hit me—he truly didn't believe our home could be saved.

I shrugged off the feeling as Pria finally made her way over.

I nodded to her and then moved my gaze to the remaining undecided people. Grandfather, Augustine, Mrs. Supart, a few people whose names I couldn't recall, and oddly enough, Trevor, still stood, looking back and forth between me and Boone. I was unsure of what Grandfather would do—I knew he wanted to help, but we couldn't escape the reality of his age. If we returned and something resembling a war ensued, well, I couldn't blame him if he went with Boone. I hoped Mrs. Supart would come with us, and I could see Augustine talking rapidly with those who remained.

At that moment, I was blindsided by a brief but strong hug from Pria. Startled, I looked at her.

"What was that?"

"It was a thank you. And a goodbye," she said, looking down briefly before meeting my gaze once more. "I'm going with Boone," she said.

The impact of her words was like a punch to the gut.

She continued talking, her words coming more quickly. "I just need to be in a place where I'm not known as Tyrann Kane's daughter. I need to be able to be me, and Boone's group will need someone with medical expertise... I'll be thinking about you, all of you."

The others mumbled a series of surprised and saddened goodbyes. I couldn't get any words out. We were depending on her. Surely, she had known that, right? We were going back into the Heights and we would need her contacts, her knowledge of the city, her saber skills, her friendship...

Daphne rushed forward and wrapped her in an embrace. They exchanged a few whispered words that I couldn't make out, and then both wiped at their eyes as they broke apart.

Pria gave us one last look, then walked away.

A loud tone sounded from the group of drones, followed by a mechanical-sounding voice that said, "One minute."

Boone's group had swelled to nearly a hundred people. We had five, and only five were left to make a decision. One went with Boone, and the other four made their way over to us. That made eight. Eight out of a hundred. Eight to take on Rosewood. I tried to tell myself that we had taken on Ville with less, but even in my head, it didn't sound convincing.

Mrs. Supart walked quickly toward us, as did Grandfather, Augustine, and, strangely enough, Trevor.

Mrs. Supart, stunner in hand, beamed a strong smile at us. It was a smile that said she knew we would do it, and she knew we would succeed. She had that effect on people. And not to mention her comfort level with stunners—especially with Pria gone, she would be a huge asset to us.

"Where's Jeffrey?" Alex said, looking around.

"He's with Boone," she said, sadness overtaking her face. "Which is where I'll be going here in less than a minute, so I'll make what I have to say short."

That brought us to seven.

"Oh, don't look at me like that." She shook her stunner at us. "An old woman like me would only slow you down. And heaven knows I've shot a few errant stunner blasts in my days, but you'll need more than that when you're up against that Rosewood hag."

"But—" Daphne started.

She held up her hand and continued speaking.

"Every parent tells their child stories, stories to teach them lessons, stories to help them dream. When you take down Rosewood"—she locked eyes with me, eyes that were fierce, eyes that knew sacrifice—"yours will be a story that parents tell to inspire. It's a rare thing to be able to stand up for what is right, especially when the price is high. And that is why you will win. You will win."

She gave us a final smile, a final twirl of her stunner, then walked to join the other group.

As she left, Grandfather, Augustine, and Trevor joined our group. Grandfather placed his hand on my shoulder and squeezed. Augustine reached out and pulled Daphne into a strong embrace.

"Twenty seconds!" Boone called out. Then, in a slightly shakier voice—"Trevor?"

Trevor didn't turn around. I looked at him and nodded, a nod that he returned.

The drones, which had been spectators for the last few minutes, now began to move, forming a sort of curtain between the seven of us and the others. I glanced over briefly at Daphne and Augustine. They were still holding each other tightly. A knot grew in my stomach.

"Victor," Grandfather said. "I love you."

It was something he had told me time and time again, but this time was different.

He released my shoulder and took a step back. Augustine released Daphne and joined him. They both took another step back. And then another.

And another.

It was a goodbye, a proper one this time. Augustine turned his gaze briefly from Daphne to me, then back to his daughter. He reached up and wiped a tear from his eye.

"You've grown into a fine young man," Grandfather called out, as the wall of drones came closer to us. He stopped where he was. "Your parents would be immensely proud. They live on through you. Best of luck, grandson."

The wall of drones made its way around him, then blocked him out completely.

Like an ominous storm front, the drones continued their path. I wiped the wetness from my face and steeled myself. I felt Daphne's fingers interlock with mine and squeeze.

The drones surrounded the five of us, and we were forced to move —a mobile prison cell shepherding us directly into enemy territory.

10

Conversation happened around me, but I was still reeling. The five of us, only five of us, walked the overgrown path back to the city.

Pria wasn't coming.

Mrs. Supart and Jeffrey had decided to stay behind.

Grandfather had said goodbye.

Augustine had abandoned us.

I was shaken, to say the least.

When we made our final stand against Rosewood, I had anticipated we would have more, a lot more. But it didn't matter now.

I took a handful of deep breaths, steadying my mind and steeling my nerves as I did so. Five of us, plus whoever we could recruit in the Heights. There, I knew we could gain numbers. We would head back to the events center, then get to work. I found myself wishing Tyrann were still alive. This would be a moment where he could shine, an instance where our plans could have actually lined up.

My mind moved on to other options, other scenarios, as we trudged along on our drone-guided path. It was the only way I could distract myself from the pain I felt. Daphne and I had stopped holding hands a while back.

She was quiet like I was—I assumed she was thinking, trying to figure all of this out. I glanced over at her, her hair in a low ponytail, swinging side to side as she walked. I hadn't had much time to process it, but Rosewood knew. How could she have known that we were more than friends? And would she use that against us? We had kept our distance from each other before. "No distractions." It had been a mantra, but it had mostly been an excuse. We had been, well, I had been, afraid to let something so good happen when everything around us was so bad.

I glanced over at her again.

"I really thought we'd have more," she said quietly while Alex and Zeno chatted in front of us.

"I did too," I said. "You think they'll be okay without us?"

Daphne scoffed.

"Boone was probably right. They're probably safer now that we're gone." She looked away from me. "Can you believe Pria, though? She would have loved all of this."

I knew she was trying to keep it light, but I could hear the betrayal in her voice, and it wasn't just because of Pria.

"I'm sorry your dad didn't come with us," I said.

She didn't respond—she wiped once at her face and kept walking. I reached for her hand, but she didn't take it. And maybe, with Rosewood, that was the right call for us. I staggered my steps so that I wasn't exactly in line with her. She probably needed some time. I probably needed some time.

So much had changed in an hour. Rosewood knew about us—she knew where we were, where we were going. She knew we would do everything in our power to stop her, and still, she was letting us come back. Was it possible my worst fears would still come true? Could we survive this? Could our relationship? What would Rosewood come up with to use against us?

Fear mixed with anger at the thought, but at the moment, I wasn't sure which emotion was more powerful.

"So, are we going to use this time to plan our attack or what?" Alex said. "Because let's not kid ourselves, the inside of a black drone tornado is a pretty unique creative space, am I right?"

"What?" Zeno said, glaring at Alex. "Come on, man—plan of attack? There is no plan of attack. These drones are watching us, bro. And listening!"

Alex's face fell slightly.

"It doesn't matter," I said. "She already knows. There's no reason for us to come back except to go after her. The only reason she'd let us come back was if she thought she'd already won."

"And she hasn't," Alex said with a nod. "Idiot. All right, let's plan."

"Yeah," Zeno said, "still no reason to spell it all out for her. Let her do some of the work, right?" He eyed me. "How about we get to know our new bro, Trevor, here a little better first?"

Zeno skipped forward and patted Trevor on the shoulder. He jumped at the contact.

I knew him as Boone's lackey—someone who did all of his bidding, someone who took his assigned task, whatever it may be, very seriously. His short, dark hair, dark eyes, and my inability to recall him ever laugh only enhanced his no-nonsense persona.

But that was all I knew about him, and if he had chosen to join our group, we needed to know him better. Besides, we had the time. From what I could tell, the drones were taking us the long way back to the Heights, probably to keep us as far away from the Capital as possible or just wear us out in general.

"Sorry, bro, didn't mean to startle you," Zeno said, turning back toward me with a grimace. "So, Trevor, why are you here? Out of a hundred people who followed Boone, I would have thought you'd be first in his line, and yet you're here. With us. And all these drones."

Trevor took a moment to respond, his silence almost to the point of awkwardness. Before speaking, he cleared his throat.

"Have any of you ever been a servant?" he said, his voice rough.

His question caught me off guard. I knew he was from the Flats, and there were no servants in the Flats, or anywhere that I was aware of.

"I have," Trevor continued, clearing his throat again. "My family was. We made sure the extremely wealthy Nobles were taken care of. The truly powerful relied on us to ensure their lives didn't fall apart. Our DNA wasn't as Noble as most in the Flats. We didn't rank high enough to be anything other than trustworthy, so that's what we were."

"Whoa," Zeno whispered. "Bro, that was kind of heavy."

"I didn't know people in the Flats had servants," Daphne said.

"They kept it quiet." Trevor shrugged. "I always felt it was wrong to be classed like that, and I wanted to help fix it, which is why I left the Flats in the first place."

"Did you work for Boone before leaving the Flats?" I said.

"No." He said the word shamefully. "But it's what I'm good at—attending to the needs of others. It was a comfortable role to play. If I had stayed, I would have continued to help Mr. Boone like a servant, and I kept asking myself, 'How is that any better than what I had before?' It wasn't, so here I am. At my own service."

The drones continued their unending orbit around us in the silence that followed.

"Any questions?" he said.

"Yes," Alex said, as if he had been waiting patiently for him to ask. "How old are you?"

"Twenty."

"Wait, really?" Alex said. "Man, you seem, I don't know, older. Maybe even twenty-one or twenty-two or something."

Trevor gave him a confused look, but Alex continued unabated.

"Favorite color?"

"Yellow."

"Favorite food?"

"Donuts."

"Ahhh…" Alex placed a hand on his stomach and closed his eyes. "Trevor, we're going to be good friends." He punched Trevor lightly on the shoulder, and Trevor jumped again.

I was beginning to suspect that Trevor wasn't used to much physical interaction. Alex didn't notice and gave him a smile, which Trevor didn't return at first, but then, his posture relaxed, and he did.

It was transformative. He instantly became warmer. But more importantly, he believed things could still change. It was in that moment I had a realization. The five of us, out of everyone in that camp, believed change could still occur. That's what we had in common, that's what bound us together.

I smiled at the back of his head. He was going to be a good addition to our team.

———

The terrain beneath our feet, the only terrain we could really see, began to change once again. I thought I had glimpsed a tall building a few minutes back, but the circling drones did an excellent job blocking our surroundings, not to mention that darkness had fallen over an hour ago.

We had gone from thick underbrush to sparsely growing weeds and dirt, which transitioned into asphalt and pavement, which transitioned yet again to cracked roads and loose gravel with the occasional weed here and there.

We were in the Heights now, or at least near it. Which part of the Heights was difficult to say—our contingent of chaperoning drones had taken us on a detour, but lucky for us, Daphne knew her way around as well as anyone. We'd be back to Augustine's compound in no time.

"Guys, we're close," Alex said. "I can smell it."

As if to confirm his words, the drones began to break formation. Thirty or so flew forward and created a path that ended in a chain link fence, the space illuminated only partially by a flickering lamp post. The message was clear. This was where our escort ended.

I could make out nearby buildings that rose up into the sky, blocking out the stars. I glanced behind me to find a wall of drones, apparently blocking any thought of escape, which was unnecessary, seeing as the Heights was where we wanted to go. There was only one path here, and it was forward, into the Heights.

"Finally," Alex said, throwing his arms up. "My feet are killing me."

"We're not done walking yet," Daphne said.

The drone-enforced path to the fence was only wide enough to accommodate one person at a time.

"Seeing as you know where we are," Zeno said, "how about ladies first?"

Daphne smirked and looked out past the fence. Broken sidewalks, cracked roads, decaying buildings, not to mention some of the unsavory people who lived here—I never thought I'd be so relieved to see it.

"Home sweet home," Daphne said.

She disappeared over the fence in a matter of seconds. Alex went next in a significantly less graceful manner.

"You ready, bro?" Zeno said, turning to Trevor. "Ever been to the Heights before?"

"Never," Trevor said. He looked tense as he stared at the fence, but then again, he had looked tense almost the entire time we had been walking.

"Well, you're in for a treat. I'll have to introduce you to Gina. Let's go."

Zeno slapped him on the shoulder and took off down the pathway. Trevor followed. After a few moments, they, too, had made it over the fence.

I could see them waiting for me on the other side, free from the drones beneath the unreliable yellow glow of the lamp post. I was ready to join them, ready to be free of our temporary moving prison… well, almost ready.

I eyed the drones that lined the path and remembered the most recent damage they had done, as well as the near-constant paranoia they had caused over the last few weeks.

I was certain that the drones had recorded everything we did and said for the entire walk. I was certain that a team of her people would analyze it to try and figure out what we were going to do. But with even greater certainty, somehow, I knew Rosewood was watching me right now. This wasn't something that she would watch later, she was viewing me live, this very second.

"Well, Victoria," I said, beginning my walk down the line of drones. Each step was slow and deliberate. "I can't say this wasn't fun."

The drones remained silent.

"I'm going to make a bold claim," I said. "Whatever you have planned—it's not going to work."

I took another two steps in silence before the nearest drone came to life.

"There is nothing worthwhile about bold stupidity." Rosewood's voice came through like ice.

"Believing that good will win isn't stupidity," I said, taking slow, measured strides. "Besides, I was once told that fortune favors the bold."

I started to climb the fence. The nearest drone began to ascend with me, keeping Rosewood's voice right in my ears.

"Indeed it does, Victor," she said, her pronunciation of my name sending goosebumps cascading down my neck. "But you know nothing of boldness. But rest assured, you will. There is nothing you or anyone can do to stop what I've put in motion. If only you knew what I have planned." She paused as I reached the top of the fence, clearly calculating her final words.

"I'll enjoy watching you suffer through it very much."

I could hear the malice and yearning in her voice.

I looked down to where they all stood, all of them ready and waiting. Rosewood had nothing like this, she had no one like them, she only had fear and deception.

"It's too bad," I said, turning to face the drone. I wanted her to get one more good look at me before she made her biggest mistake yet. "You won't have the chance." I swung my legs over the top and dismounted, landing hard on the pavement below.

I motioned to Daphne.

"Lead the way."

11

"We haven't been gone *that* long, have we?"

There had been a few odd things about our walk back to the compound. First, it was dark, but the threat of being abducted by a sweeper was gone. Jahko had assured us such would be the case weeks ago. Even so, the streets were vacant—I assumed out of habit more than anything. Secondly, each step closer to the compound seemed to be slightly cleaner than the last. Not that things had been terribly dirty before, but it was different, somehow. Things had been eerily quiet, but as we approached the old events center, the noise level increased.

Now I knew why.

The courtyard was completely filled with people, hundreds of them. People of all ages—small pockets of people our age to entire families—were spread throughout the open space. I noticed a few green canvas tents scattered about—not unlike the tents we had used in the forest. But even stranger than all of that, at the end of the court-yard, backed up against the facade of the events center, was a small stage. It was constructed of an assortment of mismatched wooden pallets that, at first glance, didn't appear all that sturdy. A single figure illuminated by an array of lights stood on it, holding a microphone.

He stood tall, his arms spread wide, a large spotlight shining behind him, casting his larger-than-life shadow over part of the crowd. His face was obscured in the darkness, but his words rang out loud and clear.

"There is nothing wrong with being Sinister!" The man spoke with a powerfully charismatic voice, not a deep voice, but one that was filled with emotion. He paused in interesting places and placed emphasis sporadically, and the people here loved it.

The crowd cheered. Some clapped. Some nodded their heads in vigorous agreement.

"You must accept yourself!" the man continued, his voice booming throughout the clear night. Then, in a comparative whisper: "And you must learn to love yourself."

Clapping broke out again.

"Well, this is new," I said.

"Yeah. And weird," Daphne said out of the corner of her mouth.

"Did you say this was weird?" Alex practically shouted as people around us began to clap once more. The person closest to us shot him a look of outrage, which he didn't notice. Daphne threw Alex a look of warning, her eyes going fierce and wide at the same time.

"Couldn't agree more!" Alex said with a slight but confused nod of his head. He leaned over to me and looked both ways before speaking in a quieter voice. "She's really got to work on the nonverbal cues."

I looked over at him as he mimicked Daphne's expression of warning.

"This," he said, pointing to his now fierce, wide eyes, "does not mean weird."

Next to me, Daphne shook her head. I laughed, which only elicited more incredulous looks.

Trevor had been mostly subdued, which I had come to recognize as his baseline, but at this, he nudged my arm.

"I am not familiar with the Heights," he said. "I take it this is not normal."

This was *not* normal. This was Augustine's home, a place he, Daphne, and Zeno had lived for years after being forced into exile. The crowd, the lights, the noise—it was all very out of place.

"In my experience," I said, "Sinisters don't congregate, at least not like this."

Trevor nodded and returned to observing his surroundings.

The crowd grew silent as the man up front began speaking once more.

"My friends," he said. "Free yourselves from the guilt forced upon you by those who would call you their betters. Difference is not wrong. Difference is not inferiority. Believing those things is wrong. Believing those things is inferiority!"

Cheers rang through the courtyard again.

"I will end as I began, with love. Each of you is worthy of it, no matter what anyone else says. And remember this—peace is not attainable in your own lives until there is love. Thank you."

Applause broke out once more as the man exited the stage and spotlight. A woman took his place. I couldn't make out her features from here, but she seemed to be the director of the event.

"Before we all turn in for the night," she said, her voice much higher than the average woman, "there are a few announcements. First, there are more and more people arriving each day. A building about ten blocks from here collapsed just this morning."

Muttering broke out in the crowd. To my knowledge, that hadn't happened before, but judging from the snippets I could hear from those nearby, it wasn't a first.

"Another one?"

"That's the second one this week!"

The director held up her hands.

"I know, I know. It's devastating, and we expect many, if not all, to come here to stay. Everyone, of course, is welcome, so please be accommodating to the newcomers. As you know, supplies are still slim, but we're all helping each other. Share what you can. Have a good night."

Normal chatter began to break out as people started to disperse, some of them into the events center and some of them to their tents in the courtyard.

The five of us stayed where we were for a moment.

Zeno was the first to speak.

"All right, bros, I feel like we've walked into a parallel universe. What was that?"

It had all felt foreign. It was like it didn't fit here in the Heights, and I couldn't tell whether it was a good thing or not.

"I kind of liked it," Alex said. "Who doesn't love love?"

Trevor cleared his throat.

"It reminds me of religion," he said. "We don't really have much in the way of religion now, but there was one family I served that kept a few rather ancient-looking history books on their shelves. They told of a time when people would meet together to hear a pastor speak. It makes sense that the Heights would be the place it reemerges."

"What do you mean?" I said.

Trevor cleared his throat once more.

"Historically, religion often gave disconnected groups of people a common purpose, a common culture, and a sense of community. It was a great source of strength and growth for those involved. And if there was ever a group of people who could benefit from those things, it's the people of the Heights."

"So you're saying that this," Daphne started, gesturing around us, "is like religion, like a church? The man that was speaking was like a pastor?"

"It seems that way, yes," Trevor said.

We all stood there for a few moments longer, contemplating the scene.

During my brief time in the Heights several weeks ago, I didn't get the impression that many people were friendly with one another. It looked like that had changed, or maybe I just hadn't seen it before.

As the crowd continued to thin out, the "pastor" became visible, surrounded by only a handful of people.

"Well, if we really want to find out what this is all about," I said, motioning toward the stage, "let's go ask."

I started off toward him, weaving in and out of the stragglers as we made our way through the crowd. Before we arrived, however, the pastor took notice of us. His eyes enlarged, and he broke into a wide, toothy grin.

"Mr. Zeno!" he said. He broke away from the people he'd been speaking to and made his way toward us.

"Do you know him?" Daphne said, looking over at Zeno.

"Never seen the dude in my life," he said slowly, an unsure look on his face as the man approached with a hand outstretched and a smile on his face. Zeno tentatively took it, and the pastor gave it a vigorous shake.

"Kyros Zeno!" The man continued to shake Zeno's hand as he looked around at each of us.

He was, for all intents and purposes, a very average-looking man. He stood about my height. His hair was brown. He wasn't fat, but he wasn't thin—nothing about his physical characteristics stood out. But I supposed people didn't come for his looks. They were more interested in what he had to say.

"So, it's, uh, it's good to see you?" Zeno said.

The man continued to shake his hand as he answered.

"Technically, we've never met, but I did know Augustine. I nearly came to one of his classes on several occasions. This was in the past of course, but now, well…" He finally let go and motioned to the stage before turning back to us. "Is he around here somewhere?"

"No," Daphne said, fixing him with a stare.

"Oh. Well, no matter. It's a pleasure to meet you, all of you." His eyes flickered to me before returning to Zeno. "I am Benjamin."

I noticed that his strange inflection and emphasis had disappeared. And I couldn't help but think it was a little odd that he knew exactly who Zeno was, even though they had never met. And what about last names? Did people not give those out anymore?

I made a mental note to reach out to Augustine about him.

"All right, Benjamin," Zeno said, clearly unsettled by him, "it's good to meet you. This is Daphne, Victor, Alex, and Trevor."

Benjamin nodded at each of us in turn, a bland smile on his face as he did so.

"A pleasure."

"So," Alex said, grabbing a fistful of his shirt and polishing his arm, "how long have you been holding these shindigs?"

"Our *gatherings* have been happening almost nightly for the last two weeks."

"That's a lot of people just showing up overnight," Daphne said.

"Well, every group isn't as large as tonight's," Benjamin said, his smile fixed firmly in place. "Although, every day, there are new faces. I'm happy the message resonates."

"We only caught the end of your speech," Alex said, "but all the stuff about love. I mean, everyone loves love, right? Trevor, back me up."

Benjamin chuckled kindly as Trevor appeared to contemplate the request, finally giving a brief nod.

"I'd say most people do."

Alex laughed and slapped him on the shoulder, which only caused him to jump.

"Of course they do," Alex said.

"I'll admit that our message isn't for everyone in the Heights, but I do preach a message of love," Benjamin said. "We in the Heights have been looked down upon for so long—most have forgotten what it means to love themselves. It is vitally important if we are to move toward our goals."

"Goals?" I said.

Benjamin turned his gaze on me.

"Yes, Victor. Change cannot occur in a group before change happens inside the individual. Broken people trying to fix broken things doesn't end well. I believe that's exactly the problem with our friends, the Nobles."

I waited, expecting him to elaborate, but he didn't. He stood there with that same strange smile on his face as if he had completely answered my question.

"So you're saying you want change?" I said, pushing for more. "In what way?"

"It's simple, Victor. Freedom. It's in short supply here. The people you saw here this evening are only the beginning. The Heights has always been a fragmented place, but I believe freedom can be achieved through unity. A united group is always stronger than the individual parts."

Daphne and I exchanged looks. Benjamin's words were still a non-answer. What was he getting at?

"I think we all can agree with that," Trevor said. He looked beyond Benjamin to the small stage. I followed his gaze. The director woman was up there walking swiftly this way and that. I still couldn't make out her features well, but she was certainly busy, pointing at things as other volunteers did what she told them.

"Your director—" I started.

"Yes, Maggie," Benjamin finished. "My assistant. I'd be lost without her."

"Right," I said, "Maggie, she said something earlier about another building collapsing?"

"Yes," Benjamin said, adopting a somber expression, "sadly, there have been multiple buildings that have fallen in the last few weeks. Hundreds have been left homeless. It has been a real tragedy. Fortunately, our space has provided shelter to so many."

I looked at Daphne. Her expression had started to change. I looked to Zeno, who seemed like he wasn't quite grasping what Benjamin was saying, and then back to Daphne. Her face had started to take on a slightly redder hue than normal.

"*Our* space?" Daphne said. "What do you th—"

"I'm glad the events center could help out," I said, jumping in before things got too heated. "And with all the homeless people, we'll do our best to keep helping out, right, guys?"

"Uh, yeah, of course," Zeno said, glancing at Daphne. "But, I gotta say, it's been a long day for us—lots of walking—and we're about ready for some sleep, so we're going to, you know, turn in for the night."

Zeno nodded toward the closest set of doors leading inside. He extended his hand once more. "Benjamin, it was great to meet you, bro. I'm sure we'll talk again soon, right?" He looked at me, clearly still processing the situation.

"Yes, of course," Benjamin said, taking a step to the side and motioning to the door. "I look forward to it."

"So do we," I said. "Let's go."

"Can I ask why you all abandoned your home for so long?" Benjamin suddenly said. "I assume I would have seen you had you been here weeks ago when we started this. You'll find that many changes have been made to help those in need."

"What kind of changes?" Daphne said, ignoring the first question, her tone even and measured.

"The need in the community has been great. All I can offer you is a few cots to share."

"Bro, excuse me?" Zeno said. "Or uh, pastor bro? Is that more appropriate?" Zeno shook his head. "Anyways, what do you mean you can only offer us cots?"

"In our own home," Daphne added.

"As I said, things have changed. I'm sure you can understand how much need there is in the community—hundreds of homeless people with the building collapses. I'm sure you understand." His bland smile appeared once more. "Cots can be found just inside the doors. Any empty room or floor space is yours for the taking."

Daphne opened her mouth to respond, but I was quicker.

"Thanks, Benjamin," I said. "I think we can show ourselves in."

Without another word, I continued toward the doors. I glanced over my shoulder, making sure everyone was following me. Benjamin stood by, nodding a farewell to each of them in turn.

My feet hurt, and I was exhausted, but I had a feeling that sleep wouldn't come soon for us tonight.

12

———

There were people everywhere, many lying on small cots, many trying to make do with what they had. Some had rolled-up clothes to place underneath their heads. Others had small bags or nothing at all. Fortunately, no one tried to talk to us as we picked our way through the maze of hallways.

Most feigned sleep, but a few of the small groups that had gathered stared suspiciously as we passed. I did my best not to make eye contact, as did the others, but Trevor apparently wanted to observe. He looked at everything and everyone but somehow still managed to be polite about it. Fortunately, our new houseguests were about as eager to meet us as we were to meet them. I watched as Trevor passed by a small family—a mom, dad, and two kids, all attempting to sleep under a single blanket.

Surely, this was a lot to take in.

Daphne led the way. As we moved along, we began to encounter fewer and fewer people. I knew she was mad—the rest of us had grabbed cots when we walked in, but not her. She strode silently but purposefully down each hallway.

I glanced down at the cot I was carrying. It looked like an oversized pillow that had lost most of its stuffing. I looked at the cot Alex had picked up—lumpy and discolored. At first, he had been carrying it, being careful not to let it touch the floor, but now he dragged it behind him. I would have said the floor was dirtier, but looking at both Zeno's and Trevor's cots, I wasn't so sure.

As we picked our way down the hallways, Daphne stopped periodically to peer into rooms just off the hallway. Each time, she huffed, slammed the door shut, then increased her pace. Trevor didn't seem to notice, but Zeno, Alex, and I exchanged looks. We let her stay a little bit ahead of us after the first couple of slams.

Daphne turned down another hallway, one I hadn't been down before, which, finally, was completely empty.

We passed by a couple of doors, which, surprisingly, Daphne didn't open.

Zeno nudged me and nodded to Daphne, who was still walking with a very frustrated air.

I nudged him back and nodded at her, too, but he shook his head vigorously.

"Hey, Daphne," Alex said, looking over at Zeno and me before turning to her. "Since we've got the hallway to ourselves, can we—"

"Not yet," Daphne said, cutting him off, her eyes searching up and down the hallway. She let out a deep breath. "Sorry, I'm searching for something."

"Uh, what are you searching for, Daph?" Zeno said, his tone light. "There's nothing down here but empty hallways."

"Contrary to what you may believe," Daphne said slowly, her eyes searching up and down the walls, "you don't know every secret this building has to offer." She moved over closer to the wall and ran her hand across a stretch of faded and chipping paint. She stopped. "There it is."

She moved her fingers into a slight crease in the wall. Carefully, she dug her nails into the crease and pulled. A small section of the wall popped out and slid to the side, opening just wide enough to let a person through into the darkness beyond. Daphne reached her arm into the void and waved it around. A light flickered to life, illuminating the narrow passageway.

"Yes!" Alex exclaimed, bounding forward to stick his head in through the opening. He popped back out. "We were due for a secret passageway."

With a weary grin, Daphne stepped past him and disappeared inside.

"Follow me."

"Is it common for buildings here to have secret passageways?" Trevor said, stepping forward to peer inside.

"More common than you'd think," Zeno said as he made his way through the opening, squeezing his cot in with him.

I brought up the rear of the group, glancing up and down the hallway before I stepped inside. As soon as my body was in, the panel behind me slid back into place.

In front of me and around a corner, a light flickered, casting an intermittent elongated shadow of Zeno's afro across the wall to my left. The floors were dusty, and our shoes left footprints on the ground, or at least the part of the ground Alex's cot hadn't swept.

Clearly, this hadn't been used in ages. I followed the passageway around two gentle curves until I came to a stop at the top of a rather lengthy staircase that descended straight down into the dark. Daphne was already at the bottom.

A light fluttered to life, illuminating the space below.

I had no choice but to stop and stare.

"Dang," Zeno's voice echoed all around us. "This is some place."

He was right.

The only way I could describe it was like a very large closet. From the top of the stairs, the ceiling stayed at a consistent height over the entirety of the room. What looked like stacks of old mattresses, boxes of who knew what, and a pile of what appeared to be molding blankets covered most of the floor. Things smelled musty, even from the top of the stairs, and I imagined it was worse at the bottom.

"Are you waiting for something?" Daphne said, already beginning to make her way across the room below.

"Just taking it all in," Zeno said.

By the time the four of us had reached the bottom of the staircase, Daphne was pulling down a few of the old mattresses from one of the piles. The moment they hit the floor, clouds of dust billowed up into the stale air.

Daphne squinted and coughed as she waved the particulate-filled air away from her face.

"It's been a few years since I've been down here." She pushed past a stack of boxes. "A year or two after we first moved in, I started getting some supplies together, just in case. Dry food, mattresses, blankets, medical supplies—just some basics."

"I'm surprised Gina kept this place from me," Zeno said. "She's got the whole compound mapped out in detail."

Daphne smiled. It wasn't easy to beat Zeno at something, especially if he had Gina helping him out.

"And I'm impressed," Trevor said. "You did all this by yourself? Your father didn't help?"

Daphne's smile faltered at the mention of Augustine.

"Sorry, I know this isn't the arrangement we were expecting coming back to," she started.

"Um, yeah, no, it's great, Daph," Zeno said. "We're going up against Rosewood. We need some privacy, and this place has it." He grabbed a mattress from the pile and started to pull it to the ground. "That and a good night's sleep, and we'll be golden."

The mattress dropped to the concrete floor and a cloud of dust ballooned from it and into the air. "As long as we don't all get bronchitis," he coughed. "You know we don't have time for that."

He pulled out his phone and checked for a signal. "Good." He paused and looked up toward the ceiling. "Good." He turned his focus back to his phone and began a series of taps.

"As far as I'm concerned, this is way better than some regular room or hallway," Alex said.

I tried to catch Daphne's eye to let her know I approved, but she wasn't looking my way.

Next to me, Trevor craned his neck to get a better look at Zeno's phone.

"What's he doing?" he said.

"Probably something useful," Alex said, flexing his mechanical fingers. "That's his thing. I do cool stuff. He does useful stuff. Victor, well…" Alex shrugged. "You'll figure it out."

"Alex's other thing is giving compliments," I said.

"Look, not all of us were blessed with good looks and multiple skills like you and Daphne, okay?"

I looked over at Daphne and smiled, but still couldn't catch her eye.

"Oh, I've got looks," Zeno said, his fingers continuing to blur across his screen. "Looks for days, style for weeks, and cool for months. Annnd…" He gave a few final taps to his phone. "Solutions for always."

A faint sound could be heard, and the stagnant air in the room suddenly became less so.

"My girl, Gina, is up and running!" Zeno said, pocketing his phone. "In incognito mode, of course. Don't want to disturb the new locals. I've got her filtration system engaged and targeted for this area. The air should be clean in about thirty seconds."

I tossed my cot aside and reached for my own mattress, immediately releasing a cloud of dust, which was sucked upward into the air vent above.

"See," Alex said, nudging Trevor, "useful."

"I see that," Trevor said. "Who's Gina?"

"Gina's the brain of this building," Zeno said. "Surveillance, security, comfort—she's in charge of it all. Well, I'm in charge of her, so technically, I'm in charge of it all, but..." His phone buzzed. He fished it out of his pocket, read the screen, and scoffed. "You've made changes since I've been gone?"

His phone buzzed again. He looked down at the screen and then back up at the ceiling. I assumed there was a camera somewhere, or at least a microphone that he was yelling at. "Why would you think I abandoned you?"

Another buzz.

"I did too say goodbye!"

Another buzz.

He shook his head before looking back up this time, his face stern like a frustrated parent. "You know I don't like threats, but if you keep this up, I'll reprogram you, you hear me?"

He looked back to his phone, daring it to vibrate again. When it didn't, Zeno shoved his phone back into his pocket with more force than was necessary.

I looked at Trevor, who didn't seem at all fazed by Zeno's fight with a voiceless computer.

"Sorry you all had to see that," he said. "She gets a little testy without constant oversight." His phone buzzed again. He sighed and fished it out. "And did I mention needy?" After a brief pause, he looked up. "Yes, Gina, we should be back for good."

"Speaking of being back," I said, grateful for the opportunity to interrupt. "We need a plan." I looked at Daphne again. A nagging voice in the back of my mind told me to ask if she was okay, but I decided to wait. In my pause, Alex spoke up.

"Daphne, you doing okay over there?" he said.

All eyes were on her. You could see the tension in the way she stood. Her eyes darted quickly around at all of us, and finally, she let her shoulders slump, the look on her face melted, and I knew we were about to see something that few had.

Tears came to her eyes, and before they could begin their course down her now-red cheeks, her hands were there, wiping away the evidence.

I rushed over to comfort her, but she waved me off. I stopped awkwardly in the middle of our little circle and retreated back.

"I'm okay," she sniffed. "Really, I'm fine." She took a deep breath and forced a smile. "I thought my dad would be with us, but... it's okay. The rest of the camp needs someone like him. What we need is to figure out what to do with this Benjamin guy, and also Rosewood."

We all stared at her for a moment. I wanted to say something, but after being waved off, I didn't think that was what she wanted. When no one spoke up, Daphne talked again.

"Seriously, I'm fine. Let's figure out this Benjamin guy."

Alex was the first one to break the silence.

"Not having your dad around sucks. I'm sorry."

The rest of us muttered our agreement. Of everyone, Alex knew what it was like to have your dad choose not to be with you. Daphne wiped at her face a final time.

"All right, let's talk Benjamin first," Alex said. "He's got a good message. Can't argue with love, right?"

And just like that, we were back on track.

I was jealous of Alex's casual nature. He said things in a way others wouldn't, and it was helpful in a way I often couldn't be.

"Right," Zeno said, jumping in, "Pastor-bro *was* talking about unifying the Sinisters. I know we didn't do much planning on the way over here, but if we're going to go against Rosewood, we're going to need all the help we can get."

"Strength in numbers," I said, turning away from Daphne. "Yeah, I had the same thought. If we're planning on bringing everyone together anyways, why not use Benjamin to our advantage?"

"Excuse—I mean, forgive me." Trevor shook his head. "Old habits." He exhaled. "In my opinion, he is a strange man to be a unifying figure."

"How so?" Daphne said.

"The way he spoke was intriguing," Trevor said, "but his clothes were slightly mismatched, he chews the fingernails on his thumb and forefinger of his left hand, and I would say he hasn't bathed in over two days."

"Well, that's the Heights for you, I guess?" Alex said, looking around with a shrug.

"No, it's my experience that people of influence are rarely gifted in a single area or so sloppy in the way they present themselves."

"What are you saying?" I said. "He's a fraud?"

"I'm saying that there's more to learn about him."

We all took a moment to digest Trevor's words.

I hadn't noticed those things about Benjamin. Granted, I hadn't ever been a servant, and it made me wonder exactly what Trevor had done and who he had done it for.

"I don't think we should rock the boat," Daphne said, "or at least not yet. He could be useful to us."

"Not to mention," I started, "if buildings have been collapsing and people have come here for shelter, Benjamin might actually be doing something good for the people here, right?"

"Right," Zeno said, eyeing me. "What are you thinking?"

"I'm thinking that we should get to know him better," I said, a plan beginning to take shape in my mind. "We need to understand our surroundings if we're going to use them, right?"

I was met with a series of nods.

"We also need to get reacquainted with the Heights and find out what's really going on here. So who's doing what?"

"I can stay here," Zeno said. "I've got to make sure Gina's operating correctly. If we're going after Rosewood, we'll need everything Gina can give us. If I've got some spare time, I'll see what I can learn about our boy Benjamin, too."

"Makes sense," I said. "You get Gina up and running and get to know Benjamin. We'll go out into the city tomorrow and see what we can learn."

"Sounds like a plan," Daphne said. "I have some ideas for the Heights." A wry smile took hold of her face. "It's good to be back."

13

———

After picking our way silently through the still-sleeping bundles of people scattered about the rooms and hallways, it was good to be outside. Goosebumps covered my arms, and the cool air felt refreshing on my face.

"You realize normal people don't wake up this early, right?" Alex said, stifling yet another yawn.

Beside me, Trevor glanced at his watch with a look of confusion on his face.

"First off," Daphne said, "it's not that early. And second off, out of everyone, you should be the least tired. You started snoring the moment your head touched the mattress."

Alex shrugged.

"What can I say, I *am* very good at sleeping."

We turned a corner, and the welcome feeling of warm sunlight enveloped us. I looked around at the cracked streets and the faded brick facades of the buildings—there was a certain beauty to it in the stillness of the morning. After the time we spent in Ville and the time we spent in the woods, this felt more familiar than anything had in a while.

For a moment, the only sounds I could hear were our footsteps, and everyone's slightly labored breathing. Daphne led the way, her dark hair turning golden in the sunlight.

"Forgive me for—no, sorry." Trevor exhaled. "What I mean to say is, do we have a plan? I know Zeno is working on getting, is it, Gina?" He looked at me for confirmation. I nodded. "Gina up and running while trying to learn about Benjamin, but what about us? I'm not sure I understand what we are doing exactly."

"If we're going to take down Rosewood," I started, looking at Daphne as she continued to trudge along, "we're not going to do it alone."

"I thought we were considering using Benjamin as a means of acquiring help?" Trevor said.

"He might be helpful," Daphne said, not bothering to look over her shoulder at us. "But we still don't know much about him. And the people at our home aren't the ones who really matter."

"Come on, everyone matters," Alex said. "Everyone deserves some love." Alex shook his head. "Man, that Benjamin guy—he's got me seeing things in a whole new light!"

"No," Daphne said, a slight irritation to her voice, "that's not what I mean. When Tyrann died, it left a power vacuum. I want to see who filled it. Right now, those are the people who matter." Daphne brought us to a stop at an intersection. "Brick and Jonny should know better than anyone, but first, there's a stop we need to make. Come on, this way."

Charred brick, chunks of plaster, and generalized debris covered the entire area. It was as if there hadn't been any effort whatsoever to clean it up. The scene made me ill. I had hoped that it wasn't true, that the Chairman had just made it up, for Pria's sake.

From where I stood, I could see right into what used to be Tyrann Kane's home. Once white carpet was covered in black ash. Overturned furniture lay strewn about. Glass shards were everywhere.

"What happened here?" Trevor said softly.

"An explosion," Daphne said tersely, picking her way through the exposed front room. "Once Zeno has Gina up and running again, we can have her help us do some analysis, but my guess is that the bomb went off right here."

She stood as close to the sidewalk as possible while still being inside the perimeter of the room. I could see burnt markings on the floor shooting outward from the spot. It was maybe the only clean spot of ground in the area.

"Why has no one cleaned anything up?" Trevor said, studying the area more closely.

"My guess is that people are still scared of Tyrann, even though he's gone," Daphne said, making her way back over to us. "I'm sure there are rumors floating around that he faked his death, and no one wants to be on his bad side if those rumors turn out to be true. But..." Daphne surveyed the scene once more. "I don't know... this was a pretty devastating explosion. Brick and Jonny will know more."

"What about Dax?" I said.

"And Printh?" Alex added.

"Supposedly, they were all with Tyrann when the explosion went off."

I pulled out my phone and took a picture of the scene. I couldn't help thinking that it would have been good for Pria to see this, even though I was sure it would have been painful. Sometimes, that was how closure worked.

I wasn't certain she'd get the message if I sent it. Odds were she wouldn't, but the least I could do was try.

I typed out a quick message on my phone and sent it along with the picture to Pria. I slid my phone back into my pocket as Daphne made her way out of the wreckage and back to the road.

"Let's go."

The rest of us were still picking around, but apparently, our time here was done. I jogged to catch up with her.

"Hey, you okay?" I said quietly. I knew that her relationship with Tyrann and Printh and Dax was anything but ordinary. This had to impact her more than she was letting on.

"I'm fine."

I continued to walk beside her. Daphne wasn't someone I could push into talking. We walked for another block. Trevor and Alex chattered behind us, mostly Alex recounting his version of what transpired in Ville. From what I could hear, it was mostly accurate, with a few embellishments.

We made a left turn and continued on. I found myself searching for the personal transports that Tyrann once had. All this walking felt like a waste of time.

"I have a hard time believing it's real," Daphne said suddenly. "Tyrann being 'confirmed' dead." She shook her head. "I'm sure they spent time in that room, but it wasn't like that was their entire living space or their only living space. And for it to get Dax, Printh, and Tyrann?" She led us down an alleyway.

"You think they could still be alive?" I said.

"I don't know," she sighed. "I wish Pria was here."

We walked for another couple of minutes in silence, winding down unfamiliar alleyways until we emerged onto a sunlit street. Daphne brought us to a halt.

"And that's when I knew for sure that Jahko wasn't crazy," Alex was saying.

"Sounds like it was quite the adventure," Trevor said.

"And I'm only just getting started—"

"And you'll have to finish another time," Daphne said, cutting him off. "We're here."

"Here?" I said, surveying the row of large buildings in front of us.

"This is where Brick and Jonny live. I know they're a couple of idiots, but if anyone knows what's really going on in the Heights, they will." She looked back at all of us with a smile that didn't quite reach her eyes. "And I know I can get them to talk."

14

———————

The door to their building was larger than average and long since boarded up, as were all of the windows on the ground floor. Here, the bricks were a rich, dark brown, but they turned lighter the higher up you went. Toward the top, they were nearly white from all of the sunlight over the years. Other than a couple of spots with missing bricks, the building appeared to be in decent shape.

"This used to be one of Tyrann's main buildings," Daphne said.

"What do you mean, main buildings?" Alex said. "Didn't we already stop by where he used to live?"

"Tyrann had several buildings—no one really owns anything in the Heights, but as much as someone could, Tyrann did. If you lived in one of 'his' buildings, he made sure it was protected, and he made sure he was compensated. Part of the way he did that was to place members of his crew in them to protect and collect." Daphne looked up. "Which brings us here."

She rapped her knuckles on the large, wood-covered door.

After a moment, a window, about ten stories above us, opened up, and a pair of binoculars peeked out.

In the still morning, even the smallest of sounds made their way down to us—a sigh, then a chuckle.

"Well, I'll be." Then, a bit louder. "Stay where you are."

The window slammed shut.

Daphne rolled her eyes.

"Who was that gentleman?" Trevor asked.

"Gentleman is a strong word," I said. "He's got bad teeth, bad grammar, and worse morals."

Daphne turned to face Trevor.

"His name is Brick, and he's as dumb as his name sounds, but he is mean. He used to be part of Tyrann's inner circle."

"And you know him..." Trevor paused. "Well?"

"Better than most," she said, turning back to the door.

"Don't worry, Trevor," Alex said quietly, "we'll be fine. She's meaner than Brick is."

"Meaner?" I said, looking back at Alex.

"It's true," Daphne said nonchalantly.

Alex gave me a knowing smile.

Before I could respond, a metallic clanking followed by the sounds of turning locks and gears made its way through the door before it started to swing open on noisy, rusty hinges.

"So it took four of ya to muster up the courage to come and see me, did it?" Brick smiled his trademark yellow grin, albeit with a few more holes in it than last time. "Victor Wells and Daphne Pendleton. A lot has changed since you've been gone. I thought you'd be dead by now."

"Sorry to disappoint," Daphne said. "Are you going to let us in or keep us standing on your doorstep?"

Brick's eyes darted over his left shoulder.

"Here's fine."

Daphne eyed him suspiciously.

"Great. We're not here to catch up anyways. We've got questions."

"And what makes you think I'm going to answer them? Huh?" Brick stared at us, eyes narrowed. We all stared back.

"Come on, Brick," Daphne said, almost bored, "your tough guy look never worked with me before. What makes you think it's going to work now?"

"Things are different now," Brick said, his voice tightening as he said it.

"Yeah?" Daphne said. "How so?"

"Mr. Kane ain't top dog 'round here anymore." Brick puffed his chest out.

"From what I hear, he's not around, period." Daphne leaned back slightly and eyed him.

"Some would say that, yeah."

"*Some* would say?" Daphne said. "I thought you were part of his inner circle, Brick. So what do *you* say? Is Tyrann really gone?"

Daphne folded her arms. Brick stared back, unblinking. Daphne waited. The silence stretched on into uncomfortable territory.

I looked to Alex, who had started fidgeting. Alex opened his mouth, but I elbowed him. He closed his mouth noiselessly.

Finally, Brick spoke.

"I might, secretly, agree with what some may say."

"Let me guess, you want everyone to think that he may still be around. It's good for business, right?"

Brick shifted his feet and folded his arms as well.

"You might be onto something."

I looked over at Trevor, who seemed content to observe.

"So you think that you and Jonny are going to take over Tyrann's old operations? Just like that?" Daphne said, starting to smile. "You and Jonny?" She gave a small laugh of disbelief.

Brick stiffened and let out a short, rattling breath.

"Jonny's not part of the picture anymore," he said, his tone changing radically. There was true pain in his voice and true sadness.

Daphne paused. I was taken aback, too. I barely knew the two of them, but I had gotten the sense that they were inseparable.

Brick looked at the ground and scratched at his eye. Or was he wiping a tear? He coughed and sniffed loudly before looking back up.

"Allergies," he grumbled.

"Brick," I said slowly, "is Jonny gone, like Tyrann?"

Brick looked my way. Our eyes met.

I could see the sadness in them. "Look, we've all lost people and—"

"I didn't lose him!" Brick said, cutting me off. "He's in that building right over there." He pointed across the street from where we stood. "We're just not business partners anymore."

He kicked at the ground and then threw his head up toward the sky. "Oh, who am I kidding? The two of us, we're not even on speaking terms anymore!" He threw up his hands and let his head slump toward his chest.

Daphne rolled her eyes and took a step closer to him.

"Stop that," she said, her voice a terse whisper. "If anyone sees you, you'll lose all credibility."

Brick straightened up slightly.

"Wait," Alex said, lines of confusion riddling his brow. "Jonny? Sunglasses, stunner, real quiet type, right?" He paused for validation, which I gave with a weary nod. Where was he going with this?

"I didn't know he could talk," Alex continued, turning his attention to Brick. "I thought you were never on speaking terms."

Daphne stared daggers at Alex.

"What? I'm not wrong, am I?"

"No one ever understood us!" Brick threw his arms up in despair once more. Then, speaking to the ground in a much quieter voice, "It was a friendship for the ages. No more intimidating people together. No more beating people up together. No more—"

"Pull yourself together!" Daphne said, grabbing him by the shoulders and shaking him. "Right now! Stop being so dramatic. You act like you've never had a fight before."

"F-first one," Brick said. "I don't know if we can ever come back from it."

I stared at Brick. I was struggling to reconcile the man before us with the man I had known—mean and merciless versus distraught and depressed. Honestly, I wasn't sure which version I preferred. One thing was for certain—we weren't going to get much more information out of him in his current state.

"Maybe there's something we can do," I said, taking a half-step forward.

"L-like what?"

"We'll talk to him for you," Alex said simply. "Trust me, we'll take care of it. You guys will be friends again in no time."

"Really? You think, you think there's a chance?" Brick said, visibly lightened by Alex's words.

"Absolutely," Alex said. "But first, we need a little help from you."

"O-of course!"

Alex nodded to Daphne, who smiled, then turned back to Brick.

"We need to know about the buildings that are collapsing," she said.

Brick wiped at his nose and performed a hard, mucous-filled sniff before speaking.

"There's been over a handful of them so far. Seems like it was only a matter of time, though. All these buildings were built around the same time. No one's sure what's causing it. Some say structural integrity."

"What do you say?" I asked.

"Don't know for sure, but it seems like the only buildings collapsing are the ones with people in them. Infestations is what I hear. People are dirty. Not in my building, of course, but other people."

"So just the buildings with people in them, nothing else?" I asked.

"As far as I know," Brick said. He gave another powerful sniff.

"All right, next question," Alex said, jumping in. "How's the food situation since we've been gone? Any better? And remember, your friendship with Jonny depends on this."

Brick gave him a confused look.

"I, well, I don't do much cooking myself and, well, my mother..." He nodded to the building behind him. "Well, there's no one better and—"

"You live with your mother?" Daphne said.

"Yeah, so?" He crossed his arms.

"I wasn't expecting—"

"Look here, you live with your father, so I don't want to hear another word!"

Daphne took a half step forward, her mouth open, ready to retort, but I was quicker.

"You're right," I said.

Daphne's head whipped around at me, her eyes wide in disbelief.

"Ha!" Brick said, then folded his arms with a triumphant smile.

"Yeah, yeah, you're both the same," Alex said. "But we've got a few more questions."

"Right," I said. "Tyrann used to run the Heights, but what happened after he died? And," I added more quietly, "what do you know about Printh and Dax?"

Brick sighed and looked at the ground, then up at Daphne. He swallowed.

"I haven't heard a thing about them, one way or the other. People say the three of them were incinerated together—nothing left. The Nobles who came to check it out stopped running DNA samples as soon as they ID'd Mr. Kane. But I know the three of them were supposed to be together when it happened. You ask me, they all went down together."

My heart sank. I had been holding out that they weren't really gone, that somehow, Printh or Dax had gotten away.

Brick continued. "Probably just the way Mr. Kane would have wanted to go." Brick looked up to the sky, then shook his head. "As for the rest of the Heights, most everyone else struck out on their own. Some formed alliances, some didn't."

"Alliances?" I said. "Like gangs? People formed gangs?"

"Yeah," Brick said. "Well, nothing like what Tyrann had with us. I've got my crew. Jonny... Jonny's got his. And others teamed up too."

"Why didn't everyone just join together and make a super group?" Alex said. "That's what I would have done."

"I dunno," Brick said, scratching his cheek. "Mr. Kane kept everyone under his thumb, but now, I guess everyone wants a piece of the power." Brick paused. "I'm not used to giving out information for free," he said. "I don't like it." He turned to Alex. "You said you can make things right between me and Jonny. I'm going to hold you to that."

Brick looked Alex up and down, his eyes pausing on Alex's mechanical arm.

"One last question then," I said, looking back and forth between them. "What do you know about this Benjamin guy who is taking over the events center?"

Brick growled, and a dark look passed over his face.

"I don't like him. He's taking a lot of people from our crews. People say his message 'resonates,' whatever that means." Brick sniffed hard and spat on the ground.

"Do you know anything else about him?" Daphne asked.

"I didn't know him before, and I don't plan to know him now." Brick took a step back. "All right, I can't be out here talking all day. Mother's inside waiting to help me collect. It's collection day!" he finished, a little more aggressively than was necessary.

"Well, thanks for the info, Brick," Alex said. "We'll get this Jonny situation figured out for you ASAP."

"You better," he said, stepping back to close the large wooden door of the building.

"We're going right now," Alex said. "You said this building, right?" He pointed across the street to a building that matched Brick's in both size and appearance.

"That's the one."

Alex nodded and started walking.

"All right, let's go."

Before I had time to object, a terrible, earsplitting noise filled the air, and it was coming from Jonny's building. I'd never heard anything like it. It was like something massive was dying, screaming out as it fought for its life. But as I looked up, I realized it wasn't a fight. It was a knockout.

Brick was suddenly beside me, his open door forgotten.

"Jonny!"

Twenty stories up, windows shattered. Bricks rained down and exploded on the pavement all around us. The scream of metal twisting and bending shattered the stillness of the morning.

The top of the building swayed like a tree in the wind. Instinctively, I threw my hands up and started spraying. An errant brick caught on the invisible beads just inches from my head.

"Run!" I yelled.

Daphne had already moved. She had Alex in tow. I pushed Trevor, his eyes wide in fear. I started to sprint, dragging him along with me. Brick could do what he wanted.

Debris continued to fall all around us. I let out a trail of spray with my off hand. There was no question—Jonny's building was coming down, and if we didn't get far enough away when it collapsed...

"Jonny!"

Brick's terrified yell barely registered above the noise of the groaning building.

I looked over my shoulder, past Trevor's terrified features, and back to Brick. He stood there, rooted to his spot.

He wasn't going to move.

I let out a yell of frustration and threw Trevor in front of me.

"Keep running!" I yelled. I skidded to a stop and ran hard the other way.

"BRICK!" I yelled. He didn't hear me. I kept running, one arm up, a steady stream of spray releasing out over my head. "BRICK!"

A falling piece of glass fell right through my wispy spray trail and glanced off my arm, slicing an inch-long gash just past my right glove. It surprised me more than caused me pain, but I could tell the blood was flowing freely. And Brick still hadn't moved.

The building let out another almighty groan, followed by a snap that you could feel. Whatever metal support structure there had been, it was now gone.

People had started swarming out from the ground floors. Some had even decided to jump from the windows. Their screams carried to my ears. I knew I couldn't save them, but I could save one.

"BRICK!"

I grabbed hold of Brick's jacket and tugged. He stood there, staring up at the teetering structure, terror and distress in every feature. He stumbled forward, but caught himself. We locked eyes.

"LET'S GO!"

Finally, he moved.

I pushed him as we sprinted, gray beads materializing around us like raindrops in a storm.

I had never run so hard in my life. My legs burned. My lungs burned. My arms burned—one from the cut, the other from pulling Brick along.

I looked over my shoulder just in time to see the top third of the building break free, falling over onto the road beneath. The sound was deafening, like a thousand boulders clacking together while a bomb exploded.

A loud whoosh sounded, and I could feel the air change, and then an airwave of dust and debris nearly swept me off my feet. The debris consumed us as we ran, blocking out the sun and covering us in darkness. And for a moment, all was quiet.

15

"Daphne!"

I couldn't see anything in the haze. The farther away from the building we got, the clearer the air became, but we still had a ways to go. Brick kept a hand on my shoulder as we stumbled through the semidarkness. His hand trembled in time with his gasping breaths that had nothing to do with us running. I knew if I looked behind me, I'd see tears running down his face.

I yelled again. Surely, they were all safe, right?

"Daphne!" I paused to cough out all the particulates I had just inhaled. "Alex! Trevor!"

"Victor!" Daphne's voice floated through the dirty air.

"Over here!" I yelled again.

Ahead of me, three sooty figures materialized. Two of them raced forward, and the three of us embraced. A cloud of dust erupted from my clothes at impact.

"You're okay!" Daphne said with a relieved sigh. She must have caught sight of Brick because she let go and took a step past me. She didn't say anything, but I could hear her pat him on the shoulder as his ragged breathing continued.

I didn't know where to start. A building had just collapsed. A building full of people. How many had died? *We* had almost died.

"We've got to go back," Alex said suddenly. All I could do was stare at his dust-covered features. "The building isn't going to fall more. We have to go back."

I looked around our group. Shock registered on every face. But Alex was right. I nodded to him, then faced Brick.

"We're going back."

The dust took what seemed like hours to settle.

The lower two-thirds of the building appeared to be somewhat intact. Bricks, rubble, and surprisingly few scattered personal effects littered the whole area. It looked more like a construction site rather than a multifamily dwelling that had collapsed.

I picked my way through the debris, searching for Jonny or anyone who needed help. We had split up to cover more ground, and so far, Jonny hadn't been found.

Dozens of people milled about, some of them in small groups, others by themselves. A few of them hugged one another, but most stood there talking and occasionally kicking at the rubble. I had honestly expected more screams and more crying, but it was virtually nonexistent.

"Hey," I said as a small boy walked past me, his attention focused on the ground, his hands full of what I assumed were other people's possessions.

He looked up at me in alarm, his eyes wide. He glanced down at the trinkets in his hands. He couldn't have been more than ten.

"I, I, um, there's a—"

I waved my hand dismissively.

"I'm just wondering if there is anyone who was hurt when the building fell."

"Mighta been a few," the boy said, eyeing me suspiciously. "But the part that fell was mostly empty."

"Empty?" I said.

"Yeah," the boy said simply. "Empty." He shrugged and quickly skirted away, his attention back on the ground.

Brick's distraught voice cut through the lingering haze for what had to be the twentieth time in the last five minutes.

"Jonny!"

Part of me wondered if Jonny would respond in a situation like this. I'd never heard him speak—I didn't even know if he could speak.

I returned to my search and walked over to the nearest group of people. It was a mix of guys and girls, I guessed a few years older than me. They all took a step backward as I approached.

I held up my hands.

"I'm looking for a friend," I said slowly. "His name is Jonny. I think he was in charge of the building."

Understanding dawned on a few faces.

"Haven't seen him," one of the girls said. Then, as one, they all turned their backs on me.

"Hey," I said, a thought striking me. "What's everyone going to do? Can you still live here?"

"The whole roof is gone, what do you think?" the girl said, turning back around.

"Uh, right," I said awkwardly. "Well, where's everyone going to go?"

"Do you live here?"

"No, I um, I—" I sputtered. The girl continued to stare at me. "I don't really have a home," I finished.

The girl let out a slightly less annoyed sigh.

"Look, you know where the events center is at?"

I nodded.

"It sounds like you can get help there. I think that's where most of us are going."

"Okay, thanks," I said before a shriek from Brick filled the air.

"Jonny!"

I made to say goodbye to the girl, but she had already turned her back on me.

Without another word, I moved quickly toward Brick's cry. It didn't take me long to find them. It was an interesting scene.

Alex knelt on the ground, clearly talking to someone. Trevor and Daphne looked like they were arriving about the same time as me, and Brick stood behind Alex, staring down at the ground, his eyes as wide as I'd ever seen them.

Jonny, lanky as ever, his dark jacket coated in brick dust, lay on the ground, pinned from the waist down by what used to be an interior wall and door.

"You have to trust me on this," Alex was saying. "I've been best friends with someone for a long time, and there can't just be one good communicator. You both have to talk."

Alex made fierce eye contact and nodded as if agreeing with himself.

Jonny continued to stare at him, a somewhat bewildered expression on his face.

"Look," Alex continued, "Brick has been carrying the two of you this whole time, and clearly, it's caused some stress between the two of you. Am I right?"

Jonny tried to push some of the wall off of himself, but Alex put his hand down, thwarting his efforts.

"Alex!" Daphne said.

"Give me a second, Daph," he said without looking at her.

Daphne looked on incredulously.

"You see what I'm saying?" Alex continued, unabated. "Brick came here when he didn't have to, looking for you. What I need you to do is step it up. You've got to pull your weight. Can you do that?"

Jonny looked to Alex, his face weary, probably because of pain or exhaustion or because part of a building was on top of him. His eyes moved to Brick, and I thought I heard an affirmative sounding grunt.

"You really mean it, Jonny?" Brick said, rushing over and kneeling by his side.

Jonny nodded, and Brick let out an excited yell.

"Come and help me get this off of my best friend, will ya?" Brick said, looking up at all of us.

With a smile and a nod, Alex got down on the ground, and then together, they held the section of wall up, and Jonny wriggled free.

Alex stood up, and Daphne punched him in the arm.

"What were you doing keeping him stuck under there?"

"I was working," Alex said. "*And* I checked to make sure he wasn't hurt, *and* he said he wasn't."

"He said that, did he?" Daphne said, her eyes narrowing.

"Yeah," Alex said, perplexed. "Why wouldn't he tell me if he was hurt?" He shrugged. "Plus, friendship is important, right, Victor?"

Jonny pushed himself to his feet and squatted up and down a few times, apparently injury-free.

"Couldn't agree more," I said with a smile. I looked over at Daphne as well, but she was watching Jonny move around. I walked over to her.

"For a second, I thought you were going to jump in there and free Jonny yourself," I said. I leaned into her, gently bumping her shoulder with mine.

She didn't bump back into me like she normally did. She didn't even look at me. My smile faltered. I looked around. Trevor caught my eye, but I quickly looked away.

"Well," Brick said, apparently wiping a happy tear from his left eye, "all it took was for the building to fall over, and we're friends again." He nodded to Alex. "You're all right, kid. I won't forget this." He turned back to Jonny and started walking. "Let's get you back to my place. Mom's got some soup on and…"

His voice trailed off as the two of them walked away. Jonny looked back briefly and nodded at Alex before he and Brick disappeared into the haze.

"Well," Alex said, smiling around at all of us. "Don't you feel that?" he said, looking around.

I took a half step away from Daphne. It felt awkward to stand so close to her when there was definitely something going on. Alex continued to smile at all of us.

"We did a good deed, you guys."

I smiled back. Trevor fixed Alex with a curious stare.

"Yes," Daphne said, her voice flat. "Brick and Jonny are reunited. All is right in the universe."

Her cynicism was starting to wear on me.

"Come on, Daph, he's got a point," I said. "We did do something good, even if it was for a couple of degenerates."

"Good deeds always come back around," Alex said.

"Mmhmm," Daphne said, staring coldly in the direction Brick and Jonny had disappeared in. "We'll see if *they* ever come back around."

"You're different," Trevor said, still staring at Alex. Calling it an awkward silence was an understatement. "I meant it as a compliment," he continued. "The Nobles I used to serve had a slightly different world view."

"Oh, thanks!" Alex said.

I relaxed internally.

"You're welcome. Do we know why it fell?" Trevor said, turning to face what was left of the building.

"Jonny wasn't sure," Alex said. "It was the second thing I asked him, *after* finding out if he was hurt." He glanced at Daphne, who gave him a look.

"Did Jonny literally speak and tell you this?" I said. "Because I've never heard him say a word."

"Oh, he talks," Alex said. "Believe me, he talks."

All I could do was shake my head. What was it with him and the weird ones?

"So we still don't know why the building fell," Trevor said, bringing us all back. "And it's not the first building to fall. If this is a pattern, wouldn't it make sense to figure out what's going on?"

"Honestly," I said, "the buildings intrigue me, but I don't know if they hold the key to us stopping Rosewood, and if it's not connected to that, we don't have time for it."

"So no one else saw the black things that got tossed out of the windows near where the building fractured?"

"What things?" I said.

"What did they look like?" Daphne asked.

"Due to the distance," Trevor said, "I can't give an accurate description, but they all looked to be fairly small—maybe the size of a small suitcase?"

"I didn't see anything that looked like that when I was looking around," Daphne said. "Or in any of the debris on the ground. Any of you?"

I shook my head. Alex and Trevor did the same.

"Look," Daphne said, "the buildings *are* old. Most of them were built around the same time. It makes sense for a few to go around the same time." She glanced quickly at me. "I'm with Victor. It's unfortunate that this is happening, but we've got other priorities."

"Speaking of," I said, "let's get back to the events center. We can check in with Zeno, too." I looked at the wreckage of the building and the small groups of people still picking their way through it. "If this means that even more people are going to show up there, I think we should have a talk with Benjamin sooner rather than later."

16

———

The sun was starting to fade as we entered the courtyard.

"Victor!" An unusually high-pitched voice pierced the air, but due to all the people, I couldn't quite tell where it was coming from.

"What is that horrible screeching?" Daphne said.

"Screeching?" Alex said, looking around. "Nah, I don't mind it."

"I agree," Trevor said. "It has a pleasant, familiar quality to it." He and Alex looked at each other and nodded in mutual agreement.

"Victor Wells!"

I winced as my own name nearly damaged my ears. There was only one voice I'd ever heard like that, and it was distinctive enough to recognize immediately: Benjamin's assistant. I scanned the surprisingly crowded area and located her almost immediately.

She was walking toward us, her steps short and quick. She couldn't have been more than five feet tall. She had a somewhat angular face, and her hair was a bright yellow-gold. She came to a quick stop before us.

"He said to be on the lookout for you. I'm certain he'll be wanting to talk to you," she said, turning and motioning for us to follow. "Come, I believe he's just around here."

"A little light on the introductions," Daphne muttered.

"My name's Maggie, by the way." She flashed us a warm smile. "I've been working with Pastor Benjamin since the beginning. Such a visionary."

Alex nudged me and gave me a look. *Pastor?* He mouthed. I shrugged.

I guess, I mouthed back. We had been right, after all.

We followed Maggie around a set of pillars, making our way in between and around multiple groups of bystanders. It was almost alarming how many people seemed to be here at all hours of the day. The events center courtyard was full. People were everywhere—some rested in makeshift tents while others conversed together in groups that grew quiet as we walked past. I couldn't decide if it was because of Maggie or because of me.

All but a few seemed to have a screen of some sort in their hands. As we passed by, I caught a few words of whatever it was they were watching, but the odd thing was, it seemed as if everyone was watching the same thing, at least from what I could tell. I never got a good look at their screens, but it sounded like the same voice speaking everywhere we went.

Maggie continued to weave us in and out of the different groups until we passed through a set of double doors and entered a long hallway.

"I can tell you take good care of Benjamin," Trevor said as our footsteps echoed down the hallway. "He's very lucky to have you around."

Maggie let out what I could only describe as a poorly suppressed giggle.

"It's been quite a day so far," Maggie said without looking back, although if the color of her neck was any indicator, she was definitely blushing. "Word is getting out about what we're doing here. We had nearly fifty new faces show up today!" Finally, she turned around. "Isn't that great?"

All of us but Trevor offered a mumbled agreement. He felt the need to go above and beyond.

"It's always great to help our friends accomplish their goals." Trevor smiled serenely, and Maggie blushed once more. "What exactly is it that you're trying to accomplish here?" Trevor said.

"You don't know?" Maggie said, bringing us to a stop.

"We only arrived yesterday," Trevor said.

"Well, I would love to tell you, but I am certain Pastor Benjamin would want to explain it to you himself. I won't spoil the surprise." Maggie smiled and gave us a small bow. "He'll be in his office, just behind that second door on the right. Go ahead and walk right in. He'll be happy to see you." She pointed to the nearest door. "I wish I could stay," she said, her eyes gravitating toward Trevor, "but I have other things I need to attend to. I enjoyed our walk."

Without another high-pitched word, she turned around and sped back the way we had come.

"Well," I said, looking at the others, "I know we wanted to get to know Benjamin better. Shall we?"

"Yes," Daphne said with a nod.

"First," Alex said, turning to Trevor, "there was a little something going on with Maggie, wasn't there?"

Trevor looked at Alex, a look of confusion on his face.

"What do you mean?"

"I wasn't the only one who saw it, right?" Alex said. "Daphne? Victor?"

"Okay, there was definitely some chemistry," Daphne said.

I looked over at her, but again, she didn't look back.

"Compliments are the quickest way to make someone comfortable enough to talk," Trevor said.

"Oh, come on!" Alex said, giving him a shove.

Trevor didn't say anything but turned a shade of deep red.

"It's not exactly like that," he said. "I won't deny that she was, well, attractive. And I like her voice," he added.

At that, I tried to catch Daphne's eye but couldn't.

"Amen to that," Alex said, slapping him on the back with his metal arm. Trevor flinched but smiled. "Well," Alex continued, looking around, "should we do this?"

I nodded.

"Let's go."

I took the lead. The hallway was well-lit. There wasn't any trash here, but the floor had more scuff marks than usual. Did a lot of people come to see Benjamin on a regular basis?

As I neared the door, I could hear voices inside. It sounded like there were two voices, both male. I held up my hand and put a finger to my lips. It occurred to me that before all of this, I would have never thought to eavesdrop, but now, it just seemed prudent.

I didn't recognize the first voice.

"... if they ask questions?"

"The questions won't matter at the end," Benjamin said. "Don't lose faith now."

"But, what if—"

"There isn't room for 'what if,' Damien."

"Yes, Benjamin."

Almost like she had a sixth sense, Daphne stood up and started ushering a surprised Alex and Trevor back.

"Go!" She said, pushing them both.

From inside the room, I heard footsteps, and they were coming our way.

We all disappeared around the nearest corner just as a squeak from the rusty hinges met my ears. I held my finger to my lips once more.

The door squeaked its way back closed, and a single pair of footsteps made their way down the hall opposite from us.

"I'm going to follow him," Daphne whispered. "The rest of you, talk with Benjamin."

"Are you sure?" I said.

"After that conversation, yeah. Catch you back at our place." Without another look, she took off silently down the hall after him. I poked my head around the corner to watch as she disappeared.

Before I started toward the office, my phone buzzed, drawing my attention away from the hallway.

"You still get texts?" Alex said.

"I guess so," I said, tapping on the screen. It was strange—I hadn't gotten one in a while.

"Who's it from?"

I squinted at the screen for a moment as the message opened up. I couldn't believe it.

"Pria," I said, surprised.

"Well, what's it say?"

"Thanks." I tried to scroll, but that was it. "That's all it says. 'Thanks.'"

"One word?" Alex said, his expression one of distaste. "What happened? I thought you two were friends?"

"We are," I said. "I sent her a message after we visited her old home."

"Oh," Alex said. He shrugged. "Honestly, it's a miracle she even got your message. Maybe she kept it short to give it a better chance of arriving."

"Maybe," I said.

"Shall we move this along?" Trevor said.

"Right," I said, pocketing my phone. "Benjamin." But I was still contemplating Pria's single-word text. Maybe Alex was right—a single word had a better chance than a paragraph or a picture. Hopefully, wherever she was, wherever they all were, they were doing okay.

"Let's do it," Alex said.

Trevor simply nodded.

We all stepped out from the corner and strode the few steps that brought us back to Benjamin's office door. Both Alex and Trevor stood back, silently signaling it would be me who was responsible for knocking.

I held my fist up and rapped on the door three times. No sound came from within, and then silently, minus the rusty hinges, the door swung open, revealing a serenely smiling Benjamin waiting to greet us.

"Ah, your timing is perfect," he said. "I just finished a meeting with a rather inspiring volunteer."

"Volunteer?" I said, pausing in the doorway to take in his office. A desk sat in the middle of the room, completely devoid of anything except for a single screen, which was pointed away from us. Other than that, there were no papers, no writing utensils, no pictures or decoration of any kind—just a flat space with a screen.

Two chairs sat opposite the desk, which Benjamin motioned to. Alex plopped down comfortably in one while Trevor and I remained standing.

"Yes," Benjamin said as he moved around the desk to his chair, "we have a few people who help me in my efforts."

"Like Maggie?" Trevor said.

"Exactly," Benjamin said. "Among others."

"She said that you wanted to talk to us," I said, eyeing him as he sat down in his chair.

"Indeed I did." Benjamin clasped his hands together and leaned in, fixing me with a serious stare. "How are you adjusting since being back? I know this must be a difficult transition to find things not quite the way you left them."

He kept eye contact, and it was odd, but he seemed genuinely concerned. It caught me off guard.

"Well, I haven't been back long," I started before regaining my composure. "And this wasn't really my home. But it was my friend's home. Why did you take it over?"

"Couldn't agree more, Ben," Alex said casually, making a show of crossing his legs. "Can I call you Ben? Pastor Ben? Benji?" He looked up questioningly.

Benjamin leaned back in his chair, continuing to keep his hands clasped, and allowed himself a small smile.

"Benjamin is just fine, Alex, thank you. And to your point, Victor, yes, I can see how that would be more than a little disconcerting." He leaned forward once more. "Do you know what I am trying to do here?"

I stared at him, not sure whether it was a rhetorical question or not. Before I could decide, he answered.

"Unity. Peace."

"Love it," Alex said. Benjamin smiled and stood.

"But it starts with acceptance of oneself," he said, beginning to pace. "How can we come to love each other until we first love ourselves?" He raised an eyebrow.

"You can't," Alex said with a shake of his head.

"Correct. We in the Heights are different from those in the Flats." He looked at each of us in turn. "And that's okay."

"Absolutely it is," Alex said. I gave him a look.

"Yes and—" Benjamin started.

"And then what?" I said, cutting in. What he was saying had the feel of a rehearsed speech, something he had practiced a hundred times. Benjamin looked at me, mouth still open.

"What do you mean?"

"I mean, after everyone loves themselves, then what? You say we're different from the people in the Flats. If we really want peace, shouldn't we, I don't know, 'love them too?'"

"We need to start with ourselves before we can look outward," Benjamin said.

"Makes sense to me," Alex said.

Beside me, Trevor fidgeted.

"But what's the end goal?" I said, starting to get frustrated. "I don't know if you know much about us or why we're here, but there's more at stake than just a few people feeling good about themselves."

"I have a feeling my end goal will be made clear soon enough," Benjamin said, returning to his seat. "It really was good to meet all of you," he continued, looking up and locking eyes with me. "I can tell that the three of you have a unique energy, a persistent energy. It will serve you well in the days ahead. Remember, peace through unity."

He smiled his customary serene look and turned his attention completely to the screen on his desk.

Apparently, our meeting was over.

"Come on," I said, nodding toward the door.

"I didn't like that," Trevor said as we walked.

"Me neither," I said. All of Benjamin's non-answers—it didn't feel right.

"I could listen to him all day, though," Alex said. "Know what I mean?"

"Did you really like him?" I said, giving him a sidelong glance. I had my gut feeling about him, but Alex had a way about judging people.

"Benjamin?" he said.

I nodded.

"No way," Alex said. "Something is definitely off about that guy, but how good is his message?"

"Yeah," I said. "Good stuff."

Benjamin was a new type of person, one I wasn't sure I had encountered before. How were we supposed to regard him? Was he a friend or an enemy? Could we trust him?

These and other thoughts floated around my head as we wound our way back to the secret room, making sure no one was watching as we entered through the wall and pushed the panel back in place.

We made our way down the steep staircase and found Daphne already there, waiting for us. She sat on one of the many musty mattresses on the floor.

"Hey," I said tentatively. "You okay? Where's Zeno?"

She stood, the look on her face grim.

"He's still trying to get Gina up and running. Apparently, she's sustained some 'pretty heavy neglect,' and it's caused her to rewrite some of her own code."

"Dang, Gina..." Alex said with a shake of his head. "What'd she do this time? Must be bad."

"What makes you say that?" Daphne said.

"Oh, I just figured, by the look on your face—"

"Yeah, well," she said, her face falling. "This is worse. You'll want to sit down for this."

17

———

Daphne wasn't normally one for hyperbole. If she said this was bad, it was. I sat down on a mattress next to Alex. Trevor remained standing as Daphne began talking.

"You know that guy I followed? Damien, I think his name was?"

"The volunteer?" I said.

"Volunteer?" she said with a confused look on her face.

"Benjamin uses 'volunteers' to help him get his work done," I said. "He said Damien was one of them."

"Okay, sure," Daphne said, "well, I followed him—we ended up behind the events center. I couldn't see perfectly, but I saw enough."

"Enough of what?" Alex said.

"I saw him talking to a drone."

My stomach dropped.

We all stayed quiet for a moment.

"Lots of people use drones," Trevor said, breaking the silence. "Do they not?"

"Not like this, and not in the Heights," Daphne said. "There's only one person we all know who uses drones here."

I met her eyes. She nodded.

"Rosewood."

Behind me, a new voice could be heard, along with his rapid footsteps.

"Don't worry, Gina! I'll be back!"

Zeno's voice preceded his entrance down the stairs. As he burst into view, he vaulted down the first several steps and continued skipping them two and three at a time as he barreled toward us. He kept one hand on his glasses to keep them in place. Moments later, he slid to a halt in front of us. His chest was heaving, and beads of sweat coated his brow.

"What. Is. It?" he said in between gasping breaths.

"I said it was urgent," Daphne said, looking at her phone, "not be here in thirty seconds or the world ends."

"I don't think you understand the seriousness of the situation," Zeno said, his breaths becoming less ragged. "Gina, *my* Gina, the brain of this whole building plus a bunch of other stuff you know nothing about, is in distress! Girl's code is all over the place!" He took a deep breath. "What I'm trying to say, is whatever you've got, make it quick, because my girl—"

"I thought Ivy was your girl?" Alex said.

"Look, I didn't birth Ivy out of my brain, okay?" Zeno said while poking himself repeatedly in the afro. "Gina is my first love—I created her, and where she used to be such a sturdy girl—"

"Is that a compliment?" Daphne said. Zeno didn't hear her.

"Now, she's... fragile." He fearfully looked up to the ceiling.

I'd never seen Zeno like this. Eccentric? Sure. Excited? Absolutely. But frantic? Never.

"Do we need to be worried about this?" Trevor said slowly. "It sounds as if the building is going to attack us."

Zeno laughed nervously.

"No, psh, man, come on." He waved his hand dismissively, then wiped his brow. "So, uh, you guys said you had something urgent to talk about."

"Yeah," I said, trying to catch Zeno's eye, "Daphne was just filling us in."

Zeno said something under his breath and pulled out his phone. His fingers flew across the screen while the rest of his body fidgeted.

"Is there, um, anything we can do to help?" I said slowly.

"Huh?" Zeno said, not taking his eyes off his phone.

Daphne rolled her eyes.

"Zeno!" she said rather loudly.

"Oh, yeah, uh, sorry," Zeno said, looking up to find us all staring at him. Slowly, he slid his phone back into his pocket but continued to fidget all the while. He kept glancing down at his pocket like it was going to start moving on its own. Daphne cleared her throat and gave him a look.

Zeno looked around at each of us and then finally took a deep breath and let it out slowly.

"Look, I know you guys rely on me for my dope ideas and cool tech, but Gina is built on a relationship."

"And?" Daphne said.

"And," he continued, "her basic programming is centered around bonding with a few people—that's what keeps her stable—and since she hasn't had those people around—"

"She got lonely," Alex said simply. "Makes sense. I hate to think how my personal assistant at home is doing—Vivian's probably gone and erased all my gaming data... or worse." Alex looked off toward the ceiling.

Zeno didn't miss a beat.

"Exactly. And after she got lonely, she had to accept her new reality, so being the bundle of resourceful and ingenious code that I created, she made some changes to her internal logic. Specifically, now she thinks that people just abandon each other all the time."

"I thought computers generally did what you programmed them to do," I said. "Isn't there a master override or something?"

"Irrevelant," Zeno said. "We need her capabilities—things she's developed herself over the last few years. If I override her, all of that goes away. So we need Gina to let us in, and if I don't get back to her soon, she'll shut me out completely, and that might be the end of it. Forever." He looked at us all with a somber expression.

"Can't you just apologize for being gone?" Alex said. "Or get her the computer equivalent of flowers or something?" He paused and looked up at the ceiling, then smiled. "I once got Viv a new graphics card, but I don't know what Gina would want. Something..." Alex paused and glanced at Zeno. "Dope?"

"I think you're onto something there," Zeno said, starting to nod. "You know what?" He said with a snap. "I bet Ivy would know!"

"Great idea!" Alex said.

"Yes," Zeno said, his eyes getting big. "Yes! How did I not think of this before? She's a girl—Ivy *would* know!" Without another word, Zeno bolted right back up the stairs in multiples.

"So, is everything going to be okay?" Trevor said, watching him go with some degree of suspicion. "From what I know about Zeno, I imagine this 'Gina' is fairly advanced. Does he need help? I do have some experience with computers."

"I don't know," Daphne said, "he's pretty particular, especially with Gina. It's probably better to let him work on it alone. I'd imagine Gina is multiple generations ahead of anything in the Heights, or the Flats for that matter."

"Agreed," I said, "so let's get back to Damien."

"Okay," Trevor said with a shrug. "This Damien, you said he was talking to a drone?"

"Yes," Daphne said, nodding emphatically.

"And you think that him talking to a drone means they're working with Rosewood?" Trevor said.

Daphne nodded again.

"I don't know of anyone else in the Heights who has drones like that. If Tyrann was still around, maybe he'd be a suspect, but no one else comes to mind. And he never used drones. I doubt Brick or Jonny could figure one out."

"And they're probably busy doing best friend things," Alex said, using his shirt to polish his hand again. I glanced at him and then back to Daphne.

"Did you hear what this Damien guy was saying?" I said.

"No," Daphne said. "I was too far away, and he had his back to me."

"I don't know, guys," Alex said. "Rosewood isn't all about helping people, right?" He continued to polish his robotic hand. "This Benjamin guy is helping tons of people. If you think about it, all the people we saw last night—they'd all be homeless without his help."

"And without our home," Daphne said.

"Alex has a point," I said slowly. "It's inconvenient for us, but he *is* helping a lot of people. That's not really Rosewood's MO."

"Can we at least agree to treat him with some level of suspicion?" Daphne said. "He's new, he's influencing a large number of people, and one of his 'volunteers' was talking to a drone." She gave us all a pointed stare. "I'm not going to just trust him."

"That's fair," I said. "He's on the list of potential bad guys, but that doesn't help us with Rosewood. We keep getting sidetracked."

"I'm sorry someone stealing our home and buildings collapsing for no reason is diverting our focus," Daphne said.

I let loose an impatient sigh. Yes, the things she mentioned were kind of a big deal, but they were still a distraction. Rosewood wasn't distracted. The only reason I could come up with for why she would even allow us to return to the Heights was if things were already so far in motion that she felt like there was nothing we could do to stop it. If that was the case, we didn't have much time. We needed to focus. I glanced at Daphne. She was still fuming.

"So what now?" Trevor asked.

Alex moved over to the mattresses and plopped down. Trevor and I stayed standing.

"We plan," I said. "We've got to figure out how to take down Rosewood, before it's too late."

18

———

"You're suggesting civil war?" Trevor said.

I paced up and down the small space in our bunker. I looked back at Trevor and nodded. It's exactly what I was suggesting. I didn't see any other way.

"Nobles versus Sinisters." Trevor shook his head. "Are there any other options?" He had become increasingly concerned the more we had talked. He had sat down and clasped his hands tightly together, I imagine, to keep himself from fidgeting. I could see his white fingers and knuckles from where I stood.

"The five of us can't do it alone," Daphne said. "With all the support Rosewood has, plus anything new she has planned, I don't think flying under the radar is going to be in the cards.

"Agreed," Alex said. "And while my arm is pretty powerful, I don't know if it's that powerful." He held it out and examined it. "Well, maybe."

"Let's talk worst-case scenario," Daphne said, turning away from Alex.

"Let's start with facts," Trevor said, standing back up. "Rosewood has more resources, better infrastructure, and more than likely, a very united group of people behind her, and we—"

"We have a disjointed group of degenerates without any means," I finished.

"And?" Alex asked, pushing himself up off the mattress.

"And what?" Daphne said.

"Exactly!" Alex said. "And what? We're a disjointed group of whatever, and we've got you, and Victor, and this guy." He pointed to Trevor. "And my arm! And Zeno and Gina and whatever ideas we come up with. No one's been a match for that combo yet." Alex glanced at Trevor. "If you didn't already know, you're now part of a very elite crew."

Trevor considered Alex's words for a moment, his head leaning this way, then that.

"Well," he said, "what else do we have? Can we expose Rosewood for who she really is?"

"There's those ideas I was talking about!" Alex said.

"Would anyone believe us?" I said. "The moment they find out where the information came from is the moment they would dismiss it."

"Agreed," Daphne said.

"No," Trevor said, "Victor, you're onto something." He started to nod. "Would anyone believe us is a good question." We all looked at him. "Are there any Nobles who would believe what we could tell them?"

I looked around the group and shrugged.

"I don't know, maybe? You'd know better than I would. What are you getting at?" I said.

"A simple Sinister versus Noble fight is a lost cause," Trevor said. "But what if we were able to get a significant number of Nobles on our side? Enough to tip the scales?"

"So it'd be us, all the Sinisters, and some Nobles?" Alex said. "If my metal arm could get goosebumps, it would have them right now."

"Assuming we can get all the Sinisters," Daphne said.

"I was under the impression that all Sinisters would be against the Flats," Trevor said slowly. "Is that not the case?"

We all looked to Daphne, who hesitated.

"Generally speaking, it's true," Daphne said. "But it will take some convincing. With Tyrann out of the picture, I doubt everyone will be so quick to back our plan. They're not an easy bunch to convince of something, let alone unite."

"Even if we did get all of the Sinisters on our side and some Nobles," I said slowly. "Would it be enough?"

Rosewood's legion of drones flashed through my mind. I looked around at their unsure faces.

"It'll be enough," Alex said. "Probably more than enough."

"Do we have any other options?" Trevor said. He looked around once more.

The more we talked, the smaller our chance of success seemed. But I didn't see another alternative except to abandon our cause. Silence met Trevor's question.

"So we're all agreed then?" I said. "Recruit the Sinisters and as many Nobles as possible in preparation for war." I looked around again. Three uneasy faces met mine, but there wasn't any dissent. "Okay then," I said. "Let's figure this out."

Nearly an hour had gone by. Parts of a plan were coming together, but other parts weren't.

I was drawing a blank. How could we recruit Nobles? There was no way I could reach out to anyone in the Flats. No one would believe me, anyway. Daphne had been in the Heights for so long that

I was certain she didn't have any contacts there. That left Alex and Trevor.

"I don't think it's as far out an idea as you think it is," Trevor finally said, breaking the silence. "The people at the camp were the ones who were brave enough to act. I imagine for every one person who acts, five or ten more have similar feelings."

I mulled it over.

"It's a good thought," I said, trying but failing to do some quick math in my head. "We'd have to get a significant portion of the Flats to turn against Rosewood. I don't think we'd need a majority, but a pretty good chunk."

"So again," Daphne said, "the question remains, how are we going to convince a bunch of Nobles that their beloved leader is a murdering liar?"

Alex had been unusually silent. I glanced at him. He was staring off, apparently lost in thought.

"This is where some of Zeno's expertise would come in handy," I said. "What are the odds he steps away from Gina to help us brainstorm?"

"Low."

Silence hung over us as we all fought for a shred of creativity. We needed to figure something out. And fast. Whatever Rosewood's plan was, I had the terrible feeling it was days away, not weeks.

Since the moment Rosewood's drones destroyed our convoy, I had been actively repressing any feelings of doubt. But now, I felt my defenses weaken. Zeno should be here. Augustine should be here. They weren't. Who else was there? A thought struck me. Why hadn't I thought of it before?

"What about Jahko?" I said suddenly.

"Jahko?" Trevor said.

"He's the crazy, not crazy one," Alex said. "Responsible for this." He held up his mechanical arm. "Well, not responsible responsible, you know what I mean? But it's because of him, well more Ivy, I guess, that I don't have nothing here." He wagged his arm again and grinned.

Trevor gave him a confused look. I'd gotten used to him over the last couple of days—I forgot how little he knew of what we'd been through.

"Jahko is the leader of the city to the south," I said. "Ville."

"Oh, yes," Trevor said, his eyes registering understanding. "Alex was telling me that you were all imprisoned together?"

"The good old days," Alex said, as if reliving a fond memory.

"Well then," Trevor said, looking around at us. Each of us met his gaze. "And you think he can help us?"

"He hasn't been much help since we left, and he's nearly impossible to contact," Daphne said.

"But worth a shot," I said, turning to Trevor. "If he could loan us a few sweepers, it could make a big difference. And having Ivy's help would be huge—especially if Zeno is..." I glanced up the staircase. "Otherwise occupied." I nodded at Daphne. "I think it's your turn."

Daphne sighed, pulled out her phone, and started typing. We'd gone back and forth texting him for help and advice, but it usually didn't amount to much. Even Alex hadn't had much contact with him. I continued.

"The way I see it, if we're going to recruit Nobles, we need a way to communicate with them. And we need to do it under Rosewood's radar."

I looked around the room. Everyone was lost in thought.

"What about the Toddlers?" Alex said.

Daphne shook her head.

"They were destroyed, remember? Zeno nearly cried when Ivy broke the news to him."

"Right," I said.

Silence returned.

Alex raised a finger, his mouth open, about to speak, but stopped. His hand fell back to his side. Then, just as quickly, it shot up again.

"What if we didn't need the Toddlers?" he said. "What if we didn't need anything?"

More silence as we all stared at him. He held up his hands in defense.

"Hear me out—what if something like what we're talking about already exists?" He looked around at each of us, excitement showing in his voice. "We need a way to get a message to a bunch of Nobles on an underground network, right?"

"Right," I said slowly.

"Well," Alex pulled a small screen out of his pocket. "It just so happens that an underground network for Nobles already exists." After a few taps, he flipped it around for us to see.

His screen was taken up by a single large icon. Two concentric circles were the backdrop for a small square box through which glowing particles passed in and out of, like a stream.

"Isn't that just a forum for one of your games?" I said. "I've seen you on there before, all the time, actually."

"No," Alex said. "It's more of a forum for people to discuss things. Threads, videos, all kinds of stuff. It's called the—"

"Sandbox," Trevor finished, almost in a whisper. "Of course." I gave him a look, but he didn't see me. He was staring off, apparently already lost in thought. I looked to Daphne. She shrugged.

"So there's a lot of people on it?" I said, turning back to Trevor.

"Over half of the Noble population," Trevor said softly.

"Wait, seriously?" I said. "I've never been on there in my life."

"Not all of us dedicated our lives to saber fighting," Trevor said, coming out of his reverie. "In fact, most of us did not."

I looked at Daphne again. She shrugged. She was in the same boat I was in. I looked at Alex, who was smirking.

"So you're saying we could use this to tell people about Rose-wood?" I said. "And they'll listen?"

"For sure, as long as the right people notice it," Alex said.

"I'm sure my grandfather knows people who might listen to us—" I started.

"It wouldn't matter," Trevor said, cutting me off. "It's about who in the community notices it, not necessarily a person in the government."

"Yeah," Alex said, "the Sandbox is totally anonymous. No one knows who anyone else is on there." He let loose a yawn. "My dad could be on there, and he could either be a really influential account, or he could be a complete nobody. There's no way to know."

"So then, how do we know who to target?" I said. "And how do we target them? And how do we get our message out and—"

"Victor," Alex said, yawning again, "don't worry about it. I got you."

I looked over at Daphne.

She shrugged. "I want Zeno's take on it, but—"

"He's going to love this," Alex cut in.

"And we can talk with him about it later," Daphne continued, "but it seems like it's worth a shot. I can work on the people in the Heights. You two can do the Sandbox thing. I say we all get started first thing in the morning."

"The Sandbox," Trevor said. Daphne gave him a look. He shook his head and smiled. "This could really work!"

I stared at him. How could this forum, The Sandbox, how could it be the answer if Daphne and I had never heard of it? I looked at Alex.

"I knew Rosewood was no match for us." He let loose another yawn. "But"—he laid his head down on his mattress—"for my money, it's bedtime. Saving friendships and brainstorming really takes it out of me. Anyone got any bedtime snacks?"

Daphne and Trevor both shook their heads, then stood up.

"That's it?" I said, looking around.

Alex gave me a look as he laid back on his mattress and kicked his feet up.

"Did I mention we walked like ten miles today, too?" He lifted his head up and brought his voice down to a whisper. "But seriously, food? I would eat anything right now."

"No, sorry," I said, shaking my head. "I know it's late, and we're all tired, but..."

Trevor and Daphne stopped in their tracks.

"The Sandbox. That's it? That's the answer?"

Trevor continued his walk toward a stack of mattresses.

"We'll have a few bugs to work out, I'm sure," he said, pulling down two mattresses in a single tug. "But we'll need fresh minds for that."

"Yeah," Alex said, the grogginess really starting to kick in, "we'll start planning what you're going to say tomorrow." His speech slowed. "It'll have to be good. I'm thinking video message—really intense, no smiling—you know, something to really draw people in."

"Video message?" I said.

Alex nodded with his eyes closed.

Daphne made her way toward a different stack of mattresses. Trevor's was about five feet past where Alex was at. Daphne's spot was across the room.

Alex's eyes popped back open. "No, I take that back. I wouldn't eat spinach right now. Or arugula. Or kale. But anything else." His eyes closed once more, and he began to snore gently.

Normally, his ability to sleep with such ease wouldn't irritate me, but this plan... We didn't have time for a do-over if it didn't pan out.

I followed Daphne to the other side of the room.

"What do you think?" I said.

"I think," she said, sitting down on her mattress. A puff of dust emitted from around her and was immediately siphoned up and into the vent. "I think it's something."

"What does that mean?"

"You saw how Trevor reacted," she said.

"So?"

"So, there's got to be some merit to it, right? And if half of all Nobles are on there, it sounds like the best shot we've got."

I stared at her, and she held my gaze.

"And what about Benjamin and Damien?" I said. "If we don't unite the Sinisters, it won't matter if the Sandbox does its thing anyways."

She kept her back turned as she did her best to fluff the mattress.

"You're right," she said. "I think we talk to Benjamin in the morning, first thing—try and catch him off guard."

"Good idea," I said.

But it didn't really sound good. It felt like we were putting too much stock into something we didn't know anything about.

"There's nothing else we can do tonight," Daphne said, finally turning around. One hand slid to her hip, and she fixed me with a stare. It wasn't a cold stare, but it wasn't a warm one, either. This wasn't the Daphne from the past several weeks. What had changed? What had gone wrong?

"Well, good night then, I guess," I said. Daphne nodded.

"Goodnight."

Without another word, she crawled onto her mattress and pulled an old, musty blanket over her. Conversation over. I stood there for a second, working through my thoughts. I should be able to talk to Daphne about this and also about us. But apparently, we couldn't do that now.

I had grabbed a mattress earlier and positioned it closer to the stairs. It was the only way in and out of the room, and it made sense for someone to be there. Not to mention, it now gave me a little bit of extra space to think. I glanced back at Daphne as I started walking toward my bed, racking my brain for any explanation of Daphne's reactions to me.

Upon arriving at my musty old mattress, I removed my gloves, tossed them on the bed next to where a pillow should be, and laid myself down.

I felt the exhaustion come upon me the moment I pulled the slightly dusty blanket over my body. The extra weight and warmth were comforting. I hadn't realized how sore my feet were from walking. I wasn't going to figure out Daphne tonight. I attempted to push her from my mind and tried to focus on the problems at hand.

To defeat Rosewood, we needed to unite the Sinisters. Our obstacle—Benjamin. Maybe. And then there was the Sandbox. I wasn't convinced. But Alex was, and so was Trevor. And Daphne seemed to be on board.

Daphne. Why? She had started acting cold after we left camp. But for what reason?

I closed my eyes harder, trying to squeeze the thoughts away.

We needed to get the Nobles on our side. Somehow. A sandbox?

My mind struggled for sleep.

There was so much to do. Tomorrow was like a weight crushing down on me. How much time did we really have?

19

———

My phone vibrated, jolting me awake.

Getting a message was a rarity anymore—especially with the phones Zeno had given us. Less than ten people knew how to contact me, and most of them were in the room with me now. And the other ones, well, Ville apparently had their own problems to deal with, and I doubted whether reception was really possible with the camp. I was eager nonetheless.

I wrestled my phone out of my pocket and brought it up close to my face, squinting into the bright light of the screen. It was from Zeno.

    Bro. Hallway.

I checked the time.
2:30am.
I took a deep breath and let it out slowly.
My phone vibrated again.

Come on, my man—I've only got like two
minutes. Gina's needy.

I pushed my blanket off and rolled out of bed. Hopefully, he was in a better state than earlier.

I did a quick check of the room. Alex's gentle snoring could be heard throughout the room. Daphne's and Trevor's breathing remained undisturbed.

I made my way quickly but quietly up the massive staircase.

Moments later, I slid open the panel to find Zeno standing entirely too close to the entrance.

"Jeez, man," I said, jumping back.

"Sorry, bro," he said quickly. "I don't have long." He looked down the hallway. "I've managed to get away for a few minutes—I think I've got her trust back, but I've got to build in some independence again. It's a delicate balance." He looked back at me. "You good?"

I stared at him, not sure if my face had woken up enough to glare.

"You do realize it's two-thirty in the morning, right?"

Behind his glasses, Zeno's sleep-deprived eyes blinked in disbelief.

"You're kidding me," he said. "That's it?" He let his head hang. "I was really hoping it was closer to four."

I stared at him.

"You said you only had a couple of minutes," I said.

"Oh right," he said, shaking his head clear. "I wanted to ask—did you guys make any progress figuring out how to take down Rosewood?" When I hesitated, he continued talking. "Look, man, I know I wasn't much help earlier, but as soon as I get Gina back to a hundred percent, it'll be like having two of me."

I exhaled. How long would that take? And hadn't he hacked out of Ville with his phone? I didn't quite understand, but I also didn't have the energy to debate him.

"No worries," I said. "We have a plan. Well, sort of."

"And?" Zeno checked the hallway again and then leaned in.

I gave him a quick recap of Daphne trying to unite the Heights, coupled with Alex's idea. He didn't ask questions but instead nodded appreciatively.

"My bionic armed bro—he never ceases to surprise me." Zeno chuckled, then looked at me seriously. "It's a good plan, Vic. It could work, it could really work."

"Really?"

Zeno gave even more credibility to Alex's idea. I shifted my feet, feeling uncomfortable.

"Yeah, bro—it's pretty ingenious, provided we can get the attention of the right people. You won't be able to just post a video, though." Zeno straightened his glasses. "We'll need some heavy lifting to get past the security protocols that prevent people in the Heights from posting to places Nobles can view it." He locked eyes with me. "And for that, we'll need Gina up and running."

"I've never even heard of the Sandbox—"

"Don't underestimate the number of closet nerds there are out there, bro. Trust me, there's a lot, and they're more powerful than you think."

Zeno looked up and down the hall again. I knew he'd have to leave soon. And if we needed Gina to make this work, I didn't want to keep him long.

"There's two more problems," I said.

"Can you make them quick?" Zeno said, his eyes locked on something down the hall I couldn't see. After a moment, he shook his head. "Sorry, bro, yeah, I mean, whaddaya got?"

"If I get on this Sandbox, people aren't going to just believe whatever I say, right? Plus, Alex said it's all anonymous. How do we make whatever I say credible? How will anyone believe it's actually me?" Zeno opened his mouth to respond, but I wasn't done. "And," I continued, "if this is really going to work, we're going to need more than just me."

I had a few doubts about Alex's plan, but this was the biggest one. If I said what was on my mind, it would make it real. We would have to do something about it, and I had no idea what that was.

I exhaled and continued. "The only person who can really defeat Rosewood," I continued, "is herself. I think there will be some people who believe what I say, but to really take down Rosewood, we need everyone to believe. We need a video or a sound bite of her incriminating herself. I've got no idea how to get something like that. I was thinking we could use something like your Toddler tech—"

Zeno let loose a groan and then sighed.

"Sorry, bro, it's just, me and Ivy, you know, we created the Toddlers, and now they're just gone. It hurts, it hurts deep, right here." He poked himself in the chest.

I nodded, unsure of what to say. After a couple of seconds of silence, I continued.

"What I was getting at is I don't know how we're going to get Rosewood to incriminate herself. And get it on video. Any ideas?" I paused. "And I can't help feeling like the clock is ticking. I honestly don't know how much time we have left."

Zeno pondered the question for a moment.

"I don't know, bro," he said. "Honestly, once I get Gina up and running like she's supposed to, we'll have a better shot at it. Let me think on it. Deal?"

I nodded.

"All right, so you said you had two problems—what's the second one?" Zeno said, glancing down the hall once more.

"Yeah," I said. "The Sinisters. They've never been united, and they're still not. If we're going to have a chance, we're going to need everybody together. I don't know if that's something Daphne and I can do."

"Benjamin might be the answer, bro. Seems like he's got quite the following. And it seems to be growing. I'd use that."

"But what if we can't trust him?" I said. "There's still a lot of people who haven't come around to him. Brick and Jonny don't like him. And they seem to have a bit of a following, too. Tyrann's name still seems to hold some clout."

"I don't know how much stock I'd put in what Brick and Jonny say, you know what I mean? My gut tells me to use Benjamin somehow. But the Sandbox idea is solid."

Zeno had stopped looking at me at this point. His gaze was fixed back down the hallway.

I sighed again and shook my head.

"Go," I said.

"You sure, bro?"

"Yeah, I'm sure," I said.

Zeno let out a breath he had apparently been holding and smiled.

"My man." He held out a fist. We knocked knuckles, and he started walking.

"Hey, Zeno," I said.

He kept walking backward.

"Thanks," I said. "And good luck with Gina."

He nodded and then took off in a run.

I stepped back through the panel, made my way down the stairs, and slipped into bed. By this point, the tiredness had worn off, and I was left to my thoughts once more.

I had a feeling I wouldn't be getting much more sleep tonight.

20

"You sure he'll be here?" Alex said. "I feel like we got up even earlier than we did yesterday. He's probably still sleeping."

I opened my mouth to respond but closed it.

We stood outside Benjamin's office. It had been light for at least an hour, and although I had gotten almost no sleep, everyone else seemed well-rested. The walk through the hallways to Benjamin's door had been mostly silent. The plan was to catch Benjamin off guard. After last night, I wasn't convinced this was the right thing to do. Unfortunately, Daphne hadn't seemed like she was in a talkative mood this morning.

"If he's not," Trevor said, "perhaps we can track down Maggie. She'll know where he is."

I stepped up to the door and knocked three times, then stepped back.

The door was thick, and we couldn't hear anything behind it. For several seconds, there was nothing.

"Well," Trevor said, "let's go find Mag—"

The creak of the door handle brought my attention back. It turned slowly until it clicked, and the door swung inward. A smiling, albeit weary, Benjamin greeted us, wearing the same clothes from yesterday.

"Hello all. Please come in."

"Late night?" I asked.

"What? Oh, yes," Benjamin said, taking his chair behind the desk. "As you know, another building collapsed yesterday. Each time has been very busy." He smiled. "It's a blessing in disguise, I think." He motioned to the chairs in front of us. Alex immediately plopped down in one. The rest of us remained standing.

"How so?" Daphne said.

"Another hundred or so people showed up yesterday," Benjamin said. "I'll have the chance to address them all later today, and perhaps a few of them will feel uplifted by what I share." He tapped a few times on the screen at his desk. "But enough about me and my late nights, what brings the four of you to my office at this hour?"

I was most curious about this Damien character and why he was using drones, but Zeno's wisdom from last night continued to scratch at my thoughts. And the more I thought about it, the more I felt like we should try and be friendly to Benjamin rather than surprise and accuse him. Benjamin was already gathering and uniting the Sinisters. Like he had said—this could actually be a blessing in disguise.

"We're here—" Daphne started. I cut her off.

"Because we wanted to learn more about what you do here." I gave her a look. I hoped it said, "Trust me," but all I saw was the beginnings of a scowl as I turned back to Benjamin.

"Is that so?" Benjamin set his elbows on his desk, clasped his fingers together, and smiled.

"Yeah," I said. "You mentioned yesterday that you had volunteers helping you." I looked around at our group. "How does it all work? You've got a sermon you're working on for later today. Is that right?"

Daphne bumped my shoe with hers and gave me an angry look. I gave her a brief shake of my head while Benjamin looked down at his desk.

"That's right. I divide my time between delivering messages and caring for those whom I am able to help."

"And what about your volunteers?" I said. "What do they do? Does anyone go out and recruit?" If I did this right, maybe we could befriend him and find out about this Damien character.

"Recruitment?" Benjamin shook his head. "No, we let people come to us. And we hope our message will inspire people to stay."

"Sounds nice," Alex said.

Benjamin gave him a smile.

"It is."

"So let's say," Daphne said, finally deciding to sit in one of the open chairs across from Benjamin, "that most of the Sinisters like and agree with your message, and they've all come to stay. Then what?"

"Then, Daphne, things can begin to change."

"What do you mean?" Trevor said.

Benjamin leaned back in his chair to a more comfortable sitting position.

"I believe that part of the problems that Sinisters face is their own doing. Because they are 'Sinister,'" he put air quotes around the word, "they expect that others will treat them poorly, or take advantage of them, or betray them. They expect to make poor decisions. They expect to be hurt."

Benjamin took a deep breath, which he exhaled slowly. "In short, they expect to be inferior. And they expect everyone around them to act that way as well."

It took me a moment to digest his words. I had never thought about it that way. Sinisters normally blamed the Nobles for where they were. Benjamin was basically saying they only had themselves to blame. Was this the type of stuff he was telling everyone? Augustine had tried to change how Sinisters thought about themselves, but it never gained any traction. Maybe Benjamin's method just resonated better? And if he was proposing a way out of inferiority, well, the Sinisters would like that, wouldn't they?

"You're talking about a change in perspective," Daphne said.

Benjamin nodded. "Yes." He rested his elbows on the desk and clasped his hands together.

"And then what?" Daphne continued. "If everyone did change, what would that achieve?"

Benjamin smiled

I listened intently—this was what I really wanted to know. How far did he want to go?

"Harmony in the Heights," Benjamin said, "and ultimately, the Flats as well."

"Do you have a plan for that, too?" Daphne said.

Benjamin leaned back in his chair once more.

"One step at a time, Daphne."

Daphne crossed her arms.

"Does one of your steps involve your volunteers sending drone messages to the Flats?"

I stared hard at Daphne. So far, Benjamin had taken her hostility well, but I couldn't imagine it continuing.

"Whatever do you mean?" Benjamin said. His cadence remained unchanged, as did his smile, but there was a nearly negligible difference to his tone. I almost didn't catch it, but it was there—a slight coldness.

"I mean that yesterday, after your volunteer, Damien, left here, I watched him talk to a drone for a few minutes before it flew off."

The lines between Benjamin's eyebrows creased in confusion.

"I struggle to see any inherent evil in sending messages by drones."

"And there's not," I said, jumping in, trying to soften the tone. I could immediately feel Daphne's glare. "It just seemed a little odd. You don't see much of that happening around here."

"Or in the Flats," Trevor said. "We only know one person who uses them, especially in this area."

Benjamin raised his eyebrows in question.

"Rosewood, Benji," Alex said. "And we've got some pretty personal experience with her drones." He made an explosion sound, which he dramatized with a couple of hand gestures for effect.

"And do you think that a growing congregation of Sinisters isn't a concern to Rosewood?" Daphne added. "You know as well as we do that tensions between Nobles and Sinisters are at an all-time high."

"I am aware of the tensions," Benjamin said. "If anything, I would hope that what we're doing here, should it get back to President Rosewood, would be encouraging." He stood. "Additionally, I can assure you that drone usage for sending secure messages is not exclusive to the President."

"Do you know what Damien was doing, then?" Daphne said.

"I do not." He paused. "However, I know that Damien has used drones in the past to send messages to other parts of the Heights."

Daphne responded with a look. Clearly, she wasn't satisfied with the answer.

"That's how I'd do it," Alex said. "Text messages can be so boring, but if a drone shows up—major style points."

Benjamin looked at Alex and smiled.

"I appreciate the four of you stopping by. Now, if you'll excuse me, I do have some preparation I need to do for my sermon later today."

"Of course," Trevor said.

Daphne stood up.

"Thanks for your time," I said.

I reached behind me and opened the door, allowing everyone to exit before me. I tried to catch Benjamin's eye before I left, but his eyes were glued to the screen on his desk.

I stepped out and shut the door behind me. The very moment that the door latched into place, Daphne started talking.

"He's lying about Damien," she whispered.

"You sure?" I said as we made our way down the hall. "I don—"

"I'm with Daphne on this," Trevor said.

I looked at him. He shrugged.

"Call it experience or intuition, but I agree with Daphne."

"Alex agrees with me, too," she said.

"Is that so?" I said.

"Yes," Daphne said. "We have an agreement. Alex always chooses my side."

"I do?" Alex said.

"You do," she nodded.

Alex looked at me and shrugged.

"Seems like the safest way to go for me."

"So, what now?" Trevor said.

"I talked with Zeno last night," I said.

"I thought he was too busy with Gina?" Daphne said.

"I had him for a whole five minutes, and he was on the verge of leaving the whole time, but we did get to talk," I said.

"Well, what did he say?" Alex said.

"He thinks the Sandbox is a great idea, but in order to make it work, we'll need Gina." I turned to Alex. "I don't think we have a lot of time, and Zeno could use some help."

"Wait, like, what kind of help? I use computers. I don't fix them." Alex held up his hand. "Sometimes I just break them."

I shrugged.

"No idea. I just know the sooner we get Gina back up and running, the more useful he becomes."

"And less crazy," Daphne mumbled.

"I could do it," Trevor said. "I actually have a fair amount of experience with electronics in general."

"Great," I said. "We'll take you there now." I started to walk, and everyone followed. "While they're working on that," I continued, "the rest of us need to figure out how to get everyone in the Heights on the same page." I looked back over my shoulder. "I think we need to pay Brick and Jonny another visit."

Daphne and Alex both nodded. I pushed through a set of doors and started down a new hallway.

"Good, they owe me big," Alex said. "They'll help us."

"They're going to have to," I said. I looked back at Daphne, but she avoided my gaze. I came to an abrupt halt. "Actually, Alex, can you take Trevor to Zeno and then meet us out front? I want to talk to Daphne for a minute."

Alex didn't skip a beat.

"Yeah, sure thing. Come on Trev—Gina's a friendly computer. Well, at least she was. I don't know about now, but you guys'll figure it out."

He and Trevor turned a corner, and their voices and footsteps faded.

A mix of fearfulness and resolve hit me. She stared at me, her face devoid of emotion. I didn't know how this was going to go, but as we locked eyes, I got the feeling it wasn't going to be fun.

21

———

"Are you going to say something?"

Daphne stood, her arms crossed, her gaze darting repeatedly from my eyes to anywhere else. The rest of the hallway was empty. The off-white linoleum floor had a cold, vacant feeling to it, and the lighting in this particular hallway was dim—not the ideal setting for what we were about to talk about.

Initially, I had been worried, but watching her, I was confused. There was something in the way she stood, the way her weight shifted back and forth, the way she wouldn't hold my gaze.

Daphne was uncomfortable.

But why? She was never uncomfortable, not in high-stakes situations. She was always ready for action, even if it was potentially harmful. Why was this different?

"Well?" she said, adjusting the way her arms were crossed.

"Well, I, um." I searched for the right words. Daphne started to glare. "Things have felt off lately," I said a little hurriedly. "I don't know why or what I did, but things haven't been, no, you and I haven't been the same since we came back here."

Finally, she held my gaze, but she didn't speak. There was more I wanted to say, but it was difficult. I waited another few seconds, but she still didn't respond.

In the moment, I thought about ending it, about walking away, but this mattered to me, maybe more than it should, but it did, so I locked eyes with her and continued.

"It's almost like we're not even friends anymore," I said. "And... it hurts."

She broke eye contact and stared at the floor. I waited. The buzz of the fluorescent lights above us was the only sound I could hear. Daphne shifted uncomfortably again, but still, no words.

"So is this it then?" I said. "Our friendship? Our relationship? This is it?"

Daphne stared at me, her face indecipherable.

I wanted to go. Anywhere. Her lack of an answer, her coldness— this hallway was quickly becoming the last place I wanted to be. Daphne looked back down to the floor.

"Okay then," I said with a nod, a difficult mix of emotions beginning to grow inside me. "Well, I'll meet you out front when Alex gets back."

I stood where I was, awaiting her response, but she continued to stare at the ground.

This really was it.

I started to walk, each footstep taking me farther and farther away from what I wanted. But what choice did I have? I had attempted a conversation. I had put myself out there, and this was the result.

Up ahead, a pair of metal doors with small glass windows loomed closer. The light beyond the windows called to me—anything to get me out of this dark hallway.

"This," Daphne suddenly said, her voice scratchy, "this isn't a real relationship."

I stopped in my tracks, fire flaring up inside me. The door in front of me was so close. One more step, and I'd be through it. But part of me wanted to fight, to defend myself.

"A real relationship?" I said, my back still to her. I fought to keep the incredulity out of my voice. I fought to keep from reaching for the door handle and walking through. My emotions warred against logic.

She kept talking.

"I don't want a fleeting, 'we're about to die' relationship," she said. "And that's what this is. We've spent every moment escaping death or preparing for it." I closed my eyes and sighed, my anger starting to dissipate. Daphne continued. "I want something real, and we can't have that until we get out of all of this. If we get out."

I turned back around.

"It's just too much," she said, her voice softer than before. It barely carried the distance between us, but I heard it. I took a few steps and closed the gap. Our eyes met.

I had rarely seen her so vulnerable—there was so much fear there, so much uncertainty. So often the warrior—she was never the one who needed comforting. She looked back at the ground, ashamed of her emotions.

"When we get out," I said. The silence stretched between us. I tried to meet her eyes, but she wasn't looking at me. "When we get out," I said again, "I'm going to take you on a real date."

Something in her look had changed. The fear was still present, but so was my support. If this was what she wanted, if this was what she needed—a break, a pause, whatever this was—then this was what we'd do.

And she could see that.

I gave her a half smile.

"Well," I said, "you ready?" I held out my fist.

Not a hug, not a kiss—we were about to truly start our fight against Rosewood, our final fight, and there was only one way to begin a fight.

Daphne looked from my fist to my eyes, then slowly, a soft smile graced the corners of her mouth, and she bumped her knuckles to mine.

"Let's go," she said. She started to walk, and I followed.

As we pushed through the doors and into the hallway beyond, I glanced back.

The light that shone through the small windows wasn't so dim, and the hallway didn't seem so cold. I felt a calm between us that had been missing. It felt good to know. It felt good to have even more to fight for. I allowed myself a smile as we continued walking.

Rosewood wasn't ready for us.

22

———

"Where even are we?" Alex said, looking around.

I had been about to ask the same thing. I had never been to this part of the Heights.

The street was teeming with people—there seemed to be even more Sinisters here than at the events center. The buildings here looked to be newer than the ones that had recently collapsed. Things were slightly less worn and slightly cleaner. The buildings weren't quite as tall, either—still taller than anything in the Flats, but nothing over fifty stories.

"We're at where I assume Brick and Jonny's backup home is," Daphne said. "We're going there." She pointed at a pair of black doors across the street. "It's one of Tyrann's old places." Two very large individuals stood to either side of the double doors. Both wore sunglasses and scowls. Both had the sleeves of their shirts torn off to reveal body-body-builder-sized muscles.

"There?" I said. "How do you know that's where they'll be?"

"Because I don't know anyone else in the Heights that would use bodyguards like that," Daphne said. "Come on, I know how to handle them."

Daphne took the lead, and we followed, weaving our way through the river of people. It was obvious where we were headed, but it was tough to tell whether or not the bodyguards had noticed us. Neither of them moved an inch as we approached.

Daphne opened her mouth to speak.

"We're here to—" she started.

"That's him!" The big man on the right said, pointing at us.

I assumed he was pointing at me—it wasn't like my face hadn't been plastered all over the news for the past several weeks for being a carrier of TᴨD or causing mayhem in the Flats.

Daphne sighed and gave me a look of supreme annoyance. I shrugged. I guess there were some perks to being semi-famous, even if it all was a big lie.

"Look, it's no big deal," I said. "We're just looking for—"

"No, it's not him," the other man said, ignoring me completely.

"Yes, yes it is," the first one said. "Look, Jonny said they always travel together. And I wasn't pointing at him." He pointed at me. "That's Victor Wells, and *that's* Alex Trabue." He pointed at Alex, who then pointed at himself in question.

The first man nodded vigorously, then smiled and gave him a wave. Alex returned the gesture.

"Our bosses have been expecting you, Alex." The two hulking men took a step back, clearing themselves of the door. "They're just inside —up the stairs, and it's the first door on your left."

This was definitely not the turn of events I was expecting.

"Cool if my friends come?" Alex said as he started walking toward the door.

"We were told that for you, anything." The second man gave Alex a little bow as he said it. Alex inclined his head in return.

"Thank you, gentlemen."

The two men opened the doors as Alex approached. He stopped in the doorway. The guy on his right tried to give him a fist bump, which Alex did not see. I shook my head in disbelief.

"You guys coming?"

"There he is!" Brick said, standing to meet us as we walked through the door. He smiled his set of crooked, yellow teeth as he came to meet us. He walked right up to Alex and grabbed him by the shoulders. "Alex Trabue," he said, smiling once more. "See, Jonny, I told you he'd come eventually! Come on in, sit down."

Jonny sat on a sofa across the room, his feet up on a large wooden coffee table and a drink in hand. He gave his glass a brief raise before taking another sip.

I shared a look with Daphne as we entered the room. She shrugged back at me. Never had I seen Brick so excited or cordial toward anyone. I decided in that moment that as soon as I could, Alex was getting a dozen donuts just for himself.

Maybe this would be easier than we thought.

The room was large—it had to be forty feet by sixty feet. It had the feel of an old-fashioned library, minus most of the books. Shelves lined the walls and were mostly filled with decorations of one kind or another. It was surprisingly classy. The furniture was sturdy and clean —all built from wood, all ornately carved. There was an element of comfort throughout, at least until my eyes reached the corner that had been obscured by the open door, which was now shut behind us.

Daphne elbowed me, maybe a little too hard, but I had already seen it. A body, an unmoving body.

"This is nice!" Alex said, continuing to walk forward. Daphne and I had frozen.

Brick eased himself into a large chair near Jonny and picked up a drink of his own.

"What can we say?" Brick said. "Business is good. Especially now. Ain't that right, Jonny?"

"Because of him?" I said, motioning to the corner of the room.

An overweight man, probably around forty years old, lay in what I hoped was an unconscious heap, slumped up against the wall. He had dark hair and a piece of black tape over his mouth. His wrists and ankles were bound with a cord of some kind.

"No idea who he is," Brick said. "We just got here an hour ago, and there he was, all unconscious in the corner. We're just waiting for him to wake up."

"So you checked to make sure he's *just* unconscious?"

"What are you trying to say?" Brick said, his eyes narrowing at Daphne.

"I'm trying to say, is that a dead body in the corner?" Daphne glanced at the body, then fixed Brick with a stare. Brick looked back confusedly.

"Why would someone dump a dead body in our office?" Brick said.

I glanced over at Daphne. I didn't think it was out of the realm of possibility—this was the Heights, after all—but clearly, this worried her. She glanced over at the body again.

"Obviously, it's an unconscious body," Brick said, "and we'll figure it all out when he wakes up."

Alex took a few steps toward the body. I almost told him to stay back, but I held my tongue.

"Have you at least tried waking him up?" Daphne said.

"Have you ever had someone wake you up after being knocked out?" Brick said, giving her a look. "It ain't polite. Last time someone clocked me good—it was the best sleep I got that whole year. Ain't that right, Jonny?"

Jonny nodded.

"See, Jonny knows. Similar thing happened to him a few years back."

Jonny nodded again.

"You're kidding!" Alex said, his head snapping back around. "Someone kidnapped you, knocked you out, and then left you in someone else's house all tied up?"

Jonny nodded again. Alex mouthed the word "wow" and turned back to the body, moving even closer.

"But if you just tried to wake him—" Daphne started.

"Put yourself in his shoes," Brick cut in, nodding to the corner of the room. "He's going to wake up and realize he's somewhere he don't want to be. The least we can do is let him get some decent sleep."

Daphne rolled her eyes.

"Did you guys see the note?" Alex said, bending over, his face entirely too close to the man's hands.

I looked to Brick.

"Like I said, we haven't disturbed him."

Alex fished a small piece of paper out from in between the man's hands and made his way over toward Brick.

"Not sure what's wrong with him," Alex said. "He's got some serious BO, though. I mean, really, what died?"

Daphne's eyes shot to Brick.

"I knew it!" she said, starting over toward the body.

"Knew what?" Alex said.

"He's dead, Alex! That's why he smells!"

"Nah, it's something else. Something sort of familiar..." Daphne gave him a disgusted look. He shook his head. "Anyways, he's not dead, he's snoring."

"Snoring?" I said.

"Yeah, you can hear him when you get up close, right, Daphne?"

Daphne, in the process of stooping over the unconscious man, straightened up and turned around.

"Right," she said with some measure of relief. "But seriously, what is that smell?"

Alex closed his eyes and gave the air a good sniff. His eyes shot open. "I knew I recognized the scent from somewhere. It's those snacks!" Alex said, clapping his hand to his forehead. "But what are they called?" He looked to Brick and Jonny. "Come on, help me out. They smell so bad, but they taste so good. They're like this big and yellow and salty and..."

Brick's face lit up. "Corn Nuts!"

"That's it!" Alex said. "Corn Nuts. The greatest treasure of the Heights."

Understanding dawned on Daphne's face, which quickly turned to disgust. "How many of those do you have to eat to smell like that?"

"Well, that settles it. Told you he wasn't dead," Brick said, a triumphant grin on his face.

Daphne didn't respond.

"I believe this is for you," Alex said, handing over the note he had plucked from the unconscious body.

Brick unfolded the paper and stared at it for a long moment.

"Well," Alex said, "what's it say?"

"Hold on, hold on." Brick smoothed the paper and cleared his throat. "Ahem. It says, 'Don't forget everything I've done for you when the time comes.'" Brick looked at Jonny. "Just like the others." He crumpled it and tossed it on the floor. Alex bent over and picked it up.

"What do you mean, 'just like the others'?" I said.

"Third or fourth one we've gotten," Brick said.

"Third or fourth note, or body?" Daphne said.

"Second body," Brick said.

We all stood there and stared at him.

"Who is Brock Thorton?" Alex said.

"Where did you hear that scumbag's name?" Brick said, his head whipping around.

Alex held up the piece of paper.

"It was written on the back."

Comprehension dawned on Brick's face, and he stood up.

"So that's Brock Thorton, eh?"

"Who is he?" I said.

"Never met him before," Brick said, not bothering to look at us. "Some of our main competition—keeps to himself mostly, but he's got some influence. Nothing like what we've got, of course."

Daphne was the first to respond.

"So you've got one of your biggest competitors tied up in your room. It's not the first time this has happened, and you're this nonchalant about it?"

"What did you call me?" Brick said, his voice dropping again.

"It means you don't care too much," Alex said.

"Oh." Brick shrugged. "Guess that's about right then. Why question a good thing?"

Daphne let out an exasperated sigh.

"So what does this mean?" I said. "He's tied up in your room. Who would do it? And why?"

Brick looked pensively up at the ceiling.

"Don't know. Must just be someone out there who believes in what we're doing and wants to help us out."

"Believes in what you're doing?" Daphne said. "As in controlling rents, threatening people, and taking over more property?"

"Exactly. We provide some really nice services. Can't help it if people want to help us." He looked over at Brock's unconscious form. "And this'll help us lock in the whole southern half of the Heights, won't it, Jonny?" Brick sat back down in his chair and let a serene smile take hold of his face. He looked over at Jonny. "We sure are blessed, ain't we?"

Jonny raised his glass and nodded.

"Congratulations to the two of you," Daphne said. "But we don't have time for this. We're here to talk business."

"Not so fast," Brick said, getting to his feet. "We just knew Alex would be stopping by, and I... Jonny, well, I have something I'd like to say."

He looked around the room, a bit of earnestness in his face that I'd never seen before. He cleared his throat again. Daphne shook her head but took a half step back. Brick looked around again and took a deep breath.

"We owe Alex here a great debt," Brick began, glancing over at Jonny. "Our friendship was on the rocks, our businesses were competing instead of working together, and now look at us." He spread his arms wide. "We have it all. And we owe it all to our good friend, Alex Trabue."

"What did I tell you guys?" Alex said. "A little communication was all you needed, right?"

"Yes," Brick continued rather shakily. Apparently, his speech wasn't over. He glanced over to Jonny again, who nodded. Brick reached into his pocket and pulled out another piece of paper, which he tried to smooth out. He looked down at it as he spoke, deliberately pronouncing each word. "Alex Trabue, we would like to extend to you the hand of professional friendship and offer you full partnership in our business dealings in the Heights." Brick stopped and folded up his piece of paper and gently tucked it back into his pocket. "Well?"

Alex pointed at himself. Brick nodded, and Alex smiled.

"Guys, I'm honored!"

I had the unmistakable urge to laugh—two grown men, Tyrann's old cronies, wanted Alex to be their business partner. I must have been smiling, and Alex didn't need anything beyond that.

He turned back to Brick. "I accept!"

"Great!" Brick said with a smile. Jonny, too, cracked a smile.

"Whoa, hold on a second," Daphne said, taking a step forward.

"What do you mean, 'hold on'?" Brick said, his voice dropping to a growl.

"Oh, right," Alex said, glancing at Daphne. "I accept later. Today, we're here on our business, but later, we can talk about," Alex paused and leaned in, "our business."

Brick let loose a sigh of relief.

"Right down to it," Brick said with a nod. "I approve."

"Thanks," Alex said, taking a seat across from Jonny. Daphne and I followed suit. I glanced back at the body in the corner before getting comfortable. I was always amazed at how at ease Alex found himself in any situation.

"I'm going to let these guys take it from here," Alex said, leaning back in his chair. "They have my full support, but we need help."

"Just say the word," Brick said, leaning forward. "Partner."

Alex nodded to me, and Brick and Jonny's attention shifted my way. I nodded to Alex. I had been debating on my strategy to persuade them, but seeing as time wasn't on our side, I hoped Brick valued directness.

"We're going to take on Rosewood, and we need your help," I said.

Brick stared at me for a long time before he spoke.

"Tyrann always said he mostly liked you."

"Mostly liked?" I said.

Brick chuckled.

"TΠD ring a bell? Breaking into the Capital, maybe?" He paused. "Hanging out with his daughter?"

"Mostly liked makes sense," Alex said.

I nodded slowly.

"He always liked your bold plans," Brick continued. He looked over to Jonny, who nodded. "What kind of help are you looking for?"

My original plan was to explain things to them—how Rosewood is planning something, how we need to be united if we were going to stand a chance—but I knew they respected Tyrann, and as they said,

Tyrann liked my bold plans. I looked to Daphne and Alex, then back to Brick.

"We need an army."

I could feel Daphne shoot me a look, but I didn't break eye contact with Brick.

He leaned back in his chair. The corners of his mouth twitched, almost like he was trying to hide a smile.

"An army, huh?" He looked over at Jonny. "Says he needs an army."

"With Tyrann gone, you two are the most powerful people in the Heights, right?" I looked over to Daphne for validation. "Unless I was wrong?" I shot my eyes back over to Brick.

He sat forward as fast as I'd ever seen him move.

"You know you're not."

It was my turn to conceal a smile.

"Sounds like we've come to the right place, then."

"You want to do something about Rosewood," Brick said. "When?"

"I need an army before I give you a timeline," I said. "Rosewood is planning something, and the only way we come out on top is if we band together."

"You mean work together? Who? Everyone in the Heights?" Brick said. He looked over to Jonny again, who shrugged and took another sip from his glass.

I nodded and continued to stare at him.

Alex didn't look up from polishing his arm when he spoke.

"Are you wasting our time here, *partner*?"

"No, no, of course not," he said quickly. "We've wanted to make a move against the Nobles for a long time now."

"And we're here to offer you that opportunity," Daphne said. "If you're on board, it shouldn't take too much persuading to get the lesser players on our side, too. So, are you in or out?"

"What do you think, Jonny?" Brick said. "Is it time?"

Jonny stared over at him, raised an eyebrow, and gave a slight incline of his head.

Brick broke out his toothiest, yellowest smile yet.

"You're right, maybe it's past time." He looked at me. "It's not going to be easy." He turned to Daphne. "You know everyone down here doesn't like to play nice."

"We figure you can be persuasive," she said.

Brick smiled slowly.

"In one way or another." Then his smile faded. "But we still have Benjamin to deal with."

Across the room, Jonny's face shifted into a frown.

I looked back at Brick and leaned forward.

"So you do know more about him than you told us last time?" Brick's face turned sour and he shook his head.

"All I know is I don't like him," Brick grumbled. "He came out of nowhere. Since Tyrann, people have been coming out of the woodwork to make a power play, and I know 'em all. But this Benjamin fellow—nothing. Never heard of him before a few weeks back."

"So you don't really know anything about him?" Daphne said.

"I'm saying there's not much to know," he growled. "Like I said before, he's new."

Daphne scoffed. "That's all you know?"

Brick fidgeted and shot Alex a quick glance.

"Look, all I heard was that he's got a voice people like to listen to. Plus, he's cutting into our business." Brick looked over to Jonny, who gave another silent but emphatic nod. "Any time a building goes down, the people seem to turn to him instead of us. We're the ones that control the buildings, not him!"

"Any reason why that's happening?" I said. Brick leaned forward, his voice growing tighter as he spoke.

"I just said he's got a nice voice, didn't I?"

"I was talking about the buildings coming down."

"Oh," Brick said, leaning back again. "Like I told you last time, infestation is what I keep hearing. Old buildings. Supports are starting to rot. But Jonny told me he didn't see anything when his building went down." Brick glanced at Jonny, who nodded, then pushed himself to his feet. "Speaking of, we've got to run ourselves a little errand. Some kind of commotion over in the North Heights that we've got to take care of."

"What are you going to do with Brock Thorton over there?" I said.

"He'll be here when we get back," Brick said dismissively.

Beside me, Daphne shook her head.

"Can we come?" Alex said.

"Why?" Brick said, eyeing him.

"Well, seeing as we're partners now," Alex said. "I know I said later, but we could help now."

"Is that so?" he said, turning to me. I nodded.

"Absolutely," Alex said. He pointed across the room at one of the bookshelves behind Jonny. "Do you need that white statue thing?"

"I, well—"

It was too late. In a blinding flash of light, half the bookcase exploded as Alex shot a single blast out of his hand. The statue had been turned to dust. Books went flying, their pages floating through the now dusty air. Behind us, in the corner, the unconscious man snorted.

Brick's eyes went wide. Jonny brushed a little debris off of his shoulder and took a final sip of his drink before setting it down. He stood up and walked past Brick, patting him on the shoulder as he did so.

He made his way past us but paused at the door. What happened next was easily the most surprising thing that had happened all day.

Jonny spoke.

"Coming?" he said.

23

—————

"We've gotta stop by here first," Brick said. Up to this point, the walk had been mostly uneventful. Brick had showered Alex with question after question about his arm. Alex had obliged by blowing off the corners of several abandoned buildings and scaring multiple birds.

I had tried, without luck, to get Jonny to speak again, but I'd still learned a few things, mostly through Daphne pestering Brick during his conversation with Alex.

"Where is 'here'?" I said.

We were, yet again, in an unfamiliar part of the Heights. We had come to a stop at what was clearly one of the older buildings in the Heights. It wasn't the tallest or the shortest, but it did seem to be about on the verge of collapse. The exterior brick was crumbling, and the windows had long since been boarded up. One blast from Alex's arm might be enough to bring the whole place down.

Brick looked around, then lowered his voice.

"It's a Noble news station." He pushed the door in, and we followed him inside.

The door shut behind us, and a single, large screen came to life at the back of the room.

"See, tensions have been running high, higher than normal, between the Nobles and Sinisters," Brick paused as the screen filled with static. "Tyrann used to come here every day. He knew more about what was going on in the Flats than anyone else here."

The screen flickered, then Kelly Straunton appeared. Brown hair, eye makeup, and an almost blindingly white smile filled the screen.

"... week into the ban on Sinisters entering the Flats continues," she said. "Experts had predicted more opposition to such a move, but President Rosewood's policy has been met with little resistance. Perhaps it's her promise of future genetic modification for Sinisters, or maybe...."

Her eyes flicked to somewhere off camera, and for a microsecond, her normally composed face fell before returning to a smile. "Or maybe the people of the Flats have come to see the Sinisters for what they really are."

I looked to Daphne, whose eyes were glued to the screen. I could barely process what I was hearing. Never before had I heard anything like this on the news. There had always been some degree of strain between the Nobles and Sinisters, but this was completely different. This was bad. Beside me, Brick growled.

"Nobles." He said the word like a curse and shook his head.

"But hope for the future remains strong," Kelly continued. "President Rosewood's research continues to show promise. To date, five Sinister individuals have undergone genetic modification, apparently to great success. However, in an exclusive interview from earlier this week, President Rosewood mentioned that not every Sinister will be a candidate for such modification. We are still unsure of what the future will hold."

The screen cut to some prerecorded footage of Rosewood. She wore a white jacket with a high, stiff collar that covered most of her neck. Her hair was pulled back tight against her head, but she had a comfortable look about her. She was sitting in a chair, leaning back slightly—as casual as I'd ever seen her appear. She had no fears, no worries. Everything was going according to plan.

And it made me furious.

"We have made great strides with our genetic modification," she said smoothly. "However, our continued research and testing has proven that only a small subset of the Sinister population will be compatible with the process. Yes, it is unfortunate, but any amount of progress in the right direction is a victory."

Off camera, another voice spoke.

"What about the rest of the Sinisters?

"Them?" Rosewood said. "It is an unfortunate path that they have inherited. The question is whether or not that same path should be allowed to propagate to further generations."

I felt the air change. I looked over at Daphne and then over to Alex. Daphne's face had grown stern. Alex remained staring at the screen, his face neutral, but as I looked at his hands, his fists were clenched.

"Can you elaborate on that?" the voice said.

Rosewood allowed herself a small smile.

"Rest assured that we are doing everything we can to further our research and save as many people as is possible. Thank you."

The screen cut back to Kelly.

"This brings us to the conclusion of this morning's news update." She gave a weak smile. "As always, I'm Kelly Straunton. John, back to you."

The screen turned off.

"Don't know why he did this every day," Brick muttered. Clearly, he didn't really grasp what was going on. Brick shook his head. "Anyways, let's go." He turned toward the door.

I didn't move. I was speechless.

"Are you coming?" he said.

Beside me, Daphne hadn't moved either. Alex stayed put, too.

A ban on Sinisters entering the Heights was one thing, but Rosewood was planting seeds more dangerous than that. She was preparing the Flats for something.

"Has Rosewood said something like that before?" Daphne said, turning to face him.

"Like what?" Brick said. "Every week, it's the same smug nonsense."

Daphne turned to me.

"You caught that, right?"

I nodded.

"Yeah, that was bad," Alex said. "Bad, worse, and ugly. She's got to go. And soon."

Brick looked around at all of us, mild confusion showing on his face.

"Brick," I said. "Rosewood is going to make a move. Soon. How about that army we mentioned?"

"Okay, okay," Brick said. "One news update, and you think the world's ending." He turned to Jonny, who shrugged. "Like I said, we've got a matter to attend to first, and then we'll get onto your army."

Brick winced as Alex slapped him on the back with his metal arm.

"Well then, let's go!"

I couldn't stop thinking about what Rosewood had said. Should Sinisters even be allowed to propagate what they inherited...

So much had changed. And so quickly. I shook my head and squinted as a beam of light reflected off of one of the buildings in front of us.

"So you're saying the number of gangs has decreased since Tyrann died?" Daphne said. She walked next to Brick, pestering him with questions. So much had changed in the Heights, and we needed to get a handle on it quick.

"Are you going to question everything I say?" Brick said with a sigh.

"Yes." Daphne's face turned smug.

"Fine," Brick said. "Since Tyrann disappeared, a few of the smaller gangs decided to join together and see if they could take some of our territory."

"Annnnd?" Alex said, drawing it out. He looked back at me and shrugged. "Gotta make sure my business partner is making good moves."

I smiled.

"You know the answer to that," Brick said with a gruff smile. "Our territory's bigger than ever."

"Thanks to whoever is knocking off your competition," Daphne said.

"Tyrann always said to never question a good thing," Brick said. "Just be grateful."

"So who's doing it?" Daphne said. "You said all the other gangs are trying to come after you."

"What part of just being grateful are you not understanding?"

"It's infuriating that you don't care who is helping you," Daphne said.

"It's just some good karma," Alex said.

"Good karma?" Daphne scoffed. "For what?"

"Helping us," Alex said simply. "We can't take Rosewood down without them."

"Speaking of," I said, "I know everyone here hates Rosewood, but how difficult is it going to be to convince them to work with us?"

"To be honest," Brick said, steering us down a new street, "I don't think many people here have thought too much about it."

"That's not an answer," Daphne said.

"Well then, I guess we'll all find out together, won't we?"

Daphne went silent.

"Come on," Alex said. "We just want to know what we're up against. Is this going to be an easy sort of thing, or am I going to have to use my arm blaster a lot?"

"And if everyone really does hate Rosewood, then ultimately, they want the same thing, don't they?" Daphne said, jumping in before Brick could speak.

"They don't all want the same thing," Brick said.

"Then what do they want?" I said. "Do they not want to be free?"

"If Rosewood is gone, then what?" Brick said. "Isn't it just some new Noble who's going to take over? What's really going to change? And besides, they all want to control the Heights. They want our buildings." He pointed to himself and Jonny. "They want money and power. They want to be feared."

It was hard remembering that they just didn't think like we did. They believed in the Noble-Sinister dichotomy. They thought the only way to change things was to reverse the power structure. More likely than not, the rest of the Heights felt the same way. Could we appeal to them somehow? Could I trust their hatred for Rosewood being so strong that they would look past their beef with Brick and decide to work together? Or would they see it as a pointless endeavor—something that required a lot of work but ultimately changed nothing?

In my pocket, my phone vibrated. I fished it out and quickly read the text. It was from Zeno.

"Looks like Trevor has a knack for helping out with Gina," I said. Daphne and Alex turned my way. I held up my phone. "Zeno just sent me a text. Apparently, Trevor has skills. With a Z."

"I knew he'd be good," Alex said. "He's part of our team, right?"

I nodded my agreement as Brick steered us around the next corner and slowed his pace. The street we were on dead-ended into a clearing that was bordered by a tall wire fence. Just beyond that lay the Inner- belt. We were approaching the official border of the Heights and the Flats, and all thoughts of uniting the Heights vanished from my mind.

Normally, people didn't spend time in areas like these. The buildings nearest the Innerbelt on our side were generally vacant, but today, things were different. Four or five dozen Sinisters congregated near the fence. On the opposite side, I had expected the police, but instead, I saw a group of about ten black-clad figures.

They looked like Sinistrali.

Black boots, pants, shirts, body armor, and helmets. They were impressive. Maybe it was the fence separating the Sinister protesters from the Sinistrali, but the protestors didn't seem scared in the slightest. Their screaming, their signs—if there wasn't a barrier, I wondered if they wouldn't have already rushed the Noble side.

"Let's stop here," Brick said, holding his arm out. He looked at each of us. "Just so you know what you're getting into," he said, pointing down the road. "This ain't no kid's commotion. You hear that?"

We all nodded.

"That's a bunch of angry Sinisters," Brick said.

"Yeah, and what are they protesting this time?" Daphne said, her tone bored.

"Rosewood, of course." He gave Daphne a look. "I thought that much was obvious."

"I thought they didn't care about her that much?" Daphne said. "All they want is your power." She gave him a look.

"Some care more than others," Brick growled.

Clearly, it annoyed him, but it gave me hope. Their discontent for Rosewood, their hatred—we could use that.

"What are you planning to do?" Alex said.

"Nothin'." Brick shook his head. "This ain't the first time they've done this. A few of them'll get stunned, and the rest'll run back with their tails between their legs like the dogs they are."

"So we're just going to stand and watch?" Daphne said. "I thought they were on your side. I thought you 'had matters to attend to.' Why else would you come here?"

"It's just business," he said. "Alex gets it. These guys run around causing havoc—breaking windows, picking locks, stealing things—but we don't want them doing it on our property. That's part of the security we provide." He looked over at Jonny. "Now, if they were doing it on someone else's property at our request, well, that'd be a different story." He looked up the street. "Maybe today is the day we convince them."

"And to join us against Rosewood," Daphne said. "Right?"

"That too," Brick said, continuing to stare up the street.

I could see the greed in his eyes, but I didn't care. Whatever convinced them to join us, I'd take it.

"Good," Alex said with an official nod. "I approve of this plan."

I kept my eyes on the Sinistrali. So far, none of them had moved, and that was a good thing, but if the protesters kept it up or intensified their efforts, I couldn't imagine the Sinistrali would stay put for long.

"We need to get them away from the fence," I said.

"Easy there, Tii" he said. "No need to rush into this. Trust me, one stunner blast, and they'll come running back this way."

I wasn't fond of the new nickname, and this was more serious than Brick realized. We needed to do something—warn them somehow.

"Those aren't regular police officers," I said.

"The Flats only have one set of police officers," Brick said. "Must just be a uniform change. Probably some stupid order from the old hag."

"It's not a uniform change," I said. "It's the Sinistrali. We need to get them out of there."

Brick chuckled.

"Sure it is, and good luck with that," Brick said.

I stared at the protesters. They all chanted something I couldn't quite make out, laced with intermittent yelling and screams. I continued to watch. Up to this point, all of the protesters had stayed in a fairly tight group. Now, one broke away, and the yells and screams grew louder.

He was riling them up.

"Damien's a real unreasonable type—nothing like me and Jonny," Brick said. "If he wants to be there, ain't nothing you can do to convince him otherwise."

My head snapped back around.

"Wait, Damien?" I said.

"That's right," Brick said, pointing. "He's the tall one at the back of the group. He's their leader." He was pointing to the person riling everyone up. Brick shook his head. "Lead idiot, more like. Maybe he'll be the one that gets stunned, and we can talk to the rest of his crew. Funny, though, I wasn't sure we'd make it in time to see this part. They're usually pretty quick to get stunned—one usually tries to climb the fence, and then it's all over." Brick chuckled to himself. "Idiots."

Damien made his way to the front of the chanting group and began pacing back and forth, throwing up his fist and punching the air periodically. Each movement was punctuated by a new round of yells and chants. I kept my eye on the Sinistrali—they continued to maintain their position.

"Hey Brick," Alex asked, "do you know any other Damiens?"

"Just the one," Brick said.

I turned to Daphne.

"How about you?"

"I don't know anyone else named Damien," she said.

"Me neither," Alex said. "But I guess I only know like ten people in the Heights, so..."

"You said he's unreasonable—do you think he'll talk to me?" I asked. A plan was forming in my mind. If this was the same Damien that Daphne had spied on earlier, he could be useful to us, very useful.

"Oh, he'll talk to you all right," Brick said. "Talkin's all he does, but he won't listen to a word you say."

The loudest cheer yet stole my attention. The Sinistrali started maneuvering. Alarm bells went off in my mind.

Too late.

I took off at a run.

"Victor!" Daphne yelled. "Wait!" I looked back briefly, but she had started running, too.

I sprinted as hard as I could, my eyes jumping back and forth between the protesters and the Sinistrali.

"Get back here!" Brick yelled.

The chanting grew louder, drowning out anything else Brick had to say. The Sinistrali took a few concerted steps backward and tightened their ranks.

I sprinted past building after building, alleyway after alleyway. Another hundred yards and I'd be in the clearing. I started to yell. "Damien! Dami—ughf."

Out of nowhere, I was hit with a force that was both hard and soft at the same time, right in the stomach. It was like running into a horizontal pole that was padded. The wind was knocked out of me. All my forward moment stopped as my feet left the ground, and I folded forward over the invisible spot.

Daphne crashed into me at a full sprint. She should have bowled us both over, but instead, gray beads materialized all around me. A gloved hand reached out and grabbed me by the collar and pulled me hard, dragging me into an alleyway.

"Run away from here!"

The raspy voice, the dark clothes, the blurred face.

I stared into the bloodshot eyes of none other than Kratos himself.

Shock, confusion—I, I didn't know—where had he been? Why was he here now?

"Kratos?" Daphne said, recovering more quickly than me.

Finally, my diaphragm relaxed, and I took a gasping breath.

"That's the Sinistrali!" I said, pointing.

Kratos didn't bother to look.

"Leave. Now!" he said, releasing his grip on me.

Kratos stumbled and braced himself against the alleyway wall. Something was off. Something was wrong.

"Are you hurt?" Daphne said.

Kratos held out a hand, keeping her at a distance.

"Go, now! Far away!" He pushed off the wall and stood on his own wobbly feet. "GO!"

"We need them! I'm not just going to let them die!" I said.

I took off running again, but I hadn't gone two steps before I ran into another invisible barrier. I tried to push through it. Beads dropped around me like rain, but I wasn't making any progress. I tried to go under it. I punched and kicked at it, but it held me in place.

I tried to back up, but there again, I was blocked.

Kratos stood off to the side, his arm out, palm facing me, a constant, barely discernible hiss emitting from his gloves.

Daphne stared at him and then back at me.

It was clear he was intent on holding me here, but I wasn't going to give up.

"Daphne!" I shouted. "Do something!"

She took a step forward, and then she, too, ran into an invisible barrier. Kratos's other hand shot up to reinforce it. He let his body slump against the wall as he held his hands out.

We were stuck.

"What are you doing?" I yelled.

Kratos ignored me completely.

The loudest chant yet—more of a battle cry—rang out. I snapped my head around to see the protesters rush the fence. On the other side, behind the Sinistrali, an Innerbelt train approached. It clicked—this is what they had been waiting for.

The Sinistrali held their position. I had expected to see people start dropping like flies, but no shots had been fired, and no movement had been made. Behind them, the train continued to approach. Ten more seconds and it would be rounding the corner, and two seconds after that, it would be gone.

One of the protesters from the back lobbed a small metal projectile into the air. One of the Sinistrali raised their weapons and pointed it upward. The metal projectile was headed well over the fence, past the Sinistrali. Except it didn't make it past the Sinistrali.

A gray beam shot out from the end of the Sinistrali's raised weapon and connected with the projectile, freezing it in midair. It was like a long gray strand of cloud had wrapped itself around the projectile and connected it directly to the Sinistrali's gun. I watched in awe as the man moved his gun, and the projectile followed suit, all the while encased in the gray tendrils of the gun.

Then, in a single, sudden motion, the man jerked his gun downward. The gray beam broke, and the projectile flew back toward the oncoming protestors.

None of them had time to react. No one had time to move.

A lone scream rang out before all of them were consumed by an explosion.

Flaming bodies went flying in all directions.

The shockwave and blast of wind hit my face a second later, showering me with even more beads.

I stopped struggling against Kratos's barrier and just stood there.

None of the protesters could have survived, not a blast like that.

Yet the Sinistrali stood, as they had before, unharmed. The Innerbelt train flew on by, uninterrupted.

"Kratos," I said, unable to tear my eyes away. He didn't answer.

"Kratos!" I said, louder. He was nowhere to be seen. Daphne was still struggling to get out of her beads. "Where'd he go?" I said.

Daphne's face fell. I fought against the beads, working desperately to free myself. My eyes searched the alleyway—nothing.

Finally, I broke free and sprinted past Daphne and into the shaded alleyway. I saw no doors or windows, only bricks. I kept running, but I knew he was gone. I came to a stop and yelled in frustration.

My mind raced.

Kratos had just saved my life. Those people had all died, and Kratos had known about it. How? And then he disappeared! And where had he been?

I jogged back to where Daphne stood. She was staring at the scene, an almost blank look on her face.

The Sinistrali had retreated. Only a few had yet to disappear behind the nearest building. Dozens of Sinisters were dead, and their effort had been minimal.

This was what we were up against. A group of fifty didn't stand a chance against just a few of Rosewood's crew.

"He knew," Daphne said softly. "He knew."

Alex, Brick, and Jonny skidded to a halt behind us.

No one spoke. A soft breeze blew, sending the rancid smell of burnt death swirling around us.

Brick started to speak but instead stopped and shook his head. After a few more moments of silence, he tried again. "You all saw that, right? The gray beam of whatever?" We all nodded. "I've seen stunners before. It's always been non-lethal with protestors. But this, this was outright murder," he said quietly.

Brick let loose a deep breath and glanced over at Jonny before turning back to me. "Maybe you were right. Maybe those weren't regular police officers." He paused. "Was that the Bounty Hunter I saw?"

"Yes," I said.

"And he stopped the two of you from going out there?"

I was still trying to make sense of it all.

I started to walk.

"Come on, we need to get back."

Silence. No one moved except me.

"But what does that mean?" Brick said, staying where he was. "The Bounty Hunter showing up to stop you from getting blown up? He saved you—he's on your side, too?"

"Something like that," I said, continuing to walk. I could still feel the heat on my face from the explosion.

Murder. Dozens of people gone in the blink of an eye.

"What do we do now?" Brick said.

"Get the word out," I said, turning back. "Maybe now you understand just how serious this is."

24

"And he just came out of nowhere?" Zeno said. He took his glasses off and rubbed his eyes before replacing them. "Bro, how? It sounds like he knew what was going to happen, but like, before it happened."

We stood in our secret room back at the events center. Zeno's eyes were bloodshot. Trevor let loose a yawn, which he tried to stifle before speaking.

"And they're all dead? All of them?"

The image of the blast seared my mind again. I shook it off.

"How did, was it, 'Brick?'" Trevor looked around for validation. "Yes, Brick. How did Brick take it?"

"I think it opened his eyes," Daphne said. "He now knows that one or two groups of Sinisters won't be able to stand against Rosewood. It's going to take everyone. And even that might not be enough. It's a big deal that he agreed to help us, though," she said. "Thanks to Alex."

Beside me, Alex puffed out his chest but said nothing.

Zeno nodded. I could tell he was still thinking about Kratos.

"Word is going to spread about what happened," I said. "Fifty people died, probably on direct orders from Rosewood. I don't know if a peaceful resolution was ever on the table, but it certainly isn't now." I turned to Daphne, "Do you think more people will protest after what happened?"

"I don't know," she said. "It's possible, but I honestly don't know if this is going to make people fearful or angry. I guess we'll see."

I shook my head, still trying to process everything.

"Okay, but back to Kratos," I said. "How did he know? And if he's not here, where did he go?" I turned to Zeno. "You said you had Gina working? Could she track him somehow?"

Zeno looked at the floor and shook his head.

"If Gina was at a hundred percent, we might have a chance, but right now"—he fished his phone out of his pocket—"this is where we're at. Gina sent this to me after I asked her to do some slightly taxing tasks. Nothing big." Zeno held out his phone for us to see.

You only love me for my brain.

Zeno sighed and shook his head.

"It's a warning. I can't push her that hard yet, but we'll get there. Besides," he slid his phone back in his pocket, "keeping tabs on Kratos was never easy, and even with Gina at full capacity, it wasn't always possible."

"So she can't track Kratos, and you're afraid that she is going to shut you out?" Daphne said.

"Yeah, that about sums it up," Zeno said. "But we made a lot of progress last night, thanks to my man Trevor here." He stepped over and slapped Trevor on the shoulder.

"What do you mean by progress?" I said, envisioning Gina alternating between aiding our plans and sabotaging them.

"Well, bro, what I mean is that we can now make your broadcast happen."

"You guys figured it out?" Alex said.

"Ivy's input was invaluable," Trevor said.

"She may have helped a little," Zeno said, "But Trevor and I did ninety percent of the work."

Trevor gave his head a minute shake of disagreement.

"Regardless, we're moving in the right direction. Oh, hold up." Zeno reached into his pocket and fished his phone back out. He peered at the screen for a moment. "See, she's already back on our team. Pertinent news announcement incoming." He smiled and began unfolding the extra sections of the screen from the back of his phone. "Guess we better watch." He moved around and held the phone so all of us could see.

Kelly Straunton appeared, her hair and makeup as pristine as ever. She appeared to be walking near the fence line that divided the Heights from the Flats. The camera view swung in and out, up and down, giving a dynamic feel to the scene. No doubt, the camera was actually a drone. Behind her, a stretch of dirt turned into a group of meticulously maintained buildings in the Flats.

The camera focused in on Kelly and came to a still frame shot of the news anchor. She forewent her normal smile and began her report.

"Less than an hour ago, tragedy struck at a stretch of border fence just like this. As you all know, our fearless President, Doctor Victoria Rosewood, has been consistent in her message and actions—Sinisters represent a threat to our way of life.

"For their good and ours, restrictions have been heightened, and everyone has been safer as a result." She forced a smile. "We were warned of how an uncivilized group of people may react, and although we hoped it wouldn't come to pass—the day has finally come."

Her hand went to her earpiece.

"I'm receiving details from the police crew on site this very instant." She nodded and continued, her hand sliding down to her side. "A large group of Sinisters, over a hundred strong, saw fit to rush the border fence earlier today, in clear violation of recent orders. Fortunately, our police force was aware of the situation and were in place to deter them.

"What should have been a peaceful showing of disagreement soon turned violent. After our Noble officers warned the rebellious group numerous times of the new restrictions, the Sinisters attempted to employ deadly force by launching an explosive toward our police force. However, the explosive malfunctioned and backfired." Her eyes grew slightly wider. "Permanently incapacitating the group of protesting Sinisters. Fortunately, none of our courageous police officers were harmed in the blast."

"Permanently incapacitated?" Daphne whispered. "They're dead."

On screen, Kelly's hand shakily rose to her ear again.

"I'm being told that our beloved President Rosewood is on the air with us this very moment." Kelly paused, a tone of surprise in her voice. "President Rosewood—your thoughts on the events of today?"

The screen transitioned, and Rosewood appeared, dressed in her customary white, striding across a large hall in what was certainly a building in the Capital. She was flanked on both sides by bodyguards, their uniforms matching those I had seen worn by the officers at the protest down to the last detail.

Anger boiled within me at the sight of her. She was evil, wrapped in a cold, white veneer, surrounded by her own personal death squad who would carry out her every order without question.

As she walked, I could tell something had changed about her. It was a cockiness, an arrogance that hadn't been present previously— almost like she was on the verge of smirking at any moment.

The muffled voice of a reporter echoed Kelly's question, and a microphone was pushed into the frame. Rosewood nodded in front of her.

"The people deserve to be addressed by me directly," she said.

The camera panned to capture a small drone that hovered a few feet in front of Rosewood, a small lens pointed at her every movement.

An unidentified voice answered.

"Of course, Madam President."

The screen transitioned once again, and we were met with a head-on view of President Victoria Rosewood, apparently from the drone.

"What happened today," she began, her voice like ice, "was regrettable. Any life lost is a tragedy, and to lose nearly a hundred is unthinkable. Having been around as long as I have, you learn about human nature. Unfortunately, the Sinister nature is often, but not always, irredeemable.

"In spite of my best scientific efforts, I have concluded that the vast majority of Sinisters are incompatible with genetic modification. This may be difficult news to hear, but as your President, I have taken an oath to speak the truth, regardless of its popularity, in order to protect that which we hold dear.

"Another difficult truth I must share—this attack may have been the first of its kind, but it will not be the last. We must be prepared. Fear not, follow me, and we will prevail. Thank you."

The view of Rosewood transitioned away from the drone and back to what I assumed was the news crew's camera. She continued walking, the drone adjusting its position to float above her shoulder, seemingly ready to beckon to her every command. The view transitioned one last time back to Kelly Straunton.

"Strong words from our strong leader. How lucky we are to have her," she said, lacking her normal gusto. "Back to you, John."

Zeno's display went dark, then lit back up with bolder text.

End of transmission. How did you ever get by without me?

I would have laughed at Gina's quip had I not been so angry.

So many lies.

A hundred Sinisters?

The officers tried to warn them?

The device malfunctioned?

Blatant, inexcusable, manipulative lies.

No doubt this news clip would be played over and over until there wasn't a single person in the Flats who hadn't heard it or believed it. The longer Rosewood's filth circulated around, the more damage it would do on both sides.

Zeno pocketed his phone. The rest of the group stood there in silence. For me, I had clarity. We couldn't let her lies go unopposed.

"Zeno," I said, breaking the silence, "you and Trevor get everything ready for the broadcast." I turned to Alex and Daphne. "Let's figure out what I'm going to say in the Sandbox. We're doing it tonight."

25

———

"Are you ready?" Zeno looked at me over the blinking light of his phone.

Alex, Daphne, and Trevor all stood behind him, watching me intently. After our brainstorming session, we had all reconvened here, in our secret room. It felt momentous what we were doing, yet somehow I had imagined it going differently.

I hadn't imagined a carefully placed pile of mattresses behind me to obscure the background and improve the sound quality. I hadn't imagined that out of all those who were against Rosewood, it would only be five of us who were attempting to truly fight back.

"The Sandbox," Alex said fondly. "It's been waaaay too long since I last played there."

"Don't you mean post?" Daphne said. "Or visit or read or something? I thought it was a forum, not a game."

Zeno shook his head.

"Sorry, bros, I feel responsible for Daph's lack of knowledge here. I should have educated her when I had the chance." He gave her a wistful look.

"You play in a sandbox, Daphne," Alex said in his best teaching voice. "You don't post in a sandbox or read in a sandbox. You play in it. See what I mean?" He lowered his voice slightly and mumbled. "I mean, this is really just kindergarten level stuff we're talking about…"

"So then answer me this," Daphne said, her eyes narrowed at Alex, "When we're finished with the video, what's Victor going to do?"

Alex and Zeno looked at each other, then spoke in unison.

"Post it."

Daphne looked at both of them.

"Post where?"

"In the Sandbox," Alex said. "Honestly, Daphne, try and keep up."

Alex and Zeno looked at each other with confused looks on their faces and shrugged.

Daphne let out an "ugh" sound.

"Anyways," Alex said, "we're going to do this live. No do-overs. If you mess up, just go with it. It'll give the video the best chance of getting noticed."

"Right," Zeno continued, "the feed goes from my phone, through Gina's encryption, and then into the Sandbox. It'll have a slight delay, but there are only a couple of people I know of that could crack her code, and I'm here, so…"

"Ivy could figure it out with relative ease?" Daphne said with a smirk.

Zeno didn't respond. I continued to go over what I was going to say in my head. There were lots of people back home who loved posting videos of themselves. They could talk for hours and were comfortable in front of a camera. I hadn't been one of those people. And that was the least of my worries. Would this even work? Would my video get noticed? From what Alex and Zeno had told me, the Sandbox was an incredibly large place—thousands of pieces of content posted every hour. I needed to cut through it all. We needed everyone to see this, everyone.

"Are you sure this is the right tactic?" I said, licking my suddenly chapped lips. "Shouldn't I just tell everyone how I was there today at the explosion and that Rosewood lied about it?"

Never before had I felt so nervous. The buildup before a saber fight was a comparative breeze.

"Anyone could get on and say Rosewood isn't telling the truth," Alex said. "My Uncle Stephano is doing that right now, and everyone knows he's crazy. We've got to establish credibility." Alex made intense eye contact with me. "Trust me."

He had said it with such conviction. He knew he was right, and if Alex had proved anything to me, it was that he was worthy of my trust, especially when it counted.

I nodded.

"Alrighty then, bro," Zeno said, "are you ready?"

I nodded again.

"Time to play."

The blinking light on the camera turned red, and Zeno pointed at me. I was live.

"Hello," I said, feeling as awkward as I ever had. "My name is Victor Wells." I paused and swallowed. The red light continued to blink. Behind the camera, Alex nodded encouragingly. The knot in my stomach loosened.

"A lot has happened in the last few months," I continued. "People were Marked. People died. President Keltan was replaced. My DNA was manipulated. It's all related, and here's how it happened as it happened—not through some filter, not what your friend said or what you heard on the news." I paused and tried to stare into the lens with feeling. Anyone who saw this had to know that this was real, and it had to grab their attention.

"I am not a Noble." I took a deep breath. "But I'm also not a Sinister."

I let the statement hang there in the air for a moment before continuing.

"In fact, nobody is Noble, and nobody is Sinister. There are no Noble or Sinister people. There are just people, and people act in accordance to what they believe. In our society, we've been told what to believe. The Nobles have been told to believe they are inherently good and that being good is built into them. So they act like it. Sinisters were taught to believe the opposite."

Daphne had moved behind the camera, too. She gave me a small, encouraging smile and a nod. I continued.

"Right now, our future looks grim. Right now, our future looks like a place where people in the Flats and people in the Heights can't coexist. I know why that is, who's responsible, and how to fix it. The story I'm about to tell you is why I was Marked. The story I'm about to tell you is why I was kicked out of the Flats. The story I'm about to tell you is going to change how you see the world, and you won't ever be able to go back."

I stared deep into the camera.

"From me to you, this is how it happened."

I started from the beginning—that first abnormal scan on Grandfather's car, my terror at being chased by that small metal ball—my Marking.

I was so caught up in what I was saying that I didn't see Alex until Zeno snapped his fingers at me.

Alex was waving his arms behind Zeno. I met his eyes, and he motioned across his neck with his hand.

I finished my sentence and looked back to the camera.

"That's all I have time for tonight," I said slowly.

Alex nodded at me, but there was one thought, one last thing I needed to share before I ended.

"But before I go," I said, "I have seen good everywhere—from my friends and family in the Flats to my friends and family in the

Heights. Nobles don't own the good, but Sinisters don't own the bad. Something is coming, and our only chance of surviving it, Nobles and Sinisters alike, is to work together for good. I'm Victor Wells, and I'm signing off. Goodnight."

Zeno pressed a button, and the red light blinked off. I stood up.

"Did I do something wrong?" I said.

"No, you did great," Alex said. "I mean, for your first time, it was great, but no, I stopped you because we have to leave something to tell them tomorrow."

"Right," Zeno said with a nod. "Leave the people wanting more."

"Oh, they'll want more," Alex said. "Trust me. I don't know if you guys know this, but our stories are a level above cool. I mean, if our stories were like an object, they'd be like this." He held up his bionic arm like a trophy and showcased it with his other hand.

Zeno gave me a thumbs-up.

"Truly awesome work, my man. Wait until people hear about Ville. It's going to blow their minds."

Of that, there was no doubt. I had meant it when I said I was going to change how people saw the world.

"So what do we do now?" I said. "Do we just sit here and wait? How do we know if people are watching it?"

"Gina's still synthesizing the video and encrypting it," Zeno said, squinting at his phone. "It's still technically a live stream—it'll just have about a minute delay on it. Looks like it's got about thirty seconds before it finishes up, so for now, we wait."

"And then we'll wait some more," Alex said, failing miserably to stifle a yawn. "Man, this whole changing public perception and getting the truth out there—it's hard work." He shook his head in a vain attempt to wake himself up. He only looked more tired, but he continued. "We're posting at the perfect time. Right now is when the Sandbox gets the most traffic it's gotten all day. Tomorrow, we'll start looking at the comments and see what everyone thinks about it. As for me, I'm going to get some sleep. Anyone else?"

"I could go for some shuteye," Trevor said.

"Me too," Daphne said.

I was wired after telling part of our story. I didn't have an inkling of sleepiness in me. But what could I do except wait? I had never cared so much about a video message. It needed views. A lot of them. It needed to be seen.

"I know everyone is tired and needs some Z's," Zeno said, "but—"

"Here we go," Daphne said.

"What's Gina up to now?" Alex said, already lying down on his bed. "Has she—"

"No, she hasn't found a donut place nearby," Zeno said. "No, this isn't about Gina. It's something else, something potentially lucky."

I gave him a look.

"What do you mean?" I said.

At this, Alex sat up, and Daphne and Trevor made their way back over.

Zeno rooted around in his pocket and pulled out a tiny strip of white paper.

"This showed up earlier today, like right before I came down here to help with the Sandbox vid." He unfolded the slightly crumpled scrap and smoothed it out before handing it over to me.

THE DRONE IS THE ANSWER.

The writing had been printed rather than written. I flipped the paper over. Nothing—no signature, no signs, no other information of any kind. I flipped it back over. "The drone is the answer." I looked at Zeno with a raised eyebrow, then looked around the room. "The drone is the answer. What does that mean?"

Zeno shrugged.

"Where did you say the note came from?" Daphne said after a brief moment of silence.

"No idea," Zeno said. "It just appeared on the table while I was working on Gina."

"I can attest as well," Trevor said. "I haven't seen any paper like that anywhere here. I didn't hear or see anyone or anything enter."

I examined the paper again.

"Why didn't you tell us about this sooner?" Daphne said.

"We had the video to work on, and I didn't want to derail it."

"So, what does it mean?" I said.

"I don't know..." Zeno trailed off. "But maybe that newscast from earlier had the answer."

"What do you mean?" I said.

"Remember when the camera switched to Rosewood, and it jumped from a side view to a head-on view?"

I nodded.

"Well," Zeno said, drawing out the word, "that camera was on a drone, and I think *that's* the drone that is the answer."

"The answer to what?" Daphne said.

"To the question of how to incriminate Rosewood!" Zeno looked around again. "Bros and Daphne, if I'm not mistaken, that drone is a disciple drone—it's programmed to follow Rosewood around, probably everywhere all the time—*but* it only transmits when she wants it to."

"Okay," I said, starting to understand where this was going. "So you're saying you want to get it to transmit something when she doesn't want it to be listening?"

"Boom! Exactly—preferably when she's talking about her plans with one of her many goons," he said. "Can you imagine getting it to broadcast without her knowing about it?" He looked at me, then at everyone else. "That would be enough, right? People believe anything she says, so catching her in the act of saying something crazy, like she wants to enslave the human race—it has to be enough, right?"

I stood there contemplating the idea, doing my best to not get too excited. Slowly, I started to nod my head in agreement. I glanced at Daphne. I could see her considering it, viewing it from different angles. Alex, on the other hand, was all in.

"That's it!" he said. "Can't be that hard, right?"

"I don't know," I said. "Won't she know if someone's trying to hack her drone? It's not like it was easy for us to hack her searcher drones back at camp, and I can only imagine her personal drone has some extra encryption on it."

"Yeah, my man, but we're not at camp now, are we?" Zeno had a glint in his eye. "You just wait until I unleash the powers of Gina on it. We'll be golden."

"Provided we can actually get her to let us do that," Daphne said.

"From what I see," Trevor said, "we're getting close."

I nodded again. That was encouraging. Getting Rosewood to incriminate herself via a surprise broadcast to the news. It was good, wasn't it? We were talking about irreparable damage. Could we really hope for a fatal hit like that?

I allowed myself a short moment of optimism. We had to. At this point, hope was all we had.

There was only one question, one that itched at my mind, but Daphne beat me to it.

"What if one of Rosewood's people dropped that off?" she said.

"They didn't," Zeno said.

"How do you know?" I said.

"Because, bro, I can feel it."

I raised my eyebrows.

"And Gina ran some security scans. No life forms in or out other than Trevor and me. Nothing electrical or motorized, either," he added before I could open my mouth.

"So you're saying it just appeared?" I said. "Like magic?"

"Hey man, I don't question where the wisdom comes from. I just recognize it when it comes, and then I act."

"You sound like Brick," Daphne said.

Zeno shot her a look of befuddled disgust.

"What if it's from the same people who are helping Brick?" Daphne said.

"Then let's just hope they're on our side," I said. I turned to Zeno. "I think this is a good plan."

He smirked and lowered his voice. "You know this is a good plan. We've got to attack Rosewood from every angle we've got, and this is a good angle."

I nodded.

"Let's do it."

"Good man," Zeno said, a smile covering his face. "I know you and Daphne and Alex need to go out and try and unite some Sinisters tomorrow. Trevor and I will stay here and work on this." He crossed his fingers. "By the time you guys get back, Gina should be up and running at full strength, and with any luck, we'll have Rosewood's drone in our pocket."

I couldn't help but feel like Zeno was serving us a big slice of unwarranted optimism, but I forced a smile nonetheless.

"I hope so, too. Now, let's get some sleep," I said, easing myself onto my mattress. "We've got a big day ahead of us tomorrow." I glanced at Zeno, who nodded back at me, "on more fronts than one."

26

———————

"So you're saying that guy is in charge of the second biggest gang in the area?" I said. "*That* guy?"

Alex looked down at him.

"I could take him."

Brick chuckled while Daphne rolled her eyes.

"Yeah, that's the one," Brick growled. "Erik Vo—skinny little runt is what he is. But he's scrappy. I'll give him that. And he's only got one building. We've got what?" He looked to Jonny, who held up several fingers. "Yeah, eight and all the people with it."

We stood on top of the tallest building in the area. Brick had agreed to meet us here to talk about a "potential acquisition." Apparently, the man we had come to meet was Erik Vo. He and a small number of his crew were meeting on an adjacent building's rooftop like they supposedly did every week around this time.

"So, how did you find out about their rooftop meeting?" Daphne said. "Vo and his guys are notoriously secretive."

"There was a note," Brick said simply.

"This one come with a body, too?" I said, keeping my eye on the rooftop below.

Erik was surrounded by a handful of people, and even from this distance, his height discrepancy was noticeable. He was tiny.

"No, it didn't," Brick said, and the way he said it made me think that he was disappointed in that fact.

"And you still have no idea who is dropping off the notes to you?" Daphne said.

"Doesn't matter much, does it?" Brick said. "Besides, if whoever is helping us wanted us to know who it was, they would have just shown up themselves, right? If he wants to stay hidden, least I can do is be accommodating, ain't that right, Jonny?"

"I wonder if it's the same guy who's leaving us notes, too," Alex said.

Daphne and I both threw him a look.

"What's that now?" Brick said, his attention back on Vo.

"Nothing," I said. Jonny glanced in my direction and fixed me with a squint.

"You wouldn't happen to have the note with you, would you?" Daphne said.

"What?" Brick said. "Uh, yeah, course we do. Jonny's got them." He nodded to Jonny, who slowly reached into his jacket pocket and produced a tightly folded piece of paper. He eyed Daphne as he handed it to her. I took a few steps closer to get a look.

> Erik Vo meets with his crew each week on top of their building. Watch them for two weeks. Figure out how much time it takes them to get from the roof of their building to the street below. Choose a day to confront them on the street. Vo and his team are weak and don't do well being

*caught off guard. Meet with them, and take what's
yours.*

The note was significantly longer and more detailed than what we had gotten. And in a completely different font and on different paper. And very specific. Ours simply said, "The drone is the answer." This had step-by-step instructions.

"Thanks," Daphne said, handing the letter back to Jonny. She gave me a look, one of relief rather than concern. She'd come to the same conclusion I had. Their letter and our letter were unrelated. Or at least that's how it seemed.

"So, Brick, did you see the Noble newscast after the explosion yesterday?" I said.

"Filthy liars," Brick said. "It's nothing new, though. They've been lying about us for as long as I can remember."

"Yeah, it's not right," Alex said. "But can we talk about Rosewood looking real ugly, though? People say it isn't true, but the camera adds ten years."

"Ugly or not," I said, "she's getting ready to make a move. The whole thing was designed to make sure the Nobles are on her side."

"Of course they are!" Brick said. "Not like they need much convincing. I haven't met a Noble yet that didn't eat out of her hand." The brisk air swirled around us as he spoke. I pulled my jacket tighter around me.

"You sure about that?" Daphne said, nodding to Alex.

Brick's eyes went wide. "You're right. Jonny, we're business partners with a Noble!" Brick shook his head. "Strange times... but that's why we're here. It was a shame to lose all those people. We've got thousands of people all around the Heights who are loyal to us because we protect them, or they fear us more than they fear other people, you see?"

He nodded toward Erik. "Vo's got a lot of loyalty too, probably second in size after us. We get him, and the rest will fall over like dominoes." He turned to me. "But you're the one that's got to do the talking."

"Why's that?" Daphne said. "He doesn't like you?"

"Course he don't!" Brick said, smiling. "I wouldn't be doing my job if he did."

Brick continued to flash his yellow, crooked teeth.

"Is there anyone left who does like you?" Daphne said.

Brick let loose a gruff laugh.

"Jonny and I aren't here to make friends." He glanced at Alex. "Well, except in rare situations. We're here to take what's ours."

"Because that's what the note told you to do?" Daphne said.

"No! Because that's what we're here to do!"

"And get everyone in the Heights on our side," Alex said. "To take down Rosewood?"

Brick glanced at him.

"Of course. We haven't forgotten."

"Good," Daphne said, "because if we can't figure out how to put a defense up against Rosewood, there may not be a Heights for you to try and run."

"Well then," Brick said with a grin. "Let's go talk to the skinny little runt."

We descended from our building down onto the street. Apparently, it always took at least ten minutes for Vo and his crew to leave the building, sometimes longer. The plan was to position ourselves where he couldn't miss us, in public, in front of his building. He wouldn't be happy, but he also wouldn't be able to run.

While we walked, I took in my surroundings. We were, yet again, in an unfamiliar part of the Heights, at least to me. This area was newer. The bricks were less faded, fewer windows were boarded up, and there was more asphalt on the street than there was vegetation, which I couldn't say for everywhere else.

A few dozen people could be seen on the street and sidewalks around us. About three-quarters seemed to be either coming or going from Vo's building. All of them avoided eye contact. I couldn't tell whether it was because they recognized Brick and Jonny or because they didn't recognize us as regulars here. Either way, they steered clear.

Brick walked proudly down the street like he owned it. It was still odd seeing him like this. I remembered him as Tyrann's underling. Now, everything had fallen to him. He didn't have Tyrann's flair for the dramatic, but he wasn't afraid to take charge.

"So that's the one, right there, right?" Alex said, pointing to the building up ahead. Brick had informed us that it loomed thirty-eight stories high and housed around five hundred people. Brick nodded. Alex shrugged. "I'm not impressed."

Brick let loose a crooked grin and a chuckle.

"Let's wait here for them," Brick said. "This is why I get places early. I like to see them walk to us—tells me what kind of meeting we're in for."

An odd tactic, but I guessed I could see the wisdom in it. That, or it was a way to ensure the meeting started off on the wrong foot, and based on what Brick had told us, we could be waiting on that wrong foot for several more minutes.

We came to a halt in the middle of the street, about a hundred yards from the large ground floor doors of Vo's building. A soft buzzing sound met my ears that coincided with the vibration I felt in my pocket. I jumped at the sound and sensation.

I fished my phone out as Daphne looked over my shoulder.

"Zeno?" she said.

"Looks like it," I said, tapping on the message. I was half hoping it was from Pria with an update about how things were going on their end. The last message from her was a single word, and even though only a few days had passed, well, we all knew how much could happen in that time.

"Well, are you going to open it?" Daphne said.

"Oh, right, yeah." I tapped on the icon, and his message popped up.

It's working.

"It's working?" Daphne said. "What's working?"

My phone vibrated again, and a new message popped up, this time containing some sort of link.

"Let's find out."

I clicked on it.

A thumbnail picture of my broadcast from last night appeared, along with around a hundred comments. I started scrolling through them, reading a few here and there. What I saw did nothing to improve my mood.

"I'm not sure why he said it was working," I said, handing my phone to Daphne. "Take a look at these."

"You talking about the broadcast?" Alex said. I nodded, my eyes darting to and from Brick.

"That's right! We haven't told him yet," Alex said, turning to Brick. I started to say something, but Alex was already committed.

"We're trying to convince Nobles to join us, too," he said. "Not just Sinisters."

Brick laughed without mirth.

"You're even crazier than Tyrann was."

Alex took a step closer to me.

"Let me guess," he said, "Zeno sent you a link to the Sandbox, and all the comments are bad?"

"That about sums it up," I said, surprised at his foresight.

"I wouldn't worry too much about it. The real influencers usually wait to do the influencing. They let the crazies do their thing before weighing in. I'm telling you," he continued, "it'll turn around, just give it time."

"Time isn't something we have a lot of," I muttered, feeling the pressure again of not knowing exactly when Rosewood would strike.

"Speaking of," Brick said, looking at the watch on his wrist, "the little runt is taking his sweet time." He turned to Jonny. "I hope he enjoys it."

The corner of Jonny's mouth twitched in reply.

Another minute passed, and finally, Erik Vo appeared, his entourage of six surrounding him.

"Here the weasel comes," Brick said.

I watched them as they came. Vo was flanked on either side by three significantly taller men. They all appeared to be in a good mood as they strolled down the street. The people who passed them on the street made sure to acknowledge him, though not in a cordial way—it was in fear. Already, I didn't like him.

Vo was the first to see us, and I could see a change in his walk the moment he did. He reached out immediately and hit the person on either side of him in the stomach. For any normal-size person, he would have hit them in the chest, but Vo really was tiny. His men straightened up, and Vo stared straight ahead, his eyes never wavering. The six people surrounding him weren't so laser-focused—all of them glanced repeatedly at each other and between Vo and us as they walked.

Beside me, Brick chuckled.

"They're worried about him, the runty little rat. He must be in a mood today." He raised his voice. "Now that's close enough!"

Vo and the rest came to a halt about ten feet from us. Almost immediately, the rest of the street cleared of people.

Erik Vo couldn't have been more than four and a half feet tall, but Brick was right—he looked mean. His hair was dark but short—nearly shaved. His face was covered in nicks and scars, and his expression seemed to be a perpetual sneer.

"You're up," Brick said, nodding to me.

I took a step forward, then another. I could tell Vo was sizing me up, just like I was him.

"And just who are you?" he spat as I continued to close the gap between us.

I stopped where I was—not quite close enough to shake hands.

I had fought guys like him before—always ready to swing. Often, they intimidated their opponents with their ferocity, but for me, it just made them more predictable.

"I'm Victor Wells," I said.

"And you speak for Brick now?"

"Do you speak for all of them?" I nodded to his entourage.

"I do," he said, puffing his chest out. "And they'll do whatever I say, whenever I say it."

At his word, the guy to his right tugged back the corner of his jacket. I caught the glint of a clearly modified stunner. It probably kept you unconscious for an additional thirty minutes, and I wouldn't have been surprised if it left a burn mark where it hit. Or worse.

I knew the spray in my gloves protected me from regular stunner blasts, but a modified one might be a different story. Hopefully, I wouldn't have to find out.

"We want to make a play against Rosewood," I said. "It looks like you would be a good addition to our team." I nodded to his friend's hardware.

He surveyed me in silence. His men fidgeted around him. I maintained eye contact. Finally, he nodded. The fidgeting stopped. In the background, a loud crack sounded, like two rocks being thrown together or a slab of wood being dropped onto concrete. I was caught off guard and nearly jumped, but none of them did.

"We would be a good addition," Vo said, "if that was something we wanted to do."

"You're saying you don't?" I said. "You'd rather wait around for Rosewood to make her move? I assume you keep track of the broadcasts?"

"Course." Erik shifted his weight to his other foot.

The other thing I knew about people who were always ready to fight—they were always in the know, they were never wrong, and they would never admit anything to the contrary.

"Then you know that Rosewood is getting ready to make a play in the Heights, right?"

"So?"

"So, do you want to react to her move or be the first to strike?" I said.

Behind them, another loud crack sounded, louder than the first. It was followed almost immediately by two more. A series of muffled screams met my ears.

At this, even Erik broke away from our staring contest. My heart began to race. Erik's men began to mutter.

"You guys see anything?" I said over my shoulder.

"Nothing," Daphne said.

The main doors to Erik's building burst open. Dozens upon dozens of people spilled out, yelling at and pushing one another. What they were running from, I couldn't see, but the sinking feeling in my stomach told me I knew what was happening.

Another sound erupted—so loud you could feel it.

And then, I saw it.

Erik and his men turned as a giant fissure appeared in his building. It ran vertically from the ground up, just off center until it reached the roof.

It was like déjà vu.

Part of the building started to sway and lean. The building groaned as chunks of concrete and glass broke free and rained down from above. Like a terrible symphony, the percussive sounds of a cement avalanche mixed with the cries of people attempting to flee.

Even if I had wanted to, there was nothing I could have done. Another ear-splitting noise sounded, and then, nearly half of the building broke free and began to fall sideways. The uppermost portion of the building collided with the building across the street, but the bottom couldn't handle the strain. With an almighty wrenching noise, the middle portion of the building gave way and started to collapse in on itself.

People, furniture, possessions—all could be seen falling from the part of the building that was still standing, but even that was short-lived as it began to sway and then finally collapse.

Thirty-eight floors disappeared into a cloud of dust, the noise of implosion sucking the air out of every scream or cry being uttered.

A brief blanket of stunned silence filled the air as a powerful gust of wind and dust hit us. I was in such a stupor of surprise that I didn't even put up a shield of spray to protect myself. The dust filled the air around us, nearly succeeding in blotting out the sun. I couldn't see more than ten feet in any direction, but what I couldn't see, I heard.

The screams and cries were almost more than I could take.

Erik Vo stood before me, his back turned. I could only imagine what was going through his mind.

Slowly, he began to turn back around. Anger had contorted every feature. His eyes were wide as he extended his finger to point past me and directly at Brick. His words were barely more than a whisper.

"You! You did this!"

It took me a moment to realize what he was saying.

"YOU DID THIS!" he screamed.

"Me?" Brick pointed at himself, then shook his head. "You stupid, tiny—"

His sure-to-cause-a-fight insult was cut short by a swarm of people who had started to engulf us. Dozens of people fleeing from the scene ran past us screaming.

I jumped back and threw out a concentrated burst of spray that shunted people to either side of us as they fled. Dozens and dozens sprinted or stumbled past us. Each person who ran past was another person who had survived the collapse. The last building hadn't had anywhere near this number of people nearby.

After several moments, the fleeing slowed down, and I stopped spraying. Our area was clear once more, and in front of me, Vo and his crew were nowhere to be found.

I was stunned. It had all happened so fast—the building, the people.

How?

At that moment, I didn't even remotely care about Vo and where his crew had disappeared to. I stared into the dust cloud in front of me. My mind shifted gears. I hated to even imagine what we might find or if we could even help.

As if they had read my mind, Alex and Daphne started walking past me and disappeared into the haze.

27

"And that's a wrap on part two," Alex said. The blinking light on Zeno's phone died out. Alex and Daphne sat behind the camera, watching intently. Or at least Daphne was. Alex pulled out his phone and went silent. Trevor was up in Gina's mainframe room, monitoring things—making sure nothing was tampered with. Considering all the new people that had shown up in the last few hours, someone was bound to stumble onto all of Gina's inner workings.

I stood up and stretched. This livestream had been both harder and easier than the first time. The words flowed easier this time around, but I wasn't sure if it was because it was my second time or because my mind was preoccupied.

"Not a single news story," Zeno said, shoving his phone back in his pocket. "Bros, believe me, I checked them all. Apparently, like trees, if a building falls in the Heights, no Nobles hear it. How long were you guys there for?"

"Almost two hours," Daphne said.

It had been an awful two hours.

We had done what we could, but it wasn't much. We helped

people gather belongings, consoled those who needed it, and did some minor first aid, but some were far beyond that. I had seen things I only wished I could forget. Pria would have been able to do more, but even she had her limits. The best we could do was send everyone to the same place we were going—the events center—our home.

At least there was shelter, but even here was starting to feel crowded. It hadn't been easy to slip into our room without anyone noticing. I wasn't exactly sure where Benjamin was getting all of his supplies or if people were just starting to share, but either way, everyone here seemed to at least have a blanket and a place to sleep.

"Two hours is plenty of time for the news to cut a story, especially on something like this," Zeno said.

"Were there any stories after the last building fell?" I said. "Or any of the buildings?"

"Uhhh," Zeno pulled out his phone and held the sound as he scrolled. His face fell. "No."

"Are you surprised?" Daphne said.

"Guess not," Zeno said. I looked over at Alex, who was still glued to his phone, and that's when a thought hit me.

I tried to shake it off. It was worrisome, but it was viable. I stood up.

"Is it me?" I said, starting to pace. I was working it all out in my head.

"What do you mean?" Daphne said.

"You know—is it because of us? I mean, we show up at two different places, and both buildings go down. It's not an infestation that's bringing these buildings down. It's us."

"Yeah, I'm not buying it," Alex said, still not looking up from his phone.

I wasn't sure if he was talking to us or to whatever was on his screen. We all looked at him and then back to each other.

"So you're saying someone is tracking us, and they're bringing down the buildings right in front of us?" Zeno said. "Why?"

I shrugged. I hadn't worked that out yet.

"You think Rosewood is making this happen, don't you?" Daphne said.

I nodded slowly, still trying to connect the dots. Who else would do something like that?

"I don't know, bro," Zeno said. "I kinda get the feeling that if Rosewood was the one behind it, and she's tracking our movements, wouldn't she, I don't know, collapse a building on us or while we're inside? Kinda seems like poor planning on her part, you know?"

I met their words with silence. They were skeptical, but something itched at my mind, and I couldn't quite pin it down. Was Rosewood keeping tabs on me like that? Could she bring down buildings whenever she wanted? Was she somehow following me around and then causing mass destruction right in front of me? The more I thought, the more questions came.

"I don't mean to be, you know, callous," Zeno said slowly, drawing me out of my spiral of questions, "but we've gotta talk next steps. What's the plan for the Sinisters now?"

"That's a good question," I said, sitting back down. I let out a sigh. "I don't know."

"It's looking like we talk to Benjamin again," Daphne said. "No point in trying to track down Vo. I think I actually saw him when we got back here. Some leader—he was probably the first of his crew to arrive."

"Yeah," I said. "And since we sent every person we came across this way—"

"This is by far the biggest concentration of people in the Heights," Daphne finished.

"Right," I nodded.

Benjamin seemed like the logical answer, and I wasn't excited about that, especially after how our last conversation had gone. We just couldn't win, and we desperately needed a win.

I pulled out my phone, logged into the Sandbox, and began scrolling through the comments. Maybe our videos were starting to gain some traction.

I stopped reading after I had made it through a dozen comments or so.

Lukewarm, negative, or crazy. I shoved my phone back into my pocket.

"Is this even going to work?" I blurted out. "Everyone in the Sandbox thinks I'm crazy. All the Sinisters are flocking to Benjamin, and we don't know what he really wants to do. All the Sinisters hate the Nobles, and all the Nobles hate the Sinisters—"

"Bro, we knew things were stacked against us when we decided to come," Zeno said.

I exhaled a frustrated breath before answering.

"You're right." I looked at each of them. "It's just that we haven't gained any ground. Every time we try and do something, a building falls on us. How many people have died in the last few days alone? And with all of that, we're still supposed to unite the Heights and gain Noble support before Rosewood makes her move?"

I looked down at the ground again. No one said a word.

My phone buzzed. I ignored it and was about to continue talking when Alex spoke up.

"Guys, check this out," he said, his phone out. "I think something is happening in the Sandbox."

With a sigh, I pulled my phone out. I was tired. I was drained, and I was not in the mood for false hope.

There was a new comment from less than a minute ago.

User0103:

I've been doing my own research into this very subject. What he says lines up with what I've seen. If you believe me, believe him.

1 Reply...

I looked up from my phone.

"Great, one good one," I said. "But I don't think one anonymous person's comment is going to turn it all around."

"I'm with Victor," Daphne said, folding her arms. "I thought we needed to have a huge impact."

"We do," Zeno said, looking up from his phone. "But, and no offense, this is our realm, and this 0103 guy is a big deal. Dude's got a ton of clout in here."

"I don't know if he's got a *ton* of clout," Alex said.

"No," Zeno said, "you're right. He's got two tons of clout. Bro is basically a celebrity. See, check out all these comments coming in."

I looked down at my screen. Comments had started to come in rapidly.

...If you believe me, believe him.
18 Replies...

User85902: 0103 is that really you?!

User11867: You've been quiet so long! What do you know about this?

User101112: You're back! Is this real?

User54286: 0103—where have you been?

User80001: This is interesting to say the least. For once, we are on the same side of things.

Replying to User80001: User82864 Seriously?

Replying to User 80001: User 20055 No way, really?
View more replies…

I caught Daphne's eye. She was staring at her screen, looking mildly impressed. I looked over at Alex, who was gazing at his phone with a look of mild confusion.

"What's up?" I said.

"Oh, nothing, no, it's just," Alex started, shaking his head, "this user80001 guy. Weird that he's on here."

"How do you know he's a guy?" Daphne said. "I thought this was all anonymous."

"You can just tell, Daph," Zeno said. "But it doesn't really matter because he's small potatoes compared to 0103, right?" Zeno said, looking at Alex.

"I don't know," Alex said. "80001's got a pretty good following. And I think he might be from the Heights."

"But, bro, look at the comments." Zeno looked at me like Alex didn't know what he was talking about. He held his phone up for me to see. Then he scrolled. Dozens and dozens of comments all replying to 0103, and more by the second.

"All right, so we've got a bunch of comments on 0103's post, and they seem excited," I said. "So what?" I looked over at Alex. The concern from moments ago was gone, but he kept his eyes glued to his phone.

"So what?" Zeno looked back and forth between Alex and me. "So what? Alex, come on, bro, back me up—the people are excited for a reason!"

"Well, they're about to get more excited." Alex's fingers moved quickly over his screen, the metallic clicking of his prosthetic thumb breaking up the normally padded beat. "Check, this, out."

A distinctly tinny tap sounded from Alex's direction, and my phone vibrated.

User0103:

I've been having a few adventures. Can't say where, but beware of Rosewood's stories. Stay tuned—more broadcasts to come.

"Wait..." Zeno started, his eyes wide. "You, you—" He pointed to Alex's phone, then back to his. Alex stared at him and nodded, waiting for the end of the sentence. Zeno continued to stumble his way through it. "You, you hacked 0103?" he said. "The 0103? That's genius! Even I can't hack a Sandbox profile. And to hack 0103's profile... Bro." Zeno shook his head in appreciation. "I mean, long term, it's going to blow up on us for sure, but using 0103's influence might be just the juice we need! How'd you do it?"

"Do what?" Alex said, a look of genuine confusion on his face. "I didn't hack anybody. 0103 is me. It's my account. See?"

He typed on his phone some more, then finished with an emphatic tap.

Another ping sounded, and we all looked at our phones.

User0103:

But seriously, stay tuned. More to come—these broadcasts are going to blow your mind.

"So you didn't hack a big-time account," Daphne started slowly, looking from Alex to Zeno's slightly open mouth and back again, "because you are the big-time account." She glanced my way briefly.

"I guess that's one way to put it," Alex said, looking back to his phone.

Zeno finally stopped staring and came back to life. "Bro, so you…" He leaned forward. "*You're* 0103?"

Alex nodded. Zeno smiled and let out what could only be described as a giggle. He stood there for a moment with a stupid grin on his face, a goofy half-smile that zapped him of all of his normal cool. It was like watching someone meet their hero but doing it really, really poorly.

"In the mostly flesh." Alex wiggled the fingers on his robotic hand.

I wasn't surprised that Alex had a decent following in the Sandbox —of course, he did—but it seemed like Zeno was overplaying it a little. I knew Alex's social circle, and if all the people commenting were part of his Follower friends or people from school, would whatever traffic he helped us get on these videos really help change anyone's mind when it came time to fight? And, knowing Alex's other friends, would those people even fight at all?

I nudged Zeno in the ribs. He jumped and partially regained his composure, but not all of it.

"Alex," I said, "do you really think it's a good idea to keep messaging like that? I mean—"

My phone buzzed again. It was a reply to Alex's last message.

replying to User0103:

User077261: Can't wait for more! This matches up more with what I'm seeing in the Senate than on the news. Help us out! Details! (And thank you again for your help during the last session. Your input was vital.)

Alex looked at me and smiled.

"You tell me."

"The Senate?" I said. "The actual Senate of the Flats?"

Alex nodded. A small feeling of shame was starting to overcome me. He didn't notice my discomfort.

Daphne let out a laugh of disbelief. "Alex, this is amazing."

"Yeah, yeah, but look, there he is—80001 is commenting again."

I had no idea who this 80001 character was, but I also had no idea what kind of influence Alex wielded. As a teenager, he was impacting Senate hearings? I was just good with a saber.

"Well, Alex," I said, "any more surprises for us? This is incredible."

"Nah, just the one tonight." He continued to type on his phone, but I thought I saw the corner of his mouth twitch.

Zeno walked over to him and gave him an awkwardly long side hug.

"This is why profiles are supposed to be anonymous," he muttered, patting Zeno's shoulder. He gave me the kind of apologetic look a parent gives their child when they're doing something embarrassing. Finally, Zeno disengaged, took a step back, and shook his head.

"My man."

Alex eyed him warily, then looked at me.

"Is this how you felt after saber matches?" he said. "I don't like it."

"So," Daphne said, looking at Zeno with a mix of disbelief and disgust. "The Senate of the Flats uses the Sandbox and listens to this, to you?"

"Yeah," Alex said. "Well, some of the Senate, not everyone. And they don't listen to me on everything, you know, just on most stuff."

"Wait a second," I said. "So that time a couple of years back when the Senate nearly passed an initiative to decrease taxes on baked goods, that wasn't you talking with your dad, that was you," I pointed to his phone, "Sandbox you, talking to the Senate directly?"

"Oh yeah!" Alex said. "I almost forgot about that. One vote away."

He shook his head wistfully. "There would have been donuts on every corner."

I couldn't help but smile. I glanced again at my phone. It had been buzzing nearly nonstop since Alex's last message. There were over a hundred new comments. I couldn't believe it. Well, I could, but... This was a good break. This was a really good break.

"We've got the 0103 in our group," Zeno said. "This could actually work! Think of how many Nobles we can reach. Thousands," he said. "*Thousands.*"

"I don't know whether to be really surprised or not surprised at all," Daphne said, starting to grin.

I smiled at Alex and gave him a nod, which he returned. I held onto some of my skepticism, but I was feeling something dangerously close to hope.

"Let's see what kind of traction this gets," I said. "Alex, you keep doing your thing." He nodded and went back to his phone. I continued. "The moment Rosewood catches wind that some of her people are listening to someone else, she'll react, and depending on the impact, it could be on a big scale. We need to be ready." I looked around, and Zeno and Daphne nodded.

"Even if Alex can convince a bunch of Nobles to be on our side, I imagine they'll still be scared when the time comes. We need people who are ready, ready to actually resist and fight. I'll put out another call to Jahko to see if they can help, just in case we can get a response."

"Good luck," Daphne muttered.

"And speaking of Rosewood," I continued, turning to Zeno, "what do you say we start keeping better tabs on her? Would Gina be up for it, as long as you or Trevor is around?"

Zeno nodded.

"I think she is. And it just so happens that tomorrow, Rosewood is having some sort of a rally. Might be a good time to test her out."

"Good," I said. "Tomorrow, we'll get to work." I glanced at Alex. "I think we may actually stand a chance."

28

———

"That's the last one," Alex said, closing the door behind him. "Nice guy. Goes by Tyler. Says he has a girlfriend somewhere in here, but I don't know... he wasn't much of a looker." I chuckled as Alex shrugged and made his way back over to us.

The five of us stood in the room behind the stage of the events center. I hadn't been back to this room since we had left for Ville all those weeks ago. It was dusty, cluttered, and, until a few moments ago, recently occupied by a bunch of strangers.

"Who knew so many people would try to live here? It's not like it's the most accessible place to get to," Daphne said.

"They probably enjoyed the quiet," Trevor said. "Zeno and I have been working around them for the last couple of days—they've been very accommodating."

"I think it's us who's been accommodating," Daphne muttered.

"You got that right, Daph," Zeno said. He grunted as he shoved the projector into place and hit the power button.

The screen on the wall flickered to life, and with it, text from Gina.

Good afternoon, Zeno and Trevor.

Zeno and Trevor both responded.
"Hey Gina,"
"Hello, Gina."
Zeno worked on clearing off a table but continued talking.
"As you know, we've got Victor, Alex, and Daphne with us today, too."

Are they here to stay?

"Tough to say, Gina," Zeno said, depositing an armful of junk into an empty box. "Depends on how everything goes with Rosewood." Zeno lowered his voice. "We're working on setting realistic expectations."

"Makes sense," I whispered back. "How are things looking in the Sandbox?"

"Not bad," Alex said. "I mean, not my best numbers, like that one time I got your saber tournament moved. That was impressive, if I do say so."

"Wait," I said, swinging myself around to face him, "you mean that championship match against—"

"It was over a year ago," Alex said, waving me off. "Don't worry about it. Anyways, the main thing is that lots of people are watching your video."

"That's good," I said, eyeing him, but I found myself wondering exactly how much of my life had been indirectly manipulated by Alex.

"All right, Gina," Zeno said, raising his voice, "I think we're ready. Show us the rally."

You got it boss.

The projector screen turned into a television feed. Camera footage, no doubt from a circling drone, showed that a stage had been set up on one of the street corners in the Flats. The area was filled with people—I'd never seen anything like it. A few banners could be seen, but for the most part, it was a huge gathering of Nobles, easily the biggest I'd ever seen, eagerly awaiting their president. Fortunately, we didn't need to wait long.

On stage, a group of black-clad "policemen" opened up, revealing Rosewood in her usual white attire. The moment she appeared and began her strut toward the pulpit, the crowd erupted.

Almost immediately, the camera switched views—another drone provided a close-up of Rosewood's face as she approached the podium.

Her unnaturally timeless face was devoid of wrinkles or signs of aging. She surveyed the crowd, a small, toothless smile forming on her lips—more of a smirk than anything.

She held up her hands to silence the applause, but it continued unabated. And though she fought not to show it, it was clear she was enjoying herself.

"What is all of that about?" Daphne said.

"Apparently," Zeno said, grunting with effort as he and Trevor hoisted a large screen onto the table, "old Ancientwood has been having these Noble rallies every week for the last few weeks. Just a little bit farther, Trev. Yeah, all right, that's it." He exhaled forcefully and took off his glasses, wiped his brow, and gave Trevor a fist bump. "Thanks, bro."

Trevor responded with a slight inclination of his head.

"And they're still excited to see her?" Alex said. "Crazy."

"What are the rallies for?" I said.

"As far as I can tell," Zeno said, "it's kind of a pat ourselves on the back show. I think she's just trying to build more loyalty. And I hate to say it, but it looks like it's working."

I looked back up to the screen. The camera switched views a few different times—a long panning shot over the audience, a view from the stage, and finally, an aerial view. Everyone there was still clapping and cheering.

Clearly, it was meant to make any self-respecting Noble feel left out if they weren't in attendance.

"This'll be a good way to figure out where Rosewood is at," I said. "People give more away when they're talking to people who agree with them."

"My thoughts exactly," Zeno said. "Now, you all might be wondering why I brought out this huge screen that is proportionally unfit for the table it's on. Let me tell you—Gina has helped us learn that there is a network of drones that has taken over the media and has a presence with Rosewood. It's clear she likes using them, and I assume they were her idea. That being said," Zeno continued, stepping over to the screen, "the drones are sort of like Rosewood's personal network, and she literally has hundreds of them. With Gina's help, we're going to hack into a few of her drones. Their video feeds will be displayed here." He motioned to the screen.

"And what good is that going to do us?" Daphne said. "We can already see and hear everything she's saying. It's not like she's hiding anything here."

"It's a test run," I said, folding my arms.

"Right," Zeno said, "this is all about access. Gina," he said, turning to the large, blank screen on the table. "Let's get started."

As you wish. Is dynamic mapping okay?

On the screen, about fifty small dots appeared. Some began to move.

"That's perfect, G."

"So what are we looking at here?" Alex said, strolling over to get a better view.

"Drones," I said. "All the drones in the area."

As I said it, Gina overlaid a transparent version of the rally so we could get our bearings. Three-dimensional renderings of the buildings, streetlamps, as well as the stage, and podium, all appeared on the screen.

One of the dots on the screen lit up a bright red, but then went out, and another dot lit up red.

The camera view shifted in time with the dots on the screen.

"Right, that's perfect," Zeno said. "Nice work, Gina."

I would call nice an understatement.

"Forgive me," Zeno said. "Exceptional work." He lowered his voice. "High-level compliments are the way to her heart. Anyways," he said, returning to a normal volume, "all of Rosewood's drones carry a unique signature. That's what allows us to track them. I learned that back in camp. Rosewood's drones also have the ability to broadcast video, and Gina can see which drone is sending out the signal and map it out right here."

"Dang, Gina! You're awesome!" Alex said. "Right up there with old trusty." He patted his arm.

Thank you, Alex. At least someone knows how to appreciate greatness.

Beside me, Zeno sighed.

"So needy."

Onscreen, Rosewood raised her arms in an attempt to quiet the cheering masses. The view rotated through multiple different drones. It gave the impression that, for all of Rosewood's efforts, she just could not get the people to stop cheering for her—a truly beloved leader.

A liar.

Finally, the audience quieted down, and Rosewood began to speak.

"Thank you all for coming out tonight."

I had to fight the instinct to tune her out. Her voice made me angry. Every word was laced with poison, meant to deceive and manipulate.

"I appreciate your kind gestures, but it is you who deserves the applause. It is you who deserves the praise. We have become more advanced and safer than ever before." The crowd broke into cheers and applause. Rosewood tried to speak over them. "You have executed our new policies with commitment and integrity, two very Noble virtues. And so, I say again, the credit is not mine alone, but yours."

"Ugh," Daphne said. "Can we mute her or something?"

"Yeah, mute the hag!" Alex said.

"Sorry, my metal-armed bro," Zeno said. "Gotta leave the old witch on for what we're about to do."

"Plus," I said, "she might say something useful to us."

"Or not," Daphne muttered.

"So, now that we can see what the drones are doing, what comes next?" I said.

"Now," he said, making a show of popping his knuckles, "we test a theory."

Zeno sat down at the table and produced a keyboard from a nearby box.

"Trevor, you want to fill them in?"

Trevor had an uncanny ability to almost blend in with the background. His voice came from the back of the room where he stood. Probably an old habit.

"Certainly," he said, taking a few steps forward. "Zeno and I have been busy. Aside from helping with Gina, of course, I have been going over all of the drone data we've collected since we were back at camp. We have a more complete understanding of their inner workings, which has allowed us to do this." He nodded to the screen in front of Zeno.

"Right-o, my man," Zeno said. "So, the last time we saw Rosewood on TV, she had a small drone following her around." He began typing on his keyboard, a whirlwind of clicks, pausing every few moments to check the screen. "It's most likely her personal drone. It's a little smaller than the rest, and it's somehow connected to her physical person—most likely through facial recognition or a connected bracelet or something." He looked up. "Everyone following so far?"

Nods all around.

"Good." His near-frantic-sounding keystrokes returned. "I'm going to hack into one of the drones and gain access to the internal system, the idea being that once we're in, we'll be able to work our way to Rosewood's personal drone."

"And how does that work, exactly?" Alex said.

"Like this," Trevor said. "Gina, would you begin our drone take-over protocol for Rosewood's contingent of drones?"

"Drone take-over protocol?" Daphne said.

"I let him name it," Zeno said, nodding to Trevor.

`I think it's an excellent name. Initiating now.`

On the projector screen, Rosewood was still talking. The camera hadn't deviated from her since she started—no panning to the audience, just her face taking up the majority of the screen.

"There is nothing we cannot overcome together," she was saying. "It is our unity of purpose that will carry us through any trial, any difficulty, and any change." Cheers rang out once more.

"And it looks like Gina has just about got it," Zeno said.

I directed my focus to the other screen.

The dynamic model of the rally had shrunk to fit half of the screen while a new camera view appeared, different from the televised broad-cast. Probably twenty feet or so in the air, it was pointed away from the stage and seemed to be focused in on a specific area in the crowd.

"I thought you said you were going to hack into the drones," Daphne said. "Looks like Gina's doing all the work."

"Gina and I are one," Zeno said. "Isn't that right, G?"

```
We are unified, yes, but I am more "one" with
Alex, seeing as he has technology integrated
into his biosystem.
```

I gave Zeno a look as Alex started to grin.

"Thanks, Gina! I always felt we had a connection."

"Yeah," Zeno said, hitting a few keystrokes unnecessarily hard, "she's been getting real technical lately."

I continued watching the screen. The current camera view disap-peared and another one popped up. It, too, was pointed away from Rosewood.

"Wait," Daphne said, "why'd it switch?"

"Rosewood's drones have very substantial security," Trevor said, moving to take a seat at the table as well. Zeno pulled out another keyboard and slid it over to him. "We must jump to a new drone every five seconds to escape detection, but each drone we're able to board allows us to download a significant amount of information."

"The problem we've got," Zeno said, his fingers flying over his keyboard, "is that it looks like old Rosewood's using her personal drone for all the broadcasting. If we try and take over her drone while it's broadcasting, we'll be noticed for sure."

Our hijacked camera view switched again. This one was posi-tioned higher up—maybe thirty feet in the air. I could see a good portion of the crowd as well as Rosewood's stage and podium.

"So when she's done with her speech," I started.

"Or if the broadcast feed changes to another drone," Trevor continued, "that's when we'll engage. We only need a handful of seconds to get what we're after. Gina's processors are fast enough to do it in two seconds if she needs to."

`Someone's trying to butter me up. I'm flattered.`

"Hopefully, her speech ends soon. I don't know how much more of this I can handle," Daphne said.

"No kidding," Zeno said, his fingers still clicking away rapidly. "Her rallies are propaganda. She's done enough damage. Daph, can you keep an eye on the screen and let me know the moment it changes camera views?"

"On it," she said, turning to face the screen.

I turned my attention to Rosewood as well. Zeno's keystrokes clicked in the background. I shook my head. Rosewood had a skill for saying things that sounded benign but, in reality, were cancerous seeds, but with all of her support, she was getting brave. She was becoming less careful with her words. She was becoming comfortable.

"We rely on the best of us," Rosewood was saying, "to move our city forward, to make the difficult decisions. In the past, our city was led by those who were satisfied with passivity, those who allowed weeds to grow where there should be none. You all know that Nobles are not passive people."

She paused as the cheers came in anew. "You do what is necessary for our future, even when the means may be difficult because Nobles do not give up, because Nobles seek after the greatest good." A slight curl formed at the corner of her mouth as she surveyed the crowd. "Our future, is the greatest good, and I will lead you all to it."

The camera angle shifted—her personal drone flew closer and then rotated ninety degrees until the shot was directly over the podium. A DNA scanner was there. Rosewood placed her hand upon it, and a hush fell over the crowd as the dotted lines traced the outline of her hand. An audible beep sounded, the screen glowed green, and her Noble percentage was displayed for all to see—something no leader, to my knowledge, had ever done before.

99%.

She held up the scanner and its results.

At this, the crowd erupted into near chaotic support.

The shot changed, and the new camera panned out over the cheering sea of people as they began to chant.

"Zeno, now!" Daphne said. I jerked my head around to Zeno's screen.

An emphatic keystroke sounded out, and the screen went blank.

"What the?" Zeno yelled.

A text box popped up:

```
Attempting to engage. Error. Attempting to
engage.
```

"Why's it not working?" Daphne said. The error message flashed again.

"Come on, G!" Zeno said as he typed furiously. "Looks like there's some extra encryption on this one. I designed you for stuff like this. Come on, Gina! You got this!"

The view of Rosewood's rally returned to her personal drone, along with another text box.

```
Attempted engagement terminated.
```

Zeno threw up his hands in frustration and sat back in his chair. Trevor simply stopped typing.

The message disappeared, and the previous map of the area showing the drones returned.

"What happened?" Alex said.

"Looks like Rosewood's got something extra on that one," Zeno said. "You got anything, Trev?"

"Maybe," he said slowly, hitting a few keys as he did so. A few more keystrokes, and he had Rosewood's personal drone highlighted on the digital layout on the screen. A final keystroke brought up a series of small text boxes that surrounded the dot.

"From one of the other drones, we were able to download a catalog that numbers all of Rosewood's drones. Her personal drone"—he pointed to it—"here, is different from the others." He pressed another few keys, and one of the text boxes enlarged. He leaned in to read it. "It appears as though Rosewood's drone needs a unique alphanumeric six-digit key to access it. It's not found in the software." His face fell. "It says, 'PVM industries. Access code physically printed on an interior panel.'"

"So that means that—" Alex started.

"It's unhackable," Zeno finished, his tone hollow. "Unless you have the stupid code!" He stood up abruptly and shoved his keyboard away, sending it careening with a crash onto the floor.

I'd never seen Zeno lose his cool. Ever. I broke the stunned silence his actions had brought.

"Couldn't you just hack into the mainframe of the company that made the drones?" I said. "They would have a directory of the codes, wouldn—"

"No," Zeno said. He took a few steps backward, took his glasses, and rubbed at his eyes with his other hand. "These guys delete all evidence, any digital or paper trail that could have the access code. They're very thorough."

"Do you know the PVM guys?" Alex said. "Is it something Ivy did?"

"No," Zeno said, "PVM—it's one of my old companies. I designed the protocol so that even I couldn't hack it. No one can."

Silence settled over the room. An anti-hacking protocol designed by Zeno—who knew we would be our own biggest roadblock?

"Okay, so then what do we do?" Daphne said, eyeing Zeno. "I thought we needed her drone if we were going to have any chance of Rosewood saying something that we could use against her. This is kind of a major piece of the puzzle, right?"

Zeno nodded but without feeling.

"That's right," he said softly while looking up at the ceiling. "It can't be done. I can't hack it."

Up on the screen, the camera view from the other drones continued to change. Applause continued to ring out. Rosewood stood there and bathed in the sound, smirking as the entirety of the Noble population cheered her name.

Without warning, the sound of a siren blared. I slapped my hands to my ears, but just as quickly as it had come, the sound went away.

"Zeno," I said, "what was tha—" I trailed off as both screens went blank, their feeds replaced by a short message.

```
Damage imminent.
```

"Everyone take cover!" Zeno shouted, diving underneath the table. My breath caught in my throat. I held my arms over my head, throwing out a protective spray, while the rest followed Zeno's cue and dove for cover.

Seconds passed, but nothing happened.

Did Gina malfunction? And what was that noise?

I kept my spray going and looked back at the screens.

I let my arms fall to my sides.

"Guys," I said. "Gina wasn't talking about here."

The video feeds were back up. On screen, fire was everywhere.

Part of Rosewood's stage was aflame. Her personal drone was still broadcasting, shooting wild footage all around. A building in the background looked to have a gaping hole in it from which smoke billowed like a cloud.

The audio had become distorted, but the occasional scream made it through as people fled.

Zeno took one look at the screen and practically dove for his keyboard.

The camera views he controlled started to switch, although he had a few less drones to choose from now. Everyone else crawled out from under the table to watch.

Short clips of people running and screaming and shots of smoke and debris flashed across the screen as Zeno cycled his way through every drone he could.

Then, in an instant, all of the feeds went dead.

"Come on!" Zeno said, tossing his keyboard aside yet again. "Gina! I need eyes!"

`Working on it.`

"What just happened?" Daphne said.

"I don't know," I said. "A bomb?"

"Gina, let's go!" Zeno said.

"Who would do that?" Trevor said, his complexion slightly paler than normal. "Who would bomb a rally of innocent people?"

`We're back.`

A tone sounded and the projector screen flickered back to life, and with it, the shocked face of Kelly Straunton. Her eyes were wide as she stared into the camera.

"An explosion has occurred at President Rosewood's rally. Infor mation is still coming in." She put her hand to her ear. "Many people have been hurt, injured, or worse. Currently," Kelly said, her voice beginning to tremble, "the death count has reached twenty-two people. John is on site. Fortunately, he was not harmed in the explosion. John, over to you."

John, apparently, stood next to a smoking pile of cement and glass. He, himself, looked completely normal—no signs of dirt or smoke on him at all. The street looked to be largely cleared, minus Rosewood's stage, which was giving the firefighters a battle. Half of it had turned into a charred mess, while flames spontaneously burst up from the other half.

"Thanks, Kelly," he said, staring deeply into the camera. "I was fortunate enough to be on the far side of the street when the explosion happened, but others weren't so lucky." He shook his head as he glanced downward. "For those who lost loved ones or were injured, we extend our greatest sympathies."

"The blast appears to have originated from this point," he said, regaining his composure and pointing to the building to his left. The camera panned to follow. The damage was extensive—the whole facade of the building was gone. Cement pillars that had once supported it were now mere stubs of crumbling rock. It was amazing it was still standing at all.

"We can only assume," John continued, walking back into the center of the frame, "that a Sinister individual or group is responsible, although no one has taken responsibility and current evidence is slim.

"This is a fact that should scare every Noble in the Flats—the fact that someone from the Heights was able, even with the additional rules and security in place, to pass through the border and into the Flats with a bomb—and do so undetected."

"With our limited information, we believe the attacker's intended target was the beloved President Victoria Rosewood. Fortunately, she was spared from the blast and was immediately escorted away to safety. We expect words from her later this evening."

"All right, Gina, that's enough," I said. The screen turned off.

I started to pace.

"Who would do that?" I said, raising my voice. "Who do we know that would do that? Was it Brick?"

"No way," Alex said. "We asked him not to do anything crazy. This was crazy."

"Alex is right," Daphne said. "Also, Brick doesn't have the brains for something like that."

"Okay, then who?" I said. "If Rosewood was looking for an excuse to eliminate all of the Sinisters *and* have the support of all of the Flats while she does it, she just got it."

Options ran through my mind. Who would do this? And who could? We needed to find out and then hold them accountable, show the Nobles that we weren't on board with that sort of thing.

News coverage in the Flats would be nonstop, pounding the narrative into their minds. We would have to act fast if we were going to minimize the damage, but even then, how could we play catch up against the constant media blitz the Nobles would get?

I couldn't help feeling like this was the final push Rosewood needed to get the Flats on board with her plan.

But still, who?

"Tyrann would have done something like this," Daphne said softly.

"Right, but Tyrann's dead," I said. I continued pacing.

A sobering thought struck me, a thought I desperately hoped wasn't true.

"Guys," I said. "What about Rosewood?"

"What about her?" Alex said. "I hope the bomb singed off her eyebrows."

"No," I said, beginning to pace again, "what if Rosewood planted the bomb and let it go off?"

"Why?" Zeno said. "I mean, bro, she's crazy, but—oh. She's creating a legitimate way to eradicate the Sinisters. That's what you're saying?"

"Makes sense, doesn't it?"

"You mean to say that you believe Dr. Rosewood would murder dozens of her own people?" Trevor said.

"You know the Bounty Hunter?" Alex said. Trevor nodded. "Well, Rosewood is his mom." Trevor's eyebrows raised. Alex continued. "And she's the worst mom in the world." Alex shrugged as if that explained everything. Trevor blinked and looked at me.

"And," I said, picking up the explanation, "by 'worst mom in the world,' he means that she stood by and watched as one of her goons shot the Bounty Hunter, her son, in the chest with a real gun, and then continued to do nothing as he fell off of the roof of the Research Tower."

Trevor's eyes grew wider.

"See?" Alex said. "Worst mom ever."

"Not to mention that she directs the Sinistrali and has been killing Nobles for years," Daphne said. "What does she care if another twenty people die?"

"Point taken," Trevor said. "But she can't be doing it all alone, can she?"

"No," I said, "she's working with her team—her Sinistrali."

"Exactly!" Trevor said with surprising gusto. "She's working with people. She's still discussing her plans with other people," Trevor said. "I think it would be unwise to change our plan at this point. We need to gain access to her personal drone so we can provide proof to the people."

"But, bro, how exactly do you propose we get the drone's unique ID number?" Zeno said. "I mean, I dig the optimism, but the number is carved into the interior panel of the drone. I doubt the drone ever leaves her side."

"This is assuming that Rosewood even did it," Daphne said. "It could have been someone else."

"And tomorrow, we're going to talk to Brick about it and get some answers," I said. "For now, we're—"

But I didn't get a chance to finish my thought.

Alarm lights and sirens began to flash. The sound was deafening.

"Gina!" Zeno yelled. "Details!"

Incoming airborne objects.

"Objects plural? Like a batch of missiles or something? Be more specific!"

Before she could answer, the doors to the room burst open. A sea of people poured through it. Their faces filled with fear as they all tried to push and claw past one another. They all began to rush past us, a few urging us to follow them as they fled.

"Gina!" Zeno yelled. "What's going on?"

If ever there was a sentence that would make my veins run cold, it was the next few words that appeared on Gina's screen.

Drones have arrived in the courtyard.

29

———

We arrived on the scene after observing Gina's video feed for several minutes. We stood just inside the events center behind a pair of glass doors that led out to the courtyard. Automatic lights, triggered by dusk, illuminated the space.

Over a dozen drones floated outside, waiting for us. Their many rotors kicked up dust and debris as they hovered in place. Blankets, makeshift tents, and personal effects of the recently homeless had been blown into a singular corner of the courtyard, where they came to an uneasy rest in the wind.

"It's all a little creepy," Alex said. "But I will say this—that's the cleanest I've ever seen the courtyard."

"Yeah, way to look on the bright side," I said, my focus on the drones.

It felt like they were waiting for me.

"Want me to blast them?" Alex said.

"While I would absolutely love to see that happen, my man," Zeno said, "I don't think it would be wise."

The pounding of feet sounded in the hallway behind us. Moments later, Benjamin appeared, skidding to a halt.

"Oh, you're already here," he said, completely out of breath. "I had just heard about our visitors."

"Did you miss the stampede of people about ten minutes ago?" Daphne said.

"I must apologize," Benjamin said. "I was meditating."

"Meditating?" Zeno said.

Benjamin nodded solemnly. "Deeply."

We all exchanged looks as Benjamin peered through the windows.

"That must be them," he said. "I suppose there's no reason to keep them waiting." He took a step forward, but I blocked him.

"Keep them waiting?" I said. "Were you expecting them?"

"No, no, of course not," he said, smiling blandly. "But the longer we wait here, the more we delay the resolution."

We all stared at him for a moment.

"Resolution?" Zeno said. "Bro, the last time we tangoed with drones, they torched everything we had and almost us, too."

"If these drones were here to cause damage, they would have done so already, don't you think?" Benjamin continued to stare out the window. "I say we go and make contact."

Technically, he was right. We had no information other than the fact that the drones were here and they were waiting. We gained nothing by drawing this out, but I didn't want to be blindsided just in case this wasn't the passive demonstration Benjamin thought it was.

"We should at least come up with a plan," I said.

"A plan for what?" Benjamin said. "Do you believe the drones are here for you?"

"It's a pretty good bet, my man," Zeno said. "We're not exactly on Rosewood's good side."

"I can't imagine many of us here are." Benjamin turned back to the window.

"Did you think they were here for you?" Daphne said.

"I can't imagine that would be the case," Benjamin said.

"What about one of your volunteers getting killed the other day near the border fence?" Daphne said.

"What's this now?" Benjamin said.

"Damien," Daphne said. "Your volunteer. Didn't you know? He was trying to get a group of people to rush the fence. I can't imagine Rosewood liked that very much."

Silence took hold of the moment as Benjamin studied Daphne's face. I looked back and forth between them.

"What she means is that we were sorry to hear about Damien," I said, jumping in. "It's not easy to lose someone who was part of your team."

Benjamin's face took a sad turn.

"Yes, well, thank you. It's unfortunate—I had hoped for something better for him." He looked up. "We can't control the actions of others, no matter how much we would like to."

Benjamin gazed off for a moment longer. The rest of us exchanged looks.

"Well," he said suddenly, clapping his hands together. "Shall we?"

"So we're going to go with the 'no plan' option?" Zeno said, shaking his head. "All right, bro, lead the way."

I was hesitant, but what other options did we have? I took another look out the window. Benjamin was right. Had they wanted to cause damage, they would have done so already.

With a nod, Benjamin stepped past me, pushed the door open, and strode out toward the drones. I followed.

Immediately, the air was filled with the electric hum of dozens of rotors. They were imposing—an unsettling group of floating sentinels. I came to an uneasy halt after just a few steps. Benjamin took a few more steps before stopping.

The drone nearest us swiveled to face us and hovered forward a few feet. It had a single light in the center of its cube-shaped body that blinked red. We held our ground.

Suddenly, the blinking stopped and glowed a bright red. My heart was already racing, but I braced myself for what was to come, whatever it was. The light blinked off, and the remaining drones all swiveled toward us as well.

I glanced at Benjamin, who seemed unreasonably calm. Maybe it was all of his meditating. The drones completed their swiveling, and I found myself staring into a sea of blinking red dots. Like a wave, the blinking lights of the other drones turned solid, and an eerie, monotone robotic voice filled the air.

"Message to the Heights from President Dr. Victoria Rosewood: We hold Sinister parties responsible for the explosion in the Flats that occurred today at 7:18 PM. We ask you to turn yourselves in peacefully to Noble officers at the border. This is your only and final warning. Failure to comply within twenty-four hours will result in dire consequences."

Their words seemed to echo in the night sky, ringing out louder and longer than they should have. It was as if the voices of the drones had filled the Heights.

Without warning, the drones in front of us disbanded, each one flying off into the night. I watched them go but saw what looked like hundreds of other small black dots joining up with them in the sky. The message had been played to everyone in the Heights. Everyone knew that Rosewood held the people here responsible.

"Well, that wasn't so bad," Alex said, appearing by my side. Daphne, Zeno, and Trevor weren't far behind.

"I guess not," I said, grateful it had only been a message but unsure of Rosewood's motive.

"The only thing I didn't get was the final warning part," Alex said.

"Final warning for what? Has she sent drones here before? Because if so, we definitely missed them."

"So it wasn't you who was responsible for the blast at the Noble rally?" Benjamin said.

"I thought you were meditating," Daphne said. "Deeply."

"Certain alerts are allowed to interrupt my meditation, provided they are large enough in magnitude. Multiple casualties in the Flats certainly qualifies." He stared off into the night sky in the direction the drones had flown.

"So what do we do now?" I said.

"Well," Benjamin said. "Seeing as President Rosewood has put the entirety of the Heights on alert, I think it's time we prepare ourselves. Maggie!"

I looked around, and to my surprise, Maggie popped up less than ten feet away from us. I noticed Trevor perk up at the sight of her.

"Yes, Benjamin?" she said, her voice almost too chipper to handle.

"I think it's time for a little get-together. Maybe, thirty minutes?"

"Absolutely, I'll get right on it."

Benjamin smiled serenely, and Maggie disappeared into the darkness.

"Prepare ourselves for what?" Daphne said.

"Opportunity often knocks in the darkest of situations," he said. Without another word, he turned and walked back inside.

"I'm gonna say it," Zeno said as the doors clanged shut. "That was a pretty dope exit."

"I get the feeling his idea of preparing is different from ours," Daphne said. "What do you think he has in mind?"

"I don't know," I said, looking back through the doors. "Could be good. Could be less good. Regardless, it sounds like in half an hour, we'll find out."

30

"He sure knows how to pull a crowd together," Alex said.

It had been twenty-six minutes since the drones had left, and Benjamin, along with hundreds and hundreds of Sinisters, stood outside in the courtyard. His small stage had been erected, a series of lights strung up to illuminate him as he addressed the crowd, and his usual speaker system had been wired up. His team of volunteers were truly efficient, but none more so than Maggie. She was everywhere, ordering people around and giving directions like a general.

"Do you want to help?" she said, appearing suddenly in front of us.

"Yes!" Trevor said a little too quickly. He took a step forward but then retreated a half step, apparently aware of his eagerness. Maggie smiled and suppressed a giggle. Trevor fidgeted until she locked eyes with him.

"Great, follow me."

Trevor walked quickly to her side, and the two of them walked off. Apparently, she hadn't been too interested in the rest of us.

Zeno smirked.

"I knew it."

"We all knew it, Zeno," Daphne said.

I turned to the stage. I could see Maggie and Trevor bustling around, making final preparations. A soft but high-pitched "test, test" could be heard as Maggie tapped the microphone. I looked out over the vast crowd. People of all ages were present. The aggregate chatter of so many people continued to fill the air. I only caught small clips of conversation here and there, but most of it centered on either the drones or the explosion in the Flats. Word had spread quickly.

"Here we go," Daphne said. Benjamin appeared on stage, a serene smile on his face. The hum of the hundreds of voices died down almost immediately. Trevor and Maggie were nowhere to be seen. The bulk of the other volunteers were gone, too. All attention was on Benjamin. He spread his arms wide and began to speak.

"Tonight, we've assembled," Benjamin started, his voice reverberating around the courtyard, "to discuss our fear." An even greater degree of quiet settled over the crowd. "I am certain I was not the only one to see the Noble display of power tonight. For many of us, that display was a fitting symbol of our oppressors," Benjamin said, his voice booming. "And we cowered in our fortress." He held his hands up and looked over his shoulder toward the building. "But," he continued, "there were also those who were above such emotions."

For a moment, I thought he was going to point to us—we were the only ones who hadn't run away at the sight of the drones, but just as the thought occurred, a far worse thought ensued.

"I assume many, if not all by now, know of what events transpired in the Flats this evening."

The crowd was hanging onto his every word.

"Uh, bros, where's he going with this?" Zeno said, casting a worried glance my way.

My stomach dropped. I knew what was coming next, and there was nothing we could do to stop it.

"People who were above emotion," he said, slowly, emphatically, "took action."

The courtyard erupted in cheers. We all looked at each other.

Benjamin, the man who had advocated for loving yourself, the man who said that being Sinister wasn't a sin—was the same man who was now openly praising extreme violence in the Flats.

"Our true enemy is not what we face here," Benjamin continued. "Our enemy is not hunger or homelessness. Our enemy is not judgment or ridicule. Those are merely momentary stresses. Our true enemy is Rosewood."

He paused as more people shouted and punched the air in agreement. "While we have learned to love ourselves, while we have learned that being Sinister is not a crime, the Nobles have taught themselves to fear us. They have decreed that our very lives are criminal, and they are not. It's their ideas that are criminal, and those ideas must be torn from our society and buried forever." A chaotic mix of cheering and battle cries filled the air. The energy was becoming more and more frenzied. Benjamin smiled, stoking their emotions.

"A conflict is coming," he continued, "and we must be ready. Call your friends, your family—anyone you know who is not here tonight and invite them to join us. The time has come. Things will soon change."

I looked at our small group. It must have been written on my face. Zeno summed it up.

"Yeah, bro. This is a problem."

We were back in our hidden room, trying to figure everything out. Things had just escalated. We needed a next step.

"Brick says Benjamin only has about half of the Sinisters on his side," Daphne said, looking up from her phone. "And he's got most of the rest. Or so he says."

"Not after Benjamin's speech," Zeno muttered. "And where is Trevor?"

I hadn't seen him since he went to help Maggie.

"Probably still with Maggie," Alex said. "He'll show up soon."

Zeno shook his head.

Alex was right, and our current matters were more pressing. Benjamin wanted to make a move against all the Nobles. I couldn't wrap my mind around it—even with his support, it just didn't make sense. The population of the Heights was roughly the same size as the Flats, but the difference in resources was significant. And if Brick was right and only half of the Sinister population sympathized with Benjamin, then what Benjamin was proposing was suicide. Did he not realize what he was preparing to do?

"So what do we do, team?" Zeno said. "Benjamin bro has gone full-on crazy, and the people love it." He sat down on a mattress, and for the first time, I didn't see a puff of dust emit from the old bed. Small victories.

"Well, he's not going to stand a chance with only half an army," I said.

"Are we really thinking about going to war?" Zeno said.

"Well," Daphne said. "I mean, we've been trying to bring people together so that we can stand a chance against Rosewood, right? I thought it was implied that this was the way it would go. Do you see any other options?"

Zeno sighed and buried his face in his hands. Silence accompanied his gesture.

"We could leave," I said quietly. "Go back and join up with my grandfather and your dad and Pria."

"Rosewood would never let that happen, bro." Zeno stood back up and started to pace. "I bet she's got a lock on our DNA position—we step foot outside the city, and drones are headed our way."

More silence.

"What about talking Brick into joining Benjamin?" I said.

"No way," Daphne said. "Under no circumstances, even if Jonny wanted to." She held up her phone. "I already asked."

"What about the other way around?" Zeno said. "Get Benjamin to join Brick and Jonny."

"Worth a shot," I said, "but I'm not optimistic. I think this was Benjamin's plan all along—gain a following and then attack the Nobles."

"Yeah," Zeno said. "Seems that way."

We all sat in silence for a moment. I collected my thoughts.

"We could kill her," Daphne said, her voice both soft and hard at the same time. The air became thick. It was the most extreme option that we had voiced, but if I was honest, it was an option that was always there, floating around in the back of my mind. I just hadn't had the guts to say it out loud.

"She's right," I said. "With her gone, could we avoid a war altogether?"

"Nope," Alex said, suddenly standing up. "Nope. We're the good guys. We'll find another way to bring her to justice."

No one responded.

I admired his attitude. I admired his goodness. I just wasn't sure what options we had left.

"With what?" Daphne said.

"I don't know," Alex said. "Have we heard anything back from Ville?"

"Nothing," I said. I pulled out my phone to check, just in case, but there was nothing. I typed out a quick plea for help and hit the send button, but it was a faithless action.

"It's fine," Alex said, waving it off. "We have other things going for us—the Sandbox is going crazy. People are starting to believe us."

"How many?" I said. Alex pulled out his phone.

"I don't know—like maybe two or three hundred people on here. It's the start of a movement!"

He looked around at us, but everyone else's faces mirrored what I felt.

Hopeless.

A couple hundred. It was a victory. Any truth we could get people to believe was a victory. But only a couple hundred?

We needed something more—we needed Brick and Benjamin to work together. What else would work? What else would even allow us to stand a chance? A conflict seemed inevitable, and our survival depended on how we played this.

"Guys, check this out."

Zeno sat down again—his phone out and the volume up. I could hear the perfectly articulated words of Kelly Straunton.

"Information found at the blast site points to a small group of potential sources, some linked to the recently deceased Tyrann Kane. However, since his reported death just days ago, we have to assume it was someone associated with his former crew."

I stood up and walked over to Zeno.

"They think Brick and Jonny did this?" I said.

"Looks that way, yeah. They're also mentioning you on here."

Of course, they were.

Zeno held up his phone. Text in a banner scrolled across the bottom of the screen.

Kelly Straunton said the words as they appeared.

"Victor Wells's presence has once again been confirmed in the Heights. He is, of course, among possible suspects. Probably right there at the top of the list, wouldn't you say, John?"

I didn't even care about the slander. It didn't really matter at this point. But what about Brick and Jonny? Would they do that? Could they do it?

I thought for a moment.

"Daphne, what do you think?" I said. "Brick and Jonny?"

She already had her phone out.

"Doubtful." Her fingers tapped the screen rapidly. "This is definitely more of a Tyrann-level move. I don't think they have it in them." Her phone buzzed. "Like I thought. They say that they didn't have anything to do with it. Regardless, we need to talk to them and strategize. I say we go now."

"Agreed," I said. We needed to plan. We needed to talk to Benjamin, too, but he was going to be busy with the aftermath of his speech for a while. I stood up. "Alex, Zeno, you coming?"

"I'll stay with my home girl Gina and see what I can learn on my end," he said.

"Well, I'm in, "Alex said, pushing himself to his feet. "Let's do it. It's been too long since I talked with those guys anyways."

We started making our way over to the stairs.

"Would Brick lie to you?" I said, turning to Daphne. She let out a devilish grin.

"I doubt that very much," Daphne said, "I believe them. I don't think Brick is smart enough to get into the Flats to plant a bomb, especially without Jonny. Not to mention, they would have needed to know that Rosewood was going to be there in advance. It's a tall order for two people who hadn't been on speaking terms until Alex refused to lift a door off of one of them."

"What can I say?" Alex said. "I just know people."

"Who else could have done it?" I said as we made our way up the long staircase. "Is there anyone?"

"What about the Bombers?" Alex said. "They have, you know, bombs."

"I told you they dismantled weeks ago," Daphne said. "And I'm pretty sure they used the last of their supplies when they helped us out. It always used to take them a long time to recoup after an explosion."

"So," I said, pausing at the top of the stairs, "there's no one else? Just Rosewood?"

I slid back the panel but froze. There, standing in the hallway like a wraith, was Kratos.

31

———

I froze. To say I was stunned was an understatement.

"Kratos!" Alex said, a big smile wrapping around his face. "Long time, no see!"

Alex's joviality knocked me out of it. I reached out and grabbed Kratos by the cloak and dragged him into our hidden alcove.

He didn't resist.

Daphne slammed the wall panel shut and started ushering us all back down the stairs.

"Where have you been?" I said, half dragging him, half supporting him down the stairs.

Still, he didn't fight. Still he didn't say a word.

How had he found us? No one knew about our hideout, at least not this part of it. But more importantly, why wasn't he talking? And why did it feel like he could barely walk?

We reached the bottom of the stairs, and his knees buckled. I slumped under his weight.

"Zeno!" I said. "A little help here!"

Zeno was still sitting on the mattress, just like we'd left him. Startled, he jumped.

"Kratos! Bro!"

He dashed over to meet us and helped me guide Kratos to the nearest mattress. We set him down as gently as we were able, but he wasn't doing much to help.

Without our support, he fell back immediately. He made no effort to move—his body was limp.

Alex had gone silent.

No one had to say anything. We didn't have time. I could feel the helplessness in the air as my heart raced.

I was at a loss—I scanned up and down his body. He was in rough shape. He had to be, right? I watched his chest rise and fall.

Breathing. Okay, that's good. If only Pria was here.

He still had his mask on, obscuring his face and features. The only thing it didn't touch was his eyes, which were now closed.

Slower than I knew was necessary, I reached up for his mask. Alex stopped my hand.

Seeing the look in his eyes, I stood and took a step back. Alex reached for his mask and gently removed it from his face.

The once golden hair was now the color of faded straw. His skin was sallow and dull. Behind closed lids, his eyes darted erratically back and forth, this way and that.

"Kratos," Alex whispered. Then a little louder. "Kratos." He didn't respond.

With an even gentler touch, Alex attempted to open one of his eyes. I didn't want to look, but I couldn't stop. A frantically moving blue iris was surrounded by a dense web of red vessels. Never before had I seen an eye so bloodshot.

Alex gasped and retracted his hand.

"Call Pria," I said.

We all stood on the opposite side of the room, watching him.

After several tries, and with Zeno using Gina to boost her reach, Daphne miraculously had gotten a text back from Pria.

"She says to let him sleep."

From what we could tell, Kratos didn't have any wounds. No blood stains, no bruising, but he definitely looked bad. He had lost weight since we last saw him, there was no doubt about that.

"He's been out for the last thirty minutes," Zeno said. "Does she know what's wrong with him? Bro's always been invincible." His gaze lingered on Kratos's still body. Alex remained quiet.

Seeing him there—it brought back memories of Rosewood, Harvesty, gunshots, and falling. Was he as close to death as last time? I shook off the thought.

"So, how did he find us?" I said. "I mean, it's not like we've been talking to anyone."

"I don't know," Zeno said, finally pulling his gaze away and directing it toward Alex. "I mean, he is the Bounty Hunter. This is kind of what he does, right? Got anything for us, bro? Alex?"

Alex sat down, not looking at the rest of us.

"I don't know," he said. "Last time he was in this bad of shape, it was a poisoned bullet. This time—I don't know."

"I don't—" I loooked at Alex. "I don't know if Kratos—or his mind — is all right." No one responded, so I continued talking. "Last time we saw him, something wasn't right, either. And when we lost track of him back at camp—even then, Pria said something was wrong."

Kratos began to moan.

I rushed over, knowing that I had no clue what to do.

Kratos stirred. He looked like Grandfather sometimes looked in the mornings—movements were slow and painful.

He let out a grunt as he attempted to sit himself up, blinking his very bloodshot eyes half a dozen times as he did so. Ultimately, he kept them closed.

Tentatively, we gathered around. It was painful to watch.

"Kratos?" Zeno said.

Kratos flinched and shook his head softly, gingerly, almost like the sound hurt him. He brought a hand up and covered his ear.

"Sorry, bro." Zeno took a step back. He looked at all of us and shrugged.

"Should we just see if he goes back to sleep?" Daphne whispered.

"I'm awake," Kratos said, his voice rough and scratchy. He sat there on the mattress, legs out in front of him and eyes closed. "Is this real?"

"Uh yeah," I said, lowering my voice to a whisper. I took a step forward. "It's me, Victor Wells."

He didn't flinch.

"Where are we?"

"The Heights," I said.

"Not Ville?"

"No," I said, "not Ville. You got out of there a few weeks ago."

Kratos blinked several times.

Alex took a step forward.

"Hey, bud."

A confused look passed over Kratos's face.

"No one has called me 'bud' before."

"That's how you know this is real," Alex said. "Your brain isn't doing this—this is real life."

Kratos blinked a few more times and slowly turned to see Alex.

"There he is." Alex smiled and extended his robotic hand.

I wasn't sure it was a good idea for Kratos to stand, but I trusted Alex. However, rather than taking Alex's hand, he stared at it, tilting his head at different angles. When he spoke, his words were soft and filled with more emotion than I'd heard before.

"What happened?"

"I got an upgrade," Alex said. "Not the best way to get one, but no big deal, thanks to Zeno and Ivy."

"Where was I when this happened?" Kratos stared unblinkingly at Alex, his eyes still bloodshot, a ragged, distraught look on his face.

"I thought Jahko had filled him in," Daphne said, her voice almost a whisper. "Doesn't he remember when we were back at the camp?"

Kratos moved his gaze to Daphne, but it was almost as if he didn't see her, like he was staring past her. She glanced over at me, her look uncomfortable.

"Kratos," I said. "Where have you been?"

In a rapid motion, Kratos stood up.

"You need to leave," he said.

"Bro?" Zeno said.

"Leave. You need to leave!" Kratos began pacing, "Drones and buildings, Rosewood—they, they, who are they? Why? Why?" He stared at me. "You need to leave!"

He went back to pacing. His movements were less jerky but still looked painful and forced.

I took a step backward, closer to the rest.

"What do we do?" I whispered.

"I don't know... bro's clearly going through something," Zeno said.

"I just think he wants us to leave," Alex said, taking another step forward. "Hey, Kratos?"

Kratos stopped pacing.

"Where do you want us to go?"

Kratos stared at Alex for a couple of moments too long, then turned to Zeno and spoke, his tone surprisingly normal.

"Why are you looking for Dr. Rosewood's personal drone?"

"I, uh, we found it, bro," Zeno said. "We just can't hack it because we need the ID number that's engraved on it."

Kratos continued to stare at Zeno, almost as if he expected him to elaborate.

Zeno looked side to side.

"Rosewood's gotta break character, right?" he said, glancing at me. "Her personal drone could broadcast her true plans. And if we could get access to—"

Kratos shifted his gaze abruptly to me, cutting Zeno off.

"You like to play in the Sandbox."

I was getting a strange feeling.

"I guess," I said. "But how do you know that?" I said. "Have you been watching us? Is that why you were there to save me from the explosion?"

"You need to leave," Kratos said, turning away from me. He looked at the ground.

"Why?" Daphne said.

Kratos continued to pace, ignoring Daphne's question completely.

"We're not going to leave," I said. "We've got to take down Rosewood, and we could really use your help."

He stopped pacing and stared at me.

"No, I've seen this one before," Kratos said, resuming his pacing. Clearly, he wasn't talking to any of us. "Yes, they won't listen if you yell. But how?"

I was struggling to process what we were seeing. Did he not think we were here? Did he not think this was real?

Suddenly, Kratos looked up, a kind of half smile on his face.

"I just need to leave. I am here," he said slowly. "They are not. If I leave, they'll come with me."

Without any more warning, Kratos took off for the staircase in a dead sprint.

He was so fast.

His black coat was whipping out of sight before I had even reached the bottom of the staircase.

I leapt the stairs three and four at a time, but when I got to the top, the panel was pushed back, and Kratos was gone. Even the hallway was empty.

"He's gone," I said, partly in disbelief, partly in anger. Daphne was next up the stairs behind me.

"Where'd he go?" she said.

"He's gone," I said again.

"Gone?" she said.

I didn't understand it. How? Why?

Alex and Zeno thundered up the stairs behind us.

"Gina!" Zeno said, his phone out. "Track him!"

"Can she do that?" Daphne said.

"She hasn't in the past," Zeno said, coming to a stop on the landing behind Alex. "But we'll see."

32

———

We were all rattled, to say the least. Unfortunately, being rattled wasn't a luxury we could afford. Gina was doing her best to track Kratos, but we hadn't gotten any updates from her. There was no way we would be able to find Kratos by ourselves. Clearly, his mind was not right. And with his skills and knowledge, he was more dangerous than ever. Who knew the next time that he would show up or what he would do when he did?

We had decided against going to see Brick and Jonny—by the time we had finished talking about Kratos, Daphne said it was too late. They were usually "out on business" around this time and wouldn't be available for a few hours, even if Alex was coming with us. Instead, we would see what we could do with our audience in the Sandbox.

It felt like a cop-out.

It was action, but was it the most effective thing we could be doing?

"You ready, bro?" Zeno said, looking up from behind the camera setup.

"Yeah, just about," I said, reaching into my pocket. "I sent Jahko another message," I said, handing Daphne my phone. "Can you watch this, just in case?"

"About Kratos?" Daphne said, taking my phone and pocketing it. I nodded. She shrugged. We both knew it was a long shot.

"Hey, crazy recognizes crazy," Zeno said.

"Jahko wasn't crazy," Alex said, not looking up from his phone in the corner.

"Right," Daphne said, "he was just acting crazy."

"Exactly."

"Either way," I said, "he was the last person to talk to Kratos before he stumbled into camp. Maybe he knows more about his mental state. Maybe he can help."

"Maybe," Daphne said.

"Thirty seconds, my man," Zeno said.

I nodded. Even though I would have rather been somewhere else —talking with Brick and Jonny, for example—it was game time. This needed to be good and convincing.

"I'm ready," I said. "You think they'll go for it?"

"Alex seems optimistic," Daphne said.

"Oh, I am," Alex said, his face still buried in his phone.

"Me too," Zeno said. He shook his head and smiled. "0301..."

He still hadn't gotten over Alex's secret fame.

"All right then," I said, willing any superfluous thoughts from my mind. "Let's do it."

I stared at the blinking light on his phone as it turned from blue to red. I set my face. We needed this to make an impact, a big one.

Zeno pointed at me, and it was on. I took a deep breath.

"I'll make this brief," I said. "Despite what the news may have said, I was not responsible for the bombing. And to the best of my knowledge, no one in the Heights was either. If it wasn't me, and it wasn't from the Heights, I think you know where the bomb came from."

I let it sink in. At least, I hoped it sank in.

"Rosewood is using any event she can to cause a greater division between the Nobles and the Sinisters, even if she has to create the event herself. Ask yourself, where does that lead—to greater peace and safety like she says? Or something else?"

I stared hard into the camera.

"Tensions between the Heights and the Flats have never been higher, but it doesn't need to be this way. Hate, anger, fear—these are not good feelings. If any of you feel that way about Sinisters, is that right? Is that good? Is that Noble?"

I paused again. They had to get it. They had to. I continued. "Hate doesn't cure hate, and we don't cure hate with fear. Why would Rosewood reinforce that kind of thinking? What kind of leader does that?"

I wanted anyone watching to have a chance to think about what I had said. Behind the camera, Zeno motioned at me and nodded. Time for Alex's idea.

"Conflict happens," I continued, "war happens, when people believe there is no other way. And soon, very soon, Rosewood is going to make that argument, but there is another way. I don't want war. The Heights doesn't want war."

I knew there were people watching who thought I spoke for the Heights, and I knew there were people in the Heights who would gladly fight the Nobles, but what I said was true. No one here wanted to die. And if war actually occurred, that's exactly what would happen, on a massive scale.

I focused back in on the camera.

"What do you want? Do you want war? Do you want to fight and die for a corrupt system created by a corrupt leader?

"Life as you know it is about to change, but personally, I believe there is another way. It doesn't have to be you versus us, or us versus them. There is strength when we do things together. If enough people show that they're willing to work for peace, then there's hope. So long as there are willing people on both sides, there is always hope." I took another deep breath.

"Here's what I propose: tomorrow at noon, one of you needs to organize your own rally, a rally for hope. Use whatever saying or slogan you want, but protest violence against the Sinisters. Protest violence against the people in the Heights. No one is expecting something like this, which is why it will have an impact. With tensions as high as they are, a showing of support for our entire city will go a long way, maybe even to the point of preventing war." I held my gaze at the camera for a moment before looking down.

A terrible image flashed through my mind—what I thought war in the Flats might look like. There would be so much pain, so much loss. I looked back up.

"It doesn't matter what side of the fence you're on or what your DNA scan says you are. We're all just people. And if enough of us come together, we can work it out. We can stop Rosewood at her game and save each other in the process. People will notice, both in the Flats and in the Heights, and that is what can make all the difference."

I stared into the camera with all the feeling I possessed.

"People say that Sinisters don't trust Nobles. People say that Nobles don't care about Sinisters. This is where we show them how deep our goodness runs. This is where we show them how far we're willing to go for peace. This is where we begin to make our stand. So, tomorrow, may we protest for peace, for each other. We're depending on you. Goodnight."

The light on Zeno's camera blinked off. I exhaled.

We all stood there in silence for a moment. It felt like a long shot.

"Well done, bro," Zeno said. "If no one takes us up on it, I'd be surprised."

"I don't know," I said. It was still hard to gauge the type of impact we were having in the Sandbox, even with Alex's help. "You think they can put together a rally that fast? Or get enough people to do it at all?"

"For sure," Alex said. Zeno nodded, too, then pulled out his phone.

"We'll know in about thirty seconds," Zeno said, checking his watch. He looked up at the ceiling. "Gina should have it all processed and posted in the next few seconds. Comments should start coming in any moment now."

"And here they come," Alex said, his phone beginning to vibrate uncontrollably.

We all gathered around.

User58964: A protest in favor of the Sinisters? Like they'd do it for us.

User211812: I bet the Sinistrali planted the bomb!

User386018: He's got a point though. Why should we be afraid of the Sinisters? We weren't before.

User80001: A clear mistake on your part.

"There he is again," Alex said.

"Who?" Zeno said.

"80001?" I said, reading over his shoulder. "I can see why you think he might be from the Heights."

"Yeah," Alex said slowly. But a moment later, his comment was off the screen as new comments continued to come in, almost too fast to read. "This isn't going anywhere," Alex said. "I swear, it's like they're a bunch of children running around in here." He looked back down and started typing. He finished with a tap, and his comment appeared on the screen.

User0103: A movement needs to be started. A protest like this would make the news, maybe more. Who can make this happen?

The comments had stopped. I looked over at him.

"Wait for it," he said. "We just need the right person to respond." His phone buzzed again.

User86453: Get a group of Sinisters to do the same for us, and you're on.

I reread the sentence again. My stomach dropped. Get the Sinisters to protest for peace for the Nobles? It was reasonable, but it made our job exponentially more difficult. We hadn't planned for this. Getting a group of people who thought they were superior to campaign for those who were beneath them was benevolent. Getting the inferior group to campaign for their perceived oppressors... it was a tall order. His phone buzzed again.

User80001: A bold request, but I see the merit.

"Are you going to respond?"

"To 80001?" Alex said. I nodded. He shook his head. "I've always kind of had a weird feeling about him. But this 86453 guy, we can work with him."

"Is he legit?" Daphne said.

"86453?" Alex said. "Oh yeah—I mean, he's not me, but people listen to him. He's just another senator or something. Not the one from before—she actually had some pull. This guy is pretty new but shows some promise. Give him a few years, and he might make something of himself."

We all stared at Alex.

"What? That might be the best offer we're gonna get. Let's take it."

"Zeno, what do you think?" Daphne said. "Is this the right play?"

"The right play?" Zeno looked at her with incredulity. "The King of the Sandbox has spoken! Of course, it's the right play!"

I reread the message from 86453—I had really been hoping for them to just do what I asked. I hoped Alex's support would carry us through, but it looked like we had fallen short. Really short. But there had to be a group of people we could get together who would do it, right? This was about swaying public opinion. This was about stopping war. There had to be people here who wanted to avoid that.

"So all they're asking us to do is get a group of Sinisters to show their support for the Nobles," Daphne said, with a shake of her head and a wry smile.

"Easy," Alex said with a shrug.

"Right, and maybe we can get them to throw Rosewood a birthday party while they're at it," Daphne said.

"Nah, I think they would really hate that," Alex said. Daphne rolled her eyes and sighed. "But a protest, we can do that."

"This is more than we've had to work with before," I said.

"Yeah, this is big," Zeno said. "Alex is right—I don't think we're going to get a better offer."

We all sat in silence for a moment.

"Any idea how we're going to make this work?" I said.

"We'll figure something out," Alex said. "We always do."

I looked over at Daphne.

"You in?"

She folded her arms and nodded.

"All right, then," I said, "Let's do it. We'll get a group of Sinisters together. Zeno, let them know."

"On it."

Seconds later, Alex's phone buzzed. Almost immediately, his phone buzzed again.

replying to User86453 "...and you're on."

VideoCreator: You have yourselves a deal.

Almost immediately, his phone buzzed again.

User86453:

User80001:

"Hmm," Alex said, closing his phone. He looked around at all of us. "I guess we'll see what happens."

33

Sleep had been fitful. It always was lately.

I opened my eyes and stared into the darkness. That was one of the perks of sleeping in a secret room without any windows—no ambient light to keep you awake. Not that it had made much of a difference.

My mind was constantly awake, humming with thoughts and anxiety. I replayed the video I had made earlier over again in my mind. I considered the agreement we had made with the people in the Flats.

Was it enough? Would they pull through? Would we pull through?

I rolled onto my side and breathed in the stale air of the mattress. I could hear the others breathing at their various locations around the room. Normally, I wasn't alone in my insomnia. Restless movements, irregular breathing patterns—none of us seemed to be immune. And if I was right, Alex, too, was awake.

I listened hard for a moment. The faint metallic clicking of his prosthetic fingers was a dead giveaway. What thoughts were keeping him up? Was he truly without doubt, or was Alex merely playing confident? Was that why he was awake? I shook the thought from my mind. Alex wasn't the type to deceive. He had his own viewpoints and opinions, but he never lied. I hoped he could get to sleep soon.

I rolled over to the other side and shoved my hand under my "pillow" to make it more comfortable. It didn't work.

I looked over in Daphne's direction. A familiar, though confusing, mix of emotions bubbled up. I longed to talk with her about something more, something deeper than our fight against Rosewood. I knew there was more. There had to be more, or else what were we even fighting for?

I reached into my pocket and slid out my phone. The screen lit up, and I quickly turned down the brightness and covered myself with my blanket.

My eyes adjusted, and the screen came into focus. Still no new messages. The last message I sent to Jahko had gone unanswered. The last several messages were that way. I opened up my chat with Pria and typed out a message.

Looks like Rosewood is planning something soon. We're trying to gain Noble support, but to be honest, things look bleak. Alex appar- ently is a big deal in the Sandbox—we're trying to use that. I hope the new city is going great. We could use the help if everyone in the camp wanted to risk their lives for less-than-ideal odds. Anyways, best of luck.

I hit send and shoved the phone back in my pocket. I knew she wouldn't answer. I knew Jahko wouldn't answer if I sent him something, too. Sometimes, I asked myself why I kept trying to get a hold of them. The only two lines we had to the outside—Pria and Ville— didn't seem to have anybody on the other side. And I knew they had their own problems to deal with.

I tried to force myself to stretch and yawn. It didn't work. My body was tired, but my mind refused to sleep. And nothing was comfortable. I moved again.

But I wasn't the only one that was moving. A cutting chill settled over me as the sound of our sliding panel met my ears. It was distinct —like metal softly rubbing against metal. I was certain it had once been completely silent, but now, the ever so faint friction of the two surfaces cut through the silence with more strength than a scream. A pair of footsteps followed. Then another.

My blood ran cold.

But before I could move, before I could even think, Alex let out a battle cry, and what looked like lightning bolts exploded from his hand.

Blast after blast peppered the darkened stairway, lighting it up each time Alex fired.

"GINA! LIGHTS!" Zeno yelled, illuminating the room and blinding everyone. But Alex didn't care. Blind or not, no one was getting past the stairway. The blasts continued.

I put a hand over my eyes and squinted at the stairs. It came into focus, and with it, a familiar voice sounded.

"Don't shoot! It's me! Trevor!

Alex let off a final blast for good measure, then lowered his arm, his chest heaving.

After a moment, Trevor appeared at the top of the stairs, his hands up. His eyes were wide—clearly, he wasn't expecting to be greeted like this. Aside from the hour at which he had chosen to come back here, what truly surprised me was the person he was shielding.

"What's Maggie doing here?" Daphne said, her voice like ice.

Maintaining his defensive posture, Trevor slowly began descending the staircase.

"Now, I know this is, perhaps, against protocol, but she can help us."

He continued his slow descent. Maggie followed closely behind. I didn't think she posed a threat, but up until now, no one knew we were down here. Least of all, Benjamin. This was a surprisingly foolish move on Trevor's part. How could he be so shortsighted?

Finally, they reached the bottom of the stairs.

"I don't know about this, bro," Zeno said.

"And just why not?" Maggie said, taking a step out from behind Trevor. "We're all on the same side here, aren't we?" She stared around the room.

Her boldness caught me off guard, and somehow lessened the impact of her unique vocal qualities.

"And just what side is that?" Daphne said, also taking a step closer.

"To heal society," Maggie said. "You've all heard Benjamin speak." She looked around the room again. "He works tirelessly to help the people here feel better about who they are. We can't heal until we've accepted that we're broken."

Nobody spoke. There was truth in what she said, and we all felt it. The people in the Heights were, effectively, a broken people. They had been told and taught their whole lives that they were destined for inferiority because of who they were. And though it was all a lie, a lie we wanted to expose, bringing the truth to light wouldn't necessarily be an immediate fix.

Maggie's eyes were earnest.

"And you really think that's what he wants to do? Even after his most recent speech?" Daphne said.

"Yeah," Zeno said, "I know he's big on self-love stuff, but earlier, bro sounded like he wanted to start a rebellion. And not a peaceful one."

"I admit," Maggie said, looking down at the ground, "that Benjamin has, on occasion, in order to maintain the focus of the people here, reverted back to some of the baser ideals of the Heights." She looked back up and started talking faster now. "But it's just a cover —it's a way to connect with the people when something big happens. But he'll bring them back down, he always does."

"You're saying he is still on the side of peace?" I said. "Despite what he said just a few hours ago?"

"Yes," Maggie said. She said it with force. She meant it, and I knew she believed it. I looked to Trevor, who had remained silent.

"What's your take?" I said. "You've spent some extra time with people who are close to Benjamin. What do you think?"

All eyes turned to Trevor. It clearly made him uncomfortable, but as he looked down at Maggie and then back up at us, there was conviction in what he said.

"I believe her. She has spent more time with Benjamin than anyone, and Benjamin has proven himself as someone who is on the side of the people. He has high ideals and he cares about the Heights."

"So, would he help us organize a protest in the Heights?" I said. Regardless of his true intentions, that was the only question that mattered. Could he help us do this, or not?

Trevor stared at me, a puzzled expression on his face.

"What do you mean?" Maggie said.

"We have an agreement with a group of people in the Flats," I said. "They're going to organize a protest on behalf of the Sinisters, provided we get a group of Sinisters to do the same for them. And it must happen tomorrow. Things are moving fast toward an all-out civil war, and we're trying to stop that from happening." I locked eyes with Maggie. "Benjamin's speech earlier only accelerated that timeline. So if he really is on the side of peace, this is our shot, maybe our only shot. Will he help us?"

"Yes!" Maggie said, almost too eagerly. She looked around at us. "Yes, of course, he will."

She looked around with pleading eyes. I could tell she was earnest. I could tell she believed that Benjamin wasn't planning anything nefarious, but that didn't mean we felt that way. Maggie turned her eyes to Trevor, clearly asking for backup. Trevor cleared his throat.

"Based on my interactions with people over the last two days," he said, "I am optimistic, yes. I think Benjamin will help you if you ask him."

"See?" Maggie said. "He's a good man. I can set up a meeting for you. First thing in the morning?"

I looked around at the rest of the group and shrugged.

"What do you think?" I said.

Daphne folded her arms, Alex stared off at the stairwell, and Zeno shrugged.

"I don't know, my man, but I don't think we have too many options at this point. We've gotta try, right?"

I glanced one last time at Daphne. I could tell she had the inside of her cheek in between her teeth. Skeptical was too soft of a word in her case, but Zeno was right—what other options did we have?

"Set it up," I said. "As early as you can. We've got a lot of work to do tomorrow."

Maggie pulled a screen out of her pocket.

"How's 7:30 a.m. sound?" she said.

"Earlier than necessary," Zeno mumbled.

"Book it," I said.

I had already started formulating things in my mind. If he actually did help us, we might stand a chance. If not, well, we'd cross that bridge early tomorrow morning.

"Well, I think it's time we all get some sleep," Zeno said. "For a couple of hours anyway."

Everyone started to move except for Maggie, who stood there, clearly unsure of what to do. I wasn't sure how she could think of staying here with us—even Trevor barely knew her. I stared at her, and we locked eyes.

"I should go," she said.

"I think that would be wise," Trevor said, leading her over to the stairs. "And I know we would all appreciate it if you kept our situation here a secret."

She nodded vigorously and gave us all a tight smile.

"Of course." She started up the stairs.

"Maggie," Trevor said. She stopped immediately. "See you in the morning?"

Maggie smiled and nodded. "See you in the morning."

Without another word, she disappeared up the stairs. Trevor watched her go. We all stayed quiet, waiting for the sound of panel sliding back into place. An audible but soft "click" sounded, and Daphne immediately broke the silence.

"What were you thinking?"

Trevor didn't meet her gaze.

"I, she, she lives here in the building, somewhere. I," he paused and looked up. "Well, I wanted her to be safe, and I thought she could help us."

"At this hour?" Daphne said.

Trevor opened his mouth, but Zeno cut him off.

"Bro, look," he said, "I'm pumped you found someone, but man." Zeno shook his head. "This is big time. What if she goes to Benjamin and it turns out he's not happy we're down here? Or we meet with him tomorrow, and he's got more than just words for us—if you know what I mean?"

"I truly don't believe that," Trevor said. "She wouldn't betray my trust like that."

"How can you be sure?" I said. "You've only known her a day."

Trevor looked at the floor once more.

"Alex, what do you think?" I said. "You've got a pretty good track record when it comes to people we don't know well."

"She won't tell Benjamin unless we ask her to," he said. "She's on our side." He paused and looked at Trevor. "But she's especially on Trevor's side."

A grin overtook his face, and Trevor's ears and neck flushed.

The tension broke.

Zeno let out a chuckle and slapped Trevor on the shoulder. I smiled, too. Relief was evident on his still-red face.

"Well," Zeno said. "Sounds like we've got a long day ahead of us."

"And not a long night," I said. "Let's get some sleep."

The rest took a few more moments to disperse, but I walked immediately back over to my mattress and laid down. I rolled over on my side, away from everyone, so no one would be tempted to come and talk. I needed to think.

We had a meeting with Benjamin in a few short hours, and despite Maggie's insistence that he would be happy to help us, I wasn't so sure. How would I present the idea to him? How could I get him to give us the little bit of help we so desperately needed?

Zeno's voice rang out.

"Gina, could you turn the lights off for us?"

The room went black.

"That's my girl. G'night."

I pictured Benjamin's face. I pictured me talking to him, presenting my case. I pictured him saying yes, but a minute later, I found myself too tired to think, and somehow, finally, I drifted off to sleep.

34

———

We were all still half asleep, or at least I felt like we should be. The only exception was Trevor, who stood erect and awake in anticipation. We had been there for less than five minutes. In that time, the hallway around us had been still. The only sounds were the snores of those who lined nearby hallways.

"Where is she?" Daphne said. "I thought you said she wouldn't be late?" She eyed Trevor, who checked his watch.

"I did say that. She still has thirty seconds."

As if to confirm his words, Maggie appeared around the nearest corner, her short steps quick and quiet as she approached.

"Good morning," Trevor said, his voice lowered.

"Good morning," Maggie whispered. I nearly winced at the sound. Even her whisper was eerily high. That, and it was too early. Maggie smiled at Trevor, and he smiled back. It took a cough from Daphne to break it off.

Maggie pulled out her screen. "We've got three minutes before he'll be expecting us. And do be quiet; we like to let everyone sleep in as much as they can. This way."

She led us down the hallway toward Benjamin's office. Zeno had opted to stay back with Gina and see what he could do to aid us from his end, so Alex, Daphne, Trevor, and I followed her closely. Daphne followed her more closely than the rest.

"So you're sure this is the best time of day to talk with him?" she said as our footsteps echoed off the linoleum-clad floors. "We need to persuade him to help us, not make him mad."

"Benjamin? Mad?" Maggie laughed. It was a nice, bubbly laugh—a stark contrast to her regular voice. She immediately clamped a hand over her mouth. "Sorry!" she continued in a much softer voice. "No, no, of course not! He's always up early, usually to meditate. He always says his ideas to help people come easiest during his morning meditation hour. I can't think of a better time to talk with him!"

I tried to catch Daphne's eye, but she was a few steps ahead of me. From her body language, I could tell that Maggie was the unknowing recipient of an eye roll.

"So, to be clear," Alex said, "you think there's a high probability that Benji is going to help us?"

Maggie looked back over her shoulder, a single eyebrow raised. "Yes, Benjamin will help you. He is a very caring leader who wants us all to feel good about ourselves and have the freedom we deserve."

Alex punched Trevor in the arm, who, rather than jumping like he had previously, merely stared at Alex with a vague look of annoyance.

"I was worried about you in the beginning," Alex said, "but now, I mean, you helped Zeno with Gina, and now this. I'd say you're a pretty crucial member of the team." Alex winked and then nodded to Maggie.

Trevor stared at him for a moment, slightly confused, but then appeared to catch on.

"Oh, um, yes, thank you. We're just fortunate to have met someone as helpful as Maggie."

"I'd say you're the helpful one out of the two of us." She looked over at him and then back to the rest of us. "If it wasn't for Trevor, we never would have been able to get Benjamin's stage and equipment set up so quickly last night."

"Trevor is great, isn't he?" Alex said, raising his eyebrows repeatedly. He looked over at me and smiled. I smiled back. Trevor had likely never had attention like this before.

"Honestly," Trevor started, "Maggie is the great one—"

"Oh, will you two give it a rest!" Daphne said, glaring. She glanced at me but quickly looked away.

Trevor looked at Daphne, his expression one of shock.

Maggie touched his arm.

"She's probably right. We're here anyways." She knocked on the door we had arrived at.

I leaned in toward Daphne.

"You okay?"

"Fine."

Clearly not, but I didn't have time to press her further before the door opened up, revealing Benjamin standing before us, a serene smile on his face. He wore loose fitting clothes and sandals. Everything was a kind of grayish-beige color.

"So nice to see you all here this morning," he said. "Please come in."

He took a step back and motioned for us to enter.

The room was one I had not been in before. It wasn't a large room, but it was completely empty, except for a single screen mounted to the wall. The floor was the same linoleum that adorned most of the building, but a large rug had been placed in the center of the room. I imagined that was where Benjamin did his meditation.

Benjamin followed us over to the rug.

"Please, sit," he said as he lowered himself cross-legged down onto the rug. "Thank you, Maggie."

Maggie nodded and exited the room with a final look back at Trevor before she shut the door.

"Well, what brings the four of you to my door so early this morning?"

We all settled ourselves to the floor.

"We need your help," I said, pulling myself into a cross-legged position. I had planned out what I wanted to say, trying to tailor it toward Benjamin, or at least what I thought he might agree with, but I didn't want to rush into it.

"Go on," he said, his voice peaceful and slow. I swallowed.

"It's clear to me that Rosewood hates everyone in the Heights," I said. "She's made rules expelling any Sinisters from the Flats, and she's using any incident involving Sinisters as a way to change how people think about them. She's getting ready to make a move, and I'm worried that the people here won't survive it if we don't do something soon."

Benjamin brought his hands under his chin and nodded gently.

"I agree. Go on."

I explained what we had been doing—the videos—and why. I explained the importance of unity among the Sinisters. I mentioned how Benjamin had talked about it not being bad to be Sinisters and how, if that really was the case, we needed support from both sides of the fence for that to become a reality.

"What I'm saying," I continued, "is that there is a group of people in the Flats who are willing to protest on our behalf. But they want to know that we're on their side, too. At the end of the day, we're all just people trying to do our best to live our lives. I don't believe people want a war. This, this protest, could be a way to stop it from happening. It could change public opinion. It could show everyone that there's another way to move forward." I quickly looked around the room before returning my gaze to Benjamin. "We figured if anyone could help make that happen, it would be you."

All eyes shifted to Benjamin.

The entire time I was talking, his expression hadn't changed—it was the same, serene look that gave me the sense he either wasn't listening at all, or was listening very intently. I hoped it was the latter.

Without warning, he closed his eyes and drew in a long, slow, deep breath. As he exhaled, he pushed himself onto his feet. I looked around at the others, confused. I got up, too.

"I admire your optimism," Benjamin said as he stepped off of the rug toward the screen on the wall. "When we first met, I did not take you for an idealist." He didn't meet my eyes, and when he spoke, his tone had changed. "As a leader, I deal in people—emotions, psychology. Optimism leaves a crucial variable of the equation out—human nature.

"It doesn't matter whether a person is Noble or Sinister," he continued, "all are slaves to nature and habit. Nobles have despised Sinisters since the beginning of our city. A few videos aren't going to change that. Likewise, Sinisters will not come to love the Nobles based on the empty actions of a few, but they can come to love themselves."

My heart began to sink.

Benjamin started to walk toward the door.

"Are you familiar with how a ship works?" he said.

I didn't answer.

"To turn a large ship against the current is a fool's errand. Done hastily or improperly, it will capsize, but a skillful captain can maneuver with the waters. Do you understand what I mean?"

"It sounds like you're not going to help us," Alex said.

"The course of the Sinisters was set years ago," Benjamin said. "I would be a fool to try and change that. If we want any chance at freedom or equality, it will be by using the current to our advantage."

He opened the door to the hallway and held it there.

I stood in the middle of the rug, stunned.

"I wish you the best," Benjamin continued, "but I believe a better use of your efforts would be to help persuade the remaining Sinisters to join my cause. No other course of action will truly help the Sinisters rise from their current station. No other course of action leads to change."

Benjamin, with a soft smile plastered on his face, nodded gently toward the door, but I wasn't ready to move. He was an advocate for war—he had to reconsider. We had to make him reconsider. But before I could open my mouth, I felt a pressure on my arm.

"Thank you for your time," Trevor said, pulling me toward the door. The rest followed us out. Benjamin continued to stand inside his open door.

"But, of course," he said, "my door is always open should you choose to return." With a bland smile and a nod, he shut the door in our faces.

Now familiar footsteps reached my ears as Maggie approached.

"So, how did it go?"

"Not well," Trevor said with a crisp shake of his head, "not well at all."

35

After a few moments of stuttered disbelief, Maggie had stormed off and Trevor had followed, which left us standing in the hallway outside of Benjamin's door. There was no use staying there. Our job had just become much more difficult. To say I was frustrated was an understatement.

I started walking.

"And where exactly are we going now?" Daphne said. She did nothing to hide the disgruntlement in her voice. I kept my pace as she and Alex caught up.

"Well," I said, pausing as I pushed through a set of doors into another section of hallways, "since Benjamin isn't going to help us, we've got to talk to Brick."

"And Jonny," Alex chimed in.

"Yes," I said, "and Jonny." I began picking my way through the scattered sleeping bodies in the hallway toward the exit beyond.

I could hear Daphne sigh somewhere behind me.

"And you want to go now?"

"Is there any reason to wait?" I said, turning a corner. A slew of furious thoughts buzzed around my head like a swarm of angry bees. I couldn't believe Benjamin. How could Maggie and Trevor have been so blind? How could Benjamin be willing to sacrifice so many lives? What was he trying to do?

Daphne sped up and jumped in front of me, bringing me to an abrupt halt. Our eyes met. A fresh wave of frustration came easily.

Now she wanted to talk? We weren't in sync, and we both knew it. I wasn't happy, and I knew she wasn't happy, but at this point, it didn't really matter. We didn't have time for it to matter.

"They're probably still sleeping," she said. "Brick is for sure."

"Then, at least we know they'll be there when we arrive," I said as I sidestepped her and continued onward. A few more steps and a blast of cool air rushed in as I opened the door to the courtyard. Behind me, several people on the ground stirred. A few of them pulled their blankets tighter around themselves. I continued walking, making my way past tent after tent. I assumed Daphne and Alex were following, but I didn't look back.

A few moments later, Alex appeared by my side.

"I guess we didn't hear many of his sermons," Alex said, nearly jogging to keep pace. "Benjamin's, you know? Maybe that first one was the only day he talked about love."

We made our way out onto the street and turned left. Daphne stayed a half a step behind.

"Maybe," I said. "Part of me thinks this was his plan all along— build a following and then make a play against the Flats. The thing I can't figure out is how he expects to win." I looked at Alex.

He shrugged. I took a deep breath and blew it out slowly. I let go of some of my anger or, at least, attempted to.

"Regardless," I continued, "this isn't good. Benjamin's got a lot of pull, and most of the people here are ready to do something against the Flats. That's why we've got to act fast. I don't think we have much time before Benjamin or Rosewood make their move."

"I agree," Daphne said. She was still a step behind us. I didn't look back. She continued. "I don't know if Brick and Jonny are going to help. We need to be prepared if they say no."

An image of just the five of us walking up and down a street holding a sign flashed in my mind. Some protest. I forced the idea from my mind—I had no clue what we would do if Brick and Jonny didn't help.

"What do you think, Alex?" I said. "You think they'll help?"

As we passed through a gap in the buildings, a bright ray of light washed over us. I squinted one eye against it, but the warmth felt good.

"Depends," Alex said thoughtfully, holding his metal hand up over his eyes. "Are they more scared of Rosewood, or are they more scared of Benjamin."

We passed back into the shadows.

"That's a good question," Daphne said. "If I were them, I'd be worried about how the rest of the Sinisters would take it."

"I know they still have a bit of a following," I said, "but you really think there would be some major fallout, even for something small?"

Daphne increased her pace until she was level with me.

"If anyone sees Brick and Jonny put a showing of good faith with some Nobles, people they hate, they're going to lose credibility. Word's going to get out. Anyone that's left is going to go to Benjamin."

We came to a stop across the street from their building. Surprisingly, the two bodyguards from before were there and awake. Alex waved at them. They waved back.

"Well, we're about to find out," Alex said, continuing to smile and wave. "I'm optimistic."

"And you think that you can take on all of the Nobles with twenty percent?" Daphne said.

Brick leaned back in his chair, his voice still groggy from sleep. "People have done more with less."

"When?" Daphne said.

"History," Brick said, crossing his hands behind his head.

"That's not an answer," she said.

"But he's not wrong," Alex said. "It has happened before, sometime in history, right?"

Brick nodded vigorously and pointed at Alex.

Daphne shot Alex a dangerous look. I opened my mouth, but Daphne cut me off.

"Look," she said, turning back to Brick, "if Rosewood were to come tomorrow in full force, are you prepared?"

Brick met her eyes but didn't hold her gaze for long. He glanced over at Alex.

"No," he said with a shake of his head. "We keep losing people to Benj—" He paused and looked over at Jonny, then lowered his voice. "Jonny doesn't like it when I say his name. Gets him real angry." He brought his voice back up. "To you know who."

"Have you guys thought about joining forces with him?" Daphne asked.

"With him?" Brick said, nearly coming out of his seat. "Did you not just hear what I said? There are two major players left in the Heights, him and us, and we're not about to give up what control we've got." Brick settled back into his chair.

Daphne almost concealed a triumphant smirk.

"Look, Benj—" She paused and looked at Jonny. "You know who, he's going to make a move within a week. You heard the drones Rosewood sent out the other night, right?"

Brick nodded slowly.

"Those weren't to make a friendly announcement. She's going to make her move, too. Tell me I'm wrong."

Brick folded his arms and looked down his nose at her but said nothing. I looked over at Jonny, who was listening as intently as I'd ever seen him do.

"If joining forces isn't on the table," Daphne continued, "then you need time to come up with a plan. Rosewood has been working hard to get every Noble on her side. If enough Nobles protest, it will delay her timeline. And it might give you some leverage with people in the Flats, a foot in the door, so to speak."

Daphne sat back in her chair a little bit and watched.

I could see the wheels turning in Brick's mind. He glanced quickly over at Jonny, who looked over at Daphne.

A few more seconds passed in silence. Finally, Alex leaned forward in his chair.

"We all need a little help sometimes," he said. "No shame in that." He held up his arm. "I couldn't have done this by myself, but now," he gathered a pulse of energy in his hand but didn't shoot it. "Well, you get it."

Brick leaned forward in his chair, too, and uncrossed his arms. He looked over at Jonny again, then back and forth between all of us a few times before he spoke.

"So what you're saying," he said slowly, "is that Rosewood is gonna make a move on the Heights, and she's gonna do it soon. And the only chance we have to buy ourselves some time is to hold hands with some Nobles? What about, uh, you know who? You're saying he's going to make a move, too?"

"That's what I'm saying," I said. "We tried talking to him earlier, but he's unreasonable—he's going to get a lot of people killed." I paused and locked eyes with Brick. "Unless someone does something."

Daphne caught my eye and gave me an appreciative nod. Brick let out a dark chuckle.

"I think me and Jonny can think something up."

He leaned back in his chair again.

"So play nice with the Nobles, give you know who some payback, and buy ourselves some time. That's what's on the table?"

"That's what's on the table," I said.

Brick crossed his hands behind his head once more and looked over at Jonny, who nodded.

"When are we doing this thing?"

"Today," I said.

Brick eyed Jonny again before locking eyes with me.

"How many people do you need?"

36
***

It turned out that "all of his people" was an unrealistic request, but there looked to be about a hundred Sinisters in total milling about, some talking in small groups, some keeping to themselves. Several wore hoods or hats that obscured their faces. I didn't think it helped our vibe at all, but at least they were here. Maybe they just didn't want any of the Nobles watching to be able to see them. Or, more likely, their fellow Sinisters.

I honestly thought the Nobles had it easier—protesting violence for an "inferior" group had a charitable aspect to it. They could call it virtue. The people here could be seen as sell-outs, sympathizers, or traitors.

I figured we'd get a count at some point of how many Nobles protested on our behalf, but I couldn't help but wonder if the group in the Flats was more or less significant than what we had here. Would it be enough for others to take notice? Would it even make a difference? Did I dare to hope that when we got back to the events center, there would be a video of Kelly Straunton covering the whole thing?

I exhaled and looked around.

We stood on the rooftop of one of the tallest buildings in the Heights. It was Brick and Jonny's pride and joy—their crown jewel as they called it. The building was in reasonably good shape and filled with people. We had a clear view of the surrounding area. Buildings in differing stages of neglect and disrepair stretched almost as far as I could see. Most were missing bricks or windows in a few places, and some even had gaping holes that exposed the interior to the elements.

Off in the distance, I could make out the much shorter but well-maintained buildings of the Flats—no missing brick, no broken windows, and certainly no gaping holes.

What a difference such a short distance made.

"They say they're good to go," Alex said, his phone out. "As soon as our live stream starts, they'll start too."

"Good," I said. "Any idea on how many people they've got?" I looked over at him. Alex's fingers were moving quickly over his phone.

"He says he's got enough."

"Let's hope so," I mumbled, mostly to myself. I looked back over at Alex. He was no longer looking at his phone but instead appeared to be scanning the rooftop. He looked to the left, then slowly swiveled to the right, his eyes searching the crowd.

"Hey," I said, stepping over toward him, "who are you looking for?"

"Oh, uh, I actually don't know."

I raised an eyebrow in question. He leaned in.

"I've been thinking about 80001, you know, from the Sandbox?" I nodded, and he continued. "I just have a feeling, you know?"

"You think he's here?" I said.

"Maybe?" he shrugged. "Nah, I'm probably just being paranoid. I don't even know who he is or if he is actually a he. Maybe he's a she? I mean, she's a she? Maybe he's a they? Honestly, I don't know. But I do think the quicker we get this started, the better, just in case."

It was rare for Alex to be careful like this, and that worried me. I nodded, stepped back, and did a sweep of the area myself.

The noise level on the rooftop had started to increase, and not in a good way. It was clear they did not want to be here. Brick had guaranteed us thirty minutes of protest time. I wasn't sure whether the countdown had started once they had all arrived or once our protest began in earnest. Either way, it wasn't much time. I made my way back over to Zeno. His face was buried in a screen.

"Hey Zeno, how close are we?"

"I've got a relay set up over to Gina, and she'll use that to broadcast it out," Zeno said. "She's running tests on it to make sure it works. We're close, bro!"

"You better be close," Brick said, sidling up next to us, making his way through a small group of hooded Sinisters. "They're not a patient bunch."

He looked over his shoulder and yelled. "Quit your whining, and give us some space!" The noise died down ever so slightly, and the small group dispersed. Brick locked eyes with me. "This had better be worth it."

He lowered his voice and mumbled something I couldn't quite make out, but I thought I heard Tyrann's name and could only guess Brick was glad he wasn't around to see what was happening here.

Brick had been mostly unpleasant since people started gathering. It was a gamble for him, too, a big one, and I could tell—everyone could tell—that he was on edge. He stared out over the cityscape.

"You sure we shouldn't be in a building closer to the Flats? How's anyone of them Nobles gonna to see what we're doing?"

"Brick, my masonry-related man," Zeno said, holding up his screen and wiggling it. "Leave it to me. Two minutes and people are going to start seeing this thing—way more than if we were just standing at the fence."

Brick narrowed his eyes at Zeno but nodded all the same. He headed back into the group.

"Two minutes!" he yelled. "And you three, give them some space."

The three hooded figures shuffled off. I worried that some of the people here might not have the best of intentions. It wouldn't surprise me if a few of them tried to ruin the whole thing. I knew we couldn't expect perfection, but this needed to go as smoothly as possible.

"Bro," Zeno said, glancing up from his screen, "it's all good. We've got this." He nodded encouragingly and winked. It made me feel a little better.

Daphne came up next to us, looking as relaxed as I'd seen her in days. I'd seen several of our temporary protesters give her a wide berth as they meandered around up here. Clearly, she was enjoying it.

"Not a bad group," she said, looking around with a smirk. "It's really too bad Trevor isn't here. I think he'd fit in well."

"I disagree," Alex said. "He'd hate it. Haven't you spent any time with him?"

"I was joking," Daphne said.

"I wasn't. He would really hate it," Alex's eyes enlarged. "I mean, really hate it. Plus, he'll be with Maggie, and you know..."

"Bro was definitely excited to be hanging back," Zeno said with a smile. "Not sure if he and Maggie got things ironed out yet, though. She still looked pretty shook before I left."

"Either way," I said, "it'll be good to have him back at the events center. After talking with Benjamin, the more we know about what's going on there, the better."

"And he'll help with Gina," Zeno said with a shrug. "She likes him."

Zeno's phone dinged. He immediately pulled it out.

"Nice! We're ready!" he said. "Let me get into position." He took a few steps back until he was standing up against the small retaining wall that lined the roof. He held up his phone and squinted. Apparently satisfied, he nodded to himself, then called out. "You ready, Vic?"

"Almost," I said. A new group of Sinisters had formed nearby. I needed some space to operate. I looked around until, finally, I spotted him. "Brick!" I yelled. "Let's get started!"

He appeared out of the crowd and looked at me. I nodded. "Finally," he muttered. "All right, boys, you heard him. Let the protesting begin! Hold those signs up like you made them yourselves!" Without much excitement, thirty or so signs popped up in the crowd—big white ones with green letters. In our relatively short window of prep time after talking with Brick, we had headed back to the events center to strategize.

The green was supposed to symbolize our support for the Nobles —the same color the DNA scanners glowed upon recognition of their DNA. The design had been Trevor and Maggie's idea. I had been surprised that she was so eager to help. During those few short hours back at the events center, she had alternated between crying about Benjamin and throwing herself into our cause and then feeling guilty about not being there for Benjamin. It had been hard to watch.

"March!" Brick yelled. "Make it look good!"

I glanced quickly over at Alex, who gave one last cursory sweep of the rooftop and then shrugged. I glanced around the rooftop as well, but nothing was setting off any alarm bells for me.

"Captain V!" Zeno yelled. "Two more steps in, my man, and you're golden." He held up his phone, trying to frame me in for the shot.

Daphne and Alex melted into the crowd of protestors, but not before Alex gave me a thumbs up, and Daphne gave me what I could only assume was a "good luck" nod.

I followed Zeno's direction.

One, two.

He held up a hand for me to stop, then peered down at his phone. He smiled and gave me the thumbs up. I took a deep breath.

Zeno pointed at me, and the light on his phone started to blink.

Here we go.

"For those of you who haven't been here before, welcome to the Heights." I held out my arms and let them take in the scene. Zeno panned around for a few seconds before returning to me. "The people here aren't so different from people in the Flats. If you can read the signs behind me, you'll see what I mean." I hoped they could read what was on the signs.

I looked over my shoulder to check, but it wasn't the signs that caught my eye. Three protestors had broken away from the main group and were gravitating toward me. This wasn't a good sign. I quickly tried to locate Alex in the crowd, but no luck.

I turned back to the camera to see Zeno attempting to wave the three protestors out of the shot. I continued and started walking. Zeno followed with the camera, albeit a half a second late.

"If you can believe that all Sinisters aren't evil or bad or broken, then you can believe that there are some people here that believe the same about you."

I continued walking, but I was running out of room. The rooftop was only so big. Zeno was now gesticulating wildly behind the camera. I didn't know what was about to happen, but I knew it wasn't good. I had so much more I wanted to say, but I didn't have the time. The people in the Sandbox—anyone who was watching— needed to hear what I had to say before I no longer had the opportunity.

"Over a hundred people have joined me on the rooftop today to show our support—to send a message that we don't want war, that there is a better way, and that better way is only achieved by working together."

Zeno had stopped waving, and I had stopped walking.

It was like a shadow passing over on a sunny day—I felt them before I saw them. Their collective presence loomed behind me. I stared at the camera. Behind it, fear was written on Zeno's face. Strangely, I wasn't afraid. It wasn't fear I felt. It was barely intrigue.

Overwhelmingly, it was disappointment.

This was a last-ditch effort. This was all we had left to give—the only play we could make—and it was over. Our cards were spent, and it didn't matter. I sighed. It was the beginning of the end, and it had been inevitable from the start.

Zeno kept the camera rolling. I turned to face the end.

Before me stood three hooded figures of varying sizes—one of them being absolutely huge. As one, they flipped their hoods back, revealing one black-haired girl, one bald man, and one ebony-skinned behemoth. It was like staring into the eyes of a ghost—three ghosts. Dax, Tyrann Kane, and Printh stood in front of me, very not dead.

"I hope you don't mind, Mr. Wells, but we've come to commandeer your broadcast."

My muddled emotions dissolved into confusion.

"Wha, what are—how?" I said. "You're supposed to be dead."

"A very worthwhile illusion, I assure you," Tyrann said. Dax shrugged. Printh stared past me, straight at Zeno. "Now, if you'll excuse me," he continued, "you've laid my groundwork brilliantly. I promise we'll catch up later."

He made to step around me, but I blocked him.

"No," I said, still processing what was playing out in front of me. He was alive? They were alive? And my broadcast—my chance to get some Nobles on our side—this, this was what they were watching? Tyrann Kane returning from the dead. "Cut it, Zeno!" I said.

"Belay that order, Mr. Zeno," Tyrann said quickly, authoritatively, his voice growing louder as he spoke. "I have a message for everyone in the Sandbox. It is I, Tyrann Kane, User80001!"

He held his arms out wide.

Zeno gasped.

All around me, the protesting ground to a halt.

Muttering had broken out. Brick let out a whoop.

"See! I knew he wasn't dead!"

"Cut it, Zeno!" I said. "He's not on our side. He believes Rosewood as much as anyone! Cut it!"

Printh unsheathed a saber, electrified it, and took a few swift steps toward Zeno.

"Sorry, bro!" he said, holding one hand up while maintaining the camera with his other.

"Mr. Wells, Mr. Wells," Tyrann said, "carrier of TꞮꞮD—I've enjoyed our adventures together. Who knew we'd share this one as well?" He stared straight into Zeno's camera. "And me, believe the words of Victoria Rosewood?" He spat her name. "That old wench and her DNA superiority…. Mr. Wells here has done an admirable job explaining that not all Sinisters are of an evil nature, but you Nobles are not without your stains—most worse than what you think we carry. Your oppression, your high-mindedness, your arrogance—it is time for these things to end."

He surveyed the group of now silent protestors. By this time, Alex and Daphne had made their way over to my side.

"Part of me couldn't believe they were gone," she muttered. "I guess I was right. And so were you." She nudged Alex. "You did say you thought he was from the Heights."

"I did say that!" Alex said. "And 80001 is a they! I bet all three of them posted under the same account!" Alex smiled. "Man, I am really good at this."

Tyrann cast a look back at us before continuing.

"Do you really believe," Tyrann continued, staring hard at the camera, "that these protestors behind me are aligned with you? Do you think for a moment that they believe the signs they hold aloft?" He chuckled. "Of course not. I don't. But one thing I do know is that they will follow me." He raised his voice. "Isn't that right?"

As if they had been waiting for this moment all along, the

protesters erupted in cheers. As they yelled and clapped, another figure emerged from the group, this one dressed entirely in black, with his facial features blurred.

He stepped out and made a beeline for Tyrann. Like someone had pushed the mute button, the cheers died out.

The Bounty Hunter was here.

37

I could only stare as my stomach dropped.

Where had he come from? Why now?

"Well, well," Tyrann said, spinning in place to face Kratos as he approached. "This is unexpected—a visit from the Bounty—"

"You all need to leave," Kratos rasped, cutting him off.

"Leave?" Tyrann said. "Really? Isn't it you who is a little out of their place?"

"It's not safe," Kratos said, coming to a halt a few feet out of Tyrann's reach.

I looked at Zeno—he was still recording and transmitting everything. Everyone in the Sandbox was watching this right now.

"Of course, it isn't safe," Tyrann said. "Rosewood is about to pull all the Nobles into a full-scale war with the Sinisters!" He turned around. "But we won't let them take us!" Tyrann yelled amid new cheers.

"We need to leave," Kratos barked again. "Now!"

Kratos stood, but not to his full height. His posture was bent, almost like he was injured or, at the very least, weak. Daphne pulled

Alex to the side. I caught her eye and knew she was trying to get into a more tactical position should this go sideways.

My eyes snapped back to Tyrann as he adjusted his weight to his back foot and folded his arms.

He began to smile. He opened his mouth to speak, but I cut him off.

"We should listen to him," I said.

"And why, pray tell, should we do that, Mr. Wells?" Tyrann said.

"Because the last time he showed up, he saved my life," I said.

"The Bounty Hunter saved your life?" he said with a scoff. "Perhaps you're not the man I thought you were."

The air was taut with tension.

"You're right," I said, fighting to keep my composure. "I'm not the man you think I am. I don't have T11D. I never have. Nobles, Sinisters, the DNA scans—it's all a lie. The difference between you and me is that you want to believe it. You're just like the people in the Flats—it's more convenient for you to believe the lie than it is for you to accept the truth."

Silence reigned as I finished. A slight breeze swirled around the rooftop, but everyone seemed to be holding their breath.

People didn't talk to Tyrann Kane that way. No one dared cross him. But the time had come—reality needed to be made known.

Tyrann looked at me, smiled, then looked down and casually picked at his fingernails.

"And tell me, Mr. Wells, what is this truth?" he said slowly. I glanced at the camera. Maybe I'd get my moment after all.

"That there's no such thing as Nobles and Sinisters," I said. "We're all just people. We make our own choices. Our DNA doesn't matter. It's what we think, what we do, and how we act that matters. That's the truth."

Tyrann continued to work at his fingernails as his smile deepened across his face. Printh kept her saber pointed at Zeno, and Dax maintained his spot a few feet behind Tyrann. He caught my eye and nodded. Was that approval?

"We have to leave!" Kratos said, breaking the silence. "Now!"

"No, Mr. Bounty Hunter," Tyrann said. "As Mr. Wells has told us, we can do whatever we want. We all have our own decisions to make, and I for one—"

A loud rumbling shook the building, and I nearly lost my footing. Immediately, another rumble sounded, accompanied by the scream of tortured metal. Muttering broke out, but we all knew what it meant. Printh lowered her saber. Kratos staggered a few more steps forward.

"Evacuate, now!" But we were too late.

The building let loose another groan and began to sway, sending dozens of people to their hands and knees. Screams rang through the air from both the rooftop and the floors below us.

The building let out an almighty groan followed by a final, fatal crack that pierced the air like a gunshot.

And then we started to fall.

38

—————

The world moved in slow motion.

The whole rooftop scene had become a still frame. Faces were frozen in terror, and people were in various stages of falling, but gravity hadn't yet claimed its deadly hold. I cast my eyes about, slowly, too slowly, locating Daphne and Alex, who were standing next to one another, and then Zeno, who was closer to the edge than anyone else.

Kratos was frozen mid-stride, already running straight toward him. Zeno had started to fall back, his arms up over his head, his momentum about to send him backward over the edge. The blue light on his camera was still on, broadcasting everything to the Sandbox.

Time sped back up.

I moved instinctively. I saw the terror in Daphne's eyes as she, too, began to slide.

I had to get to her.

I pressed the buttons on my gloves, shooting a concentrated spray where I needed to go, and leapt. Bodies slid across the rooftop beneath me, washed away in gravity's current, but I kept my eyes focused on Daphne and Alex.

My foot made contact with the invisible beads in the air, and I leapt again, spraying as I did so.

Spray, land, leap, spray.

Things were moving too fast, and they were so far away. Doubt grabbed a foothold in my mind. Could I even make it in time?

No, and you can save more people if you leave them.

The thought stung my mind. How could I leave them? How could I do this without them?

I watched them as they slid.

I took in the dozens of strangers sliding around me, too. I fought against myself, against my wants. What was right?

But that was all the time I had to think.

The beads gave out, and I fell to the rooftop below. A sliding protestor took out my legs before I could gain a foothold, and I landed hard on my back on the rooftop, the air momentarily forced from my lungs.

And then I, too, was sliding.

In a matter of moments, I nearly flew the short distance to the small retaining wall at the edge of the roof where my feet made contact. I stood there on the short wall, briefly, as the building continued to fall, one of the few people not already in the air.

"Victor!"

Daphne's voice pierced the sky, and my eyes shot to the source.

I watched in horror as both Daphne and Alex passed over the ledge and began their free fall. Their screams chilled my bones.

I leapt toward them.

The building was no longer under my feet—there was only air, open air, that ended in pavement fifty stories below.

I willed myself to move closer, to fly to them, but even with my leap, I was nowhere near close enough. And theirs weren't the only bodies that had tumbled over the edge. I shot a burst of spray that hit me hard in the side, trying to push myself closer to them. I tried again. I willed my body towards them, but they were still so far.

The air rushing past me seemed to turn cold as realization hit me. This was their end. Even with my gloves, I could do nothing.

Tears streamed from my eyes from more than just the wind. I lost sight of Daphne and Alex and turned my vision to the ground below. I couldn't save them. I could save a few strangers, but it would only be temporary—Rosewood would see to their end. Or I could just let it all end here. The pain, the running, the fighting—it could all be done in a matter of moments if I let it. I closed my eyes.

When I opened them, the remaining sky below me had turned gray—so much so that I couldn't see the ground. It was odd—I'd never seen the air do something like that before. I watched the bodies in the air below me disappear into the gray. Soon, that would be me.

I briefly wondered what it could be before I plunged into it myself.

Immediately, I felt myself slow, like being swallowed up by a cushion. All around me, other bodies did the same, accompanied by surprised gasps and screams that were cut off unnaturally quick. The gray air turned a dark charcoal, and I felt myself slip through it, dropping a short distance until I hit another wall of gray-tinted air.

And another.

And then another.

I looked around as I continued to slow, only to find Kratos down on the ground, his arms pointed up in the air, the gray air becoming thicker with each passing second, and my descent slowing as I passed through each subsequent layer.

It was clearly a stronger version of the spray than I was using, and the fact that he could throw big sheets of it out was beyond incredible. Kratos had saved me. Again.

Tears came to my eyes again as realization hit me—warm this time —Alex and Daphne were safe, too. All was not lost.

The air was so thick with beads that it took several minutes to find Alex and Daphne. Both were unharmed, and Alex appeared unfazed. Daphne, I could tell, was shaken up.

We exchanged an awkward hug that ended far too soon. I took a step back, and she met my eyes briefly.

"I thought that was going to be the end," she said quietly, her gaze on the ground.

I looked around.

The scene was mayhem. While Kratos had been able to save us, the building had still fallen, and it had been full of people.

Debris was everywhere—broken bricks and belongings alike covered the ground in every direction. People scattered and scrambled, screaming and sobbing as they stumbled away.

But those were the lucky people, the survivors. One glance around was almost more than I could take.

"I thought it was the end, too," I said. "For all of us."

I relived those brief moments of despair. Daphne met my eyes again. I got the sense she had felt somewhat like I had. It was almost as if an understanding passed between us.

"I wasn't too worried," Alex said with a shrug. "Kratos was there. I knew we'd be fine."

I broke eye contact with Daphne.

"Fine's a generous way of putting it," I said. "Speaking of Kratos and Zeno..." I paused and looked around. "Where are they?"

Aside from the debris and fleeing people, the residual gray beads from Kratos's spray cast a haze over the whole scene that made everything look murky at best. It was like staring into a dense fog—they could be ten feet away or a hundred. It all looked the same.

"I don't know," Daphne said, looking around as well. "I'm sure they'll turn up. But more importantly, why did that building come down?" She looked at me, her eyes slightly wider than normal. "And what about Tyrann and Dax and Printh? And how about Kratos showing up again, just in time to save us?"

I eyed her as she fidgeted and folded her arms. She was off. That fall had scared her, and she wasn't someone who was used to being scared.

A small group of people ran past us. Daphne flinched but recovered quickly. As quickly as the people had appeared, they were gone. No one wanted to stay here, and I knew where they were headed.

Benjamin.

"I have questions, too," I said, eyeing her as she continued looking around. I hadn't had time to process everything—Kratos showing up again, the fact that Tyrann Kane was alive. "I still don't know about Kratos, but it kind of makes sense that Tyrann is alive, right?" I traded glances with them. "I mean, Brick and Jonny got a lot of anonymous help."

"Like those unconscious guys who showed up at their place!" Alex said, looking at me and Daphne in turn. "Tyrann!"

"Or probably Tyrann via Dax," I said, keeping my eye on Daphne.

"Definitely via Dax," Daphne said with a nod. She was starting to regain her composure. I gave her a tight smile.

"I don't think all of this was a coincidence," I said. "The building falling and Kratos showing up—I don't think Tyrann knew it was going to happen, but Kratos did—"

"Of course, he knew," Alex said. "He's still plugged into things even if people think he isn't. And now he's out there, in the wind once again." Alex looked out into the haze.

Another small group of people ran by us. Daphne didn't flinch this time. I couldn't imagine there were many people left in the vicinity at this point. I could still hear sobs and the occasional grief-ridden scream break through the beads, but most of the movement around us had stopped.

"How poetic," Daphne said, looking at Alex.

"What can I say," he said. "I am a man of great depth."

Daphne rolled her eyes. I felt some relief. She was back.

"And with your great depth," I said, "we need to find Kratos. Someone figured out where and when we were going to be here and made sure the building would go down while we were on it. If Kratos knew where we were going to be, he probably also knows the person responsible for ratting us out."

"So, was this your plan, Mr. Wells?"

Tyrann's disembodied words floated through the haze in a hauntingly playful tone. I turned toward the sound just as Tyrann appeared, strutting through the haze toward us with Dax and Printh in tow. I scoffed.

"You think this was my plan?" I said.

"Lie to the Nobles, then lie to me on camera—a truly masterful move. Although, I don't believe *I* would have brought down the building." He looked around at all the destruction and wrinkled his nose. "Though, I suppose it is quite a statement."

"I didn't do this, Tyrann," I said, letting my frustration and anger show through. "But I wouldn't be surprised if you did."

Tyrann let out a mirthful laugh.

"Me? You think I would bring down a building, especially one of the last truly habitable buildings in the Heights, killing many of my own people in the process? And you think that I'd ensure that I was on top of the building when it came down? No." He shook his head as he smiled at me. "This was not me. And for similar reasons, I suppose it makes sense that this real estate catastrophe was not by your design, either. Though you do have those gloves." His eyes skirted to my hands.

I sighed and shook my head.

A somber expression came over his face. "If not for the Bounty

Hunter, our stories would have ended far too soon. At least mine would have."

"Are you saying that you're grateful for the Bounty Hunter?" I said.

"Even people you despise have their moments of usefulness," Tyrann replied. "The more important point, or question rather, Mr. Wells, is this—what comes next?"

Before I could formulate an answer, Brick and Jonny appeared at Tyrann's side, apparently in mid-conversation.

"... tell you one thing," Brick was saying. "There aren't many places left for..." His sentence trailed off as we all came into view. "Boss, you survived again! You're back!" He came to a stop as Jonny appeared out of the haze behind him.

"Yes," Tyrann said, suddenly becoming stern, "and it's a good thing I am back. In spite of my very generous efforts, you've managed to lose a majority of the buildings I once controlled."

"I, uh, well, we... they all collapsed," Brick stuttered. "I, we did the best we could."

"Your best?" Tyrann let out a laugh. "I didn't know you had developed a sense of humor in my absence." His voice instantly became sharp and cold, and his words came quick. "Our people have moved in with an enemy, our many occupancies have been all but destroyed, and any victories you enjoyed recently were at my anonymous hands. Do you truly think your efforts are worthy of praise?"

Brick opened his mouth, but Daphne spoke first.

"Give it a rest," Daphne said, her expression more annoyed than fierce. "You chose to leave everything to these Neanderthals. That's on you. Besides, we all want the same thing, right?"

Everyone looked to Tyrann in the silence that followed. He allowed himself a smile.

"I suppose you're right. Go on, Miss Pendleton."

I watched Brick and Jonny both relax at the subject change. They slowly stepped back until they had nearly melted into the grayness.

"Okay, we all want Rosewood gone," Daphne said. "Our broadcast was an attempt to delay whatever Rosewood has planned, but I can't imagine that went over well." She gestured to what remained of the building and glared at Tyrann. He only smiled.

"And?" he said.

"And that means Rosewood's timeline isn't going to change," I said. "So we need to be ready. We need an army, and we need it now."

Tyrann locked eyes with me.

"And you believe I'm the one to help you create your army?"

"Do you have any people at your disposal?" Daphne said.

Tyrann looked down his nose at Brick.

"Not as many as I'd like. But that can change easily enough."

"I don't know about that," Alex said. "You're going to have to win them all back from Benjamin, and good luck. I mean, you both have charisma, but he's different. People love that guy."

Tyrann turned to Alex and surveyed him for a moment.

"Mr. Trabue, is it? Something in you has changed since the last time we interacted." He paused and looked Alex up and down, his eyes coming to rest on his bionic hand. "Ah, I see. Trauma can be such a catalyst."

Instantly, I felt a defensive anger surge inside me. Tyrann loved toying with people, but Alex had it under control.

He held up his hand and called a few sparks to his fingertips while looking Tyrann up and down.

"Mmhmm. Okay, well, you look older than last time—nothing big, just a couple of extra wrinkles here and there. And if it were me, I don't know if I'd choose to be bald, you know?" Alex looked around and shrugged. Tyrann began to smile as Alex finished up. "It's just not for everyone."

I wanted to laugh, but I was shocked. Never before had I heard anyone be so frank with someone so feared.

Tyrann chuckled, and the tension in the air began to dissipate.

"Only so many perfect heads exist. Hair covers the rest of them."

Alex shrugged in response. "That's one opinion."

An unsure silence followed, which Daphne finally broke.

"We were talking about Benjamin?"

"Yes, of course, Miss Pendleton. Benjamin." Tyrann nodded for her to proceed, but something in my mind had just clicked. I held up my hand to stop her.

"Sorry, Daphne. Brick, if everyone from this building went to the events center, how many people does that leave who aren't going to Benjamin? You said you still had twenty percent of the Heights on your side?"

Brick fidgeted and looked at the ground. He made to take a half step back, but one look from Tyrann and he stayed where he was.

"I, uh," he scratched the back of his head, "may have exaggerated the numbers before." Daphne threw a dagger-filled look his way. "You would have done the same!" he said. Then, he took a deep breath, shook his head and swallowed. "This was it. This was the last building. There'll be a few people here and there, but, well... Benjamin will have them all."

I ran through everything in my head. Most of the population of the Heights would be with Benjamin. Thousands of people. And Benjamin wanted to crush the Nobles. Was this his way of consolidating power? Was this his way of bringing everyone together so he could take the fight to the Flats?

I looked at Alex and Daphne. "All of the people are going to be with Benjamin."

Alex slapped me on the shoulder and winked. "I knew you'd get there."

"Elaborate," Tyrann said, a quiet command.

"It's simple," I said. "If you didn't bring the building down, and we didn't bring it down, and it didn't fall down on its own, then the only people who have a motive here are—"

"Benjamin and Rosewood," Dax said with a nod.

"So it's either a power play by Benjamin or part of Rosewood's plan," Daphne said.

I nodded.

"Then we need to go to the events center," Tyrann said. "We need to address our people."

"I agree," I said, though I wasn't crazy about the way he said it.

A smile took hold of Tyrann's face.

"Dax, Printh," he said, "I think we're about to have some fun. This Benjamin needs a challenger."

I hated to agree with him, but Benjamin was not on our side, especially if it was him who had taken down the building. Tyrann wasn't necessarily on our side either, but I could work with Tyrann. Benjamin was unpredictable. Well, so was Tyrann, but at least we were familiar with his brand of unpredictability.

"The sooner, the better," I said. "Tyrann, do you still think people are loyal to you?"

"Or at least afraid of you?" Daphne said.

Tyrann looked as if we were questioning his ability to walk.

"I believe you know the answer to that, Miss Pendleton."

With a wave, Tyrann motioned for Dax and Printh to follow. As Dax walked past me, he patted my shoulder and winked, then nodded to Daphne. Her and Alex both started to move.

I stayed put. I knew we needed to go with them—leaving Tyrann unsupervised was a bad idea—but we were forgetting about Zeno and Kratos. We needed to find them, too.

I looked at the back of Tyrann's head as he walked, then back over into the chaos of debris behind me. I made a decision.

"Alex, Daphne," I said.

They both stopped, and I motioned to them. They came to meet me.

"What's up?" Alex said, dropping his voice. "Secret plan against

Tyrann?" He looked back and forth between Daphne and me, a smile on his face.

"No," I said. His smile fell. "We need to find Kratos and—"

"I told you," Alex cut in, "he's in the wind."

"You're probably right," I said, "but Zeno isn't. And I have a feeling we're going to need his help at the events center."

They both nodded.

"So, here's what I want to do. Daphne," I said, turning to her, "I know you'll keep an eye on Tyrann, and you have a good relationship with Dax and Printh." She scoffed and wrinkled her nose. I sighed. "Okay, you have a good relationship with Dax. And you have a history with Printh, right?"

"Right," she said.

"I know you won't let them pull anything, so you go with them to the events center." I turned to Alex. "We are going to search for Zeno. If we find Kratos too, that'll be a bonus." I turned back to Daphne. "If you can stall Tyrann from doing anything crazy, that'd be great, too. Deal?"

Daphne stared at me. Her look was different from before, and I couldn't quite place it. She started to say something but then switched to a single word.

"Deal."

With nothing more than a nod, she jogged off to catch up with Tyrann and the rest. I wasn't sure what made me do it—maybe it was the fact that Tyrann was a dangerous person, or maybe it was the fact that we had all almost plummeted to our deaths, but I called out after her.

"Daphne!"

"What?"

"I'm glad you're okay," I said.

There was a brief pause, and her posture softened. Her shoulders slumped ever so slightly, and the edge left her voice.

"You too."

Then she was gone through the haze.

Alex had a dumb smile on his face.

"You ready?" I said.

He cleared his throat and nodded, exchanging his smile for something slightly more serious.

"Let's go find them."

39

———————

"Zeno!" I yelled.

It was hard to see between Kratos's spray and all of the dust in the air. We had encountered a grand total of zero people so far. It wasn't surprising considering the mad dash to Benjamin we had witnessed earlier, but I had expected to run into someone we could talk to. It made our search that much harder.

"Zeno!" I yelled again.

"Kratos!" Alex yelled.

I gave him a look.

"What?" Alex said. "'Bounty Hunter' takes too long to say. And besides, there's no one here."

At that moment, I felt a gust of air flow past my head. It was familiar, and not in a good way. I searched for the source, but whatever it was, it was gone.

"Did you feel that?" I said.

"Yeah," Alex said slowly.

"Drone?" I said.

"Maybe. Or a really big bird?" Alex said, looking up, while simultaneously pulling up the sleeve on his metal arm.

Brief flashes of our time spent in the forest came to mind.

"Yeah," I said. "Let's hope. Come on."

I continued to pick my way through the debris, a little more on edge than before. Alex followed. Drones were the last thing we needed. Although, it wouldn't surprise me if Rosewood had drones doing reconnaissance down here on a regular basis.

"Zeno!" I yelled again.

I stepped around the remnants of an old TV and sofa that had spilled out of the building. I stopped to listen. I didn't hear any drones, but as I looked around, the unnatural quiet made sense. Kratos's spray did a great job dampening any ambient noise.

"Kraaaaaaatoooooos!" Alex yelled, finishing with a huge gasp of air.

"I don't think yelling is going to help us," I said, motioning to the gray beads in the air. "I bet the sound doesn't travel more than twenty feet."

"Oh," Alex said, sucking in another breath and then letting the air fall out of his mouth. "Right."

"But they can't have gone far," I said.

"I agree," Alex said. "Zeno is not in that good of shape."

"And neither is Kratos," I mumbled to myself.

We widened our search as we made our way around the building. Every moment felt like an eternity. We needed to get back to the events center. There was no telling what Tyrann would do. Or what Benjamin would do. Daphne was good, but she would need backup at some point.

Alex yelled out for Zeno and Kratos every minute or so. I didn't stop him. The haze did seem to be dissipating, though. We spread out a little bit and continued our search.

"Zeno!" I yelled. I stopped in my tracks and looked around.

Nothing but rubble and gray air. We needed to find Zeno, but we couldn't search forever. And who knew what Benjamin would do when all of the newcomers showed up?

"Victor!" Alex yelled. "Victor! Hurry!"

There was panic in his voice.

I sprinted over to find him crouched next to a particularly large pile of bricks and debris lying on top of a large, metal door. The door itself looked to be propped up a little off the ground, but around the base of it was filled with debris.

Underneath it all, a muffled cry met my ears. Alex looked up at me, his eyes wide.

There was someone under there, and they had just been abandoned.

"It's okay," Alex said. "We're going to help you, okay?"

The whimpering stopped.

"Help," the voice said.

It sounded so weak, so feeble.

"I think it's a kid," Alex said, looking at me, his expression as serious as I'd ever seen. "She sounds hurt." He turned back to the pile. "We're going to get you out of there, okay?"

Alex moved closer and started removing brick after brick. I hated myself for thinking it, but I couldn't stop the thought from entering my head.

We didn't have time for this. Either we needed to find Zeno and Kratos in the next few minutes, or we needed to head back to the events center.

But how could we leave a kid in all of this?

I crouched down next to Alex and started to toss bricks out of the way, too.

"Just get the stuff off the top," he said. "We don't want the door to fall on top of her if we take from the sides."

"Good call," I said, grabbing an armful of bricks.

A soft whimper sounded, weaker than before. Alex and I shared a look.

"You're doing great," he said, through heavy breaths. "We'll have you out in just a minute, okay?"

But there was no answer. We worked faster.

She had to be scared. She definitely could be hurt. I tossed brick after brick aside. We had to hurry.

"Help," the voice said again. It was softer than before, but at least she wasn't unconscious or worse.

"Hold on!" Alex said, hoisting a large chunk of cement off of the door. The door itself was huge—made of metal and at least eight feet tall and three inches thick. If it hadn't been so sturdy, there's no way it would have held all the weight that was on it.

We made quick work of it, leaving only the smaller pieces of debris before we each moved to a side.

"You ready?" I said, crouching down and digging my fingers underneath the edge.

Alex nodded and did the same.

"One, two, three!" I grunted as we pulled the door up with all our might.

The door was far heavier than I expected, and we didn't have it anywhere near high enough for someone to climb out.

"I'm slipping!" Alex grunted.

I shifted my hands ever so slightly and then let go with one. Alex gasped as the door dropped an inch, but it quickly stopped as the constant spray from my free hand slowed its progress.

"Thanks," Alex said as he adjusted his grip. "I almost lost it."

I sprayed for another couple of seconds. "You ready?"

Alex nodded, hunched over, and raised his voice. "We're going to lift the door up so you can climb out, okay? But wait for us to tell you when!"

I grabbed hold with both hands once more. I looked at Alex, who nodded.

"And, now!" Alex said.

In unison, we heaved the door up. The remainder of the debris slid off of it as the door went completely vertical. I shot a few bursts of spray to stabilize it so it wouldn't come back down onto us as we let go of it. Underneath the door, I could see a small depression, almost like a crater in a pile of bricks and rubble.

I looked down into the shadows but couldn't see much—it just looked like more bricks and maybe a small piece of black furniture.

"Hello!" Alex said. "Are you okay down there?"

No answer.

I took a step down.

"Are you okay?" I said, still not seeing anything. I looked around. Was I missing something? I searched again. Bricks, a small, black coffee table without legs, but no little girl. "There's no one here." I turned back around. "You heard her, right?" I said.

Alex peered into the depression, a look of confusion on his face.

"Definitely but—whoa, what is that?"

A gust of wind hit me in the face, and the small piece of black furniture lit up and began to float. A bright light beamed over Alex, and a mechanical voice spoke.

"Identity verified. Alex Trabue."

Adrenaline dumped into my veins. I ducked as it flew at me.

"Shoot it!" I yelled.

Alex let loose a shot from his arm that went wide and smashed into the door, the door which I was under. It began to teeter, turning the remaining invisible beads gray.

It started to fall.

I threw up a wall of spray as fast as I could and dove for freedom.

The door came crashing down, hitting my shield of beads and

careening off to the side. The drone sped off into the air above us but didn't leave.

Alex let off a series of rapid-fire blasts across the sky, but most of them were absorbed in the gray mist above.

"Stay still you—"

Alex closed one eye and let off another blast. The drone dodged it. "Come on!" Alex lowered his arm as it continued to taunt us from thirty feet in the air.

"What's it doing?" I said, but the moment I spoke, a realization hit me.

The drone wanted to ID me as well.

"Uh, Victor," Alex said. "Any plans here?" He shot off another blast that missed wide.

I pushed myself to my feet, trying to formulate a plan as I wiped the debris from my forearms and legs.

The drone was too high for my spray and too quick for Alex's blasts.

"Alex," I yelled, "stop shooting at it. We need to let it get close to me!"

Alex looked back. "What? Why?"

"It wants to scan me," I said, eyeing the drone. "But it can't do it from up there. If we let it get close, we can bring it down." At least, I hoped.

Alex lowered his arm, and the drone began to circle us. I assumed it was planning out its attack.

I looked around for something I could grab—a pole or something to hit the drone with, but the closest thing was a brick.

Alex could blast it, provided he didn't hit me in the process.

"Alex," I said, "when it gets close, just when its scanning light turns on, I'm going to dive out of the way and you're going to shoot it, okay?"

"Okay," he said, adjusting his stance. The drone started to dive. I got ready, trying to position myself to give Alex the best shot, but instead, Zeno's voice rang out through the haze.

"We got you, bro!"

I turned to see him running toward us, carrying a stunner. Behind him, black cloak and all, ran Kratos.

Kratos reached into his jacket and pulled out a small gray sphere, which he threw with incredible force. The sphere adjusted its own flight to intercept the drone. Just before impact, the ball exploded, sending a perfectly spherical group of his gray beads around the drone, effectively locking it in place.

"Care to lend a hand, my man?" Zeno said, arriving at Alex's side. He raised his stunner and immediately began to unload. Blast after blast erupted from his gun, each one directed toward the imprisoned drone. Alex joined in, and a moment later, sparks flew and the drone's rotors ground to a halt. It began to fall out of the sky, its progress slowed by the cocoon of beads around it until it touched down gently on the ground.

Zeno holstered his stunner, and Alex lowered his arm as we all gathered around the short-circuited remains of the once-hostile machine.

"That's the third one we've seen," Zeno said.

Kratos walked up without saying a word and stepped on the drone. Hard. I eyed Kratos, but he didn't meet my gaze. Instead, he looked up to the sky where the building used to be.

"Come on, bro! I need one alive!" Zeno said, bending down to pick up the broken pieces.

"Where have you guys been?" I said. "We've been looking for you —Tyrann is heading back to the events center, and we need to get back there. Fast."

"We've been taking out these drones, bro."

Kratos continued to stare at where the building used to be.

"I think they're our answer to why the building went down."

"And you said you've seen three of these so far?" I said.

Alex walked over to Kratos.

"Yeah, they look like Rosewood's drones," Zeno said, letting the mangled elements slide out of his fingertips. He stood back up. "Where'd you find this one?"

"Under that," I said, pointing to the oversized door. "It sounded like a little girl, then it flew out and scanned Alex. It was trying to get to me when you guys showed up."

"Mimicking a little girl?" Zeno said. "Bro, that's cold, especially for a robot."

"You really think they're Rosewood's?" I said.

"I don't know anyone around here who would have them," Zeno said. "And the tech on them is pretty consistent with what Rosewood's been using. And these drones definitely have the ability to plant explosives or weaken support beams." He shrugged. "I'd put money on it."

"If that's true," I said, "then Rosewood has been systematically demolishing buildings here. She never does something without a purpose."

"What about Benjamin?" Alex said, breaking the silence. "Daphne *did* see one of his guys talking to a drone a few days back."

"Tough to say for sure," Zeno said. "I guess it could be Benjamin, but I don't know where he'd get all of the tech. These things cost money, or at least the skill to build them yourself. And well, I'm here, not there."

He made a good point. Besides Ivy, I hadn't met anyone who I thought could even attempt to build an advanced, well-functioning drone like this.

"What about Kratos? What does he think?" I glanced over at him. Kratos continued to stare at the sky, focusing on something none of the rest of us could see. Zeno sighed.

"I don't know, bro." He lowered his voice. "He's not in great shape

—hasn't said more than a few words to me since he saved my life. Almost like he can't talk in full sentences. You can tell he's thinking—you can tell he knows something, but it's like he can't get it out. To be fair, though, bro still has skills. Did you see him dive after me when the building was going down? It was a trip... for a second, I'm falling off a building, and then boom! Kratos grabs hold of me, and we float down to safety. And I was still broadcasting! I turned it off after I got to the ground, but everyone saw it. Anyways..."

He shook his head. "I think he'll be fine—he just needs time. And I hope we can give it to him." He looked at the remnants of the building. "But even without Kratos's help, I'm thinking we can say that the drones had something to do with the buildings coming down. I mean, they're capable, right? Weaken the right supports at the same time and—" he made an explosion gesture with his hands.

My phone buzzed. It was from Daphne.

```
It's getting crazy here. Can't find Benjamin
anywhere. I'm stalling Tyrann, but it won't
last long. Verbal fights are breaking out.
Not sure how long until things escalate.
```

"What's that?" Zeno asked.

"Daphne," I said, shoving my phone back in my pocket. "We need to get back to the events center. And fast." I looked over at Alex, who had moved over next to Kratos. "We need to go."

Like he was breaking from a trance, Kratos's head snapped around. "NO!" he yelled.

Alex jumped in surprise and stumbled on a small pile of bricks.

"Easy, my man, easy," Zeno said, taking a step back and eyeing him. "We've got to go help Daphne, and it sounds like things are heating up. Almost all of the Heights is at the events center."

"Including Tyrann Kane," I said.

Kratos made his way over to us, his steps wobbly, his eyes bloodshot. He stopped when he was just over an arm's length away. It was an eery sight to behold—I wished he would have taken his mask off.

"Do, not, go." It was like every word required great effort. "Understand?"

I stared at him. It was the only direct thing he had said to us since Ville. And if Rosewood really was behind bringing down all the buildings, then she definitely knew where everyone was right now. And that meant something big was coming. Thousands of people were at risk.

"I understand, but we can't just leave them," I said. I looked to Alex, who shrugged. "Look, if Benjamin's got control of all the Sinisters," I continued, "that's not a good thing. And if Tyrann does the same, well, neither option is good. And if Rosewood has them right where she wants them, well—we've got to do something before something terrible happens. Plus, Daphne's there. Let's go."

I started to walk.

Kratos jumped in front of me.

"No!" He appeared ready to fight if I resisted, and if the past was any proof, he was.

I stared at him.

He had saved my life before—stopping me before running into an explosion.

"Why?" I said. I met his eyes, but it was almost like he didn't see me.

Instead of answering, he just stared at me unblinkingly. I took a step forward. Kratos didn't flinch.

"What does Rosewood have planned?" I said. "Is it dangerous? Is something going to happen?"

Kratos's eyes snapped back to mine.

"Don't go."

I knew he knew more. Why couldn't he tell us?

"Look," Zeno said, "if something is about to go down, we can't just leave Daphne there."

Kratos looked up to the sky again. We were wasting time. Finally, he spoke.

"H.6.4.R.T.2."

We all shared a look.

"Uh, come again, bro?" Zeno said.

Kratos spoke again.

"H.6.4.R.T.2."

"Does that mean anything to you?" I said. "Some kind of code or something?"

"Nope," Alex said. "All of my codes start with a 'W.'"

I looked at Zeno, who had a look on his face like he was about to solve a puzzle.

"Passcode?" he mumbled to himself. "Passcode..." His face lit up, and his eyes shot to Kratos. "Is that for Rosewood's drone? H.6.4.R.T.2. Is that the code for her drone?"

Kratos didn't reply. He continued to stare off.

"Daphne says she's staying," Alex said, looking at his phone. "I told her Kratos didn't want us there because it was dangerous. She said," he paused and squinted at his phone. "It'll only get more dangerous if I leave. Tyrann is about to start something."

He looked back up. "Obviously, when I said 'I,' I meant Daphne. I mean, if I left here, it would become less dangerous too because, well, you know." He motioned to his arm. "What I'm trying to say is that we're going to go get Daphne and help everyone there. Are you coming with?"

All eyes turned to Kratos.

After a moment, his posture relaxed.

"Okay then," Alex said. "He's not coming."

My phone vibrated.

The faster you get here the better.

"We need to go. Now." I turned back to Kratos. "We'll get out of there as soon as we can, okay?"

Kratos didn't respond.

I tried one more time.

"Kratos, we want you to come with us."

He stared past me.

"H.6.4.R.T.2?" Zeno said. "Rosewood's drone? It's the right length, and it's the only thing I've been looking for. It's gotta be it, right, Kratos?"

It was as if Kratos was both deaf and blind to anything we said.

Zeno let out a sigh. We didn't have time to waste.

"All right," I said, "let's go." I started walking. I hadn't made it more than about ten feet when Kratos spoke up.

"Hurry," he said.

I stopped and turned back around.

"Hurry?" I said.

Kratos finally met my eyes.

"She's coming."

40

———————

She's coming.

His words echoed in my head.

I pushed myself to run faster.

Alex and Zeno were having a hard time keeping up. With frustration, I came to a stop and let them catch up. I looked at my watch. Kratos seemed to know, almost down to the second, when something was going to happen. Why couldn't he just tell us? I kept in my frustration as Zeno and Alex approached, Zeno with his phone up to his ear.

"What!" Zeno said, "Bro, come on, really? Like, she's not going to help unless I'm there?" He and Alex were both huffing as they came to a stop beside me. "Okay, have her ready for me. Thanks."

"Who was that?" I said.

"Trevor," he said. "I can't get into Rosewood's drones without Gina's help. I gave the passcode to Trevor so Gina can start hacking into Rosewood's drone, but Gina's refusing to do anything like that without me there. Man, I thought we had her all on board!"

I was about to start jogging again, but Zeno had his phone out—his fingers rapidly typing out a message.

"What are you doing?" I said.

"I'm sending Ivy a message," he said, still working on the message.

I let loose an exasperated sigh.

"Come on, Zeno, no one from Ville has replied in days. We've got to go!"

"I know, bro, but if for some reason we can't get to Gina, or something goes down, she's the only other person capable of doing what needs to be done. And with what Kratos said, who knows what we're running into here, bro."

I checked my watch.

"Whatever it is, we'll handle it, right?" Alex said. I glanced at him, grateful for his optimism. He nodded assuringly.

Zeno continued to type. I started to plan.

She was coming—that's what Kratos said. I just wished I knew *how* she was coming. Was she sending a bunch of drones? Was she going to be there herself? Was she even coming at all?

I figured it was wise to count on the drones, as that had been her MO thus far. There would be thousands of angry Sinisters jammed into a smaller space than they were used to, with Tyrann and Benjamin fighting for their loyalty. What kind of options did we have at our disposal? I looked at Zeno, who was still typing, then looked at Alex.

"Alex, can you get ahold of Trevor?"

"Yep," he said, pulling out his phone. "What do you want me to say?"

"See if he can get anything out of Maggie. Daphne is going to be with Tyrann. I'll ask her, but we need to know what Benjamin is planning to do as well."

"You got it." Alex went to work. I pulled out my phone and typed out a message to Daphne.

On our way. What is Tyrann planning? What do you want us to do when we arrive?

I hit the send button but kept the phone in my hand. Hopefully, she would text me back soon, if not immediately.

"Annnnd," Zeno said, his thumbs still flying rapidly, "sent!"

I watched Alex give his phone a final tap. I gave him a nod.

"All right, let's go."

We continued our path toward the events center. The streets were quiet. The buildings were vacant—it was like running through a ghost town. We ran through a vacant intersection and turned right. Five more minutes and we'd be there.

What could we do? A handful of us against Benjamin, Tyrann, and all the Sinisters in the Heights. Alone, we couldn't do much. A thought struck me.

"How many people do you think are watching our broadcasts?" I said.

"As a rough estimate," Zeno said, "a few thousand? Probably a little more?"

I looked at Alex.

"Sounds about right."

"Okay, I've got an idea. I need to do another broadcast right now."

"Right now?" Zeno said, in between breaths. "Like, while we run?"

"I don't know how much time we'll have left," I said. "I think it's our only option. Can you do it?"

"I, well, sure, but I don't have time to set up the relay to run it through Gina. Everyone will know where we are, and we won't be protected."

"It doesn't matter," I said. "If Rosewood is on her way, they already know where we are."

"Here, use my phone," Alex said, fishing it out of his pocket. "That way Zeno's is free to hook up with Gina when we get there. And use my account, too—you might get a wider reach that way."

Zeno took his phone.

"My man," Zeno said.

"I want everyone to see this," I said. "Is there a way to send it to everyone in the Sandbox?"

"Everyone?" Zeno said. I nodded. "Alright, bro, let's see what we can do," Zeno said, tapping the screen a few times. "Annnd, max radius is set. We're good."

"Perfect. Alex, you lead the way. Zeno, run next to me and just have the camera pointed in my direction."

"You got it," Alex said, putting on a small burst of speed.

Zeno fell into line beside me.

"You ready boss?"

"Let's do it."

The blue light started to blink.

41

———

"I know this is a different account than you're used to," I started, "but I want everyone to know the truth before it's too late." I looked around as we jogged along. We needed to make it to the events center as fast as possible, but if we could reach people with this video—if people in the Flats really were tuning into our broadcast in the Sandbox— maybe this was more important. I turned down a side street.

"It's usually not so quiet in the Heights," I said. "That's where we're at now. You might be wondering why we're running, but we'll get to that. Most of you have never been here. Show them what it looks like." I pointed at the buildings all around us. Zeno panned and followed my finger, lingering on a few spots before landing back on me. "The buildings are massive. They could house thousands and thousands of people and businesses." We made another turn back onto a bigger street. "But they don't. They don't house anything. A majority of the buildings aren't safe enough to live in." I came to a stop. We were all breathing heavily. "And the buildings that were safe enough to live in, well, this is what they look like now."

I pointed to my right. Zeno, again, followed my finger. The desolation of what used to be Jonny's building stood before us. Bricks were still strewn over a hundred yards from where the building used to stand. A thick layer of dust coated everything around us. Rudimentary furniture, trash, and destroyed belongings littered the ground. It was a tough sight to see.

Alex's phone started to buzz.

"Comments are starting to come in, bro," Zeno said. "A lot of them."

"Read me a couple," I said.

"Uh, you got it. Here's one: 'I didn't hear of any buildings collapsing in the Heights.' Another: 'You'd think we would have heard about something like that.' And this one: 'Who knew things were in such terrible shape.'"

Zeno looked back up at me and nodded. I continued

"Before I was exiled here, I didn't have any idea either. I didn't realize the lies that we had been told. The people of the Heights weren't taken care of nearly as well as I had thought. Until a few days ago, hundreds of people lived where that building used to stand." I stopped and pointed again. "I watched it collapse, with people inside of it. There was nothing I could do. People, children, families—they lost everything. And the worst part—no one knows why—but we have our suspicions."

I motioned to Zeno and Alex, and we started to move.

"That's not the only building that recently collapsed. Several of them, all of the major housing buildings, have fallen in the last few weeks. I don't know if you saw my broadcast from earlier, but you may have guessed what happened there. Another building collapsed, and we were on top of it. We were protesting what Rosewood has been telling everyone. We were trying to send a message that the people in the Heights don't hate the people in the Flats. We would have died, along with hundreds of others if not for the Bounty Hunter. He saved our lives—you know, you saw it. The Bounty

Hunter, protector of the Nobles, saved hundreds of Sinisters. Why would he do that?"

We turned down another street. We were almost there.

"He knew that something was going to happen to that building. He knew that we would be there protesting, and I don't know how, but he knew that the building was going to come down, and he was prepared. If we weren't innocent, wouldn't he have just let us fall?"

I looked straight at the camera.

"You know what the craziest part of it was? It was after all the dust had settled, and I had been separated from my friends. We were searching for each other, and we came across the sound of a little girl whimpering and crying for help. She was underneath a huge door that was covered in bricks. There was no way she could get herself out, and she was most likely hurt. After clearing off the bricks and lifting the door, we called out to the girl, but instead of finding a person, we were met by a drone, which scanned us and tried to attack us. And the Bounty Hunter told us it wasn't the only one he'd seen that day."

We made our way through the final intersection before the events center.

"You've probably seen the drones like this—they look identical to the ones Rosewood had at her last rally. You may have seen them flying around the city, keeping tabs on people."

I had no idea whether or not it was true, but I went with it.

"But it seems like someone has planned for all of those buildings to collapse. They didn't do it on their own. But the result is that all of the people from the Heights are now gathered in the same place, and they're there because there's nowhere left for them to go.

"I don't know why or what Rosewood has planned, but I do know something is going to happen, and if I didn't know any better, I'd say it's going to happen tonight." I motioned to Zeno and Alex, and we turned down another street.

"There's an old events center near the center of the Heights," I continued. "I have a feeling something is coming—I've seen on the news how angry people in the Flats are about the people here. I've heard Rosewood hinting at how dangerous we all are and how maybe everyone would be safer without us.

"I could be wrong on all of this, but I don't think I am. And I think we're going to need any help we can get."

I slowed my jog to a walk and then came to a stop. I could just see the roof of the events center, but there were people everywhere. Zeno panned the phone around again. The crowd of people was enormous. Men, women, children—some were gathered in groups, not talking with anyone else. Others, you could tell, had just come from their recently collapsed home.

"I'm sure many of you have wondered if what I've been saying is true. I'll let you be the judge of that. Have a look for yourselves. We're here."

42

———

"Zeno, keep it rolling," I said. "That's all I wanted to say. We need to find Daphne."

"You got it, boss. Alex, switch me. I should be on Gina's network now." They exchanged phones once more. Zeno tapped in rapid sequence on his screen, then handed it back to Alex. "Watch this progress bar," he said. "Tell me the second it hits a hundred percent, you got it?"

Alex nodded.

"Yeah, but what is it?"

"It's the link up to Rosewood's drone. It'll take a few minutes, at least, for it to work. Keep me posted, got it?"

"Got it," Alex said.

Taking over Rosewood's personal drone—the one that could broadcast to everyone in the Flats—self-incrimination was the very best we could hope for. I just hoped we'd get a chance to use it.

"Victor," Zeno said, "the comments are coming in like crazy on the video. You want me to field any of these?"

Alex walked over, peered at the screen, and started mumbling to himself.

"Don't worry, I got these." He positioned himself in front of the camera and started to speak. I pulled out my phone and started to type.

We just got here. Where are you?

I pushed the send button and waited for a response. Daphne hadn't responded to the last message, but I was still hoping for an immediate response. I knew we couldn't wait here, though. We needed to find her, or Benjamin or Tyrann.

"Let's go," I said, starting to push my way through all the people.

As we made our way through the crowd, the volume increased. Zeno held Alex's phone aloft, capturing the scene. I hadn't been able to see it before, but Benjamin's stage had been erected, and it looked like a few people were on it, people I recognized. I squinted past the multitude of heads that intermittently obscured my view. It was Trevor and Maggie.

Why were they on stage?

Where was Benjamin? And Tyrann, for that matter? Surely, one of them would have started handling the crowd.

The closer we pushed to the front, the louder it became. It occurred to me that Maggie had a microphone, but her annoyingly high-pitched voice wasn't making it through all of the noise.

A group of rough-looking people—they reminded me of the underground fights—stood nearby, talking loud enough for anyone to hear.

"We've got the numbers! Let's take it to them."

"Like any of the Nobles have lived a difficult day in their lives."

"Sabers and stunners... that's all they're allowed to have, right?"

Tyrann would love this kind of talk, and Benjamin had encouraged it. They didn't realize what they were up against. They didn't realize that right now, they were in very grave danger.

"We've got to find Daphne!" I said, nearly yelling to be heard over the noise. "And where's Tyrann and Benjamin?"

"I don't know, bro!" Zeno said. "Maybe somewhere inside?

Alex pushed up closer to us, clearly not having heard what we had just said.

"Where's Daphne?" he yelled. "And Benjamin? Look at our guy, Trevor, up there!"

Trevor stood almost nervously off to the side as Maggie held the microphone limply in front of her face. You could tell she didn't know what to do—she didn't know how to manage a crowd this size. But what she did know, if anyone knew, was where to find Benjamin. And I would bet just about anything that wherever Benjamin was, Tyrann and Daphne were there, too.

"Come on!" I said, waving Alex and Zeno behind me.

I forced my way through the crowd, pushing and squeezing through groups and thickets of people—all but a few giving me nasty glares as I shouldered past them.

Snippets of jumbled conversation flew around me, most of it decidedly different from what I had heard earlier.

"...and peace! We need peace!"

"...work it out!"

"...they're not all bad—"

The words surprised me, but I didn't have time to analyze it now. I had one objective.

I arrived at the stage, the crowd even thicker here than where we had come from. Maggie and Trevor looked helplessly over the crowd. What were they doing up there? Was this why Trevor couldn't get Gina to help out?

"Trevor!" I yelled. "Maggie!" I waved my arms and jumped until Trevor noticed me. His anxious expression melted away, and he ran toward me. I looked over my shoulder to make sure Zeno and Alex had made it with me, but it looked like I had lost them on my way up.

They'd catch up.

"I'm so glad you're here!" Trevor yelled.

"Where's Daphne?" I said.

Trevor gave me a confused look and pointed to his ear.

"Where's Daphne?" I yelled.

He nodded in comprehension.

"I thought she was with you."

I let out a sound of frustration, which he clearly didn't hear.

"No, she came back early with Tyrann."

"Who?"

I ignored him.

"Where's Benjamin?"

Trevor shrugged.

A high-pitched voice joined the noise.

"Please! Please, everyone, Benjamin will be here soon!" Maggie's voice barely carried to where I stood. Her arms dropped down helplessly to her sides.

What was she doing? The last time I saw her, she had basically been in tears knowing that Benjamin had refused to help us, and now here she and Trevor were, covering for him? What was going on?

Maggie finally took notice of Trevor and me. She immediately set down the mic and ran over to us.

"Oh good you're here!" She squeaked. "Trevor told me you'd make it!"

"Where is he?" I said. We didn't have time for any pretense. I'd ask other questions later.

"What?" She said, cupping her hand around her ear.

"Where is Benjamin?" I said more loudly this time.

She shook her head at me and then pointed to the left of the stage. She started to walk, and Trevor followed.

I searched for Zeno and Alex. I still couldn't see them.

Rather than fight my way across the front of the stage, I hoisted myself up onto it and looked for them again. Finally, I spotted them. About five rows from the front, Zeno's afro bobbed up and down as he tried to keep Alex's phone up in the air. He must have still been recording everything. I waved my arms and yelled until they saw me, and then I pointed to Trevor and Maggie and motioned for them to follow. I took off jogging across the stage.

Maggie and Trevor waited for me next to an open door behind some of the sound equipment.

I jumped off the stage and made my way over and into the room. It was more hallway than room, and it ran parallel to the stage.

Maggie shut the door behind me, and things immediately became much quieter, relegating the thousands of voices to a soft buzzing sound.

My ears were grateful for the break, but my only thought was to find Daphne and, by extension, Benjamin and Tyrann. I turned my attention immediately to Maggie.

"Where is he?" I said the moment the sound was shut out.

"Well, it's nice to see you, too," she said.

"Yes, nice to see you," I said, shaking my head. "Look, I need to know where Benjamin is now. I need to find Daphne, and I think she's with him."

She looked almost startled at my question, taking a half step back as I talked. She didn't answer, instead choosing to look at the floor in front of my feet.

"Do you know where he is or not?" I said. She continued to stare at the floor.

I was growing impatient.

"Trevor, I have to know. We don't have much time."

"Maggie?" Trevor said.

She glanced at Trevor, her eyes wide and full of apology.

Trevor cocked his head in concern.

"I thought you said he was on his way. You said he'd agreed to help us after all." Trevor said, taking a few steps forward. "You said he's been sending you messages."

Her eyes started to well up with tears.

"I'm sorry! I just, I, he did message me! He said he had decided to help you and that he'd be here to give a speech, but that was over an hour ago!"

"And you haven't heard from him since?" Trevor said.

Maggie sniffed and wiped at her eyes.

"Not since he told me to take some time off and explore the other side of the Heights," she said. Trevor's eyes grew wide. "But I told him that I knew he needed me here, and I was staying. He hasn't messaged back since."

Trevor took a step back from her as realization struck.

Benjamin had told her to leave the events center, and he clearly was not coming.

The door behind me opened wide, filling the hallway with unintelligible noise.

Zeno and Alex were on the other side.

They stepped inside and closed the door behind them. Zeno began speaking immediately.

"Bro, we need to get everyone out of here."

"No kidding," I said.

"No," Zeno grabbed me by the shoulder. "We need to get everyone out of here. Now."

There was something in his voice that made the hair on the back of my neck stand up. He held up his phone for me to see.

A large red ALERT banner flashed across the screen.

"It's from Gina."

Maggie craned her neck to see.

"What does it mean?" she said. A soft buzzing noise could be heard coming from Maggie's person. "Oh, maybe it's him!" She reached into her pocket and pulled out a small screen. Her expression was both excited and relieved. "It's him!" She tapped the screen, and Benjamin's face appeared. The background behind him was a stark white. He looked ill—dark circles under his eyes—his hair was a mess. I'd never seen him like that before.

"Benjamin!" Maggie said, "Where are you? The crowd is—"

"You're not at the events center, are you?" Benjamin said, cutting her off, his voice nearly ragged. "Tell me you're not there."

Another look of confusion from Maggie.

"Well, of course I am. I'm stalling for you—the people have been waiting."

Benjamin let loose a defeated sigh.

"I wish you would have listened to me."

"Benjamin?" Maggie's confusion turned to worry. "You're, you're not coming, are you?"

Her question was met with silence.

"Benjamin?" Maggie said again.

"I'm sorry," he said, his tone flat. "I'm so, so sorry."

With a click, the call ended.

43

———

My heart began to pound.

We needed to leave. Now.

Behind us in the hallway, one of the doors opened, and Tyrann Kane walked through it, apparently in high spirits, Dax and Printh in tow.

Daphne's voice floated through the open door.

"It won't work this way!"

"Nonsense!" Tyrann said.

He threw open another set of doors, ones that led to the stage, and noise erupted into the echoey hallway.

Tyrann continued through the doors and onto the stage, not taking notice of any of us. Daphne appeared in the hallway after him but didn't pause in the hallway as she followed after them.

"Daphne!" I yelled.

She didn't hear me but continued right after Tyrann.

I ran after her.

Even before I made it to the open doors, Tyrann's boisterous voice began to boom over the speakers. He must have picked up Maggie's mic.

"I am Tyrann Kane!"

I continued to run.

"Many of you thought I was dead, but alas, it is not so."

I skidded to a halt and rounded the corner through the doors and onto the stage. It was an eerie scene, staring at the back of Tyrann Kane's bald head with the backdrop of thousands and thousands of people, people who had once feared him.

The noise from the crowd started to die down.

"I have returned, for your sake."

I could hear the smile in his voice as he spoke.

"Nobles—they're not so different from us. I've been told that there are many of your number who would wish to maintain some sort of peace with the Nobles."

I felt a hand on my shoulder. Zeno.

"Bro, we've got to do something. This is coming straight from Gina."

He shoved his phone in front of my face as Tyrann continued talking.

The message on his phone had changed. ALERT alternated with INCOMING.

"Then there are those of you who would wish to remain oppressed. I get it," Tyrann said. "Change is hard. But now we're here together, and the time for change has come."

In front of my eyes, the message flashed again. ALERT. INCOMING.

I turned to Zeno.

"How much time?"

"Not much."

I raced out onto the stage.

"Tyrann!" I yelled.

A few boos sounded from the crowd.

"Victor Wells," he said slowly, a smile creeping onto his face.

Murmurs swept through the audience. Tyrann immediately held up a hand, silencing them.

"Give me the mic, Tyrann," I said. "Something is coming. We need to get everyone out of here."

Tyrann chuckled.

"Such demands, Mr. Wells. Something is coming, indeed. A revolution!" He spread his arms wide and looked out over the audience. About half of the people cheered, but not all with enthusiasm.

A rumbling sounded in the distance, one that shook the stage under our feet. The cheers died out and gave way to the mass chatter of before. This time, Tyrann didn't silence them.

"Zeno, did the linkup finish?" I said, still staring at Tyrann, whose eyes, for once, registered surprise as the rumbling intensified.

Zeno didn't answer for a moment.

"Zeno?" I said.

"I, I don't know. My signal just went dead."

For a moment, the rumbling stopped but then returned almost immediately and in much closer proximity.

I rushed forward and wrenched the microphone out of Tyrann's hand, but before I could yell for everyone to run, an earth-rattling cascade of noises sounded from every direction around us.

From where I stood, I could see a handful of other buildings nearby. They all started to shake. The sound of groaning metal rent the air, and all at once, the buildings started to come down.

A strange whirring noise filled the air, accompanied by the arrival of a legion of black drones.

Screams broke out. People ran and scattered, but they had nowhere to go. Bricks and glass began to rain from the sky. Hysteria ruled.

The only building that wasn't shaking seemed to be the events center.

I felt the microphone being ripped from my hands. Zeno's voice exploded through the speakers.

"EVERYONE INSIDE!"

He threw the mic on the ground and grabbed me by the wrist, pulling me back toward the building.

The nearest building finally gave way, twenty stories and a hundred tons of weight crashed down across the very back part of the courtyard. The shockwave and accompanying dust seemed to make all of the air disappear.

Through the dust and debris, the drones moved in unison, taking their positions all around the area. Each emitted a burst of red light that moved up and down the nearest walls of the events center, scanning for something.

And then we were in the hallway again. I had only a moment to get my bearings. Alex, Zeno, Daphne, Trevor—we were all here, just inside the events center, surrounded by drones, with buildings collapsing all around us.

This was it. This was Rosewood's final move.

44

———

"Follow me!" Zeno said, taking off in a dead sprint.

Without question, I followed.

The sounds outside grew even louder—the screams, the crashes.

Another thump and whooshing sound signaled the fall of another building.

I could feel the ground shake beneath my feet.

How were we going to survive this? Zeno had a plan, didn't he?

"GINA!" He yelled, throwing open another door and running through it. "GINA!"

I followed closely on his heels. Behind me, Daphne, Alex, and Trevor followed. Surprisingly, Maggie, Tyrann, Printh, and Dax were there too, and it looked as if more people were coming.

"GINA!" Zeno yelled again.

"Zeno!" I said. "Is she supposed to answer back? I thought she couldn't talk."

He came to a stop and whipped his head around, his chest heaving.

"Yeah, bro! Her protocols let her talk in an emergency!" He held up his phone again. The screen was dark. "But I've got nothing! The drones must have knocked out all of the communication apparatuses in the area, or we're starting to get some real bad structural damage."

"I thought she's supposed to be operational as long as the main room is fine," Daphne said, joining us. Alex and Trevor arrived, too.

"Yep," Zeno said, looking around.

"What is happening out there?" Trevor said.

"Rosewood is leveling the Heights," Zeno said.

"And I think Benjamin was in on it," I said. Tyrann, Printh, and Dax joined us as well. "All of the Sinisters were forced here," I continued. "They had nowhere else to go, and now that they're all here, Rosewood can come and finish everyone off without leaving a trace."

"And that's what she's going to do if we don't get to Gina!" Zeno said. "Come on!" He took off again.

We all followed Printh and Dax included, with the exception of Tyrann.

"If the buildings are all coming down, why are we going deeper into this one?" he yelled.

"When have you known Mr. Zeno not to have a plan?" Dax hollered back over his shoulder.

We rounded a corner and went down a flight of stairs. Amazingly, the lights were still on throughout the building, albeit many of them shaky or flickering.

"GINA!" Zeno shouted again.

I didn't know exactly how Gina worked, but I assumed that Zeno had put microphones all over the building. And Dax was right—Zeno always had a plan.

But Gina still hadn't answered, and as we ran deeper and deeper into the building, that was problematic.

Another huge impact shook the ground we ran on. How many buildings left until it was our turn?

We descended another staircase, and that's when I knew where

Zeno was taking us—the auditorium, or rather, the room just behind the stage in the auditorium. That was where Gina's brains were stored.

We descended a broad stone staircase that had begun to crack. The fissure widened as we thundered down it.

"GINA!" Zeno yelled. By now, his tone was frantic. Bits of rubble from the now-cracked ceiling had started to litter the floors.

Zeno was the first to hit the landing. He continued running, throwing open a set of metal double doors as he moved into the hallway beyond.

"GINA!"

As I burst through the doors, I saw Zeno stationary in the new hallway, staring up at the ceiling. He had one hand on the wall, leaning up against it for support. We weren't at the auditorium yet, but we were close.

"Come on, girl, talk to me," he said, his head beginning to droop.

I jogged over to him as everyone else filed into the hallway behind us.

"Guys, this is it," Zeno said. "There was no way we could outrun all of those buildings. We may have bought ourselves some time coming down here, but without Gina, well..." He took off his glasses and rubbed them. His eyes were red. "We'll never—"

"We should have taken our chances with the drones!" Tyrann said. "Now we're going to die like rats in a—"

"Hello, boss."

A soft feminine voice that could only belong to Gina sounded in the hallway, cutting off Tyrann's rant. Zeno looked up to the ceiling, and a smile took hold. He wiped at his eyes again. He gave Tyrann a look.

"I told you we'd never leave you, Gina! Keep your ears on me. We're coming to you!"

"I'll be waiting."

Zeno sprinted down the hallway, with the rest of us close behind.

"Gina!" he said. "Use the PA system as much as you can. Direct anyone and everyone to the auditorium, understand?" We rushed through another set of doors and then headed down another stairwell. "Have your emergency protocols ready and open when we get there."

"Of course."

"Man, it feels good to be home!" Zeno said as a particularly loud crash nearly made me lose my footing. "Last staircase!" he said, pushing through another set of doors.

The auditorium appeared before us, looking just as it had the first time I had been here. The stage was empty, although Augustine's chalkboard still stood off to the side.

"How's our integrity looking, G?" Zeno shouted as he vaulted over a few rows of seating on his way to the stage.

"Structural integrity is at an all-time low," she said.

I clambered onto the stage and sprinted to the back and through the door. The place was a disaster, but Zeno didn't care. He threw his phone down on the nearest table.

"Gina! Analyze the uplink that's in process," Zeno said, grabbing a keyboard. "Come on, come on. Trevor, help me out!"

Trevor grabbed the nearest keyboard.

"And now what?" Tyrann said. "We wait here, below ground, for the building to drop on top of us?"

"Tyrann. Outside," Zeno said, his fingers flying over the keys.

When no one responded, Zeno looked up from what he was doing, his eyes deadly.

"Go outside, Tyrann. People are going to start showing up. We need them all to stay in the auditorium. Can you handle that?"

"I'll come with you," Dax said, shifting his gaze back and forth between the two of them.

Zeno immediately went back to his keyboard.

"Come on! Gina! Status update!"

"No uplink in progress. Partial uplink noted, but unsuccessful."

Zeno hit a few keystrokes particularly hard but didn't answer. Although, with what was going on right now, I wasn't sure how much the uplink mattered.

The sounds of a small crowd started to filter into our room. I peeked my head out onto the stage to see them starting to file in. What looked like hundreds of people had started to arrive from all the different entrances, pushing and shoving to get past one another.

Their fear was palpable, and I was helpless.

"Zeno, what's the plan here?" I said, turning back. "How can we help?"

"The plan is..." He trailed off. "Come on, say they're intact, say they're intact!"

"What's intact?" Daphne said.

"Warning, critical impact incoming."

Zeno stood up, fear in his eyes.

Without any warning, the mightiest crash of all sounded. Metal groaned. The ceiling above us started to crumble. Screams began anew.

And in that moment, I knew that this was it. This was the end.

"GINA! NOW!"

"Goodbye, Zeno, my friend."

45

The sound of the impact was worse than anything I had heard before. Deafening was too soft a word. The earth shook, and the lights went out, plunging us into total darkness. Explosions erupted around us, peppering us with debris. The auditorium rang with the screams of its terrified occupants.

I felt, more than heard, the brief pause in the air before the ceiling started to fall. The loud cracks and crumbling of materials preceded the storm of dust particles that pelted our skin.

At the same time, a loud and confusing hiss sounded all around us. The rainfall of dust stopped, the screaming metal became quiet, and the thundering all around us ceased.

We were alive.

Slowly, the people in the auditorium began muttering, with a few odd laughs here and there.

I had my hands above my head to protect me, like it would have done much. I slowly brought them down to my sides. I couldn't see a thing, but I knew, somehow, that the ceiling was suspended above us, not connected to anything, just there, floating.

"Are we alive?" Alex said. "It's really dark, so is this, you know... the bad place?"

"No, it's not the bad place," Daphne said from somewhere to my right. "We're alive. I'm not sure how, but we are, at least for now."

"I upgraded our security system a year or so ago," Zeno's voice said. "There are targeted pods of my concentrated special spray for structural support. They only detonate in the case of a catastrophic event." He paused. "And this definitely qualifies."

"What did I say?" Dax said, his voice coming from my left. "He's always got a plan."

I could hear the smile in Dax's voice, but I couldn't in Zeno's.

"And a wonderful plan it was," Tyrann said. "By my account, we're stranded here, underground, with a high probability of being buried by everything around us. Am I somewhat close, Mr. Zeno?"

"You haven't been close for years," Zeno said. A light appeared by his face—his phone. "You think if I went through everything to plan something like this out that I wouldn't give ourselves an escape route? Bro." Zeno shook his head. "We're getting out of here."

Zeno started walking.

"Hold on," I said. "There are hundreds of people out there. We can't just leave them."

"How very leader-like of you, Mr. Wells," Tyrann said, his face lighting up in a malevolent grin as he, too, pulled out a phone.

"How about common sense," Daphne said. "None of them know what's happening. We do."

Guided by the light of my phone, I walked over to the door and pushed it open, revealing the stage and, beyond it, a unique scene. A sea of bodies marked by the individual white lights of cell phones filled most of the auditorium. Like our own conversation, their collective chatter was filled with confusion and relief but also fear and anger.

It was hard to tell, but the number of people who had made it down here was significantly less than those who had been outside. It made me ill thinking about it. Could many of them have survived the falling buildings? Were there literally thousands of dead people up on the surface?

The volume of chatter started to increase, with some obvious tensions starting to break out. A couple of people had noticed my appearance and were shouting out questions.

I cleared my throat. "Hello, everyone!"

A multitude of phone lights swiveled my way, and the chattering died down significantly. "Many of you haven't been here before," I started. "I know you're all wondering what is happening. We think most of the building has collapsed on top of this room. A protective barrier is in place, keeping the whole thing from caving in."

At this, more muttering broke out. I held up my hands, taking my phone away from my face for a brief moment.

"We believe we have a way out. As long as it's not compromised, we'll get everyone out of here soon."

"What about everyone else?"

"You think you can get us out?"

"Where are our families?"

I held up my hands again as questions started to come in.

"We don't have time for questions, and we don't have a lot of answers. We're going to make sure we've got a way out, and then we'll be back for everyone. That's all."

The questions continued to come, and the buzz in the room returned to pre-announcement levels as I walked off the stage.

Zeno met me and nodded.

"Me and you—let's go. I want to make sure it's safe before we take anyone else."

"I'll follow you," I said.

Without another word, he took off through the darkness toward the corner of the room by the stage.

Illuminated only by the light of his phone, he got down on his hands and knees and started to crawl up.

His light began a gentle incline through the air, seemingly supported by nothing, except I knew it was a super-powered version of the gray beads. I got down onto my knees and entered the invisible tunnel as well. Instantly, the ambient sound died out.

"Can you hear me?" Zeno said.

His voice sounded odd, almost muffled.

"Yeah," I said.

"Good, I haven't gotten to field test this version hardly at all. The math works, though. The spray should be strong enough to support double the stress that's being placed on it."

I pushed down as I crawled, testing my weight as we ascended upward. It was like crawling up through a concrete shoot without scraping up your hands and knees. Smooth wasn't the right word, and neither was soft, but it almost felt that way.

"Seems solid to me," I said.

"Sorry, bro, you're going to have to yell," Zeno said. He had a note of annoyance in his voice. "I can barely hear you—I think the beads are soaking up our voices in here."

"I was just saying the beads worked great," I said, raising my voice. Zeno didn't respond. Well, he grunted, but that was about it. Something was wrong—we were alive, and we shouldn't be, and it was because of him. His genius had saved us again. "Before everything went dark, I heard you yell for Gina to deploy all this stuff," I said. "She did it perf—"

"Gina's gone, bro," Zeno said, cutting me off, his voice taut. "The conduits containing her electronics had to be compromised if things were going to hold. It was the only way it could work."

I had just assumed that Gina was something he could access from anywhere—a remote server or something. I hadn't realized she had been contained completely within the building.

I didn't know what to say.

"I'm sorry," was all I could get out. Zeno didn't respond. We just kept crawling.

After a minute, he spoke.

"We should almost be to the top." The tightness in his voice had softened slightly.

"What's our move?" I said. "Rosewood is going to think her plan to collapse the Heights worked. She'll come to check." I imagined a swarm of drones. "One way or another. I don't know what she has planned for the Heights, but with all the buildings and people gone..." I trailed off.

"I don't know, bro. I haven't had to think my last-ditch emergency plan through this far. Small groups leave once night hits? Honestly, I don't know, but if I remember right, this is about to get real steep, and then it'll flatten back out. You might need to boost me up."

We crawled to a stop as the tunnel took a short but steep, upward incline.

I held out my palms, and Zeno kicked off of them, hoisting himself up to the final, but still invisible, level.

Zeno disappeared above me for a brief moment before his hand shot back down to lift me up.

"Thanks."

I grabbed his hand, and he heaved as I climbed. Zeno didn't move out of my way. I couldn't see anything around me. There was no moon, no stars to guide us here, just his incredible, life-saving, energy-siphoning beads.

"I don't know what things are going to look like out there," Zeno said, nodding to his right. In front of him sat a round sheet of gray beads. "But whatever it is, I don't think we want to spend much time out there. What do you think?"

"Agreed," I said. "Let's get out for thirty seconds, take a look, and then head back. We can figure out a plan for everyone when we get back down there."

"Sounds good. I designed this so that the end of the tunnel would be closed." Zeno placed a hand on the gray beads. "It's not as strong as this other stuff, but we'll have to push through it. Ready?"

I nodded and scooted up next to him.

"One, two, three!"

Together, we pushed hard against the barrier. Beads darkened and fell around my hands until, finally, it gave way.

I nearly fell through but caught myself on the lip.

A gentle light from the stars above filtered through the dust still settling in the air. I stuck my head out to make sure the coast was clear.

"Clear," I said.

Zeno grunted his assent and we crawled out to survey the landscape. I had been awed very few times in my life, but this was one of them, and not in a good way.

Decimation. Complete destruction.

"Whoa," Zeno whispered.

The Heights had turned into a brick graveyard. The night was eerily quiet and dark. The air smelled both fresh and moldy at the same time. The whole scene sent a shiver down my spine, but that shiver was nothing compared to the icy fear I felt immediately after. An unknown voice broke through the darkness.

"There's someone there!"

A series of lights flashed our way. I dropped to the ground, but Zeno wasn't fast enough.

A blast of light pierced the darkness, and he fell unconscious next to me. In a panic, I searched for the entrance back to the events center, but it was in vain. More flashes of light hit the ground around me.

"Hold your fire!"

The stunner blasts stopped. At least a dozen spotlights found their way to me, blinding me in the darkness. My mind raced.

I had my gloves on. That could buy me a little time and protection from the stunners, but what were the chances I could block them all?

And if I did manage to escape, where would I go?

"Let me see your hands!" the voice said.

I fought for another solution, another set of options. I glanced down to my left, where Zeno's body lay.

There weren't any. There wasn't another option. Running, fighting, surrendering—they all had the same outcome here.

Slowly, I raised my hands above my head.

The sound of footsteps crunching over rocks approached, dozens of them. They kept their lights on my face, effectively blinding me. I could sense their stunners trained on me. I could feel their apprehension.

The group of footsteps came to a stop, but a solitary pair continued on, coming closer and closer, and an unmistakably cold voice began to speak.

"Well, well, Mr. Wells."

A figure stepped in front of the lights, her boots coming to a stop uncomfortably close to mine. She leaned in, blocking my face from the spotlights. I opened my eyes and was met by the cold, smiling face of Victoria Rosewood.

"What a nice surprise."

Before I could utter a word, or run or fight, or even think, I saw a flash of blue light, and then everything went black.

46

———

My head pounded as I tried to blink my eyes open. I felt pressure on my wrists and ankles. I squinted and blinked again.

It was so bright.

I shut my eyes and let my chin fall to my chest. My mind did not want to wake up, but I knew it needed to. I tried to open my eyes again, but it was easier to think with them closed.

Where was I? Was that the sun I felt on my skin? And a light breeze?

A murky but terrifying memory started to resurface.

My heart started to race. My mind finally kicked into gear. Rosewood.

I struggled against my bonds, feeling them cut into my skin as I did so. They didn't budge.

Where was I?

I had to be in the Flats, somewhere. But what about Zeno? What about the others? And what were all of those sounds?

"Victor."

I blinked and squinted, unable to shield my eyes from the light source. And there was so much noise—almost like when we had arrived at the events center, last night? Yesterday? Two days ago? I had no idea how much time had passed.

"Bro, wake up."

The voice was coming from behind me and to my right and was much closer and louder than everything else. I forced my eyes open, willing them to adjust to the new environment.

Zeno sat next to me in a chair, his wrists bound to the armrests, his legs likewise bound to the chair. His glasses were broken, barely hanging onto his face, and a large welt was beginning to show on his cheek.

His eyes met mine, and he gave me a weary grin.

"Looks like we've come to the end, my man."

He spoke loud, competing with all the noise around us.

"Where are we?" I said.

"Home—ish."

Finally, I was able to take in my surroundings. We sat on a sort of makeshift stage, much like Rosewood had had at her rally in the streets, except that rather than the stage being in the middle of the street, this one connected to the building behind us.

I was surprised to see a crowd of people. Behind them stood a series of buildings, short buildings. They were well-kept, modern, and mostly single-storied.

I recognized these buildings—we were in the Capital. I craned my neck around to confirm my suspicions.

A multi-storied building, with a mostly glass facade, rose up from the ground behind us, stretching high into the sky, dwarfing every building in the vicinity. The stage I now sat on connected to the building, the one building I hated the most—Rosewood's tower.

"Well, look who's finally awake."

Another voice came from behind me and to my left—Tyrann. Tyrann's suit looked a little ragged, but other than that, he appeared unharmed. The three of us were situated in a sort of triangle orientation, with me at the point closest to the Noble onlookers.

I shook off the implications with another thought. If Tyrann was here, then...

"Where are the others?" I said. "How long have we been here?"

"If I were in her shoes, I'd save all the rest of us for a great unveiling. It would be a rather showy move for her, but judging by the crowd"—Tyrann nodded to the thousands and thousands of people here in support of her—"that's what the people want. But that's just me." He nodded to his left.

I couldn't stifle the gasp that escaped me.

How did I not see it before? It had to have been the worst thing I had ever seen.

Out beyond the stage, behind a black, protective fence, sat a massive glass box. Four completely transparent glass walls had been erected, and inside, packed together far too tightly, stood what appeared to be all of the Sinisters from the events center—maybe all the Sinisters that were left.

It was like they were an exhibit—like they were in a cage. And they were. She was making them out to be caged beasts, not human beings.

"And she calls us evil," Tyrann said, his smile turning wry.

I stared at the glass box for a few more moments. Somewhere in there stood Alex and Daphne, but I couldn't make anyone out from where I sat.

I didn't think I could hate Rosewood more than I already did, but in that moment, my anger grew.

I turned my attention to the crowd. They were all here for us, for whatever this was, for whatever was about to happen.

What promises had Rosewood made? What lies had she told them?

I glanced over at the glass box again, then back to the sea of people. Several of the people closest to us were looking up, their eyes directed beyond where I sat—not at me, not at the glass cage of survivors—something else.

Behind us, an enormous screen had been erected, and on it, a gigantic line of text moved across the screen.

"...majority of the buildings in the Heights have fallen. Sadly, many casualties resulted, though, due to the rapid response of President Rosewood, several hundred people were saved from the wreckage. Unfortunately, though all have been tested, only one of the many were compatible with genetic modification. Only one of hundreds will become Noble. The procedure will take place this evening."

An image appeared on the screen, a serene face I knew all too well. His name appeared in giant block letters below his face.

BENJAMIN.

So many puzzle pieces clicked into place.

The drone Daphne saw—it belonged to Rosewood.

The supplies he somehow had to feed and shelter all of the people —they came from Rosewood.

The single screen in his office—probably a direct link to her, giving him instructions on his next move.

He had been part of her team from the start. She had planned this. She had planned all of this. We never stood a chance.

The screen moved to a live feed.

Benjamin smiled and gave the camera a thumbs-up.

"I'm grateful to be given a chance to join all of you. I'm told the procedure is painful, but any price is worth the reward of true and lasting change. Although I've identified as a Sinister my whole life, I look forward to changing my very DNA and transforming myself into a new version of myself—the Noble version, where I can truly add to society, and no longer be a threat to those around me. Thank you, Doctor, President Rosewood. You have saved my life."

He smiled once more as the screen faded to black. The crowd cheered yet again.

Of course, that was his reward. Sell out thousands of people—be responsible for countless deaths, and his trophy: a place among the Nobles.

Tyrann barked out a laugh and shook his head.

"Well played, Benjamin, well played."

I didn't share Tyrann's sense of humor. But Rosewood had played us well. Our best efforts hadn't been good enough. They hadn't even been close.

The thousands of people cheering were proof.

The crowd quieted down as Kelly Straunton's perfectly manicured face appeared on the screen. She smiled at the audience and began to speak, her voice amplified for all to hear.

"Today is an historic day. It is a day of great tragedy but also a day of comfort. You all saw what happened in the Heights just hours ago." Her face fell into one of sadness. "But while the loss of life is regrettable, it brings with it a new age of safety for us, one where Nobles no longer need to fear. After today, we will finally be able to live in peace and safety, and it is all thanks to our wonderful leader, President Victoria Rosewood!"

Cheers erupted from the crowd.

"I have been granted a unique opportunity," she continued. "A final interview with one of the most intriguing and dangerous figures of our time. Once believed to be a high-ranking Noble, his true identity was uncovered—a carrier of TiiD. What followed were a series of events with which you are all familiar—escaping from the Flats, infiltrating the Capital, and rising through the ranks of the Sinisters to become one of their main leaders. Though just a teenager, he caused mayhem and devastation with alarming skill. His time is short, and we may never have another chance like this. I am speaking, of course, of Victor Wells."

She appeared on the stage to my right as the crowd began to boo, but I barely heard them. What I did hear was a short phrase, resounding in my mind over and over. It chilled me to the very core.

'His time is short.'

Did that mean what I thought it meant? I figured Rosewood would imprison us, but could she...?

Of course, she could. But would she?

I looked out over the crowd—thousands and thousands of raving fans. I knew the answer.

My breath caught in my throat. I felt warm, too warm. I struggled against my restraints. It was pointless.

I tried to steady my breathing but couldn't.

"Hey, uh, bro, you okay?"

I heard Zeno's voice but didn't respond.

I looked over at Kelly Straunton as she crossed the stage. A small drone floated in front of her, broadcasting her every word. I could see the enormous screen filled with her features out of the corner of my eye. And then suddenly, it was my face, not hers, that occupied the screen. I turned back around toward the crowd to find a small drone floating in front of my face as well.

I jumped.

The crowd laughed.

I tried to talk to myself, to clear my head.

This wasn't an execution. It couldn't be—not with all these people here. There were children in the crowd. It couldn't be, right? I looked over to Zeno, who gave me a bleak smile, then over to Tyrann, who was busy staring out into the crowd.

Kelly Straunton continued to walk toward me, coming to a stop well outside arm's reach, not that it mattered with my restraints.

With her smile plastered in place, she looked at me and then back to the crowd. I watched her take a few deep breaths to steady herself.

It struck me as odd, almost unsettling, that she was nervous.

She was scared of me, legitimately scared. And it was all a lie. People had been scared of me before—but only in the saber fights—never in real life. But looking at her now, it was obvious. She was terrified because of lies she helped spread.

"I think the question on everyone's mind, Mr. Wells," Kelly started, her voice mildly shaky, her face taking over the screen once more, "is why? Why would you live among us for so long? Why would you cause so much fear and pain? Why? Is it just in your Sinister nature?"

A hush fell over the crowd as my face once again took up the screen. I hesitated. This was my chance. This was my opportunity—I had to tell them the truth. I had to tell them what had happened, what Rosewood had done.

My head started to clear. I opened my mouth.

"DNA doesn't control our destinies," I started, the sound of my voice harsh and raw in my ears. A few 'boos' rang out, but the crowd stayed mostly silent. They were curious about what I—the Noble turned Sinister—had to say. "I believe people can make their own choices, and I'm not the only one who thinks like this. Others do, too, and I know there are some of you listening now, and you don't want to admit it, but it rings true."

I paused and looked up at Kelly. She almost flinched. I continued.

"There's no such thing as a Noble. There's no such thing as a Sinister. Victoria Rosewood has lied to you, to all of you." At this, some of the crowd started to boo again, but I plowed on through. "She doesn't want you to know that—"

Without warning, my magnified voice was cut off.

The screen went dark.

I looked around.

My heart continued to race. Rosewood was shutting it down. She didn't want people to hear what I had to say, but maybe it was enough, maybe it was enough to—

The screen lit back up, but this time, with an unexpected face.

Her hair was dark and short, she wore glasses, and she looked incredibly uncomfortable. But it was her eyes—they were two different colors.

"Ivy!" Zeno yelled in disbelief. He let loose an astonished laugh. "My girl!"

"We're coming," Ivy said, "but first, enjoy the show."

I looked to Zeno.

Bewilderment. Joy and bewilderment were what I saw.

The screen went black, but only for a moment. A small box popped up with red letters in it.

"LIVE"

The feed turned on, and the red letters shrank and moved to the corner of the screen.

Rosewood appeared. She sat in a large, burgundy red chair, dressed in a white suit, her lips pursed and shaded as if to match the furniture perfectly. Her cold, blue eyes were slightly pinched, giving her a look of irritation as she spoke.

"... would have done your job, we wouldn't be in this mess."

Another voice responded, but the camera stayed on Rosewood.

"Looks like it's turning out all right to me," he said, his voice deep and rough.

She rolled her eyes as he finished.

I would have known that voice anywhere. Harvesty.

"All right, would have been things going according to plan, you imbecile." Rosewood gave a withering look to Harvesty, who was just off camera. "Hundreds survived. The plan was for there to be no survivors, least of all Victor Wells."

A third voice entered the mix, one I didn't recognize.

"Um, President Rosew—"

"Quiet!" Rosewood said, her glare shifting rapidly to the right, silencing whoever had spoken. She turned her eyes back to Harvesty. "Well? What excuse do you have for me this time? You didn't kill him when I sent you to his home after his Marking. You didn't kill him on the train, or the rooftop, or any number of times you were supposed to do it. So please, tell me why you're not an incompetent idiot, incapable of carrying out the simplest of tasks."

There was a brief moment of silence, in which muttering began to break out in the crowd.

"I, uh, well, " Harvesty stuttered, "he's uh, he's been resourceful."

Rosewood stared hard, her eyes narrowing even more than before.

"Resourceful? Is that what you call it, Harvesty? You're a grown man with a trained team of assassins at your disposal, and you haven't managed to kill a teenager? Excuses." She spat the word at him. "That's all you've had—excuses. The lengths I've had to go to in order to compensate for your failures..." She shook her head. "Fortunately, after all of the mindless sheep out there cheer on this execution, your series of blunders will be behind us." She stood up. "We will discuss your future when this is over."

More muttering broke out in the crowd. It grew louder and louder.

"Dr. Rosewood!" the third voice said. "Please, wait!"

A look far past annoyance overcame Rosewood's face.

"It is President Rosewood. Perhaps we need to address your future here, as well."

I looked at Zeno, but his eyes were glued to the screen.

Our plan—it was working. Ivy, somehow, she did it!

I caught Kelly Straunton's face out of the corner of my eye.

She stared at the screen, horrified.

Rosewood started to walk, the drone following her every move.

Harvesty appeared in the frame as she moved, his face contorted in anger.

"I've obeyed every one of your orders! I played your puppet when you changed my DNA." He made air quotes with his fingers. "You made a couple of keystrokes—you're a fraud," he spat, "and if anyone finds out, this is all over."

Rosewood turned to face him.

"Oh, Harvesty," she said, her tone steely cold, "no one will find out, at least not from you."

She nodded, and then slowly, a smile began to form at her perpetually pursed lips. She started to walk again.

A handful of black-clad men rushed him. Harvesty began to yell. The sounds of a scuffle boomed over the speakers. A bright light shined, a loud thud sounded, and then Harvesty was out of the frame. However, a single sound still filtered through the speakers, and Rosewood walked down a hallway—the unmistakable sound of feet dragging across a carpeted floor.

Rosewood smiled.

Several gasps were heard, and muttering once again broke out among the crowd.

Rosewood turned to her right.

"Are they ready for me?" Her voice boomed over the speakers, silencing the audience.

No answer.

"It doesn't matter, does it?" she said as she reached for the door handle. "I'm ready for them."

Her camera swung around behind her as she pulled the door open, giving us all a picture of what she saw. In front of her was the stage and the four people on it. Beyond that, the thousands of people who were here to witness whatever this was supposed to be.

Her drone swung around to face her, her smug face taking up the entire screen, but then her eyebrows lifted ever so slightly.

Silence. That is what greeted her. She had been expecting cheers.

First, she looked to the crowd, then up to the screen, then back to the crowd.

The screen froze, and Ivy's face popped back up.

"Thirty seconds back should suffice."

The screen moved rapidly in reverse, then stopped and began playing again. She was backstage, sitting in her burgundy red chair, talking to Harvesty.

"Hundreds survived. The plan was for there to be no survivors, least of all Victor Wells."

The camera switched from the clip and back onto Rosewood. But the audio from the clip continued. What little color she had drained from her face, but there was nothing she could do to stop it.

The camera remained on her as the audio continued. I'd never seen her in such a state of discomfort. The crowd was muttering. People were pointing to the screen. The audio clip continued.

"... Fortunately, after all the mindless sheep cheer on this execution, all of that will be behind us."

The clip ended.

All eyes were on Rosewood as she stood alone at the back of the stage, her secrets exposed for all the world to see.

Hope pounded in my chest.

47

Victoria Rosewood's face looked paralyzed on the screen.

The shock was palpable, almost like everyone was afraid to let go of the breath they were holding.

"Is it true?" A man shouted out.

"Yeah! Is it true?" Another joined in.

At this point, more and more people started chiming in, the air filling with their voices. I joined them.

"It's true!" I yelled, but my words were lost. I looked to Zeno, who had done the same.

Rosewood looked over at me and almost smiled. She took a few steps forward and began to speak.

"Look how much discord he sows," she said, coming to stand almost level with me on the stage, albeit forty feet to the side. She paused until the crowd had gone silent. "It's a clever trick," she continued. "Victor Wells, in his final moments, somehow gets a completely fabricated video to play in front of all of you—is that all it takes?"

She looked up to the sky. "We have accomplished so much together—think of our city, think of your families, think of the safety we have brought about." She fixed her cold gaze on me. "And now we have the chance to finally eliminate the single biggest threat to our way of life, and you're willing to throw it all away for something constructed by a monster?"

She let her sentence hang in the air, heavy with shame for all who believed in her.

She was so good, so smart, so manipulative. But we had something on our side that she didn't—truth.

"Prove it!" I yelled. The drone in front of me took over the screen, replacing Rosewood's image with my own. "Prove it!" I said again, my voice booming over the speakers. "If I really am supposed to die today, don't I get a final request? Prove that video wasn't real."

A muttering of assent rippled through the crowd.

"I'll bet my life on it," I continued, the words flowing out of me. "And everyone who saw my videos in the Sandbox knows I'm telling the truth." I hoped for some sort of recognition from the crowd. It didn't come. "Prove to me it was fake," I continued. "If I'm wrong, when the time comes, I won't resist. I'll go quietly."

I let the words hang there. My heart rocketed around in my chest. I could feel the sweat drip from my brow. I was sealing my fate. One way or another, this was it. This was my last chance. I glanced over at the glass cage. I had no idea whether or not they could hear me.

"Where's Harvesty?" I said. "If the video wasn't real, show us the man in the video. Now."

The muttering increased. More and more people joined in. It was as if the entire sea of people was becoming more agitated, a giant undulating, irritated wave. They grew louder and louder. I added to it.

"Give us proof!" I said. "Give us proof!"

Hundreds of people picked up the chant.

Those nearest the stage were split—some yelled along with me. "GIVE US PROOF! GIVE US PROOF!"

It rang through the air like a chorus. It was beautiful.

Rosewood balled her hands into fists.

"Enough!" She said, her voice going shrill. "We will not indulge such a liar! We will not indulge a carrier of TiiD—he's caused us enough harm. It is time we end this!" She looked over her shoulder and yelled. "Do it!"

The drone that had previously been at my eye level adjusted position, sinking lower, stopping when it had become level with my chest, my heart.

I stared at it—my executioner—just out of arms reach, even if I weren't tied to the chair. I looked over at Zeno and Tyrann. Identical drones had appeared for them as well.

A small red light lit up in front of mine.

This was it.

I looked out over the crowd at those chanting, demanding truth. If this was it, if this was what I died for, there was no Nobler cause.

"GIVE US PROOF!" I yelled again.

The light began blinking.

I closed my eyes.

I felt heat on my wrist.

I opened my eyes.

My shackles melted away, burning my wrists slightly as they did so.

The drone dropped lower, and I felt the same heat on my ankles.

Ivy. It had to be.

I pushed myself up from the chair, adrenaline fueling every movement.

I was free.

"NO!" Rosewood screamed, seeing Zeno and Tyrann follow suit. "GET THEM!"

At her word, the people nearest the stage jumped the barricade and ran straight for us.

A small group of black-clad men burst out of the door at the back of the stage and ran toward Rosewood, forming a protective circle around her.

I wanted nothing more than to run at Rosewood. I wanted nothing more than to fight her myself, but I couldn't do this alone, and I wasn't sure how much support we would have with the Nobles.

I grabbed the chair I had been strapped to and ran across the stage away from Rosewood.

"Bro! Wait!"

Zeno gave his chair a confused look before grabbing it and following me across the stage.

Hopefully, this wouldn't take both of us.

I jumped off the side of the stage and continued running toward the last of the Sinisters—the last of the people from the Heights.

I glanced back to see another contingent of people cutting off our pursuers. The crowd had turned on each other. It was a miracle—people, on a large scale, must have been on our side, too.

"GET HIM!"

The unfamiliar scream matched the arrival of another mob of Nobles in front of me, cutting me off. I almost skidded to a stop at the sight.

Dozens and dozens of people had formed a blockade between us and the cage. No one appeared armed, but it didn't matter. Their sheer numbers against Zeno and me—we didn't stand a chance.

"Victor! Victor!"

I looked around for the voice—it was one I recognized, and it didn't sound angry.

"Victor!"

Finally, I located it—the voice, twenty feet away. It belonged to Gio —a dark-haired kid I knew from the saber tournaments. And in his hand, he held a saber. The mob of people behind him were advancing, and he was about to be swallowed up in it. He glanced over his shoulder and then back to me. Our eyes met, and he nodded.

"Catch!"

In a single deft move, he threw the saber to me. It tumbled once, the weight of the pommel stabilizing as it soared through the air toward me.

I took a step forward and caught it just as Gio was swallowed up in the sea of advancing people.

Zeno arrived at my side, followed closely by Tyrann. I hadn't expected him to follow us, but where else would he go?

"Where did that come from?" he said, nodding to my saber.

"There's at least one person out there who believes us," I said." Let's go free the rest of them."

I nodded toward the cage.

"You think you can take them, all of them?" Zeno said, clutching his chair like a weapon.

There had to be over a hundred people separating us from our friends, but we didn't have to beat them all, just enough of them to get through to the other side.

"We're about to find out," I said. "Let's go!"

I started running. I pounded the bottom of the saber handle. An arc of blue sparks jumped across the triangular blade. It was a welcome sizzle, and the power of it felt good and natural in my hands. I twirled the blade once as I advanced, taking in my many opponents as I did so.

I could see the fear and hesitation in their eyes, but it was too late. They were committed, but they weren't prepared.

I let loose a yell and the front line scattered, but they weren't fast enough. Reflex kicked in.

Arms and legs were paralyzed in multiples with each sweep of my blade. Most fell to the ground, some unconscious.

I fought my way forward, striking out at anyone within range. Yelps and screams met each blow, and after mere seconds, the group started to thin out—most abandoning the cause completely.

The way cleared, and I sprinted forward.

I vaulted the small fence that blocked off the glass prison. Dozens of unfamiliar faces greeted me, peering through the gigantic panes.

Where were Daphne and Alex? And there had to be a door on this thing, didn't there?

"You see an opening anywhere, bro?" Zeno's voice floated around from the opposite side of the cage.

"Completely sealed," Tyrann said from my right. "Like rats in a cage."

I raced around each of the sides—there was nothing. I slammed the pommel of my saber against the wall in frustration. The people up against the glass jumped back, but it didn't even so much as leave a scratch.

"There's got to be something!" I yelled, continuing to circle the cage until I met Zeno and Tyrann again.

I glanced back over to the stage. Mayhem reigned. Rosewood was still surrounded by her guards, and I got the feeling that our brief reprieve from the Nobles was just that—brief.

"Any ideas on how to get this thing open?" I said, staring hard at the huge crystalline structure. Tyrann stared hard at the prison, and Zeno shrugged, still out of breath from our sprint.

"Couldn't Mr. Trabue use his—"

All of a sudden, the cage appeared to be filled with smoke or dust. I couldn't tell. Muffled yelling met my ears, and those closest to the glass began pounding their fists on it.

What had Rosewood done? Had we triggered something?

"Zeno?" I said, my heart rate rising.

"Bro...I don't—I uh..."

The yelling intensified, as did the grayish-brown gas. It was becoming thicker by the second. They couldn't have much time.

I rushed to the glass and threw everything I had at it. I pounded on the glass—I hit it with my saber. Zeno dragged his chair over and threw it—all to no avail.

"Tyrann! Do something!" I yelled.

But he just stood there, a calm smile on his face, and nodded towards our friends.

I stood back, out of breath, knowing that Alex and Daphne were inside. I was helpless, but something was off. I had expected the people inside to start falling unconscious. They hadn't. If anything, their activity had intensified.

I started to make my way around to the other side of the structure. Before, people had lined the walls—every space was taken up. But now, as I turned the corner, there was one spot devoid of people, one spot where the gas was thickest. I couldn't see anything. The glass was caked in it, but it didn't look like smoke—it looked like a thick coating of dust, a layer of pulverized dirt.

The ground in front of my feet shook, and I jumped back. It shook again. And then, all at once, it caved in, and Alex's face appeared, completely caked in a clumpy layer of dust.

He spit out a mouthful of dirt and smiled at me.

"Surprisingly—not as bad as I thought it would taste." He shook his head, and more dirt fell out of his hair. "You think that means I'm iron deficient?"

"Alex!" I yelled. "Wh—how I—"

"Hold on, better stand back."

Alex took another deep breath and shut his eyes as tight as he could. Instinctively, Zeno and I jumped backward, but not far enough.

The ground in front of him disintegrated, throwing up a huge puff of dirt and asphalt.

"Fire in the hole!"

Again, another explosion of dirt and another. Then, through the mist of dust, Alex stood tall.

"I told you it would work!" he said.

"It was my idea in the first place!" Daphne said, crawling out of the now fairly large hole in the ground.

"Yeah, but it's my robot arm!"

I rushed to them and embraced them both. I felt Zeno collide into us as well.

"Yes, yes, how very resourceful," Tyrann said. "But unless I'm very much mistaken, we have some important business to attend to."

I grabbed Daphne's hand and gave it a squeeze. We locked eyes for a split second.

"Yes," I said. "And we're going to need all the help we can get."

"Did you bring one for me?" Daphne said, nodding to my saber.

"Gio—a kid I knew—he threw it to me."

"Love that guy!" Alex said. "I knew he'd be here with something."

I turned around. "You did?"

"Of course—you didn't think I'd just let your videos in the Sandbox do all the work, did you? The crowd should be packed with sabers and stunners."

"Alex, you're a genius."

"I'm beginning to see why your team has been so successful," Tyrann said.

One day, hopefully very soon, I'd get to properly thank him for all of the many times he had saved my life.

Behind us, more and more people appeared, crawling out through Alex's makeshift tunnel to join our ranks.

"Speaking of teams," Tyrann said, nodding to the cage.

"Eh, a little help here."

The deep voice of Dax drew our attention back to the glass cage. Of course, he was too big to fit through the hole Alex had dug.

"Oh yeah, sorry about that. Scoot back a bit."

A few seconds and a large dust cloud later, Dax emerged, followed closely by Printh.

"Thank you," Dax said.

"Nice arm," Printh said, in what were maybe the first words I had ever heard her say. Alex looked like he might faint, but we had bigger things at hand. I turned back toward the stage and Rosewood.

It looked like a battlefield.

Most of the fighting appeared to be concentrated near the stage but with a few differences from before.

Stunner blasts and saber sparks were everywhere. Unfortunately, it appeared as though it was coming from both sides. Rosewood's supporters had come prepared as well.

Behind the stage, the giant screen continued to broadcast the whole scene. Apparently, the drones had taken to providing aerial coverage of the melee. Rosewood was still surrounded by her people, but a much larger number of Nobles had come to provide an even larger buffer.

If I knew anything about her, I knew she was smart, and she was heartless. She cared about her survival, and that was it. If she could make a run for it, she would.

She was nearer to the back of the stage, closer to the entrance of her building than she had been before. If not for all the Nobles who had surrounded her, she would have already made it inside. We didn't have much time.

"What's the play here, Mr. Wells," Tyrann said, sidling up next to me. "They seem to look to you as their leader."

I continued to stare at the screen, trying to formulate some sort of plan, but there was nothing I could think of—nothing elegant— nothing but brute force. I looked over at Dax, grateful to have him on our side.

"Victor?" Daphne said.

"We need to get to Rosewood," I said. I raised my voice. "And it's going to take everyone. We have more allies here than you think. There are people out there who believe Rosewood is just as bad as we think she is. We need to fight together, we need to get to Rosewood, and we need to bring her to justice. Are you with me?"

Even as I stared at them all, I knew our chances were slim. I had no idea how many people were on our side. I had no idea what else Rosewood had up her sleeve. Our only chance was to overwhelm them and do so quickly. We had to break through and get to Rosewood ourselves. I didn't see another way.

A chorus of yells responded, along with some colorful language I didn't wish to repeat. I raised my saber in the air and started to charge.

48

Stunner blasts flew all around us. My saber blade clashed against anyone who got in my way. Daphne was at my side, cutting a path through the hand-to-hand war zone in front of us. She had picked a saber off of an unconscious man on the ground and was unleashing a bout of skill and fury I had rarely seen from her.

Alex and Zeno were close by—Alex shot blast after blast after blast into the ground at people's feet. No one dared get too close to them, and no one could see him through all the dust.

I glanced up at the giant screen—I was starting to see a delineation between the two groups—Rosewood versus us.

We had fought our way almost onto the stage, but we hadn't moved past that. There were too many people—Rosewood's supporters outnumbered us.

A barrage of stunner fire narrowly missed me, downing a couple of people to my left. I ducked, caught someone in the ankles, and Daphne came in with a blow to the head.

A body fell limp to the ground.

"What now?" she yelled, fending off another person.

I was running out of ideas. I had thought that we'd simply be able to cut our way through—I hadn't expected Rosewood's supporters to be so vigilant.

I tried to move forward, but two more bodies appeared where the last one had gone down. Another spray of stunner fire nearly took us out. I wished more than anything I had my gloves back, but I didn't, and Daphne and I were being forced back. We just didn't have the numbers. We didn't have the fighters. We didn't have a plan, and we didn't have another option.

I glanced up at the screen to assess our state. The inevitable was beginning to happen.

Rosewood's righteous supporters were surrounding us. Soon, any avenue for escape would be cut off, not that it would do much good. Flight from here would only delay fate. And where would we go anyway?

"Victor!"

I brought my saber up instinctively as Daphne whirled past me, sparks jumping from her blade as she made multiple consecutive contacts, incapacitating person after person.

I joined in briefly—just enough to create some space for myself. I looked back up at the screen, the overhead view furnished by an overhead drone.

Think. Come on, think!

Our numbers were dwindling. We needed to regroup, but there was no way to communicate with everyone.

I jumped back as another attack came my way. I faced a kid no older than myself. Recognition lit up his eyes with both rage and fear. He knew who I was, and he hated me for it, for what he thought I was.

"Sinister scum!"

He launched himself at me, unarmed except for his hatred. It was over before he hit the ground. I stepped to the side as he fell unconscious at my feet, a large red welt beginning to materialize across his forehead.

A kid shouldn't have so much hate.

I looked over to my left to see another one of our number fall. And another. People were even starting to close in on Alex. They were starting to realize that he wouldn't shoot them with his arm—he was worried that he would really hurt someone, not just stun them. And seeing as his arm was built during wartime, he was probably right.

The only people still making a dent were Printh, Dax, and Tyrann, but even they couldn't last long with odds like this.

I took one last look at the screen. We were nearly closed in on all sides. Once we were, it was game over.

"Fall back!" I yelled. "Fall back!"

The Nobles nearest me cheered as I turned and ran, but I ran laterally.

"Fall back! Fall back!"

Looks of confusion were immediately replaced with relief as people turned and ran, too.

Reaching the end of our ranks, I made a ninety-degree turn and headed back toward the cage—the only place where we weren't surrounded.

I checked the screen as I ran, watching us lose all the ground we had gained. We had been so close to the stage, so close to Rosewood.

"What's the plan?" Zeno said, appearing at my side, along with Alex and Daphne.

"I'm working on it. We need—"

"CITIZENS OF THE FLATS, I COMMAND YOU TO STOP!" Rosewood's voice suddenly boomed over the louder speakers.

I could almost feel the confusion in the air.

Rosewood's face took over the giant screen once more.

"CEASE AT ONCE!"

Behind us, the pursuit jogged to a halt. We continued to run. Rosewood continued to talk.

"Our common foe—the Sinisters—are running. They know they've been beaten." She paused. "We show mercy. We cannot fault them for who they are—it's in their very genes. They have no choice in the matter."

I slowed my jog as we arrived back at the glass cage. I took stock of those who had also arrived. It was a mix of people from both the Heights and the Flats. Even with all of the unconscious people in the streets and on the stage, our numbers didn't appear to have taken a hit. It was nothing short of miraculous. There were a few people I recognized from what felt like a lifetime ago. Gio had somehow made it weaponless, but a few others twirled sabers, looking unsure of what was next. But more importantly, there was family here.

"Alex! Alex!"

"Dad!" Alex caught sight of him and ran.

They embraced. It was something I had never seen before. They broke away from one another. Senator Trabue looked Alex up and down. They had been apart for weeks. I watched his face drop as he caught sight of his son's upgraded appendage.

"Alex, your arm..."

"I know, cool, right?" He gave his dad a big smile, which his dad confusedly returned.

Rosewood continued to talk.

"This fight, this war between us, is futile. Useless. As you may have noticed, there were many of our number who were deceived by the clever lies of Victor Wells."

I looked around at our group—some fidgeted at her words.

Some just looked angry.

"Not all are as strong as those of you who stayed true. We will call it an error in judgment." Rosewood smiled, with her teeth only, the kind of smile that reeked of hidden plans and retribution. "You are all welcome back into the Noble fold, provided you learn from your mistakes and misjudgments."

I clenched my teeth. Her words were well crafted.

I looked around again. People had begun to fidget and converse—they were weighing their options. It was hard to see a way forward, let alone a path to victory. If they stayed with us, the consequences would be severe, maybe even dire. If they returned, well...

Suddenly, screams broke out. I looked around for the source, but it was the big screen that caught my attention.

The screen had switched its view to the backdrop of Rosewood's building. A black-caped man with a blurred mask fell slowly from the sky. He must have come from the roof or at least one of the higher-up windows. He landed on the far side of the stage from Rosewood.

More screams and gasps rang out.

"SHOOT HIM!" Rosewood's voice boomed through the air.

Immediately, hundreds of stunner blasts concentrated on a single spot, but they seemed to have no effect on him. He stood there, somehow impervious to the blasts. The dark clothes, the effortlessness of his fall through the sky—it could only be Kratos, the Bounty Hunter.

And he scared his mother to death.

A nearby drone quickly flew to Kratos, and its feed took over the screen. Gray beads were raining down around him. His blurred features masked his emotions, but in his eyes, something had returned, something that had been missing. It was a fire, an intensity. He was here, and he meant business. As the drone's camera focused upon him, his posture changed, and he drew himself up to his full height.

He was, in that moment, just as impressive and daunting as he always had been. There was no one good who despised him and no one evil who didn't fear him. I had witnessed his supreme skill first-hand. Even in his broken state, he was a force to be reckoned with, and everyone present knew it.

One thing I knew for certain was that he wasn't here to merely draw attention to himself.

In a single motion, he threw out a hand, from which he released a tiny metal ball into the air. It emitted a bright flash of white light, then exploded into dark gray, shooting a protective wall of beads ten feet long across the stage. Not a single stunner blast made it through.

He threw out three more metal balls that mimicked the first, each one adding a new wall until he was closed inside a large beaded square. The only things inside it were him and the drone.

Briefly, the camera view switched to the aerial view, showing Rosewood's crew and their incessant stunner fire concentrated on Kratos's cube of protection.

"I spent weeks in a coma after being shot on Dr. Rosewood's orders."

Kratos's face appeared on the screen in the backdrop of gray beads as his gravely voice boomed over the speakers. "I had just learned that it was she who had command of the Sinistrali. I had just learned that it was she and not Victor Wells who carried TⁱⁱD. That was when it happened. After the bullet penetrated my armor and my skin, I fell nearly fifty stories, almost onto the very spot upon which I now stand. Miraculously, I survived."

Relative silence met his words.

The camera view switched to the aerial view once more. Some of the stunner fire died down, but not all of it. Rosewood's men and most others on the stage had surrounded Kratos's box and were blasting it from all sides. Rosewood could be heard faintly in the background, screaming out orders, but Kratos's wall muted her. He would get his message out, and everyone would hear it.

"I woke up weeks later in Ville," he continued. "My broken body had mended, but my mind was still fractured with the information I had learned. Rosewood manipulated me. She had lied to me. She had tried to kill me."

The screen showed the aerial view again. More of the stunner fire had died down. Only the black-clad soldiers remained. I almost didn't notice it, but I saw a group of people moving toward where we stood. It couldn't have been more than a hundred people, but they hadn't been there before, had they?

Kratos continued and the camera returned to him.

"I was broken, and stayed broken for a while."

It was the most emotion I had ever heard in his voice. His erratic behavior and mysterious disappearances started to make sense. He had been in pain, terrible pain. His family, his own mother, had done the unthinkable.

"But we don't need to remain broken," Kratos continued. "We can fix this, and the way we do it is by stopping Victoria Rosewood. Victor Wells has told you the truth. Rosewood has lied to you all, and I am here to help you stop her."

The gray backdrop from before had started to darken. It was weakening. The camera switched views again, this time focusing in on Rosewood's face.

It had contorted into something evil, mean, and hateful. She was screaming.

"You have no idea what I've done for all of you! He's delusional! He—"

Without so much as a warning, stunner fire lit up the air once again, and the camera switched views immediately. The stunner fire wasn't coming from us, and it wasn't directed at us. It was toward Rosewood, and it was coming from... I couldn't believe it. The aerial view zoomed in, focusing on a small group of people leading the pack.

Was that Pria? And Augustine?

And the rest of the camp?

Rosewood's people turned their attention to their new foes, and that was our opportunity.

With a battle cry, I thrust my saber in the air and advanced. I ran, my saber flashing in front of me, cutting a path through distracted opponents. I caught Daphne out of the corner of my eye, a trail of unconscious bodies behind her. Alex and Zeno weren't far behind, but they had all been forced on a different path away from the stage.

Shouts went out, alerting the rest to our attack, but the damage had been done. Rosewood's supporters started to collapse in on themselves, and many weren't even opposing us as we sprinted by.

I vaulted onto the stage. Kratos's dark gray walls were still intact. The black-clad men who had surrounded them had turned their attention elsewhere.

Then, just as suddenly as Kratos had created the walls, they disappeared, the dark beads dropping to the ground like they were made of metal.

He jumped into action, immediately engaging the closest of Rosewood's personal guard.

I would have loved to watch, but I had my own fight to deal with.

I stopped the downward saber blow of a middle-aged man, then kicked out his knee. His legs gave out, and another saber came over my shoulder and connected with his head.

"You're welcome!"

A swath of silver hair and sparkling eyes appeared in front of me.

"Glad to see you've joined the fun!" I yelled.

"Glad to see you're not already unconscious!" Pria's saber moved with practiced precision.

We continued to fight—moving almost as one. I had forgotten how well we knew each other's style and how well we complemented one another. All of our sparring sessions in the woods had brought us closer together than I had realized. In that moment, I realized how much I had missed our friendship.

"Why did you come back?" I yelled, blocking an opposing thrust.

"You really think I'd miss the chance to help you take down Rosewood?" she said, grunting with exertion as she finished the job, rending the man unconscious. "You'd take all the glory for yourself."

"This way!" I yelled, glancing up at the big screen. The tide had turned, and Rosewood was losing. And she knew it. She was trying to escape.

I grabbed Pria, and we ran back and around. We had to cut her off.

"How did you know we'd need your help?" I said, glancing back and forth between the screen, Pria, and the mass of fighting people ahead.

"We watched your broadcasts in the Sandbox," she said, dodging a stunner blast and delivering a swift and effective jab in response. "And I saw that my dad and sister were alive, so there's that."

I had almost forgotten.

"You got our broadcasts?" I said. I glanced up at the screen again. We had some work to do to get in front of Rosewood.

"Every single one," she said. I looked over at her. "They weren't that good," she said. "Especially the first one, but well, I guess it was adequate in the end."

She put on a burst of speed and pounced on a group of people in front of us, her saber blade a blur of motion. Opposing stunners and sabers clattered to the ground as their owners dropped along with them.

"Show off!"

"We're trying to cut Rosewood off, aren't we?"

I nodded and raced to keep up with her.

"Then this is the way we go!"

I rushed after her.

We had reached the back of the stage. A mere twenty feet in front of us stood the doors to Rosewood's building. Dozens of people still blocked the way, some Sinistrali, some not. I could barely glimpse

Rosewood's white clothes in the midst of her remaining bodyguards. She was fighting through, pushing ever closer to the doors to her research tower.

"Victor! Cover me!"

I looked down just in time—Pria tossed a stunner my way, then picked up an unclaimed saber from the ground, wielding one in each hand. I caught the stunner, and barely had time to react before she sprinted towards the dozens of people covering the door.

Her dual sabers shot sparks as they clashed with people in every direction. I pulled the trigger on the stunner and kept it completely depressed, delivering rapid fire blasts as best as I could.

Her progress was shown in the crumpled line of people strewn across the ground. She was nearly there—the doors were mere feet away, but she was just one person in a sea of opposition. If I didn't follow, if a lot of us didn't follow, she would get swallowed up, regardless of her skill.

I kept the stunner fire coming and looked over my shoulder as I began to advance.

Dax—that big, hulking man was right where we needed him.

"DAX!" I yelled, quickly glancing back to Pria. "OVER HERE! WE NEED HELP OVER HERE!"

Before I had a chance to check and see if he had heard me, he appeared at my side. Immediately, he knew what he needed to do.

"Pria!" He yelled, catching sight of her. He took off with a yell. "THIS WAY!"

His voice carried in a way mine didn't. Dozens of people started running past me. I let go of the trigger, tucked the stunner into my waistband, and followed.

Moments later, we had blocked the doors. I fought harder than I ever had—unconscious bodies were beginning to pile up in front of us. I found myself next to Pria once more.

Three rows of guards remained. Less than a dozen feet away, I could see Rosewood. She was screaming, but I couldn't hear it. One of the guards closest to her absorbed a stunner blast and went down. She continued to scream.

I knew there were hundreds and hundreds of her supporters still out there fighting, but we had managed to break through and into her inner circle, and she was not prepared.

And then suddenly, a drone appeared in front of her face, and her voice was amplified a thousand times.

"EVERYONE STOP!"

The fighting continued. It was a ploy, one she had already used.

I glanced quickly at Pria. Her face mirrored my own. Rosewood screamed again.

"I COMMAND MY SUPPORTERS TO STOP!" She threw her hands up in the air in apparent surrender. The fighting slowed as many of her supporters held up their hands as well.

Rosewood cast her gaze around, finally locking eyes with me. There was an expression there, something I thought I would never see in her—I could only describe it as pleading. She was scared. She knew she had been beaten.

"Lower your weapons and stop this fighting." Her voice was softer, dejected.

Everyone began to disengage, even me. I let the tip of my saber dip, but the Sinistrali in front of me stayed vigilant.

People looked around, confused at the sudden change. I kept my gaze firmly on Rosewood but felt thousands of eyes turn toward the big screen.

I imagined it showed an aerial shot. I imagined it had zoomed in on us. I imagined everyone could see the fear in Rosewood's eyes, fear that we had put there. We had cut off her escape. We had gotten too close. It would have been mere moments until she was taken down, too.

After a moment, a few people started to cheer. Then, a few more.

Then more. Then the air was filled with whoops and shouts, so loud, it was the only thing you could hear. I joined in, hoisting my saber higher into the air. I let out a yell, a yell filled with relief, and pain, and exhaustion, and excitement, and hope.

I looked over at Pria. She was screaming, too, both her sabers up in the air in victory. As the cheering continued, I looked around, searching for Alex and Daphne. If Pria was here, I assumed Augustine was too. And maybe even Grandfather? We had to celebrate—we had been fighting for this, and finally, after everything, it was happening.

But still no luck—I couldn't see anyone else. I only recognized Pria and Dax beside me. I turned to Pria, but a drone appeared in my face, and I had the feeling that it was now my turn to occupy the big screen.

The cheering started to drop off. I looked around and attempted to collect my thoughts. What was I supposed to say at a time like this?

I looked over at Rosewood. She was still surrounded by her guards —probably fifty or so men, most of them dressed in black.

Though they had stopped fighting, they hadn't lowered their weapons. I could see them all, ready to resume at a moment's notice. They were only waiting for the order. I knew what needed to happen. There was one last thing Rosewood needed to say for surrender to be complete.

"There is so much I want to say," I said, as my voice reverberated through the air. "Rosewood has asked you all to stop fighting. But her own guard continues to protect her. So what I really want to say, I say to her guards—put your weapons down."

The drone in front of my face pivoted and panned over to Rosewood and her guards. Their stunners were still at the ready.

"Put your weapons down," I said again.

Still, they didn't budge. Their lack of actual surrender made me nervous. Some yelling and booing came from the crowd.

"It looks like you're not aware that your leader has surrendered," I said, the drone quickly turning back to me. "And she surrendered because she was moments away from being overwhelmed, and still, you won't lower your weapons?" I eyed the black-clad men closest to me. Several of them had their fingers resting on their stunner trigger. "Maybe they need to hear it from Rosewood herself," I said, looking over at her. Her drone moved closer to her face. The screen now showcased both of us—me on one side, Rosewood on the other.

A moment passed. Rosewood and I locked eyes.

There was a moment in every saber fight when you knew it was over. Your opponent hadn't given up yet, but they were about to. It was a sweet, satisfying moment, the moment before they said, "I yield."

I felt that now and smiled, my eyes boring into Rosewood's. She broke my gaze and stared at the ground, then up at the sky.

"Drop your weapons," Rosewood said, her voice taut. "Now."

Cheers went up from the crowd. The drone spun in place as her guards began tossing down their weapons. The clunking sound of dozens of stunners making contact with the stage floor rang out through the massive speakers.

The guard closest to me threw his stunner at my feet. This was it—finally, Rosewood's chess game had come to an end—and we had beaten her. It was over.

"I have one last thing to say," Rosewood said suddenly. The cheers went quiet. In an instant, her features morphed from scared and beaten to malicious. Sirens went off in my mind as she opened her mouth, but there was nothing I could do to stop what came out. Her eyes turned to me as she spoke.

"Kill them all."

49

———

In a flash of movement, the guards, nearly in unison, reached inside their jackets. I realized what was about to happen a half a second too late.

The guard closest to me pulled out the metal glint of an actual gun, identical to the one Harvesty had used on Kratos, and pointed it directly at my heart.

Pria launched herself into me as a puff of fire, and smoke exploded from his barrel.

The sound of gunshots rang through the air as Pria and I fell to the ground. It was so loud. Screaming—painful screaming shattered the air around us.

I hit the floor hard and started to scramble to my feet, but I felt something warm and wet coming from my left shoulder. I didn't feel any pain—I couldn't have been shot, could I? All around me, footsteps were fleeing.

Suddenly, the screaming and gunshots were muffled as a curtain of dark gray beads expanded into existence right next to me, cutting Rosewood's gunmen off from the rest of us.

Kratos.

The beads extended all the way to the building. And the doors Rosewood had been heading for were now on her side of the barrier.

Everyone scattered. The gunshots continued.

I reached up to my shoulder to assess the wound, but my hand ran into hair, silver hair. Silver hair stained with red.

"Pria!"

She was lying on her side on the ground next to me, her hair covering her face as a pool of red formed around her.

"SOMEBODY HELP!" I screamed. I pushed myself into a crouch and yelled again.

Dax appeared a moment later, clutching his side. Blood dripped from his fingers. His eyes grew wide, and he immediately jumped down on the ground, any thought of his own wound forgotten.

"Pria!" he said. "Pria!"

She didn't respond. I looked around—there had to be something we could do... Pria would know what to do.

There was no one, no one but us.

I softly moved the hair out of her face, and Dax gently rolled her onto her back. My heart nearly stopped.

There, in the center of her chest... I had to look away. I felt my face become hot. My vision started to swim. I fought against unconsciousness.

There was nothing we could do, nothing anyone could do.

I stayed on the ground by Pria. Gunshots continued to ring out, keeping me grounded in the present, and though Dax had already been hit once, he didn't appear to care. He let out a primal yell of pain and pushed himself up to his full height. Blood flowed freely from his side. Tears flowed freely down his face. The curtain of beads was still intact in front of him, but it was clearly weakening, and each gunshot took its toll.

He surveyed the scene.

"TYRANN!" he called. "TYRANN!"

Another gunshot rang out, and Dax winced at the impact. But it didn't bring him down. And no new blood. Another gunshot. Another wince. But this time, I thought I saw the bullet bounce off of him.

Kratos's shield of beads didn't prevent the bullets from passing through, but it did slow them down.

"TYRANN!" Dax yelled again.

Except for the three of us, the area was nearly deserted. Minus the stream of unconscious bodies, everyone else had fled.

I looked over through the barrier to where Rosewood was—safe and protected by her guards. Kratos's beads clouded my vision somewhat, but I could mostly make out everything. Rosewood was still surrounded by her guards, but she was moving toward the doors.

Overhead, a colossal stuttering sound blared through the air, a sound I had heard only once before from this very same building.

A helicopter—its blades moving faster than the eye could see—flew through the air and disappeared on top of Rosewood's tower.

This was her backup plan, her contingency.

"Dax! Dax!"

Tyrann ran across the stage toward us, Printh in tow.

Twenty feet away, Tyrann let out a yell. He arrived and shoved me out of the way.

"No, no no no no, Pria, my dear, Pria, stay with us. Wake up." He gently cradled her face and began to sob. Printh dropped to her knees, speechless. Both of them were covered in cuts and bruises. Tyrann was bleeding from a gash on his cheek. His tears mixed with it as he cradled Pria's unmoving form in his arms.

She was pale, too pale.

An anger like I had never felt before started to consume me, an anger fueled by loss, by injustice.

I pushed myself to my feet and watched Rosewood's progress.

Another few gunshots rang out, keeping us all at bay. She wasn't inside the building yet, and Kratos's barrier wasn't impermeable.

I launched myself in the direction of Rosewood. I hurdled a few of the bodies on the ground and swung my saber with all my might into Kratos's barrier. Beads fell to the ground, but not enough. I just needed to make an opening I could squeeze through.

A gunshot rang out, and I felt its impact on my arm. I didn't care.

I swung again.

I just needed to get through, and then I could take down Rosewood myself.

Another gunshot.

This one hit me in the chest. It took my breath away, and I staggered backward a few steps.

I couldn't tell whether or not it had pierced my skin, but it didn't matter. Rosewood was almost through the door. I raised my saber again.

"Victor!"

Someone was screaming my name.

"VICTOR!"

As I brought my blade down, a fresh row of beads appeared. And then another, and another. Kratos must be adding protection.

So I hit the barrier again and again, even harder than I had been. I didn't even make a dent.

Another gunshot rang out, but the bullet dropped to the ground at my feet, barely having made it through the beads.

And then the gunshots stopped.

I knew Rosewood had made it inside, and her Sinistrali with her.

I let out a yell that turned into a sob and fell to my knees.

I looked back to see everyone huddled around Pria's body. Behind them, Daphne and Alex and Zeno were running toward Pria as well.

I vaguely heard my name, but it didn't really register. I knelt there, numb.

But through my tears, I saw something.

A small army of sweepers rolled down the street toward us. There were at least a dozen of them, their many arms shooting every which way, picking up unconscious or injured bodies and moving them out of their path. Anyone nearby scattered.

Jahko had sent help after all, but it was too little too late. The battle had occurred, Pria had been shot. Rosewood had gotten away. They couldn't climb a fifty story building. They couldn't bring down a helicopter. Their arrival meant nothing.

I dropped my saber and let my head sink down.

How could it happen like this?

I heard my name, but I ignored it.

She had come to our rescue, and this was her reward? I looked up at Rosewood's building, and I heard my name again, but I didn't have the willpower to focus on where it was coming from.

"VICTOR!"

Finally, I looked over my shoulder.

Zeno was waving one of his arms. The other was pressed against his ear.

For reasons I couldn't understand, Dax had swept Pria up in his arms, and everyone had moved, running away from the very spot they had just been.

Zeno screamed at me again.

"VICTOR! GET OUT OF THE WAY NOW!"

I didn't understand—there was no urgency to move. Rosewood was gone, most likely to her elevator by now.

I expected in a minute's time to hear her helicopter start up as she flew to safety.

"VICTOR, MOVE!"

Kratos appeared in front of me, and in one deft movement, picked me up and started to run back the other way, one arm out behind him.

Zeno yelled again, but this time wasn't for me.

"KRATOS!"

Immediately, Kratos dropped me on the ground and threw his body on top of mine. I watched something leave his hand and explode above us, shadowing us in protective beads.

I didn't have time to ask why, and I didn't need to.

The sounds of wreckage and shrieking metal cut through the air as a sweeper exploded out of the bottom floor of Rosewood's building. Glass and debris flew everywhere. Chunks of cement flew through the air—several of them peppering the exact ground we laid upon.

The sweeper demolished Kratos's barrier wall. Its many arms shot out, moving bodies out of the way as it skidded to a halt.

Kratos let loose a sigh, then rolled over onto the ground beside me. He tapped his wrist, and the beads around us fell to the ground. He continued to lay there, taking several deep, slow breaths.

He had saved my life yet again.

"Thank you," I said as I rolled over onto my back. I found myself nearly face-to-face with the sweeper. It sat there above me, covered in bits of building, a gaping hole behind it, and a single arm extended skyward.

And from that arm, twenty feet in the air, dangled a woman dressed in white. She didn't move. She didn't struggle. She just hung there, supported by the mechanical arm.

It was Rosewood.

She didn't get away after all.

50

―――――

She had done it. She had shown everyone her true colors. No one could deny what had happened.

I opened my eyes and closed them again. It should have been a euphoric moment. Instead, I felt a mix of emotions that I couldn't quite understand. Rosewood. Pria. Ville. So much had just happened.

Happy, sad, relieved, exhausted, distraught—they all lived inside my mind at once. I forced my eyes open again and stared up at the sweeper towering over us. Kratos still lay next to me, his breathing slow and ragged.

"Kratos, Victor!"

It was a familiar voice. I pushed myself up to my feet to find Jahko standing in front of me, a smile on his face, though it immediately turned to concern.

His eyes met mine, then flitted to Kratos, then moved over somewhere behind me to where sobs were still sounding.

He placed a gentle hand on my shoulder, understanding in his eyes.

"It takes time to heal. It all does." He gave my shoulder a squeeze and nodded, motioning behind me.

Nearby, Daphne knelt on the ground beside Pria, along with Tyrann and Printh. Alex, surprisingly, let his hand rest on Printh's back as her shoulders heaved.

Jahko took a step closer.

"I'm sorry," he said. "I'm so very sorry."

I looked down at the ground and wiped at my eyes.

"So, you got her, right? That's Rosewood?" I said, nodding up.

Jahko nodded.

"Is she dead?" Kratos asked gruffly, awkwardly joining me on his feet.

"No," Jahko said. "Just incapacitated, like most of those on the ground floor of that building." He looked back over his shoulder at the hole he and Ivy had punched through.

Zeno and Ivy walked up, holding hands; Zeno had an unrestrained smile on his face.

"From her phone!" Zeno said. "Bros, listen, I know I'm good, but I'm going to say it—she's better. The drones, the screen—it was all Ivy, *from her phone!*"

"While navigating and coordinating with the other sweepers, yes," Ivy said. "I tried to automate the drone switches using facial recognition as much as possible, but I had to take a few liberties in order to give you as much information as possible as well as keep us informed of Rosewood's movements. I hope it helped."

Zeno was smiling at me, but his grin faltered. I did my best to smile back.

"We never would have made it off of the stage to begin with," I said. "We couldn't have done it without your help."

I looked over toward Pria again, and Daphne met my eyes. Hers were red with tears, and hers weren't the only ones. Tyrann was beside himself, sobbing. Dax sat next to him, his head in his hands. I wiped my eyes again.

Zeno moved to my side.

"Bro, I know it hurts, but—"

"She saved my life," I said, cutting him off. "That bullet was for me."

Zeno wrapped me in an embrace.

"Come on, my man, let's get you over here."

As Zeno led me away, Jahko's face filled the screen behind us.

"Hello to all. My name is Jahko. I am from the city to the south—Ville. We understand this is a tumultuous time for your city. We've recently had some tumult of our own. We are here to help you through it.

"I urge you all to clean up, go home, and be with your families. Tomorrow, in accordance with the rules of your senate, a public trial will begin concerning your city's president." The screen briefly switched views and showed Rosewood's unconscious body in the pincers of the sweeper before returning to Jahko. "It will be held here and broadcasted on this very screen. Our sweepers and their drivers will assist in any way they can. Thank you."

The screen went dark.

Surprisingly, or unsurprisingly, the people obeyed. The other sweepers milled around like sentinels as people reunited with family members and started to make their way out of the streets.

Zeno walked me over to where Alex and Daphne were waiting. One after the other, they embraced me.

I felt so many emotions.

We had caught Rosewood. This nightmare could finally end. People could begin living their lives—true freedom could be restored.

But Pria. She had paid the ultimate price. And she had paid it, saving me.

I let go of Alex and looked back over my shoulder at Tyrann. He was standing now. A group of people had covered Pria with some sort of cloth and were preparing to move her body.

"So that's it, then?" I said, doing my best to sound natural.

"No, that's not it," a seasoned voice said, coming from behind me. I turned to find my grandfather rapidly approaching, with Augustine in tow. Daphne ran to her father, and Grandfather wrapped me in a hug. He let go and held me out at arm's length. His regal features were slightly more weathered than I remembered, and his hair was slightly askew, but his eyes radiated warmth. "It is so incredibly good to see you." He hugged me again.

"You too," I said. My eyes welled up.

"I was unaware the citizens of Ville would be here to help today," Grandfather said.

"Yes," Jahko said, walking over, "between Victor's final broadcast and Zeno's incessant texting, we knew we were needed beyond our own problems. I think Ivy would have mobilized the entire fleet on her own had we not come when we did." Jahko paused and extended his hand. "You must be Ulysses Wells."

"Yes," Grandfather said, shaking his hand. "I have never had much interaction with Ville over the years. Needless to say, I'm glad you intervened." Jahko smiled and nodded.

"As am I."

"I believe thanks are in order to you as well, Mr. Bounty Hunter," Grandfather said. "I hear you played a pivotal role today."

Kratos had been standing next to me in silence. He looked around at each of us for a moment before very slowly reaching up to his face. His mask fell to the ground. He still looked awful, but some of his old calm had returned.

"My name is Kratos," he said, "and I support truth." He reached into his jacket. "I believe this will be of assistance." In his hand, he held a small black block, maybe an inch in diameter. He glanced up at his mother, still dangling from the sweeper.

"A data block!" Zeno said. "Man, how many of those did you steal from me?"

"This contains all of the information I could find after I returned from Ville," Kratos said. "It should be sufficient for the trial." He placed it back in his pocket.

A short silence ensued. Around us, people continued to clear out, except for a large group that had banded together, looking altogether uncomfortable, about twenty feet away. Many people were steering clear of the large group, but there was one man who was moving in their direction.

"Hello, my fellow No—" Alex's dad caught himself. "Friends. Hello, my friends. I am Senator Trabue. We've all been through a lot, but you more than most. I hear you've all recently lost your homes?"

There was muttered assent.

"Well, let's see what we can do about that. Come with me."

I glanced at Alex and watched a smile grow on his face. His father turned and, catching sight of him, winked.

"Things are going to be different," I said. Everyone turned to me. I took another glance up at Rosewood. "No more Nobles, no more Sinisters, just people, right?"

"Seems that way," Alex said. "But what's next for us? We helped fix Ville. We helped fix our city. Now what? We're running out of cities!"

Grandfather chuckled and patted him on the back.

"But it is a good question," Augustine said. "What is next? What do we do with all of this? Jahko, it sounds like you may have some insight on how to rebuild and reunite a city."

All eyes shifted to Jahko, who smiled serenely.

"That might be a better question for someone who understands both sides of the Innerbelt, as it were. Victor?" He paused. "This question might be better suited for you. What do you see for the future?"

His question caught me off guard.

I looked all around me—the Capital, the people in it, the sweepers idling around. Beyond that—the Heights, the collapsed buildings, the broken streets, the broken people. So much needed to be done.

"I think we should start with the scanners," I said. "How fast do you think we can rip them out?"

EPILOGUE

"I can't believe she's gone," Alex said. "Well, I mean I can, she's like a hundred and fifty years old, well was a hundred and fifty—"

I grunted in agreement. It had taken two days to convict Rosewood. Augustine had predicted it would be a long, drawn-out affair, but after the Battle in the Capital (Alex's title, not mine), Harvesty showed up. Coward. He turned on Rosewood and gave a full confession in order to escape her same fate. He named every Sinistrali member as well, not just those who had been captured the same day as Rosewood. If his testimony hadn't been enough, Kratos handed over his data block. It was replete with information spanning decades. Markings, Sinistrali hits, DNA tampering, and a variety of other nefarious actions. Jahko and Ivy gave several brief statements, and several other people came forward with their stories and proof, including Alex's dad.

I didn't know if I had ever seen them so proud of each other.

Alex and I stood in a train car on the newly dubbed Intrabelt. It was a subtle change to the name, but meaningful. There was no such thing as a "Noble" car or a "Sinister" one anymore—they were all just cars, and you got on whatever one would take you where you wanted to go.

"Looks like the next one is our stop," Alex said.

I nodded and glanced up at the banner of text that snaked its way across the glass walls.

"Sinistrali granted their lives and escorted out of the city permanently.
A new era is ushered in: a time without Rosewood."

I wasn't sure of the exact details, but after two weeks in a holding cell surrounded by armed security, Rosewood had been executed earlier today, alongside Benjamin—she for her decades of duplicity and murder, and he for being a co-conspirator of genocide in the Heights. Several people argued that the Sinistrali should have shared their fate. I was just glad they were gone. And odds were they wouldn't last long outside of the city, anyway.

I had worried during the trial that some of Rosewood's network would slip underneath the radar, but Kratos made sure that didn't happen. The most important members of her team had been kept in secret rooms inside her building. Fortunately, those rooms weren't a secret to Kratos.

The text banner changed.

The last government-made scanner was removed this morning from the Flats in front of thousands of cheering people. Today to be designated as an annual holiday moving forward.

A pleasant female voice sounded over the speakers.

"Now exiting to the Future City Center."

I glanced up and smiled.

"Sounds like Zeno's finally getting to put his touch on a few things," I said.

"Yeah, I don't know how I feel about this 'new Gina' he keeps talking about," Alex said. "But, whatever makes him happy."

The tiles under our feet lit up, and glass walls from the floor and ceiling proceeded to box us in. Our car peeled off from the rest of the train and headed down a set of tracks that took us into the very heart of the Heights. It was odd being in a train car again.

For the last week or so, I had been able to go where I wanted and do what I wanted without fear. Truthfully, it hadn't been much. Grandfather and I went back to our home, although it didn't really feel like it. I could tell he felt the same way. We were still a long way away from normal.

I watched out the window. The mess of broken buildings flew past us as we made our way down the tracks.

"It's looking good out there," Alex said, his face almost touching the glass. "Zeno said he figured out how to make the sweepers go on autopilot and help with all the cleanup."

"You sure it wasn't Ivy?" I said.

"Pretty sure it was a built-in feature already," Alex said, turning back to the window. "He's just trying to take credit for it."

I allowed myself a chuckle.

"So are you going to tell me about this big installation thing you've been talking about, or just leave it a mystery?"

"Obviously, leave it a mystery," Alex said. "I don't want to ruin it for you!"

"Fine," I sighed and continued to stare out the window. Augustine and Zeno had been working on a monument of some kind, and Alex refused to give me any details about it until I had actually been down to see it myself.

"Soooo," Alex said, his tone uncharacteristically light, "have you, um, talked to Daphne lately?"

Immediately, a pit developed in my stomach.

"I, well," I paused, looking for the words.

"I'll take that as a no."

"Well, what about you and—"

"She prefers I not talk about us," Alex said, holding up a hand and cutting me off.

"Still scared of her then, huh?" I said.

"No." Alex paused for a second. "Well, okay, yeah, I am. But who wouldn't be, right?"

"Right," I said, staring out the window. Our car had started to slow down, but I barely recognized where we were at. "You sure this is the right stop?"

"Of course I am." Our car slowed to a halt, and one of the panels retracted so we could exit. "Come on, I'll show you around."

We stepped out onto a makeshift platform made of compacted dirt. Sunlight was everywhere. I had been so used to the shadows of the Heights—buildings every way you turned, blocking out the warming rays of the sun. But now, everything was brown and green. The cold grays and blacks were mostly gone, and what I assumed was a thick layer of dirt seemed to cover just about everything. I had thought everything used to be flat, but a rather large hill stood in the middle of the nearest clearing.

A handful of sweepers moved about, some pushing dirt, some planting trees. There were several dozen people spread out over the area as well.

"Britton!" Alex yelled, waving an arm. "Tyler, Tanner, Colton! Lookin' good!" They smiled and waved back. He pointed at another group. "Brock, Brody, Ryan, Tyson—quit loafin' around! Nah, I'm just kidding, do whatever you want."

I looked over at Alex.

"What? Look, spend a couple weeks down here, and you get to know a few people."

"Or everybody."

"Can't help it," Alex said with a sigh. "I've been described as magnetic."

"Are you sure that's not just because your arm is made of metal?"

"Well, this does carry a little prestige," he said, patting his arm. "But no—I'm fairly certain it's my personality. Come on, I'll introduce you."

"No, that's okay," I said quickly. "Can we just find Augustine?"

Alex gave me a look. I did my best to keep my features neutral, but I really wasn't in the mood to meet new people or put on a face. I felt like that was all I had been doing since being back in the Flats, and it was exhausting.

I used to fit in. Before everything started, I was a saber champion. During everything, I had a purpose. Now, everything we had been fighting for was done. Rosewood was gone. The Noble-Sinister dichotomy was dismantled. Anything that a "normal" teenager should be doing felt so petty and pointless.

"Uh, yeah, sure," Alex said, continuing to eye me. "He'll be over this way."

I followed him across the clearing and tried to orient myself, but it was impossible. I didn't recognize anything. The giant hill certainly hadn't been there before, and so many trees—were they trying to plant a forest here? I quickly gave up.

"Trevor!" Alex said. Up ahead, Trevor stood by himself, his head down, staring at a screen. "Look," Alex whispered, "he's still feeling a little self-conscious about the whole Maggie thing, all right?"

Trevor saw us coming, and his face lit up.

"Alex, Victor! It's so good to see you both."

"It's good to see you, too," I said. I hadn't had the chance to talk with him since, well, since right before the Heights collapsed.

"Where's Maggie?" Alex asked.

I shot him a look. He shrugged.

"Around here somewhere," Trevor said. "Look, I never was able to apologize about what happened just before," he paused and motioned around with his arms, "well, all of this."

I waved it off.

"None of this was your fault," I said. "I'm just glad you're doing well."

Trevor gave me a smile.

"Thanks, Victor."

"Anyways," Alex said, "we're looking for Augustine—any idea where he's at?"

"Yes." Trevor looked down at his screen and tapped on it a few times. "He should be just on the other side of the hill." Trevor pointed. "Just walk around it until, well, you'll see it. He should be there."

I followed his finger. The hill was fairly large—maybe a couple hundred feet across and forty or fifty feet high. It had a relatively steep incline that turned into a gentle slope as it reached the top. Trees had been planted all over the huge mound, more there than anywhere else.

I heard a soft pair of footsteps approach us from behind, followed by a thud.

"Ow!" Alex said. "What was that for?"

Printh Kane stood there in her customary black. Her look had changed very little, but it had changed, and it was significant. Previously, she had had a few strands of bright pink flowing through her black hair. Those were gone. In its place was silver.

"Just saying hi," Printh said, her voice soft and low. I was still getting used to hearing her talk, but it was becoming more and more common as her and Alex had been spending a lot of time together.

"Well, hi to you, too," Alex said, pulling his fist back.

Printh caught his fist with her hand and stared at him.

"You wouldn't dare."

Alex glanced quickly at me and dropped his hand.

"Yeah, you're right,"

Printh smirked.

"Good, let's go. We're having lunch with my dad."

I thought I heard Alex swallow, his eyes slightly wider than usual.

"Great, um, Victor, you're okay, to you know—find Augustine, right?"

I suppressed a smile as best I could.

"Yeah, of course, you go ahead."

Printh nodded, grabbed Alex's hand, and tugged him off in the other direction.

"You two have fun!" I said.

Alex waved, but it sort of looked like a plea for help.

I looked over at Trevor.

"Would you like me to accompany you?" he said.

I glanced over at the hill.

"No, thanks. I think I can manage." I gave him a nod and started walking.

The walk was deceptively far. I steered clear of most of the people along the way, but I did overhear a few people talking as I passed by, and it was informative.

The giant hill was on the exact spot where the events center used to stand, which meant that this whole clearing was where most of the people of the Heights had died.

Jahko's crew of sweepers had apparently brought in ton after ton of dirt and had worked to cover all of the death and debris.

There were no individual gravestones, but I was strolling through a cemetery.

I hadn't been sure how I would feel coming down here again, but this... this was a lot.

Regularly, over the last few weeks, I would wake up in the middle of the night with pieces of my dreams still intact in my mind. Mostly, they were comprised of that night when I thought we were going to die... all of us. That was part of the reason I had been so hesitant to come down here. I didn't want to relive it; I didn't want to hear the screams of thousands of people as buildings began to collapse around them.

But this—the sunlight, the trees—it was like I was in another place. I didn't know if there was a more beautiful resting spot in all the city.

I continued my walk around the mound. It had been a couple of minutes since I had seen anyone, but if Trevor said Augustine was here, that's where he was, so I continued on. The hill was more or less in the shape of a rectangle, and I was nearing the end of one of the short sides. I avoided a small cluster of trees, turned the corner, and that was when I saw it—the installation.

It was large—larger than I had expected. Large, black metal struts supported the structure, and the entire back side of it was black. It was at least half the height of the hill and probably half the length. I walked around the front of it. It was made up of thousands of small glass tiles that had been placed together. Only Zeno could be the architect of such a thing.

"Victor!" I looked over to see Augustine and Zeno thirty feet to my right, waving me over. I jogged over to meet them, but Zeno met me halfway.

"Bro!" he said, holding out his hand for a fist bump. "Long time no see!"

It had been a couple of weeks, but it felt both longer and shorter at the same time.

"How's life back in the real world?" I said. Zeno smiled and nodded over toward Augustine.

"Well, after faking my death all those years ago, it's kind of nice to be back in society. And someone's gotta fix all the tech infrastructure

—you guys were all hopeless without me. Where's all the cool stuff, you know? Ville is making us look bad."

Augustine greeted us as we approached.

"Is Zeno telling you his plans to make Ville look like the Stone Age compared to us within the year?"

"He was just getting started," I said.

"It's best to stop him early. He'll talk for hours," Augustine said with a smile.

"Hey, I've got big ideas," Zeno said. "Come on, boss, you know that."

Augustine nodded and smiled.

"Yes, yes, I do."

"Glad to know that a little competition isn't crushing yours and Ivy's romance," I said. "Is one of you ever going to make the move up here or down there?"

"I wouldn't call it a competition," Zeno said, "but let's just say something is in the works."

"Is that so?" I said.

Zeno nodded and winked.

"But, bro, in other news, I'm bringing Gina back! And she's a hit!"

"I heard her voice on the Intrabelt for the first time today," I said.

Zeno closed his eyes like he was savoring something particularly good.

"Man, it makes me feel good to hear you say that. I managed to save a portion of her code on my phone before, you know. I'm rebuilding her how she was intended to be built—she'll be able to run everything in the entire city by the time I'm done."

I smiled.

"Ivy better watch out," Augustine said.

"What about Dax?" I asked. "How's he doing?"

"Good," Augustine said. "He's just about all healed up, and he too has reentered society. I don't think Tyrann is too happy about it, but he's got his own past to deal with."

"Speaking of Tyrann," I said slowly.

"Yes," Augustine said, "I've heard rumors that he's going to more or less go back into hiding." Augustine paused. "Everyone grieves in different ways."

The only sound was the tapping of Zeno's fingers on his screen and a few leaves rustling in the trees.

"Uh, bro," Zeno said, looking up from his screen, "you've actually shown up at the perfect time. We're about to give this thing its first test run. I think you're going to like this." He alternated between looking at his screen and looking up at the installation. "The black on the back of it is actually made of solar cells," Zeno said. "This thing'll run itself forever. Well, unless it's perpetually cloudy, but otherwise, you get the point, right?" He looked down at his screen. "Okay, let's fire it up."

With a single tap, the whole installation lit up in light.

"There she is," Zeno said.

"Wow," I said. It was hard to take it all in, especially standing so close. It looked like lines of text were scrolling across the enormous screen from top to bottom. I was told pictures would be interspersed as well.

"Just wait till you see it at night," Zeno said. "I know there are some cool monuments out there, but you know, I think we've got the coolest there is."

"Ninety percent of the DNA scanners in the Flats went into making this," Augustine said. He grabbed my shoulder and gave it a squeeze. "It was a good idea to have them all removed. Come on, let's go have a look."

Zeno stayed where he was, his focus switching back and forth between his screen and the installation.

Augustine guided me out until we could see the entirety of the monument. I looked up and down the glass wall in front of me.

Name after name after name scrolled in front of my eyes. Pictures accompanied the names where available. They were names I didn't recognize—people I didn't really know.

"It's sobering, isn't it?" Augustine said. "To think, all these people lost their lives mere weeks ago."

I didn't respond. I just stared at the names and occasional faces.

"Zeno said that new names are being added all the time—anyone who lost their life due to Rosewood. Pictures are being submitted as well. This will be a living memory for anyone who knew them and a reminder for everyone of what power in the wrong hands can do."

We stood in silence for a few moments, watching the names float by.

"It is also a reminder of what the brave actions of a few good people can really accomplish," Augustine said.

I looked over at him, and he met my gaze.

"But what now?" I said.

"Now, we rebuild, we re—"

"No," I said, cutting him off. "I mean…" I trailed off. I knew it would sound stupid if I said it out loud, but Augustine seemed to understand. He nodded at me and squeezed my shoulder once more.

"Have you talked with Kratos lately?" he said.

I shook my head.

"I talked with him last night," Augustine said. "Do you know he hasn't worn his mask in almost a week?"

"Oh?"

"Can you believe that he often didn't take his mask off to sleep?" Augustine chuckled and shook his head. "No one knew who he was, no one except his mother."

"And she almost killed him," I said.

"Yes," he said, "and when that long-lasting human connection he had was gone, well, you saw what happened to him."

"Where are you going with this?" I said.

He held me out at arm's length, a hand on each shoulder. "Purposes come and go. There are precious few things that really matter in life. For someone who nearly lost everyone and everything, multiple times, if I am to believe everything my daughter has told me, you know what those things are, probably better than most." He paused and looked past me for a moment.

"Victor, people are free to make their own choices, and what we do with those choices is the real measure of who we are." He paused again, but this time held my gaze. His eyes were so intense with belief when he spoke, his voice so full of feeling. "Don't close yourself off from those around you—that's where the richness of life is truly found."

He held my gaze for a moment longer, until I heard footsteps. Augustine turned to look.

"And speaking of."

Daphne appeared from behind a clump of trees. She looked up and, catching sight of me, stopped.

Our eyes met. I paused and looked up at Augustine. He smiled softly, then dropped his hands from my shoulders, and I started to walk.

ACKNOWLEDGMENTS

I believe strongly that there is a trait, an aspirational one, that calls to us all. I call it the oul of the Adventurer. It's what drives individuals to take risks, explore the unknown, and boldly state outlandish claims that turn out to be full of verified truth. The Adventurer takes risks, does the ill-advised, and somehow, inexplicably, comes out the other side unscathed. We all want to be that person. It calls to us. We long to be the one with the stories, the one with the experiences, and the one with the truths nearly too fantastic to believe.

But there exists, in the homes of many, a different type of trait, a different soul. I call this the Soul of Samwise. This is a constant soul, a quiet companion content to simply watch and support in their own special way. And in some ways, though their names will not appear on the same placards, though their speaking engagements will be nonexistent, and though their fame will likely never rise above the level of the pre-k art wall at my son's school, it is they who deserve the credit for that one final push that gets you across the finish line. It is they who deserve the accolades for a race well run or an expedition that returns safely home. Without that special, constant, and sometimes uncommonly tired soul, much of what has been accomplished would be left to die on the final step of the staircase of completion.

There are moments when the path forward is obscured, your footing is unsure, and your resolve is failing. And that is precisely why the Soul of Samwise is so valuable. And so, it is with a grateful heart that I acknowledge the Samwise in my life.

The innumerable nights spent behind the keyboard were made slightly more bearable with you at my feet. It's possible you went through a stint of pre-diabetes due to my snacking habits, but the additional effort that would have been required to clean off my own plate was able to be poured into my work, and I think, when I look into your deep brown eyes, you understand how much that mattered to me.

Every crumb was important to you, and you showed care for each sugary morsel that I aspire to show for my own work. You spent countless hours in slumber nearby, usually under the desk, hiding from the glaring light of the computer screen. Yet, even in those moments, you carried me onward. If you could sleep through my furious keystrokes in the dead of night, knowing with a sure calmness that tomorrow would dawn anew, then surely I could restart my efforts fresh again on the morrow and know that all would be well.

So, Zeus, our cherished golden doodle, I write this ode to you to say thanks for your company during these many years of writing. Your presence has been both a comfort and nuisance, depending solely upon what human food you managed to steal from our plates that day. Your name will not be on the cover of this book, but your contributions will not be forgotten.

Speaking of contributions, I cannot neglect to mention my wife here. For, without her incredible love of animals, we would not have a dog. To my son, I admire your ability to stare 90 pounds of danger in the face and tell it to sit, all while taunting it with a treat that is only narrowly out of the domesticated beast's grasp.

To my usual team of editors, artists, and proofreaders, I know you're all dog people at heart. Were it not so, we would have parted ways long ago in a bitter manner and would forever more not be on speaking terms. I would also anticipate that your critique and feedback would have fallen flat, it being petty and rootless at its core. Yet, I can sense, simply from the quality of your suggestions, that you know, as I do, that a dog is man's best friend. Thank you for your rationality and love of goodness and truth.

All that being said, I suppose I won't hold it against you if you like cats. We can still be friends. Just know that one day, you will come to the realization that there truly is a superior house pet. Or maybe the realization will be mine... Who knows?

Finally, and on a slightly more serious note, I offer a sincere thank you to the readers. I hope my stories have brought you hours of entertainment, excitement, and captivation. I hope that you took your book into the bathroom to read for a few minutes and ended up sitting there until your legs were numb. I hope you stayed up too late and woke up too early. I hope you skipped lunch, and I hope you fell asleep with a book in your hand.

Stories teach, correct, inspire, and entertain. They become a part of you and influence your thoughts. I hope you choose to never give up. I hope you take control of your lives and define them yourselves instead of letting others do it. I hope you choose the good part and fight for truth, and I hope you make incredible friends along the way.

I bid you farewell with a final phrase, one that can't be said enough. To all involved, in any way and at any time, thank you.

Until the next one,

—JA

ABOUT THE AUTHOR

Sidenote:

These were all so fun that I couldn't pick just one, so for your edification and enjoyment, here is me, as told to you by myself with or without the input of others.

Raised in Idaho, where the locals say, "If you don't like the weather, wait a minute," Jordan grew up and moved to Ohio, where he found the locals say the same thing. He then moved ten minutes away from Ohio and has yet to hear any of his neighbors say anything about the weather...

Jordan has never eaten an octopus, swam with a shark, or jumped out of a perfectly good airplane. He has also never enjoyed the taste of mushrooms, the feeling of getting his nose waxed, or what is known by a mysterious and untruthful few as "the runner's high." And he has no plans to do so.

Jordan Allen was born in Utah, raised in Idaho, and now claims to be a resident of Ohio or maybe West Virginia (although no one knows for sure) with his wife, son, and dog. A lover of pink lady apples, any clothing containing elastane, a still evening on the golf course, and that patch of interstate he knows is never under radar surveillance, Jordan spends his days drilling on teeth, staring lovingly at his wife, wrestling their four-year-old, and scheming in a general manner about the future.

Jordan has been bucked off a donkey, chased by an emu, smothered by his two golden doodles, blinded by the beauty of his wife, and body slammed more times than he can count by his son. He has also had a staring contest with a llama, meditate on a mountaintop, swam less than a mile, and lost his lunch on an airplane.

After a lifetime of adventure, he now lives in West Virginia with his lovely wife, energetic son, and slumbering dog. Together, they enjoy a slew of appropriately aged animated shows, riding bikes exclusively in warm weather and constantly attempting to figure out how to get adequate sleep.

Jordan is a dentist by day, asleep at night, and groggy in the mornings. He enjoys a good protein shake (somewhat shamefully, with almond milk), whipped cream with a little bit of pumpkin pie (but only around Thanksgiving), and the taste of Gatorade when dehydrated (honestly, there's nothing better). He married way out of his league and has thus far managed to keep that secret from his wife for over a decade. When he's not spending time making children cry or extolling the virtues of flossing, he hangs out with his wife and son, practices his short game, and practices his long game. He can occasionally be seen practicing his medium game as well. He is constantly on the lookout for well-made joggers, another pair of shoes, and an exceptionally comfortable pair of socks that provide adequate cushion but also don't make his feet sweat. Jordan can sometimes be seen walking at undisclosed locations, running in place, but never jogging at a pace normally reserved for walking, but one way or another, he is always on the move.

www.ingramcontent.com/pod-product-compliance
Lightning Source LLC
Chambersburg PA
CBHW021228190726

48289CB00005B/1216